CAUGHT IN A KISS

Anna's heart beat faster as his lips reached her throat. When he kissed her, she thought nothing could be better; then his tongue moved against hers, and she thought she'd swoon. She tried to put her arms around him, but they were trapped under his body. It was as if he were possessing her. Thank God he didn't know who she was.

"Anna, tell me what you're doing here," Rutherford whispered into her ear.

"How did you know it was me? I thought you were just kissing . . ."

He stared at her in disbelief. "You thought I'd just kiss any woman? What the hell do you take me for?"

She struggled to sit up, but his body weighed her down. "I haven't even given you leave to kiss me, and you're doing even more!"

"Harumph." He bent his head to kiss her again. "And I plan to continue."

"Sebastian!" She wiggled to get out from under him.

"Anna. Be still. I'll let you up when you tell me what you're doing here. Until then . . ."

He moved his hand over her breast again and an ache started between her legs. His mouth covered hers and she opened to him. His tongue skated over her teeth, before caressing the inside of her mouth. She'd never imagined a kiss could be like this . . .

Books by Ella Quinn

THE SEDUCTION OF LADY PHOEBE

THE SECRET LIFE OF MISS ANNA MARSH

THE TEMPTATION OF LADY SERENA

Published by Kensington Publishing Corporation

THE
Secret Life
OF
Miss Anna Marsh

ELLA QUINN

KENSINGTON BOOKS
KENSINGTON PUBLISHING CORP.
http://www.kensingtonbooks.com

KENSINGTON BOOKS are published by

Kensington Publishing Corp.
119 West 40th Street
New York, NY 10018

All Kensington titles, imprints and distributed lines are available at special quantity discounts for bulk purchases for sales promotion, premiums, fund-raising, educational or institutional use.

Special book excerpts or customized printings can also be created to fit specific needs. For details, write or phone the office of the Kensington Special Sales Manager. Kensington Publishing Corp., 119 West 40th Street, New York, NY 10018. Attn.: Special Sales Department. Phone: 1-800-221-2647.

Kensington and the K logo Reg. U.S. Pat. & TM Off.

eISBN-13: 978-1-60183-165-1
eISBN-10: 1-60183-165-X
First Electronic Edition: November 2013

ISBN-13: 978-1-60183-217-7
ISBN-10: 1-60183-217-6
First Print Edition: November 2013

Printed in the United States of America

To my mother-in-law,
Margaret,
who has supported my
decision to write in
both words and deeds.

Thank you so much.

Acknowledgments

Writing *The Secret Life of Miss Anna Marsh* was an exercise in organization. One cannot have two converging love stories, spies and smugglers without it. Thanks so much to the Regency Romance Critique group as well as Romance Critiquers for bearing with me as they patiently reviewed several versions of *Anna Marsh* while I tried to figure it all out. To Courtney Milan who graciously offered up the name of her editor, Robin Harders. Robin edited the first few chapters when I needed her most and did it quickly. To the members of the Beau Monde Chapter of Romance Writers of America who are always available for advice and support.

As always to my wonderful agent, Elizabeth Pomada, and my editor at Kensington, John Scognamiglio, without whom this book would not be published, and the talented staff at Kensington.

Prologue

Lord Florian Iswell, the fifth son of the Marquis of Wigmore, entered his rooms on Jermyn Street after eating dinner at his club in the convivial company of some old school friends. He spied a sealed letter propped up on the fireplace mantel.

His heart thudded painfully. It had been months since he'd seen his name in that bold scrawl. Gingerly, he reached out his trembling hand. Using two fingers, he plucked the missive up as if merely touching it might harm him, and broke the unadorned seal.

As he read the note, his stomach roiled. He should have never eaten the lobster patties.

> *My dear Florian,*
> *Meet me at the Cock and Crow at eleven o'clock this*
> *evening. Do not, my friend, be late. We have matters of Great*
> *Urgency to discuss.*
> *G.*

"Envill," Florian bellowed to his valet, "when did this arrive?"

"About an hour ago, my lord."

Florian shook the letter. "Why did you not send for me? I'll barely make the meeting as it is."

"I'm sorry, my lord. I told him you were out. He didn't say it was urgent."

Forty-five minutes later, dressed in a shabby brown frieze coat and well-used hat, Florian entered the dingy tap of the Whitecastle inn a few minutes before the appointed time. The pungent smell of unwashed bodies, gin, and ale made him wish he could hold his handkerchief to his nose.

He glanced around the room. A man, indistinguishable from the other patrons, sat in the far corner, nursing an ale. From this distance, he was very like Florian, not much above average height, medium brown hair, and a forgettable face, though in the man's case, it was a ruse. Florian should have seen about killing Georges long ago.

Trying to maintain a casual appearance, Florian walked to the table and assumed a polite smile. "Georges, how are you?"

The man motioned to the chair opposite him. "I'm glad you could meet with me."

After so many years in England, Georges's French accent was almost nonexistent.

"I didn't know I had a choice," Florian said, dryly, eying the seat with disgust. Who knew what was on it.

The smile on the other man's lips didn't reach his dark eyes. "You did not. I merely thought to be pleasant."

Florian ordered a tankard of ale and sat. "What's all this about? I thought we were finished."

"Yes? Many thought the same," Georges said. "One must not underestimate the Corsican."

Sweat broke out on Florian's forehead. Napoleon? He was in exile on Elba. "I take it some small changes are expected?"

"How perceptive you always are." Georges took a pull of his ale. "Then again, it runs in the family, does it not?"

"You would know." Florian's stomach clenched. Between the smells and the unwelcome news, he was starting to feel ill. "Tell me what I can do for you."

Georges leaned forward and lowered his voice. "We need to bring in some rather large packages. Your part is to contact the sort of people who can be helpful to the endeavor."

Tightening his lips into a thin line, Florian asked, "Do you have any particular area in mind?"

"We"—Georges grinned wickedly—"rather like the cliffs of Dover and farther east along the coast."

Florian nodded. "I can't go anywhere until the week's end. I'll contact you when I return."

"My dear cousin." Georges's cold gaze bore through Florian. "I knew I could count on you."

Only because of the mistake he'd once made in trusting the wrong people. "I want this to be over. If I get caught . . . the scandal."

"You should have thought of that before." Georges stood. "I shall await word from you."

"Yes, of course."

Georges left the tavern. Florian waited a few minutes before quitting the place himself.

Bile rose in Florian's throat. He was to have been done with this. Where to find a smuggling gang? There was only one he knew of he might approach. What if they balked? No, they'd help bring the French spies in, or he'd threaten to expose them to the Home Office. He had too much at stake now to be caught. If his father found out, Florian would be cut off without a penny.

Despite what he'd told Georges, Florian decided to leave for Thanport tomorrow, after he made arrangements to rid himself of his demanding cousin.

Chapter 1

Miss Anna Marsh was in her parlor reading, when her maid, Lizzy, entered and held out a grubby piece of paper.

"Came from my brother, Kev, this morning," Lizzy said.

Anna nodded, took the note, and opened it. She perused the contents, then closed her eyes. "I'm going to have to find a way to convince Mama to allow me to remove to Marsh Hill before the Little Season has ended. Though I cannot do anything until after Lady Phoebe's wedding."

"That bad, miss?" Her maid screwed up her face. "You might have a time of it. I heard Lady Marsh was planning to go to some country house next week."

Anna sighed. Ever since her brother Harry's death, Mama had become difficult. "She probably expects me to go with her." Anna shrugged. "Well, I cannot. Someone has been sniffing around Thanport. I don't like the sound of it." Anna rose and walked over to her mahogany writing desk. She opened a drawer. Eschewing the neat stack of elegant pressed paper, she pulled out a piece of the distinctly rougher type. "I'll write Kev and tell him to lay low until I can get there."

K

No information exchanged or meetings scheduled until I arrive.

Mr. A

She sealed the message and handed it to Lizzy. "Make sure this goes out today, even if you have to take it yourself."

"Yes, miss."

Anna pinched her upper nose. "I do hope this is not going to make our lives even more complicated."

"What do you think that other man wants?" Lizzy asked.

"I don't know." Anna shook her head. "But I have a feeling whatever it is will do us no good. I'm going to Mama and try to talk her around. I do wish she and Papa could settle their differences."

Lizzy nodded. "It does make things a bit more difficult."

"That it does." Anna smiled grimly.

A few minutes later, she knocked briefly on the door to the morning room in the back of the house, and tripped in only to stop. The gentleman sitting on a chair next to her mother's chaise rose. Anna curtseyed.

Sebastian, Baron Rutherford, rose and bowed. Anna fought the urge to smile. He was tall and rangy. The cut of his coat molded to his broad shoulders, and his pantaloons clung to his muscular legs. He had hair the color of a hazelnut and impossibly gray eyes. When he was angry, they shone like molten silver. Anna frequently made him angry.

She'd loved him since she was a child. If he'd asked for her hand when she'd first come out, she would have accepted him. Now, at one and twenty, she was wiser.

Sebastian—he hated his given name—had spent the last few years dangling after Anna's best friend, Phoebe, who was now marrying Lord Marcus Finley. With no more cover and his mother nagging at him to wed, he'd turned to Anna. Yet, the past two years had made it impossible for her to marry him unless he truly loved her and all she was. She wasn't sure they even knew each other anymore.

Anna met his gaze coolly. "Lord Rutherford, pray, what brings you here?"

"Oh, Anna dear," her mother said. "Lord Rutherford has very kindly offered to help by escorting you to Charteries for Lady Phoebe's wedding."

Anna raised a brow and stared at Sebastian for a moment before turning to address her mother. Lady Marsh reminded Anna of a wraith. Her mother's dark brown hair was still unmarked by silver. She always dressed in flowing gowns and draped gauzy shawls around her shoulders, giving the impression she would blow away if one breathed hard enough. Mama desperately wanted Anna married and could not understand how it was she'd reached the age of one and twenty still single.

As objecting to Sebastian's escort would do her no good, Anna kept the smile on her face. "Yes, Mama, very kind of him." She glanced at him and thought she saw the remnants of a smug look on his face. "How do you think of these ideas?" she asked sweetly.

His lips twitched slightly. "I really couldn't tell you, Miss Marsh. It just popped into my head. We *are* both attending the wedding after all."

It did not auger well for him that he had used her mother to get his way. "Yes, we do have that in common."

"Well, my dear," Mama said, apparently oblivious to the tension between Anna and her guest. "Lord Rutherford would like to leave fairly early. He is to stand up with Lord Marcus, you know."

Anna's expression didn't change, nor did her dulcet tones. "Indeed? How interesting. I trust you're not doing it for the practice, my lord."

The innocent expression in Miss Marsh's large blue eyes belied the stubborn set of her lips. Rutherford turned his choking laughter into a cough and looked down so she couldn't see his expression.

When he raised his head, she was in negotiations about something with Lady Marsh. He took the time to admire her. As always, Anna was elegantly attired. She wore a day gown in printed mulberry, and he could make out the lean lines of her slender figure. Lately, his fingers had itched to touch her in ways they never had before.

Gleaming chestnut curls were allowed to escape the loose knot held by combs at the back of her head. During the past year, her heart-shaped face had lost much of its youthful roundness. When she stood, the top of her head was below his collarbone. Rutherford had kicked himself at least a dozen times in the last few weeks for not having made a move to engage her affections sooner.

He had simply always just assumed she'd be available when he was ready, but he couldn't have been more wrong. To his chagrin, after Anna had made it very clear he'd have to win her heart, he'd noticed other gentlemen of his ilk also vying for her hand. He wished she'd go home to Kent where he'd have a better chance. At least he'd have her alone. The only other gentleman of marriageable age living in their area was that insufferable pup, Percy Blanchard. Rutherford had nothing to fear on that score.

"But Mama," Anna said reasonably, "the Season is almost over. There are only two weeks left, and it will be terribly flat with Phoebe gone. Papa is at Marsh Hill, and so is Aunt Lillian. I'll be perfectly fine. I can leave from the wedding. If we take the coast roads from Sussex . . ."

"Anna," her mother interrupted, "I will not hear of you taking that route. It is too dangerous. You will stay on the highway where it's safer."

"Yes, Mama. Of course, you're right. Should I take everything with me or will you send it by courier?"

Rutherford frowned slightly. Anna had just won the argument and had really made no concessions at all.

"You will never fit all your baggage in the coach," Lady Marsh said. "Have your maid pack your trunks, and I shall send them."

"Thank you, Mama. I can make the arrangements. There is no need to put yourself out over it." Anna bent and kissed her mother's cheek.

"Very well, my dear. Thank you."

Rutherford wanted to shake his head. When he'd proposed last week, and she'd refused, he had thought it was out of pique that he hadn't asked earlier. It had been clear she was no longer a scruffy little girl in pigtails wearing grown-up clothes, but in fact was ready to take on the role of his wife.

Was something else going on?

"Lord Rutherford," Anna said. "I shall be ready to leave when you are. I'll see you in the morning."

He watched her walk out of the room, and a sense that she had walked out of his life passed over him. *Drat the girl.* She was up to something, and he needed to find out what it was. Perhaps he should have been spending more time with Anna and less hiding behind Lady Phoebe's skirts. He was being ridiculous. He'd known Anna since her birth. That was one of the reasons he wanted to marry her. During the past few years his life had been complicated enough. With her, there would be no surprises.

He almost offered to escort her to Kent, but he'd received a message from the Home Office to hold himself ready, so he needed to return to London after the wedding.

He bowed to Lady Marsh. "My lady, I trust I shall see you in the morning. I am glad I could be of service."

"My dear, Lord Rutherford, I cannot thank you enough for offering to keep an eye on my poor little Anna."

Rutherford gave her his most charming smile. "Not at all, my lady, it will be my pleasure."

He took his leave. Poor little Anna, indeed. The minx. What could she be up to that necessitated an early return to Kent?

Rutherford arrived at his town house in Berkeley Square to find a letter waiting for him asking him to attend Lord Jamison of the Home Office. He immediately set out again. Whatever it was, it had to be important for them to contact him after he'd sold out.

Twenty minutes later he entered Jamison's chamber.

Jamison stood and motioned Rutherford to a seat. "Glad you could come."

Rutherford regarded the large, buff, fair-haired gentleman with a sapient eye. "What is it you need me to do?"

"We think we've a bit of a problem in your area of Kent." Jamison glanced through some documents on his desk. "All along the coast actually. You're not the only one we're calling in." His bushy brows drew together. "We've heard rumors out of France that some of Napoleon's former officers might take up his cause. I've no doubt they'll be trying to run information through the smuggling gangs. That's where you come in." Jamison put his elbows on his desk and leaned forward. "Harry Marsh used to keep track of the smugglers in your area. You'll have to do it now."

Rutherford frowned. "I thought they'd disbanded. That was the reason Harry could leave to work elsewhere."

Jamison shook his large head. "No, my boy. Harry had got

someone else to take them over. Never told us who it was. All he said was the man was responsible and would have good control over them. After all, it was only to have been for a few months."

Rutherford leaned back in his chair and blew out a breath. "I wonder who? I'll have to scout around and try to find out who the smugglers' head man is. Harry always took the lead with them. I went a few times, but I'm not even sure they'd remember me." Rutherford sat up and scowled. "I wish to hell he'd stayed and not gone over to France."

Jamison nodded. "He was a good man. Reckless, but good. A shame his family can't be told the truth about his death."

"I've no idea how they'd feel about his being an intelligencer. Better to let them think he died in Badajoz rather than on a mission." Most Englishmen thought spying the lowest form of vocation. If they only knew the military could not have won without its spies and the information they gathered. "I'll be able to travel to Kent in a couple of days." Rutherford stood. "I've a good friend getting married. I'll go after the wedding."

Jamison rose and held out his hand. "Thank you. I know you don't have to do this."

Rutherford clasped his former chief's hand and smiled. "I'll accept your thanks. You're likely the only one to offer them."

"Rutherford," Jamison said, "let me know if you need reinforcements."

"You can be sure that I will."

Damn Harry Marsh for going off and getting himself killed. Who the devil did he find to take his place? A mental review of the men in his area capable of handling the task came up with nothing. Two years ago, they had all either been too young, gone off doing other things, or incompetent.

The only good thing to come of this was that he would be able to escort Anna home after the wedding ceremony. He wondered how she'd take that bit of news and decided not to tell her until they were already at Marcus's family's estate.

Anna entered her bedchamber to find Lizzy packing. "Did you send the note off?"

"Yes, miss, I had a footman take it." Lizzy said. "Told him it was a letter from me to home."

"Good. We'll be traveling home after the wedding." Anna looked at the clothes spread around the room. "You've no time to lose. Everything must be packed this afternoon. I shall make arrangements for the courier to pick the trunks up in the morning."

"Yes, miss. I have to say, I'll be glad to be home."

For the first time that day, Anna relaxed. "Yes, it will be good to be back in Kent again. Do you want me to help you?"

Lizzy grinned. "No offense, miss, but you're no hand at folding. I'll have it done in a trice."

"Very well, then," Anna replied. "If you're sure you don't need my help, I have some shopping I should complete."

"No, miss." Her maid shook out a gown. "You go on."

Anna found a footman to accompany her, left a message for her mother with the butler, and walked out the door in the direction of Bond Street. She had several items of clothing she needed to fetch and a new hat to buy, as well as silk stockings and other small items she'd not find anywhere closer than Dover.

Two hours later, pleased that she'd found all she needed in such a short amount of time, she returned to Marsh House in time for tea.

Her mother handed her a cup, and Anna helped herself to some of the various biscuits as well as a scone with clotted cream and jam. "I've finished my shopping, and Lizzy is packing. The carter will pick up my trunks in the morning."

"I hope you have a wonderful time at the wedding, my dear," Lady Marsh said. "I was so pleased to hear that Lady Phoebe is finally marrying. She certainly has taken her time settling on someone."

"Yes, Mama. We are all delighted for Phoebe." Mama had in no way approved of the license Phoebe had been given and could not fathom any lady's waiting for a love match. Mama's match had been arranged, and she and Papa had got along very well until Harry died. Then it all seemed to fall apart.

Lady Marsh frowned. "I don't understand why Lady Phoebe had to pick the most eligible gentleman available this Season. Really, Anna, I think you could have done something more to interest him."

Anna valiantly forbore sighing. Lord Marcus Finley, Phoebe's intended, had been the topic of conversation since early September. "Mama, I've told you. He formed an attachment for Phoebe years ago," Anna said. "The only reason he danced with me, that one time, was to aid her. I never had a chance, and I would have looked ridiculous trying to set my cap at him."

"Please do not use that vulgar term," her mother replied. "There *is* Rutherford, my love. He is very eligible, and his mother told me that since he didn't do a good job attaching Lady Phoebe . . ."

"Mama," Anna interrupted. "Phoebe had no interest in Rutherford. They are friends. That is all."

"As I was saying, my dear, Lord Rutherford is free and in need of a wife. I am sure, if you would only make yourself *agreeable* to him, he'd be happy to make you an offer."

Anna resisted the urge to cast her eyes upward. She missed the intimacy she'd had with her mother before Harry's death. Everything was so different now. Anna certainly wasn't going to tell her mother Sebastian had proposed. Trying to turn the conversation away from marriage, Anna said. "Mama, why do you call him Lord Rutherford, when you've known him all his life?"

"That is what we do, my dear. You would be well advised to remember he is no longer a schoolboy, but rather a very eligible gentleman."

"Yes, Mama," Anna replied meekly, and rose. "I must check on Lizzy. She has a lot to pack and not much time. I shall see you at dinner."

"Oh, my dear, I forgot to tell you. I am dining with Lady Worthington. I do not plan to make a late evening of it, but if you have retired by the time I come home, I shall see you in the morning before you leave."

"Please give Lady Worthington my best wishes and enjoy yourself." Anna kissed her mother's cheek and left the room.

Anna walked to the library. If she was to spend the better part of two days in a coach, she'd need books. After searching the shelves, she selected a novel she hadn't seen before. She looked more closely at the cover, opened it, and tilted her head. The pages were full of pictures of naked couples doing the most shocking things *and* directions as to how to do them. She shut the book, then opened it up again, fascinated by the pictures.

Oh my, Mama certainly didn't buy this book! It must have been Harry's. Anna put it back on the shelf. Tears filled her eyes. She wished Harry were here. He'd know how to help her. Even though he was ten years older than she, they had always been close. She remembered him holding her when she was very young. He had always been the first one to arrive when she woke terrified at night.

Even when she was five and he was fifteen, although he didn't really want her following him and Sebastian around, Harry had never tried to stop her. When he'd left, Harry had made her responsible for the smugglers he'd led. Granted he had thought it would only be for a few months, but he'd taught her well. Anna had held the group together for almost three years without mishap, and she would continue to lead them.

She wondered briefly how Sebastian would take that part of her life. The secret part. Only Lizzy, her brother, Kev, and Harry's old groom, Humphrey, knew Anna's identity and that she was female. Her position in the smuggling gang was one of the many reasons Sebastian must be in love with her before she could agree to marry him. He'd have to accept her as she was now.

Anna remained in the library curled up in a chair. When she was ten years old, she had decided to marry Sebastian. That he was twenty hadn't bothered her a bit. That he might wed someone else had never entered her mind. Even now, marriage to someone else wasn't a consideration. She'd marry him or no one. Unfortunately, no one was now a real possibility. Anna stared into the fire trying to envision her future without him and got absolutely nowhere. He was such an integral part of her past.

A footman came in, closed the drapes against the late afternoon gloom, and lit the wall sconces and candelabras.

"Please ask Cook if dinner can be served earlier."

"Yes, miss."

He came back a few minutes later, to assure her Cook would be happy to bring dinner forward.

Once the footman left, she got up and went back to the bookshelf. Anna found a couple of novels before leaving the room and, after some hesitation, took Harry's book as well. If nothing else, it would make her feel closer to him.

October 26th, 1814, London

Rutherford decided not to tell either Anna or Lady Marsh he would accompany Anna to Marsh Hill. She'd accepted his escort, albeit unwillingly, to Charteries, Marcus's family's estate. Rutherford had no desire to push his luck any further until he had to. Miss Marsh would discover he intended to escort her to Kent when he did not turn off the post road to London, and by then it would be too late for her to object.

Arriving the next morning shortly after eight o'clock, he discovered that early was a relative term. Anna was ready at eight o'clock. Lady Marsh had not yet come down.

He paced the entry hall and checked his pocket watch, again, before addressing Anna. "Do you think she'll be much longer?"

"I'll send someone to fetch her. It's not good to keep the horses waiting like this." Anna hailed a maid and gave her instructions.

Thirty minutes later, Lady Marsh appeared on the stairs. "Good morning, Lord Rutherford. I do hope I have not kept you waiting."

He took the offered hand and bowed. "No, my lady. Not at all."

Anna glanced up at the ceiling. "Mama, we must depart if we are to reach Charteries by noon."

Lady Marsh fluttered over Anna like a hen over a chick. "Do you have everything you need?"

"Yes, Mama."

Anna turned to go out the front door, and her mother embraced her. "My dear, child. How I will miss you."

Anna returned the hug. "I will miss you as well. We must leave."

Tears sprang into Lady Marsh's eyes. "Yes, of course. How silly of me."

She stood in the door weeping and mopping her eyes with a lace-trimmed handkerchief as Rutherford helped Anna into the coach. You'd have thought Anna was going to Russia and Lady Marsh would never see her daughter again. "I don't remember your mother being like this."

Anna frowned slightly. "Ever since Harry died she has been."

"Lady Marsh has never recovered?"

"No. Not really," Anna said sadly.

Rutherford couldn't imagine how painful losing a child would be. The death of his friend had been hard enough to bear. Rutherford closed the door and gave the coachman the signal to start. He mounted his horse, waiting until the outriders Lady Marsh had hired flanked the carriage, before following after them. They made their way through London's morning traffic, then on to the post road without incident.

The trip would take approximately three hours. They stopped midway to refresh themselves. It would be a good time to start getting back into Anna's good graces.

He handed her down from the coach. "I've reserved a private parlor, if you'd like it?"

She glanced around. "Thank you, but I think I'd prefer to stand for a while."

"Very understandable. Would you like hot cider?"

"Yes, please."

He found a servant to bring their drinks. "Anna, it's occurred to me that I could have been of more help since Harry died. I'm sorry I was not."

She glanced suddenly at him, her brows drawn together. "It wasn't your fault you kept being called away to your other estates."

"I might have left it in my steward's hands." He should have quit going on missions and paid more attention to Anna.

"That is never the answer. You owe a duty to your dependents."

This conversation was not going at all how he wanted it to. While he was trying to think of what else to say, the coachman came up.

"Miss, it's time we were going again."

Anna put her cup down on a bench. "I'll be right there."

When Rutherford and Anna arrived at Charteries, Lord Marcus Finley, second son of the Marquis of Dunwood, met them. Rutherford had known Marcus since Eton and could think of no one better to confide in regarding his problems with Miss Marsh, particularly since Marcus had managed to bring Lady Phoebe up to scratch after her six years on the Marriage Mart.

"Welcome to Charteries." Marcus handed Anna down from the coach. "Phoebe will be with you directly. I've sent a message to her."

Anna smiled. "Thank you, my lord. If you'll have someone show me to my chamber, I'll be ready for her."

Marcus addressed his butler. "Wilson, please have Miss Marsh and her maid escorted to her room."

Rutherford dismounted and greeted his friend. "I'd like to have a word with you if I could."

Marcus raised a brow. "Yes, of course. Wash your dirt off, and meet me in the morning room."

Rutherford shook his hand. "Thank you."

A half an hour later, Marcus handed Rutherford a glass of wine. "Please have a seat. What do you wish to discuss?"

Rutherford heaved a sigh. "Finley, you're getting leg shackled. Can you tell me how to do it?"

Marcus laughed.

Rutherford grinned ruefully. "Yes, I know. That *I,* of all people, should be asking that question, but Finley, I am quite serious."

Marcus struggled to regain his countenance. "What in God's name has brought this about? I thought you were sure of Miss Marsh?"

"I thought so as well," Rutherford said, chagrined. "However, it turns out she is not coming round as I'd hoped. Sometimes it seems as if she's avoiding me."

Marcus dropped into a chair. "I suppose you'd better tell me about it."

"I thought she would just accept me," Rutherford said.

"Are you telling me"—Marcus leaned forward, with an incredulous look on his face—"you expected her to accept you, when you'd been dancing attendance on Phoebe for years and then gave Miss Marsh no reason why she should marry you?"

Rutherford wouldn't have put it quite like that. "Well, you see . . ." He paused, trying to find the words. "I've known her all her life. I thought she was already in a fair way to being in love with me, or at least liking me a good deal. It never occurred to me . . ."

"Never occurred to you," Marcus retorted, "she might not appreciate being treated as a sure thing?"

Rutherford heaved a sigh. "I suppose I didn't think of it in those terms."

Marcus shook his head. "What a sapskull. I don't know Miss Marsh that intimately, but I know her well enough to expect she'd bridle at that sort of arrogant behavior."

Perhaps Marcus had a point. "I thought I'd leave well enough alone until I needed to marry, or until I thought she might be forming an attachment for someone else." Something seemed to lodge in his throat, and he coughed. "She was very young, and as long as her heart wasn't otherwise engaged . . ."

"Rutherford," Marcus said. "You've rushed your fences and taken a fall. It appears to me you need to start over. You, my friend, will have to undergo the humiliating experience of courting the woman you could probably have had without effort three or more years ago, when she was not so knowledgeable."

Rutherford remembered Anna smiling at him and then accepting another gentleman's offer to dance, or to escort her to supper. He couldn't believe he'd been so blind. "Now that you've said it, it all makes sense." He groaned. "The way she's hung back from me and kept me at arm's length. She plans to go home to Kent when she leaves here. I shall accompany her, but I don't intend to tell her."

Marcus asked. "Are you sure she is the one for you?"

"Of course she is. Despite her recent behavior, I've known her all her life. Marriage with her would be comfortable. There'd be no surprises." Rutherford picked up his glass and twirled the wine before taking a sip. "She's poised and fits well into Polite Society. I've heard that since her brother's death, she's assumed all the household responsibilities at her home. I'm sure we'll have our little disagreements from time to time, but she is used to taking her lead from me." Rutherford nodded his head. "Yes, I believe she is now ready to take her position as Lady Rutherford."

In fact, he couldn't imagine his life without her. For years he'd resisted the lures thrown out by other ladies as he waited for Anna to mature. Then lately, there were the less chaste desires he'd been having about her as well. He wanted to spear his fingers through her dark chestnut curls and run his tongue down her supple neck. Somehow he had to convince her to marry him.

Marcus regarded him dubiously. "I wish you luck."

Rutherford stopped himself from running his finger under his neck cloth. "It may take a little time, but I'm sure she'll come around."

Chapter 2

Anna reached the morning room door and stopped when she heard Marcus ask how Sebastian felt about her. Mama always said one should never eavesdrop, but this was too tempting not to. Then he spoke, and Anna wished she'd not given in to the lure. If Sebastian expected her to be comfortable and take her lead from him, he didn't know her at all. If that was what he wanted in a wife, it was not she. Even if she "came around," she wouldn't be what he wanted, and did she really wish to marry him at all? When had he become so stodgy?

She'd never even thought of marrying anyone but Sebastian. Her head swam for a moment as the reality of what he'd said struck her. He'd never be her husband. The dream she'd had since childhood of her future shattered like thin ice. She rapidly blinked back the tears pricking her eyes. She'd never felt so lost.

"Anna, there you are." Phoebe said. "I'm glad you found the way."

Anna took a breath and smiled before turning to her friend. "It was really no problem at all. I'm very good with directions."

"If you don't mind, I want to see Marcus before our stroll in the gardens."

"Not at all."

Anna and Phoebe entered the morning room. Sebastian and Marcus both stood. Marcus said something about walking with them. Anna prayed the gentlemen would not accompany Phoebe and her. When Marcus changed his mind, Anna let out a little breath of relief. She really could not deal with Sebastian right now. Not after what she'd overheard and when her feelings were so raw.

After her shawl was fetched, she and Phoebe meandered around the gardens.

"Is anything the matter?" Phoebe asked.

Anna wouldn't ruin her friend's day with worries over her. She smiled. "No. I'm just thinking about tomorrow and how happy I'll be for you."

Phoebe patted Anna's arm. "You'll know the same joy some day. Do not doubt it."

Anna kept the smile on her face, even though she knew it wasn't true. She'd probably never know love like that.

That evening she met the rest of the guests in the dining room. Rutherford started to approach more than once, but Anna stayed with a group of ladies, chatting as if she hadn't noticed him. When it was finally time for dinner, a Mr. Matthews escorted her in. Thankfully, they were seated several places away from Rutherford on the same side of the table, so she'd not have to see him.

The best thing she could do was keep her mind busy with the problems at home and on her smuggling gang. That would keep her occupied.

After dinner, she excused herself early and went to her room. Sitting in the window seat, she tried to shake off her disappointment over Sebastian. She never really thought of him by any other name, though she called him Rutherford now. Tonight he had been perfectly dressed as always. His black jacket fit snuggly setting off his magnificent shoulders, with not a wrinkle to be seen. His shirt points were high enough for fashion but not so high he couldn't turn his head. *And his cravat.* Anna wanted to sigh. No one but Brummell could tie a cravat like Sebastian.

Quickly, she turned her mind to the smuggling gang's problem, and desperately hoped it wasn't serious. She rubbed her hands over her face, trying to think of any explanation for Kev's urgent message. She could do nothing from here. Since they had to take the toll road back toward London, the trip would take two days. She was not due to leave Charteries until the day after tomorrow. No matter how she worked it out, it would still be at least three more days until she arrived home. That was too long. She'd send a message to Kev as soon as she returned. They could meet that night.

Lizzy entered carrying a large pitcher of water. "Time for you to wash up and get ready for bed." She poured water into a basin. "I thought you might want to know, Lord Rutherford's man, Robertson, was asking when you'd be leaving here."

"What did you tell him?"

Lizzy grinned. "I told him we'd leave when you gave the order."

Anna returned Lizzy's smile. "I've decided to leave sooner than I'd planned. We'll depart as soon after the wedding breakfast as we are able."

"That'll put us on the road overnight."

Anna nodded. "We shall stop at Seven Oakes. I just want to go home."

And away from Sebastian.

"We'll be in Kent," Rutherford said to Marcus as they shared brandy in his study after dinner. "No balls or other parties. No other gentlemen."

Thank God for that.

Marcus raised a skeptical brow. "Miss Marsh has been ignoring you pretty studiously today. Do you really think she's that stupid?"

"That is part of the problem. She's too damned smart for her own good. Trust me. Once I have her to myself, she'll change her mind."

"She's never struck me as being a particularly malleable sort of female. You know her best, of course."

Rutherford frowned. "You may be right. She always was an obstinate child, but I thought she'd become less stubborn. At least she appears that way. There must be something I can offer her."

Marcus's lips tilted up. "Love?"

"How can you," Rutherford demanded, "utter that word out loud and not shiver?"

Marcus shook his head. "Blame it on my falling in love with Phoebe when I was twenty. Neither the emotion nor the word has ever scared me."

"Yes, well, you must be the only gentleman of my acquaintance who can say that."

"Probably." Marcus agreed. "Do you love Anna?"

"Of course I do. She's been like a sister to me." Except recently his thoughts had not been at all brotherly.

"How do you plan to approach her?" Marcus asked.

"I've not quite made out my plan of battle yet." Rutherford took out his pocket watch and rubbed it. "I intend to use this weekend to think about it. Until then, I will stay as close to her as possible. I don't want anyone else to decide to use the break between the Seasons to catch her interest." Rutherford was beginning to wish for a return to arranged marriages. Surely their fathers would have betrothed them. In fact, they should have done it when she was born.

"When do you plan to tell her you're already in love with her?"

"I have told her. At least, I must have at some point over the years," Rutherford replied.

"Don't expect to succeed. Ladies need to hear it, often." Marcus grinned. "Remind me to tell you I told you so."

Rutherford glared at his friend. For God's sake, he'd brought down an entire branch of Napoleon's spy apparatus. How hard could it be to discover the key to one recalcitrant female, who might not be so comfortable and easily led after all? Perhaps he really didn't need a calm life. He raised himself to his full height of over six feet two inches. "I have no intention of failing. *I* am descended from Norman warlords, I'll have you know."

"Aren't we all," Marcus replied dryly. "Just who do you think she's descended from? Think about it. I must get back to the rest of my guests."

After Marcus left, Rutherford stared into the fire, thinking about Anna's dark curls and creamy skin. God how he wanted to bury his face in her hair, then slowly kiss his way down her neck to her breasts, tasting as he went. He shook himself. Anna had definitely changed.

He left the library and found the billiards room in time to join a game.

"Rutherford, your turn," his friend Huntley said. "What are you in such a brown study about?"

"Nothing. Nothing at all." Rutherford had the uncomfortable feeling he was going to pay for being so sure of himself with Anna.

He missed his shot.

October 27th, 1814, Charteries, Sussex

The next morning Anna wished Phoebe happy, before taking a seat in the small chapel and watching Phoebe marry. Phoebe's joy and her love for Marcus radiated from her. He had eyes for no one but her, and when they said their vows, it was as if they were in their own private world.

Despite what Anna had heard Sebastian say, her childhood dreams were not going away as she wished they would. She wanted the same happiness. She still wanted Sebastian to gaze at her like Marcus looked at Phoebe. Anna's throat tightened. Perhaps she could have a love like that with Sebastian, but only if he could accept her and her secret. Who was she kidding? He wanted a safe, comfortable wife. One he could order around. Even without her duties to the smugglers, she'd never be that. She smiled through her tears as Marcus kissed Phoebe. A small part of Anna thought there might be hope after all, but her head told her it was a dream.

A few hours after the ceremony while the festivities were still continuing, she and Sebastian were talking with Phoebe and Marcus when they learned Marcus's gravely ill brother had finally passed away. Anna watched as Phoebe drew her new nieces to her, and Anna and Sebastian left them to grieve with their family. Now Anna was more than glad she'd already made arrangements to leave.

They were making their way down a corridor when she turned to him. "Did you know Evesham?"

"Not well. I know he and Marcus were very close." Sebastian put his hand on her shoulder. "Evesham has been ill for a long time."

"I know." Tears stung her eyes. "But that knowledge doesn't make it any easier when it happens."

"You're right, of course," he said solemnly.

Anna glanced at him. "I should go."

"What are your plans this evening?" he asked.

"I will not be here. I'm leaving for Kent."

"Are you?" He opened his eyes in shock. "I thought you weren't departing until tomorrow."

"No. I'd already made the arrangements. If I remained, I'd feel as if I were intruding."

"You know you aren't. Though, I agree, leaving soon might be a good idea."

Why did he have to keep pressing himself on her? "You should stay. I'll do quite well on my own."

"No, not at all," Rutherford smiled. "I am happy to escort you."

She tried and failed to think of a reason he could not accompany her. Why did he have to smile at her like that? If only she could extinguish her feelings for him like one blows out a candle. Especially now, when she wanted so very much to be held and comforted. "Be ready in half an hour."

He bowed. "I'll be waiting."

Anna swept up the stairs to her room. At least he was going on to London, and she wouldn't have to see him until Christmas, if at all. She opened the door. "Lizzy, are you ready?"

"One satchel left, miss. The trunks are in the coach. Turn around and let me unlace you."

"Lord Rutherford has decided to escort us."

"Is there a reason we don't like his lordship anymore?" Lizzy asked.

"He is a very nice man," Anna said, holding back her tears. "But he would not make a good husband for me. Unfortunately, he doesn't realize it."

"Ah, I see." Her maid fell quiet.

"What is it?" Anna asked.

"Well, I did have some hopes for Mr. Robertson, his lordship's valet," Lizzy said prosaically. "But if you're not going to marry his lordship, I'll have to give them up."

Anna didn't know whether to laugh or cry. She stepped out of one gown and into the one she'd travel in. "I'm sorry to have spoiled your hopes."

Her maid shrugged. "Likely I'm not highborn enough for him anyway. He speaks much better than me."

"Lizzy, you'd make anyone a good wife. For all you know he might have learned how to talk like that."

"Doesn't matter any way. There you go. All laced up. I'll just get the bag, and we're ready to go."

Part of Anna wanted to try to sneak out before Sebastian arrived. It was not to be. He stood waiting at the bottom of the stairs.

Taking her hand, he bowed over it. "I shall add punctuality to your list of accomplishments."

Three years ago, her heart would have fluttered if he'd said that to her. Now, it contracted painfully. "Let's be off. I want to get as far as possible today."

After handing her into the coach, Sebastian mounted and ordered the coachman to spring the team. They made good time on the post road back toward London. When they reached Crawley, Anna leaned out of the window to say good-bye to Sebastian. Now that she knew marriage was out of the question, she couldn't stand his being so close. It abraded her already aggravated nerves. She forced herself to smile. "I bid you a good journey to Town."

"I'm not leaving. I'm going home as well."

If Anna's jaw hadn't been clenched, it would have dropped open. This was the worst possible news. He'd always run tame at Marsh Hill, and she'd have to try to avoid him. "How lovely. Do you intend to remain long?"

He stared at her for a few moments, and she fought not to fidget.

"That depends on how my plans prosper."

He meant her. This just got worse and worse. "I plan to remain overnight in Seven Oakes."

He smiled. "Perfect. I'll see you there."

After he left, Anna slumped back against the squabs as they drove east out of town. "I have got to figure out how to stay out of his way."

Lizzy glanced at Anna. "From what I've seen, he's pretty stubborn."

She nodded. "Yes. He is. If only he'd realize that we won't suit."

"Why don't you show him?" Lizzy asked.

"What do you mean?"

She scrunched up her face for a minute. "Well, if you don't think you'll get along, then, if he spends time with you, he's bound to see it after a while."

Anna frowned. "You mean *spend time* with him so that he doesn't want to marry me?"

"That's it," her maid said. "Whatever it is that you or he don't like will come out." Lizzy grinned. "Like five day old fish."

Anna held her nose and laughed, but Lizzy might have a point. Yet, could she do it? How many times would her heart break before he discovered his mistake, or she fell into his arms and made the worst mistake of her life?"

By the time their party reached the Brook Inn in Seven Oakes, Anna had decided she would be completely herself. That should soon send Sebastian running back to London to look for another lady to be his wife. Fortunately, acting the way she normally did would not be difficult. Except recently, when she had been trying to hold him at arm's length, she'd never pretended around Sebastian. He merely hadn't seen her lately anywhere but in Town where she conformed to the role expected of her.

Sebastian helped Anna and Lizzy down from the coach. "I have to say I'm glad for the outriders," he said. "They make us look respectable."

"I don't think I've ever been anything but respectable."

"I can think of several episodes you engaged in."

"Well, since I've come out I mean. One cannot count my childhood antics." The smugglers might be a different issue.

He cocked his head at an angle. "True, you always appear perfectly demure in London."

"Yes, well, ladies don't have much of a choice."

He stared at her for a few moments, before glancing up. "Have you an objection to my arranging our rooms?"

She wondered what he'd really been about to say. "If you wish to be useful, I shall require one room for myself with a trundle bed for my maid and a private parlor, as well as rooms for the coachman and outriders. While you're doing that, I'll organize the baggage and consult with the landlord's wife about dinner." She pursed her lips. "You're welcome to dine with me."

He bowed. "A comradely gesture. Do you intend to keep your maid with you during dinner?"

"Of course," Anna replied. "You need have no worries over the proprieties." Or lack of them as the case may be. There was no way she'd be caught in a room alone with him.

They retired shortly after ten o'clock and left early the next morning.

It was late afternoon, almost dark, when they turned into the drive of Marsh Hill. Anna leaned forward to glimpse her family's early Georgian house built of white stone. The manor was designed in a square *U*. A large portico graced the front, and the last rays of sun glinted off the long casement windows of the west wing, her wing. She used to share it with Harry, but now she was alone. Which was a good thing as no one watched her comings and goings.

The coach drew up to the front door. Ledster, her father's butler, greeted her warmly.

"Welcome home, miss. We're happy to have you back."

Anna grinned. "I'm happy to be home. How are my father and aunt?"

"Everyone here is well."

"Just as it should be. I've told Lord Rutherford he may dine with us. Will you please tell Cook?"

"Yes, miss, I'll send a message to her. You should change for dinner. The master and your aunt, Lady Tully, are already in the drawing room."

"Yes, of course. Please take Lord Rutherford to a chamber. He'll want to wash and change as well," Anna said, as Rutherford walked into the main hall.

He greeted the butler. "How much time do I have until dinner?"

"Not long at all, my lord."

Anna ascended the main staircase with him. They parted in the hallway. "I'll see you in the drawing room."

She left as Sebastian bowed. He'd never been so polite to her before when they were in Kent. Was all this courtesy part of his courtship plan?

When she arrived in her room, Lizzy was directing a groom as to where to place Anna's trunk, then rummaged through it and took out an evening gown and shook it.

"Here, this will do," Lizzy said. "Would you like a bath after dinner?"

"No, I won't have time." Anna stepped out of her traveling clothes. "I'll leave the drawing room soon as possible after tea is served and change to meet Kev. Send a message to him to meet me in the grove by the cliffs."

"Yes, miss. I'll do it as soon as you're dressed."

Twenty minutes later, Anna walked down to the drawing room, the last to arrive.

"Well, my sweet girl," Sir William Marsh said, giving Anna a kiss. "I'm glad you're home."

She warmly returned her father's embrace. He was a little taller than medium height with dark hair in which only a bit of silver showed. He smiled down at her, and she could see the blue of her eyes reflected in his. He'd dressed fashionably in knee breeches and a well-fitting black coat, as if he didn't spend most of his time in Kent these days.

"I missed you, Papa. I'm glad to be home." Anna turned toward her paternal aunt, whom Anna greatly resembled, gowned in rich brown silk trimmed with cream lace, and embraced her. "Aunt Lillian, I'm so glad you're still here. Why can't you ever come before I leave for the Season?"

"Maybe next year," Lillian said. "I am very happy to see you, my dear. You look lovely. Are you well?"

Anna smiled. "Yes, I am and *so* glad to be home."

Lillian's brows drew together, questioning.

"Not now, please. I'll tell you all about it later." Her aunt would want to hear about Anna's mother. "Rutherford, you remember Lady Tully?"

"Yes, of course, my lady." He bowed. "How have you been?"

"Very well thank you, my lord."

Ledster announced dinner. Rutherford offered his arm to Anna. "Please allow me."

She placed her hand on his arm. "Thank you."

They sat informally at the dinner table with Lillian on one side of Anna's father and Anna on the other. Rutherford took a place next to Anna. She glanced at him, and his well-molded lips curved up. He was so close, heat radiated from him to her.

Until two years ago, when Harry died, her father had represented the area in the House of Commons. Then news of her brother's death had come. After that, Papa was unable to concentrate on anything and gave up his seat. The talk, naturally, turned to the latest legislative session.

"I have to tell you, Rutherford, I'm not at all pleased with the job Mr. Cloverly is doing representing us."

"I agree about Cloverly," Anna said. "He's very old-fashioned, and the party needs new ideas."

Rutherford raised a brow. "Indeed?"

Anna raised one of hers in response. "In this modern age, we need more advanced thinkers."

Her father chuckled. "Anna would run if she could. Though she'd be likely to represent the Radicals."

Now was her opportunity to show Rutherford they'd not suit. Anna turned to him. "At least they support school for all children and universal suffrage. If all large landowners established schools and encouraged their dependents to attend, it would make a start to education for all."

Sebastian's brow furrowed. "Though I support the underling sympathies, I think them unrealistic at the present time. Too many of the peerage are afraid of the same type of uprising as occurred in France."

"I find that thinking runs counter to good sense. If the French peasants had been provided more opportunities, they might not have rebelled. Though one cannot discount the stupidity of their king."

Sebastian laughed. "We have nothing to be proud of in this country."

"You've just taken your seat in the Lords," Anna said. "How will you vote?"

His steady gray gaze regarded her for a moment. "There is much to be said for the more forward thinkers in our party. I shall consider all sides before I make a decision." He took a sip of wine.

"Could you see," she forged ahead, "your views being swayed by a wife, if she had valid arguments to put forward?"

He took a drink of wine. "With the right lady, of course."

She was not going to let him off that easily. "Do you plan to become more involved in politics?"

He gave a small sigh. "If I had the proper support. You know it's impossible for a single man to have much influence. One is not taken seriously until one marries."

"You would not marry for that alone."

"No. There are other reasons I wish to wed."

Well, he'd danced around that very prettily. "Do you have schools on your estates?"

He stared at her again. Good. Maybe soon he'd leave her alone.

"It is something I've been considering," Rutherford said. "Though our need is not as pressing as in other areas of England."

The soup was served. Anna picked up her spoon. "Indeed, I assume you are referring to the opportunities the children have for employment in our area."

"Of course."

"I believe education must always be something to be desired," she responded, "whether it leads to a job or not. It would not be possible for me to condone keeping one's dependents in ignorance."

Rutherford held his soup spoon suspended for a moment before dipping it in the bowl. "I cannot disagree with you. I suppose you would require all landlords to provide schools?"

"I would. Though I doubt the proposal would make it through the Lords," she said, chagrined.

His lips tilted up in amusement. "That is a debate I'd like to see."

"Yes." She sighed. "I, as well. I wonder if it will ever happen, schools for everyone."

"An interesting thought. I very much doubt it."

"I hope you're wrong. This country cannot properly develop if its people are kept in ignorance." She'd finished her soup, and it was removed. "Someday, there will be universal suffrage."

The silence stretched until the second course was served, when Anna, her father, and Rutherford once again picked up the debate.

After dessert, Aunt Lillian asked, "Do you gentlemen plan to drink your port in here? Or will you join us in the drawing room?"

Sir William rose. "We'll come with you if Rutherford has no objection."

"Port in the drawing room sounds fine to me, sir." Rutherford stood and held out his hand to Anna. "Shall we?"

Anna glanced quickly at the clock in the corner of the room. "Of course, though I'd like to retire early. I'm feeling a little tired."

Rutherford did not stay long after tea was served. He thanked Sir William, bowed to Lillian. Anna walked him to the door.

He took her hand and raised it to his lips. "Thank you for the use of your coach. I'll have it returned in the morning. Would you do me the honor of riding with me tomorrow afternoon?"

She wished he hadn't asked. Surely he could see she was not the wife for him. Anna smiled. "I'd like that. Come for me after luncheon."

"Until then."

She closed the door after him. Unfortunately, it would be fun to ride with him again. Her groom always went too slow. She wished her horse, Thunderer, was here and not still in London.

Anna walked back to the drawing room, preparing to make her excuses to retire, but her father and aunt weren't ready to let her go just yet. It was another half an hour before she could make her escape. She hurried up to her chamber. "Lizzy, what time did you tell Kev I'd meet him?"

"You've got less than an hour, miss," Lizzy said. "Here, let's get you out of your gown."

Anna was soon dressed in a serviceable pair of breeches, linen shirt, scarf, and dark brown wool jacket. Lizzy braided her hair and pinned it up to fit easily under her hat. Anna pulled on her boots and donned a warm frieze coat. Her maid handed her a muffler, which she wrapped around her throat and the bottom part of her face, before putting the wide-brimmed black felt hat over her braids.

"I'll not be long, maybe an hour." She picked up her gloves from the dressing table and slipped down the back stairs and out a side door.

Fortunately, her wing was on the stable yard side of the house. Taking long strides, she reached the stable door. Humphrey, Harry's old groom, helped her mount, then swung up on to his hack.

"Humphrey, I'll be fine by myself."

"Yes, miss, so you always say. I promised Mr. Harry I'd take care of you. That's just what I'm doing."

Anna sighed. "Come on then. Let's go. Remember, you must stay back once we see the stand."

"Yes, miss. Just like all the other times."

She didn't know why she bothered. Humphrey would do exactly as Harry had instructed. They walked as quietly as possible out of the stable yard to a nearby meadow, before allowing the horses to canter. Once Thunderer, her horse, arrived, Humphrey wouldn't be so protective. Thunderer could outrun any steed for three counties. She hugged the horse with her knees, guiding him. As she leaned low, the cold wind rushed by, stinging her cheeks. Moonlight lit their way, and before long she could smell the salt air. Anna inhaled the scent deeply. This was one of the parts of her Rutherford wouldn't like, the wildness she felt when she rode by the sea.

When she and Humphrey arrived at the grove, Kev was waiting. "Thanks for comin' so fast, Mr. Arnold."

Mr. Arnold was the pseudonym Harry had used and passed to her when he'd gone away.

"You're welcome," Anna said. "Now what's happened?"

"T'were a man, a Town swell. Come snooping around looking for a smuggling gang. Petey, he directed him to me. Told me he had some wool he wanted to ship to France. I said I weren't the leader, and I'd have to talk wi' my man."

Anna's concern grew. This could be the very thing they were trying to avoid. "Wool? I don't believe it. There are no duties for him to ship out of England, and the French are still in a state of flux."

Kev shook his head. "Didn't sound right to me neither."

"Did he tell you when he wanted to meet with me?" Anna asked.

"No, said he'd be back. Didn't give no time. He were mighty fixed on leavin' fast like."

Anna frowned. "With luck we won't hear from him again."

Kev scratched his head. "Can't say I think we're goin' to be lucky."

"I must do all I am able to keep him from using us for the wrong purpose. Keep your ears open, and let me know if you hear anything else. What else do we have going?"

"Well, we got some brandy a-comin' in two days, on Saturday night. Might you be wantin' to call a meetin'?"

"Yes, we'll need to ensure that if anyone else is approached, they know what to say," Anna said. "Let's meet at the old barn near the cutter's cottage at eleven o'clock on Saturday. That will still give the men plenty of time to take delivery of the brandy and unload it."

"Yes, that'll do it," Kev replied. "You'd best be gettin' back now. I don't want Lizzy upset. She'll give me what for if you're late."

Anna nodded. "Kev, you take care. I'll see you Saturday."

Kev made his way down the trail to the beach. From there he'd walk, keeping close to the cliffs, to the docks in the village.

"Humphrey, you heard?"

"Yes, miss. Looks like we'll be seeing some action. Sure wish Mr. Harry was still here."

"You're not the only one. We'll just have to make him proud." Anna blinked back her tears. "Here, help me up."

She let her horse have its head, but it wasn't fast enough to outrun her grief.

By the time they'd snuck back into the stable, Anna had herself under control. She brushed down her horse and watered him before walking to the house.

Lizzy was waiting for her.

"What's happened, Miss Anna?"

"We may have a problem." She told her maid about the gentleman from London.

Lizzy nodded. "Let's get you out of those clothes. You wash up. I'll have a bath for you in the morning."

Anna cleaned herself and changed into her night rail.

"Good night, miss," Lizzy said, folding the male clothing. "You'll need to take these to the cottage. It'll be the devil to pay if you're caught in them in the house."

"You're right. There is no point in running the risk. I'll do it after breakfast."

"Yes, miss. To bed with you now."

"Good night, Lizzy." She got between the covers of her large four-poster bed, whilst Lizzy drew the curtains around two sides, leaving the side toward the windows open.

Anna's mind drifted back to her dead brother. Silent tears slid over her cheeks and down her neck. Harry had been gone over two years now. Yet she could still hear him guiding her, giving her advice. She hoped the contact at the Home Office he'd given her was still there. Once she discovered what she needed to know, she'd send a carefully worded message using the code Harry had left with her.

Her mind turned to Rutherford. She prayed he'd soon discover she was not what he wanted. She could never betray herself or Harry's trust.

Chapter 3

November 3rd, 1814, The Priory, Kent

"Hell and damnation. Is that all you were able to discover?" Rutherford paced the floor in his study. He'd been home nearly a week and had discovered precisely nothing about the smugglers. He'd sent Jeb, one of his under-grooms, to learn what he could.

Jeb shuffled his feet. "Yes, my lord. Like as much, they're all a bit leery knowin' I work here at the Priory, you bein' the magistrate and all."

"There has got to be a way to find out who their leader is," Rutherford growled. "Any idea what they're supplying and to whom?"

Jeb scratched his head. "I think it's mostly brandy, my lord. The innkeeper might know more. But he ain't goin' to talk to me."

"He'll speak with me, by God." Rutherford snapped.

The groom hung his head. "Yes, my lord."

"Jeb, you did the best you could under the circumstances," Rutherford said. "Thank you for your effort. See my steward, Mr. Stanley, and tell him he's to pay you an extra ten shillings."

Jeb's jaw dropped. "Thank you, my lord. I never expected that much."

Rutherford sat at his desk. "Don't mention any of this to anyone."

"Me mouth's shut tight, my lord."

Rutherford had a different incentive planned for the innkeeper. After Jeb left, Rutherford stared out the windows on to a lawn.

According to a missive from Jamison, things were starting to heat up. One of France's known spies had been spotted in a Whitechapel tavern. Rutherford tugged the bell pull and gave the footman a message for the stables to ready his horse and to have Mr. Robertson, his valet, meet Rutherford in his chamber.

Within twenty minutes, Rutherford was on his way to the small coastal town of Thanport. He rode into the yard of the Fish and Line, the town's main inn. After dismounting, he threw the reins to one of the ostlers. The old stone building had a sloping slate roof. The Priory had owned it since the late seventeenth century. Rutherford ducked as he went through the low doorway and surveyed the taproom, studying the crowd of men, who turned to look at him. He nodded a greeting before going to the bar.

The innkeeper, Mr. Norby, wiped his hands on his apron and came around to Rutherford. "Here, here, your lordship, no use you coming to the bar. I'll have Sally bring you what you want."

"I came here to talk to you," Rutherford said in a low voice. "Let's go into your office."

Mr. Norby licked his lips. "If it's about the profits . . ."

"No," Rutherford interrupted, "though we may discuss them later. Come." He headed toward the back, and Norby had no choice but to follow.

Once in the small office, Rutherford closed the door. "I want you to tell me what you know about the local smuggling gang. Don't bother telling me you don't know anything about them. I am well aware of where your brandy and other wines come from."

Norby shifted his eyes away. "No, my lord, you're mistaken. I got no truck with smugglers."

Rutherford raised a brow. "Try again."

The innkeeper swallowed. "I'll swear on me mother's grave, my lord. I never seen 'em."

"You do realize I can terminate your lease in one month's time, do you not?" Rutherford asked, affecting a disinterested drawl.

Norby's mouth opened and closed like that of a fish. "No, my lord, please. I've got my family to support, and me mother's sick."

"Is this the same mother upon whose grave you are willing to swear?" Rutherford asked humorlessly. "You have a week to get me a contact to the smuggling gang in this area, or you may prepare to find other employment and lodgings. My steward, Mr. Stanley, will be here to look at your books the day after tomorrow. I trust I've made myself clear."

The innkeeper nodded. "Yes, my lord. I–I'll get what you want."

Rutherford started out of the office and turned. "And Norby, I don't want it to get around that I'm the one seeking the information. I shall be extremely displeased if anyone finds out."

The innkeeper shook his head several times. "No, my lord—I mean, yes, my lord."

"Good, I'm pleased we have an understanding." Rutherford gave the man a thin smile. "Send me a message when you have what I want."

Rutherford left the office and returned to the tap where he sat with a few of the local men he knew at a long table by the thick glass windows.

Sally, the serving maid, swung her hips as she walked over to him, bending low to take his order and giving him a good view of her abundant breasts and dark pink nipples.

Trying to ignore her gaping bodice, he said, "I'll have a pint of your regular."

She smiled and bent a little lower. "Are ye sure there's not somethin' else ye might want, my lord?"

One of the other men reached out to grab her and spared Rutherford from answering. She danced deftly away. "Here now, they ain't on offer for ye."

"Ah, Sally, just a little feel is all I'm askin'. Be fair now, girl."

"When ye get made a lord, you can have a touch. 'Til then ye can keep them hands to yerself." She winked at Rutherford. "I'll get you your ale, my lord."

"She's a bold piece, Sally is," a man called Kev said.

"Hmm," Rutherford said, not wanting to be drawn into a discussion regarding Sally's dubious charms.

"You back with us for a while, me lord?" another man asked.

"Yes," Rutherford replied. "Until late March or April. I need to attend to business here. Have you noticed any problems around?"

"No, been real quiet here. Not much happening." Kev rubbed his chin. "Not like when Mr. Harry was around, kickin' up larks."

"There was no one who could get things going better than Mr. Harry." Another man said and nodded.

"Let's have a toast then to Harry Marsh." Kev raised his mug, and the rest followed. "Here's to Harry, who led a merry life and had a quick death."

"To Harry," the rest of the table toasted.

November 3rd, 1814

On the Isle of Guernsey, a young man of thirty-one years wept beside the grave of his wife and small child, buried together. He was tall, with broad shoulders, chestnut brown hair, and deep blue eyes. An older man stood next to him, his hand on the other man's shoulder.

The younger man tried to keep his tears from falling. "Why did it have to happen?" A question he'd asked almost every day for the past eleven months.

"There was naught you could have done, and it was no fault of yours, Harry, me boy. The Good Lord gives and takes as He pleases," his father-in-law, Mr. Marest, said. "She loved you, lad, and she wouldn't have wanted to see you mourn overlong for her."

He patted Harry's back affectionately. "It's been almost a year. You know you can stay here as long as you like. But do you want to, now that you know who you are?"

He glanced at his father-in-law. "I don't know. I still don't have all my memory back. There are large holes."

"That's true," Marest replied. "But you know your last name and from where you hail. You don't know if your family thinks you're dead, or are still looking for you. They could be worried about you."

Harry nodded and gave his attention to the twin graves of his wife, Marcella, and his infant daughter. He'd loved Marcella with all his heart. After her death, in his grief, his memory had begun to come back, and, with it, the image of a young woman with dark curls and laughing blue eyes. He should know her.

His heart ached when he thought of the woman. He wished he could remember why he cared so much for her, and who she was.

"If you're going to go, you'd best do it soon, or you'll not get off the Isle until spring. You still have the money?"

"Yes."

When the Marest family had found Harry washed up on to the beach, he'd had a large pouch of gold coins with him. Not knowing whose they were, Harry had used them sparingly.

His rescuers had brought him, half dead, to their large old farmhouse. Marcella, the middle daughter, had sat with him and nursed him through the worst of it. She'd fed him when he'd been too weak to hold a spoon. When she finally got around to asking his name, the only one he could remember was "Harry." The rest had been a mystery.

He'd remembered nothing about his life or where he was from, but he'd known how to sail, and quite a bit about farming. Marcella had turned it into a guessing game to try to bring back his memory. He had a lot of money, yet his clothes weren't expensive. His manners and speech marked him as a gentleman. He could recite poetry, though most of it was either erotic or romantic, which made Marcella laugh.

Harry had fallen deeply in love with her, but wouldn't ask her to marry him. How could he? He didn't know what he had to give her or who he really was. Then one night she came to him. They married two weeks later. He took Marcella's last name, Marest, French for marsh, which seemed vaguely right. She would have thought it a good joke if she had known it really was his own last name.

Harry glanced at his father-in-law. "You're right. I should go."

"I'll make arrangements for a ship to take you to Weymouth. It's the best route this time of year." Mr. Marest squeezed Harry's shoulder. "We'll miss you, son, but you know you have a family, and staying here will do you no good. Marcella wouldn't have wanted to see you like this." Marest pulled out a handkerchief and blew his nose. "How will you travel to Kent?"

"I'll buy a horse in Weymouth and ride up," Harry said. "There's no reason to hurry. Maybe I'll remember more on my way."

His father-in-law said, "I'll give you a letter to give to the innkeeper at the Boot in Weymouth. He'll take care of you and help you find what you need."

Harry's throat closed, and he couldn't speak, so he nodded. He was leaving the only home he'd known for more than two years, and returning to a life he still knew very little about.

The two men turned in unison to walk back to the house. Harry went to the room he'd shared with his wife and stayed there until called for dinner.

Marie, his mother-in-law, embraced him. "Harry, it's for the best."

"Yes, I suppose it is," he replied. If only he knew who the dark-haired woman was.

Two days later, Harry boarded the ship the *Flying Angel* for his trip to Weymouth. He'd dressed warmly in a wool frieze coat and muffler. After assuring the captain he knew his way around a ship, Harry was happy to be given a job helping trim the sails to take his mind off leaving. They arrived in Weymouth's port late that afternoon.

Harry thanked the captain, who'd given him directions to the Boot.

"Good luck to you, young man. Anytime you want a job, let me know. You're a born sailor."

Harry laughed. "I'll be sure to do that. Thank you, again, for bringing me across. Safe passage back."

After reaching the inn, Harry handed his letter to the landlord, who showed him to a large chamber overlooking the docks. The landlord promised to help Harry purchase a good horse and the other provisions he'd need for the trip home. Home, what a strange thought. Would they welcome him, he wondered.

November 7th, Marsh Hill, Kent, England

Anna had been home for just over a week and, between resuming her normal duties at home, Rutherford, her smuggling gang, and an unexpected irritant in the form of Percival Blanchard, the squire's eldest son, she'd had no time to have a good conversation with Aunt Lillian. Anna was in the breakfast room when her aunt appeared.

"Good morning, my dear," Aunt Lillian greeted her. "Are you riding with Lord Rutherford again today?"

Anna swallowed. "Yes, he should be here soon. I need your advice. How do I convince Percy that I have no interest in him? The man is a coxcomb and a dead bore."

Lillian laughed. "Get betrothed. That will stop him. Unfortunately, he is the type of man who cannot understand that he is not irresistible to women."

Anna took a sip of tea and said thoughtfully, "I wonder if I can deny him when he comes to visit."

Her aunt raised a brow. "That's rather hard to do when he brings his mother along."

Almost every day since Anna's return, Lady Blanchard had come to call, accompanied by Percy. "I suppose you're right."

"You're spending quite a bit of time with Lord Rutherford. Do you have intentions?"

Anna shook her head. "No. He does."

"I thought you liked him."

Anna set her cup down. "I do, but we won't suit."

Lillian frowned slightly. "This conversation is becoming distressingly akin to an interrogation. If you don't wish me to know . . ."

"Oh, no. It's not that." Anna rushed to reassure her aunt. It would be good to talk with someone. "Rutherford wants to marry me, but I heard him describing what he wants in a bride, and it is not who I am."

"Ah, I see." Her aunt's eyes sparkled. "A challenge?"

"Not really. We haven't spent much time together since shortly after Harry's death. He will soon come to realize I am not for him. We will be no more than friends."

Aunt Lillian brought her cup to her lips. "Are you quite sure?"

Anna sighed. "Yes. So you see, Rutherford is not the problem. Percy is."

"I take your point. He is rather a bother." Lillian's brow wrinkled. "Let me put my mind to it and see what I can come up with."

"Who is rather a bother?" a pleasantly deep voice asked from the door. "I hope you don't mind. I told Ledster not to announce me."

Anna couldn't help smiling. Having him around was like old times. Still, it hurt, and she wished he'd figure out soon that he didn't want to marry her. "Good morning, Rutherford. No, I don't mind. Would you like some tea?"

"Tea would be nice."

"Have you already eaten?" Anna asked.

"Yes. Who's a bother?"

She poured him a cup, handed it to him, and scowled. "Percy Blanchard."

Rutherford looked out from under lowered brows. "What's he doing?"

"Persistently following me," Anna said with a huff of frustration. "Percy brings his mother here when he calls, so that I must see him. He tried to catch me alone in the garden the other day. Fortunately, the gardener was there."

Rutherford's eyes turned to silver. A sure sign he was unhappy. "You may leave Percy to me. When does he usually call?"

Anna smiled inwardly. "Around tea time."

"Well, if you don't mind seeing me more often," Rutherford said, "I think I'll come to tea."

"Will you throw Percy in the fountain?" she asked, harking back to an incident from their childhood.

Rutherford gave a bark of laughter. "Rather cold this time of year, but I might. That will depend on how well Percy listens. Come, I saw Thunderer in the stable being saddled." Rutherford finished his tea and stood. "I know you can't wait to ride him."

Anna rose quickly. "Yes, give me just a few minutes."

She picked up her skirts and started to run, before changing it into a fast walk, out the door and up the stairs to fetch her hat.

Rutherford's gaze followed her until she was out of sight. How different she was here. In London Anna would never have left a room running. She wasn't at all what he thought she'd be. She expressed her political ideas more forcefully here, and they were well thought out. Of course, single, young ladies were not encouraged to discuss politics at all in Town. Rather than tame and predictable, she was turning out to be the most refreshing female he knew. Not to mention the most stubborn. He wasn't quite sure how he felt about that. Strange as it seemed, his attraction to this new person was growing, quickly. He'd always loved her, but his feelings were changing, growing deeper. Maybe he was seeing her as a separate person now, and not an extension of Harry. Perhaps he was actually falling in love. There ought to be a sign of some sort.

"Anna is one of a kind, don't you think?" Lady Tully asked.

"Yes. I do." Much better than the quiet, predictable woman he'd thought he'd wanted.

Lady Tully leaned forward and put her elbows on the table. "Tell me, what do you plan to do to dampen Percy's pretensions?"

"I shall have a brief discussion with him," Rutherford replied. And if the man didn't take the hint, he'd plant him a facer.

"You do know"—Lady Tully's gaze focused on the serviette she was refolding—"if you were to convince Anna to marry you, men like Percy would not be a problem."

Rutherford stared at Anna's aunt. She had a point. If they were betrothed, he'd have every right to protect Anna. A duty even. "I'm working on it."

"You must decide whether you want her enough to allow Anna to be herself." Lady Tully raised a brow. "Ah, here Anna comes now. I'll bid you farewell until tea."

Rutherford stood when she did. What did Lady Tully mean? Anna had always been herself. "I'll see you then."

Anna paused at the door. "I'm ready to go."

He bowed to Lady Tully and followed Anna to the stables, where her dapple gray, Thunderer, pawed the ground. The large gelding nuzzled her. Anna grabbed an apple from a nearby barrel and held it out to him.

Humphrey came over to help her mount, but Rutherford shook his head. "Allow me."

He picked Anna up and tossed her on to her horse.

The moment he placed his hand on her waist, it was as if he'd touched a live flame. When he went to place her booted foot into the stirrup, his hands shook.

Rutherford stopped and breathed deeply. Fate had it out for him. He glanced quickly at Anna. Her eyes widened, her color rose, and her mouth formed an *O*. Good, it wasn't just him. He gained his saddle. Now if she'd just realize that they should marry, and quickly.

He could control his countenance, but not the gruffness in his voice. "Let's allow them to shake out their fidgets."

"Yes, let's," Anna said a little breathlessly.

When their horses' hooves clattered out of the stable yard, Anna took the lead, jumping the fence out of the paddock and racing into a meadow. There was still a light frost on the ground. Black trees flew by as they galloped swiftly toward the cliffs.

They rode along for a good while, not speaking. Though, after his revelation, he relished the silence. In the time it took his heart to beat once, Anna had seduced him, and she didn't even know it. What he'd thought was love for her was a far cry from what he now felt. Despite his completely idiotic idea of the perfect wife, Rutherford knew he'd give up everything just to keep Anna in his life.

When she finally reined in, he reached out, needing to touch her, but she spurred her horse and rode toward the cliff before quickly slipping off Thunderer and running to the clump of trees overlooking the English Channel.

Anna crossed her arms in front of her, and her chest rose and fell as if she were catching her breath. Rutherford ambled up behind her and bent his head to kiss her hair.

"*Don't.* Please don't."

He stopped. "You felt it, I know you did. Why can't I kiss you?"

Anna shook her head. "Because kissing leads to other things, and—and we don't have a commitment. I don't know if we ever will. I am not what you want, and lust doesn't equate to love."

Lust! She thought it was lust? *Damn,* now what was he to say? "Anna, look at me."

Her eyes swam in unshed tears, and she blinked rapidly. "Don't tell me you love me now. Everything cannot possibly have changed from one minute to the next."

Nothing but the awareness of how wrong-headed he'd been. "May I hold you? I promise not to do anything else."

She nodded.

He put his arms around her, drawing her close. Taking care not to crush the small hat she wore, he propped his chin on the top of her head. "Anna . . ."

She shook her head, her voice muffled in his jacket. "No, please don't spoil this."

"All right." *I love you.* "Let's go into town. Surely you need to buy something. My mother and sisters always do."

Anna chuckled wetly. "I don't have any money with me."

"I might have some. If not, I'm sure one of us has good credit. Then maybe some cider and a coffyn," he said, referring to the local savory meat pies.

That got a laugh out of her. "You are always hungry."

Rutherford drew back and gave her his best boyish smile. "Always. I seem to remember you have a good appetite as well."

"I know that if I can't eat all of mine, you'll finish it for me," she retorted.

They walked back to their horses. Anna stood next to Thunderer gazing up at Rutherford as he leaned toward her. Her eyes widened, and she tensed. He stopped. *Damn.* If he tried to kiss her now, she'd never trust him. What a fix this was. How long would it take him to convince her that what they were feeling was not lust? And what was this nonsense that she wasn't right for him? She was the only woman he was meant to be with.

"Give me your foot." That had to be better than touching her waist. The second he touched her boot, lightning streaked up his arm. If this kept up, he'd soon be fit for Bedlam.

Chapter 4

Anna and Rutherford rode into town and stabled their horses at the inn. She draped the train of her riding habit over her arm.

"You could fasten it up."

She glanced down at her skirt and the large bone button. "I'm just used to carrying it."

Unable to take her hand, Rutherford walked protectively close, lightly gripping her elbow. She flashed him a questioning glance, but said nothing.

It was market day, and the town was crowded with people. Everyone in the countryside must be here. As they turned on to High Street where most of the shops were located, a tallish, gangly man, a few years younger than Rutherford, walked out of the haberdashers and turned toward them.

Rutherford closed his eyes in pain. The young man's shirt points were so high he couldn't turn his head, and he wore a garish yellow jacket and striped pantaloons. His highly polished boots had white tops with gold tassels. Various fobs adorned his person. A beaver hat sat at a rakish angle a-top wavy blond hair. He was so ridiculous even the Dandies wouldn't have owned him. "Is that who I think it is?"

"Yes," Anna replied. "Percy Blanchard in all his glory."

"*Bartholomew Baby*," Rutherford said with disgust.

Anna gave a little gurgle of laughter.

"You abominable girl, don't giggle." He pressed his lips together as Percy came up to them. "Blanchard, it's been a long time."

Percy scowled. Whether it was because Rutherford was with Anna, or the other man could sense Rutherford's amusement, he didn't know.

Percy bowed, pointedly ignoring Rutherford. "Miss Marsh, if I'd known you wished to visit the town, I would have been happy to escort you as well as my mother."

"But, my dear Percy," Rutherford said. "As you can see, Miss Marsh is with me. Shall we continue on, my dear?"

Percy shot Rutherford a malevolent look, and he wondered if the fool would be idiot enough to challenge him.

"Yes, there is a lot I'd like to accomplish today." She inclined her head. "Mr. Blanchard, good day."

"Miss Marsh." He bowed. "I believe I am accompanying my mother to see your aunt this afternoon. Perhaps I shall see you then."

"Perhaps." Anna's grip on Rutherford's arm tightened.

Percy continued his way down the street.

"*Coxcomb*," Rutherford growled. If Percy thought there was any way he was going to get Anna, he was out of his mind.

Anna loosened her hold on Rutherford and said, "Indeed. Come, you may help me select some ribbon."

"With pleasure."

Anna made several purchases before Rutherford complained he was going to starve if he didn't have something to eat. They each got a glass of cider and a coffyn from the baker.

Anna finished hers and glanced up at Rutherford gazing down at her empty hand. "What?"

"You ate it all."

"I was hungry."

"Yes, but you told me I could finish it," he said.

"Only if I didn't." She punched him lightly. "Go buy another one. You can afford it."

He smiled at her with a softness in his eyes that hadn't been there before. She gave herself a shake. If only he could accept her as she was. Anna found herself leaning closer, then stopped. That wasn't good. She wished he'd taken himself back to Town.

"Yes?" His brows rose.

She shook her head. "Nothing."

Rutherford called to the girl to order another pie.

While she was waiting, Anna gazed out the shop window. A strange man lingered near the Fish and Line across the street. He wasn't from here. Yet, there was something about him that was familiar. "Rutherford, look. Do you know that man near the inn? There's something about him that's not right, but I can't place it."

Rutherford turned around and peered out the glass. "Yes, I see what you mean. He is out of place. Everything about him is medium, ordinary, but . . ." He shook his head slowly.

"I know I've seen him somewhere." Anna said. "I don't think it was here."

"No, you're right, not here. London. Yes, that's it. I've seen him in Brook's."

The clothes the man wore made him appear, at first glance, more like a merchant than a member of the *ton*. The way he carried himself unsettled her. "I wonder what he's doing in Thanport and dressed like that."

"I don't know." Rutherford rubbed his chin. "We're not likely to find out standing here." He finished his coffyn. "Let's go back to the inn."

Rutherford questioned one of the ostlers. It was the second time the strange man had been in town, but other than that, they knew nothing. Anna shrugged. "Oh well, maybe it's nothing. We'd better go if we are to be properly dressed for tea."

She led Thunderer to the mounting block. If Rutherford placed his hands on her once more today, she'd fall off the horse and into his arms. That she could not do. He only thought he knew her. What would he do when he found out about the smugglers? Her whole body had prickled and tingled the last two times he'd touched her. She'd never had that reaction to him before. Why did it have to happen now?

They rode more slowly back to Marsh Hill than they'd left it. Anna trotted in first and slid down from her horse before Rutherford could offer to assist her. "No need for you to dismount. I'll see you in a bit," she said with an airiness she didn't feel.

He glanced at her curiously, but inclined his head. "I'll be back after I change."

Anna summoned a smile. "Maybe I can watch you throw Percy into the fountain."

Rutherford shook his head, but his well-molded lips curved up. "Vixen."

She stared after him as he rode out of the yard, before turning toward the house. This was not turning out at all as she'd planned.

When she got to her chamber, Lizzy was waiting for her.

"I got a message from Kev. That gent's back. He wants to meet with you. There's more cargo coming in for the next two nights, and Kev wants you to be there when it arrives."

So that was who the man was. Who said the country was quiet? Anna nodded. "Very well, tell him to plan the meeting with the London gentleman for three nights from now. I want to make sure the cargo is in and stored before we have any strangers poking around. Tell Kev I don't want anyone else to know about the man until I've made a decision."

"Yes, miss," Lizzy said. "I'll let him know."

"Good, now I have to bathe. I smell of the stable, and Lord Rutherford is coming to tea."

"Whatever for, miss?" Her eyes widened. "You just spent all morning with him."

Anna had indeed, and despite her good sense, was looking forward to seeing him this afternoon. She gave her maid a wicked grin. "He is going to rid me of Mr. Blanchard."

Lizzy let out a peel of laughter. "Now that's something I'd like to see."

Rutherford rode back to the Priory deep in thought. How the hell Anna thought the sensations they'd had today were mere lust was beyond him. Lust was what he'd felt for her before. This sudden need to make Anna his and keep other men away from her, was something else entirely. He had to find a way to make her understand the difference. There was something else wrong as well. What made her think she wasn't what he wanted? Something told him that was the real hurdle. Until he solved the riddle of her mind, he'd not get where he wanted to be.

There was something about the gentleman masquerading as a merchant that made him uneasy. With Dover, Sandwich, and Ramsgate all nearby, they didn't get many of the *ton* in this area. Whatever the man was up to, it wasn't good. He wondered what the innkeeper had discovered about the smugglers, if anything. This would all be so much easier if he could hit something or kill it. He smiled to himself. Percy. Getting rid of him might satisfy some of Rutherford's frustration.

The day Rutherford had thrown Percy into the fountain, he had been at Marsh Hill with his mother. Rutherford and Harry had acquired a pair of stilts, and were in the garden practicing, to the hilarity of Anna, who was about five years old at the time.

Percy came out, and the next thing Rutherford knew Anna was crying, and Percy was standing over her. Harry was on the stilts, and from the expression on his face he was ready to pummel Percy into the ground. Rutherford was closer. He took one look at Anna's red and tear-drenched face, then reached out, grabbed Percy, and tossed him into the fountain.

Afterward, Rutherford had picked Anna up and dried her tears. His throat tightened. When she'd seen Percy in the water, she'd laughed, thrown her arms around Rutherford's neck, and kissed him on the cheek. It was the first time he'd felt like a hero. Rutherford smiled. Maybe she'd do the same thing today. Given the slightest provocation, he'd make a repeat performance, both to enjoy punishing Percy and to receive a reward from Anna.

He entered his house to the sound of high-pitched squeals. Three girls, ranging in age from eleven to sixteen, came running down the stairs and threw themselves at him. He reached out, laughing. "How am I ever going to take you to London if you act like hoydens?"

Althea, the eldest, hugged him back. "Mama says I'm to be presented in the spring!"

Rutherford tried not to frown. "Indeed. I thought she planned to wait another year. You'll barely be seventeen."

"I know, but that's how old she was. Ruhy, what if I fall in love and someone falls in love with me? Would you allow me to marry? I mean if we were truly in love?"

He wanted a brandy. It was much too soon to have this conversation. "If you were truly in love, and he truly loved you, and he could support you in the proper style, then I'd give it serious thought."

"But . . ."

"No, I'd have to see who the hypothetical love is first."

Althea pouted. "Very well, I guess that's fair."

He chucked her under her chin. "Cheer up. I wouldn't withhold my consent unless I had a good reason. I do want you to be happy." A thought struck him. "As long as it's not Percy Blanchard. None of you will marry him. Do I make myself clear?"

Rutherford smiled as they all went into whoops.

"Percy is going to marry Anna. His mama thinks it would be a good match," said his youngest sister, Cecilia, with all the seriousness of eleven years.

"Devil a bit." Perhaps he'd just kill Percy and have it done with. "When did you hear that?"

"When Lady Blanchard came for tea a couple of weeks ago," Eloisa, the thirteen-year-old, offered. "Lady Blanchard said Anna has not taken in London, and she should come home to find a match here."

"The old biddy." He ground his teeth. If either of the Blanchards thought Percy would have Anna, they were much mistaken. Rutherford would pack her off back to Town and marry her by special license. He'd pound Percy into oblivion.

Cecilia wrinkled her nose. "I don't think Lady Blanchard is *that* old, she—"

"For your information," he interrupted, "Anna Marsh could have been married several times over, if she'd wanted. Never mind. I must change. I'm having tea at Marsh Hill." He raised his brows. "Don't you have lessons?"

Three heads nodded.

"Go then. I'll see you before dinner."

"Will you be in a better mood then?" Cecilia asked.

"Yes." Because he was going to find any excuse he could to smash his fist into Percy Blanchard's pasty face.

He watched fondly as his sisters ran off as quickly as they'd come. He didn't like to think of Althea's being old enough to come out or having her exuberance stifled by the *ton*. Yet Anna had not allowed that to happen. That was the reason he'd been so fooled about her. She presented such a serene front in Town. How did she accomplish keeping the demands of the *ton* from crushing her essence? How much did he actually know about her? He had the feeling he'd only scratched the surface. Well, if he was going to marry her, he'd better find out.

* * *

Anna sat in the small drawing room entertaining Aunt Lillian with stories from the Little Season when Rutherford arrived. Anna turned to him and smiled. For some reason he looked more handsome than usual. His coat of dark blue superfine fitted snuggly across his shoulders. His cream and light-blue striped vest was just the thing, and his pantaloons showed his muscled legs to perfection. She could probably see her reflection in his highly polished Hessian boots.

Anna rose to greet him and, without thinking, took his hand. Flames lanced through her as if she'd been hit by lightning. She pulled her hand back, but he tightened his grip. Anna glanced up at him and swallowed. Rutherford raised her hand to his lips, and she closed her eyes, waiting. A tingle started where his mouth touched her fingers and spread. She opened her eyes and met his gaze. This spending time with him was not working. Her heart would only break again when he left. She must come up with something else.

A cough caught her attention, and she turned around. Her aunt watched them, smiling.

"Oh." Anna glanced back at Rutherford.

"We can continue to stand, if you wish." His eyes danced with humor. "Though, it might appear rather odd after a while."

Anna nodded gratefully. "Yes, of course, we'll sit."

She reclaimed her seat on the small sofa, and he sat next to her.

"Is Sir William joining us?" he asked.

"No," Lillian said. "He's working on something and asked to be excused."

Anna and Rutherford related the latest *on dits* about people they all knew until Lady Blanchard and Percy were announced.

Percy wasn't dressed quite so garishly as this morning, but still wore a great many fobs and other items. Anna assumed a polite smile and rose to greet them.

Percy bowed and tried to take her arm. "Miss Marsh, please sit with me over here."

Anna avoided him by taking Lady Blanchard's elbow. "My lady, have a seat on this sofa. It is nearer the fire."

Anna escorted Lady Blanchard to the sofa Percy had indicated, then went back and resumed her place next to Rutherford.

Lady Blanchard smiled thinly and sank on to the sofa.

Scowling at Rutherford, Percy sat next to her.

"Lord Rutherford," Lady Blanchard said. "How unusual to see you here. It's been quite two weeks since I saw your mother. Is she well?"

Rutherford gave her an identical smile in return. "She is well, ma'am."

Raising his quizzing glass, he perused Percy. "Not been to London recently, Blanchard?"

Percy turned a bright shade of red under Rutherford's scrutiny.

"No," Percy answered. "I like to affect my own style."

Rutherford's lips curved up, just missing a sneer. "You certainly have achieved that."

Percy looked at Rutherford as if he wasn't sure if he'd been insulted or not. Percy attempted to ignore Rutherford and engage Anna in conversation. Yet every time Percy asked Anna a question, Rutherford answered it. She thought of interceding, but as her goal was to rid herself of Percy, she remained silent. Besides, Rutherford's manners were excellent, if ruthless.

Anna spoke softly to her aunt and Lady Blanchard, whose color became higher with each subtle barb planted in her son by Rutherford.

By the time he said, "Really, Percy, one cannot discount the benefits of acquiring a little Town bronze," Anna thought Lady Blanchard was going to have apoplexy.

Then Percy responded, "If you like, my lord, we can take our discussion outside."

Rutherford's smile made Anna think of a cat that had caught a mouse.

"Indeed, we could take a look at the fountain."

Percy's complexion paled, then grew more florid than it had been before. "I think you will find, my lord, I have grown."

Rutherford's eyes were wide and innocent. "Come then, and you can show me."

Before their not so veiled threats could go any further, Aunt Lillian made a point of glancing at the clock. "My, look at the time."

"Percy, we must be going," his mother said. "We've remained as long as is proper."

Percy's chin jutted out belligerently. "Is Rutherford leaving?"

Rutherford stood. "I will definitely walk with you to the door."

Anna and Aunt Lillian rose as well. Lillian kept Lady Blanchard engaged whilst Anna strained to hear Rutherford's conversation with Percy.

Rutherford took Percy's arm and leaned close. "Leave Miss Marsh alone, Blanchard, or the fountain will be the least of your worries."

"You have no right," Percy sputtered.

"I am taking the right," Rutherford growled.

Percy seemed unable to form an intelligible sentence in return.

Once the door closed behind the Blanchards, Anna lifted her gaze to the ceiling for a moment. "Oh, dear, that was bad. Sebastian, I think you've forever made an enemy of Lady Blanchard."

"I only hope it did the trick." He escorted Anna back to the drawing room. "You know—well you don't know, so I'll tell you, Lady Blanchard told my mother she thought Percy would make a good match for you."

"*What?*" Anna gasped. How appalling. "When did you hear that?"

"Today. My sisters told me."

She turned to her aunt. "Do you know anything of this?"

"Yes," Aunt Lillian answered. "She's spread it all around the county, or at least in our part of it."

"I cannot believe her gall. Just the thought makes me ill. I wouldn't marry Percy Blanchard if he were the last man on earth. I do hope he's not going to become more of a pest than he already is."

Rutherford, who'd been grinning with unholy glee, suddenly frowned. "He bothers you again, and I'll take him apart."

Now, that sounded like the old Rutherford. Perhaps he'd forget all this marriage nonsense and act like an older brother again.

He bent his head and said in a voice only she could hear. "No one is going to harm you."

Oh, dear. That didn't sound brotherly at all.

After Rutherford left, Anna went to her father's study. Knocking, she entered without waiting for permission. This was one of her favorite rooms in the house. All dark leather chairs and sofas, with doors leading to the terrace. "Papa, how are you? We missed you at tea."

Sir William sat back. The lines bracketing his mouth and between his eyes seemed deeper. "Good afternoon, my dear."

Anna strolled over to stand beside him.

Letters were neatly stacked in piles on his desk. "You've been locked in here so much. I've hardly seen you. What have you been working on?"

He regarded her for several moments, before saying, "Pull up a chair. Let me show you something."

Anna took a ladder-backed chair and set it next to him. "What is all this?"

He handed her a letter. "This is the letter we received telling us Harry died."

Anna opened it, and, even though she'd memorized the words long ago, she read it again.

Her father took that letter and gave her another one, saying, "Here is another one I received from the officer who reportedly signed the death notification. You see how the writing is different?"

"Papa," Anna glanced from one letter to the other. "How did you get this second letter?"

"Now that the unit is returned," he said, "I wrote the officer for more information concerning Harry's death. We'd been given so little."

She read the second missive again.

My dear Sir William,
I received your letter concerning your son, Mr. Harry
Marsh, with no little concern. I never had anyone by that
name, either officer or private soldier, in my unit. Particu-
larly not at Badajoz. I am very sorry that someone has
played a hoax on you. However, I am happy to be of any
help I may be in your quest for the truth of your son's disap-
pearance or death.
                    Your very Obedient Servant
                    Lord Edward Fanning
                    Major, 95th Rifles

Anna's hands shook. "How could this be? We received the letter from the War Office."

"I don't know, my love." Her father shook his head and pointed to the stack on his left. "I wish I did. These are all letters from other officers. None of them knew Harry. I'm going to London next week and will remain until I have some answers. If Harry didn't die on the Peninsula, then he might be still alive. Maybe in a hospital somewhere. "

"I'm going with you," Anna said.

Her father nodded. "I'd hoped you would say that. We'll find Harry, or discover what actually happened to him."

Anna hugged her father. "Yes, we will. If we stick together, we Marshes are invincible. I may have an address that will help. The question is, do we want to give them an opportunity to refuse us?"

"Let me think about it. I've got some contacts as well. I'd like to write them before we go barging into the War Office."

Anna smiled. "Would you mind if I tell Rutherford? He was Harry's best friend."

"No, I don't mind. Perhaps Rutherford will know something we do not."

"But Papa, if he did, wouldn't he have said something before now?"

"He does not know that we don't know Harry didn't die in Spain."

Anna frowned. "Yes, of course." Clear as mud. Anna went to her room to dress for dinner. In the morning, she'd speak to Rutherford.

Chapter 5

November 8th, 1814, Weymouth, England

Harry had spent a few days gathering provisions and equipment needed for his long ride to Kent. He was now in possession of additional clothing, a good horse, a pistol, a knife, cheese and bread for lunch, and letters to innkeepers along the way.

He hadn't paid much attention to the draft horses and ponies on the island. When he'd gone with the landlord of the Boot to look at horses, Harry had surprised himself as he went over each horse's points with a knowledge he hadn't known he possessed.

"Are you sure you don't want to take this one?" the stable owner had asked. "I'll take ten shillings off the price."

Harry had glanced at the showy bay gelding. He was too short in the back and would probably throw a splint. "No, I'll take the black, thanks, and a saddle."

The stable owner had nodded. "Well, I'll say this for you. You know your horseflesh. I'll have everything you need brought round to the inn."

Harry had thanked the man and gone to the store that sold guns. Though his eye had been drawn to a fine pair of dueling pistols, he had picked a larger coaching one, checking to ensure all was in order with it. Then his attention had been caught by a dagger. "I'd like to see that as well."

The shopkeeper had brought it out and handed it to Harry. The weight of the dagger felt comfortable in his hand. "I'll take it."

He had instinctively hidden it in his boot, and wondered what kind of gentleman he'd been. Knowledge of guns and horses was one thing, but a dagger?

Early the next morning, Harry thanked his host and rode out of town east toward Bournemouth, where he'd spend the night.

Late that afternoon, on the outskirts of town, he came upon a yellow chaise stopped to the side of the road. Two women stood next to the carriage. Harry reined in next to them.

He directed his question to the older woman. "What seems to be the problem?"

The younger woman glanced at him and replied, "Our wheeler has lost a shoe, and we're stuck here until help comes."

Harry judged her to be in her midtwenties; she was on the tall side, with pale honey curls peeping from beneath her hat. Her nose was small and straight, and she was considering him appraisingly.

"I see." He tore his gaze away from her mesmerizing turquoise eyes and directed it toward the coach. "Has anyone been sent for help?"

"Yes, one of the outriders." She looked down the road toward the town as if she could make help appear. "Someone should be here soon."

"If you're sure." Harry wasn't happy with what he saw. "I'll tell you what, when I get to my inn, I'll have someone sent to you. Just to be sure."

The older lady took the younger one's arm. "That is a very nice offer, don't you think?"

The young lady glanced up at him. "Thank you very much, sir. I'm certain we'll be fine, but I won't refuse your help."

Harry inclined his head. "I'd consider it my pleasure."

He took off at a trot, then urged the horse faster, and quickly discovered galloping made him feel free. A memory hovered of salt air and cliffs. *Drat*, if it would just come back all at once.

A short time later, Harry arrived at the Admiral, a posting house situated on the edge of Bournemouth. He immediately made arrangements to send an ostler off with a wheeler. That evening, while he was enjoying dinner in the common room, the younger of the two ladies from the carriage came up to him. "I wanted to express my thanks to you for your help today."

Harry stood and smiled politely. "My pleasure. I'm sure any gentleman would have done the same."

She stuck out her hand. "I am Miss Emeline Spencer-Jones. I suppose it is appropriate to introduce myself." She glanced briefly around. "Under the circumstances, that is."

Harry hid a grin and surveyed the other customers. "I think you're right. There doesn't seem to be anyone to perform a proper introduction."

He took her hand and shook it.

Miss Spencer-Jones's face fell.

"Is there something wrong?" he asked.

"Well," she replied, blushing slightly, "I was told that in England a gentleman kisses a lady's hand."

Harry bent his head so she wouldn't see him grin and kissed her hand. "Is that more what you were expecting?"

She smiled delightedly. "Yes, thank you. That was very well done."

Her companion entered the room and glanced around before saying, "Oh, my dear Miss Spencer-Jones, there you are. I've been looking all over for you. You really should not be wandering around the inn by yourself, even if it is very respectable. And the common room, no, no, no. It is not at all the thing. You must remember you're in England now."

A pained expression passed briefly over Miss Spencer-Jones's face, before she turned to greet the older woman. "Mrs. Wickham, I was merely thanking the gentleman for helping us today."

Mrs. Wickham smiled distractedly. "Oh, I see, very proper I'm sure, but not in the common room." She bobbed a curtsey to him. "Most kind of you."

Harry bowed. "As I was telling Miss Spencer-Jones, it was my pleasure."

Miss Spencer-Jones looked down at his half-eaten meal. "We mustn't keep you. Come along, Mrs. Wickham. We mustn't keep the gentleman from his dinner. Sir, perhaps we shall meet again."

Harry bowed. "If our paths cross."

The ladies left, and he resumed eating, barely noticing his now tepid food. She was pretty and seemed nice, but it was much too soon. He closed his eyes and saw his dead wife's smiling face. His heart contracted. The food now tasted like ash. Harry finished his meal and remained in the bar for a while longer. He ordered a pint of the inn's own ale and watched the other customers come and go. After a while, it occurred to him that he made a point of studying people.

Harry was on his way to the stairs when he heard Miss Spencer-Jones's voice. "Mr. Reynolds, you may not join us. I have no wish for your company."

"But Emma . . ."

"I have *not* given you leave to use my name, sir. Please go."

Harry sighed. He had enough problems without inserting himself into something that was no bread and butter of his. Still, he couldn't allow this Reynolds fellow, whoever he was, to accost Miss Spencer-Jones. "Excuse me, might I be of help?"

She smiled gratefully. "Oh, thank you. I was just telling this *gentleman* that we do not wish his company."

Harry met the man's gaze and raised a brow. "If the lady says she doesn't want your company, you should leave."

"Look here now," Reynolds said. "I don't know you, and you've no business sticking your nose in where it ain't wanted. Just leave us be."

Harry fixed the man's swarthy face with a hard look. "The lady has asked for my assistance. Take yourself off, or I'll have the land-lord remove you."

He'd not used that tone of command before, but it felt comfort-able.

"I have a room here." Mr. Reynolds stiffened.

"Not for long, you won't," Harry said firmly. "I can't think the landlord would want a man in his house who threatens ladies. The choice is yours. You can either leave Miss Spencer-Jones alone, or you'll leave this inn. Which is it to be?"

Reynolds clenched his fists.

"I wouldn't if I were you. I'm quite handy with my fives." Where that knowledge came from, Harry didn't know. Only that it was true.

Reynolds made a low guttural sound. "Very well, I'll leave. I'd better not see you around again." He stalked off.

Harry asked Miss Spencer-Jones, "Where did you meet him?"

She'd been watching Reynolds depart and turned to Harry. "He was on the ship on which we journeyed from the West Indies. I tried to keep my distance, but he kept pressing his attentions. I thought once we landed, I'd be free of him."

"It's unfortunate he doesn't seem to be able to take a hint," Harry said. "I suggest you arrange to leave early in the morning and keep as good a pace as possible to your destination."

She worried her full lower lip for a moment. "That's a good idea. Thank you."

"You're welcome. I'll bid you a good night." Harry started back toward the stairs, heaved a sigh, then went to talk to the innkeeper. Once he was satisfied arrangements were in place to protect the ladies, he found his own bed. With any luck, Miss Spencer-Jones would be traveling in a different direction from him, and he wouldn't see her again. The last thing he needed was her distracting him.

November 8th, evening, London

Florian sat at the corner table of a seedy tavern in Spittlefield. He pretended not to notice as Georges entered and raised a brow as he surveyed the room. If Georges saw the small dark-haired man seated with his back to Florian's table, he gave no indication.

Georges got a tankard from the bar and joined Florian, sitting with his back to the wall.

Once his cousin sat, Florian leaned forward, and in a low voice said, "I've set up a meeting with the only gang that appears to be at all discreet. I've had a devil of a time getting an appointment with their head man."

"Are you telling me that you do or do not have an appointment?"

"Oh, no, I've got one for two days hence. In the middle of the damned night. I'll have to take a room in one of the large towns nearby."

"What have you told them?" Georges asked.

"That I was a merchant looking to ship wool to France," Florian responded. "Time enough to tell them I want to bring packages in when I meet the head of the gang."

"Good, we'll meet when you return. *Au revoir, mon ami.*" Georges stood to leave.

Florian stayed where he was for a few minutes more, waiting for the small dark-haired man to follow Georges before quitting the tavern. Once Florian was outside, he strode quickly toward the more salubrious parts of Town, before slowing to a stroll.

When he turned on to St. James Street, the dark-haired man, calling himself Scully, joined him.

"Did you find where he's living?" Florian asked.

He felt little remorse for what he was about to do. Georges had blackmailed him into helping him during the war. Afraid of being discovered, Florian had tried to give him old intelligence reports for the most part, but occasionally, he had to give Georges something new. Mostly, Florian had used the excuse that he wasn't senior enough to have new information. Until, that is, his new position was announced in the *Gazette*. After that, he'd been required to be much more creative. Still, it was better to give in to Georges's demands than to have his proclivities brought to light. He'd lose everything.

"Yup, got him nice and boxed in," Scully replied. "A couple of me lads is watchin' him. If he leaves, he'll be followed like a tantony pig. When do you want him done for?"

"As soon as we can do it safely," Florian said. "I don't want anyone caught."

He didn't want to be caught. His father would cut him off if he found out about any of this, and Florian couldn't afford to be without family funds. Not much longer now, and he'd be free. Georges would be dead, and no one would know his secret. He continued on to Brook's.

Scully waited until the swell was out of sight and then glanced around to make sure no one was following him. Ducking down an alley, he came up against a large man and stopped short. "Didn't see you there, Guv'nor."

"That was rather the point," the man said. "What did you find out?"

Scully backed up a little. The man was not the friendly type. "We're to do away with the Frenchie as soon as it's safe."

The man frowned. "Hmm, were you given a reason?"

Scully shrugged. "Said the Frenchie was a spy."

"Well, that's true enough." The man seemed to consider what

Scully had told him and then asked, "Did you discover anything about what they're doing?"

"I got good hearin' cheats, like. I did hear someat." Scully scratched his head and his face. "But I needs some help to r'member it."

The large man dumped some coins into Scully's hand. "There's a pony for you. Tell me what you heard."

Scully quickly pocketed the money. "Clever cove, said he's going to some port, near Sandwich. Someat to do with smugglers." He held out his hand again.

"Anything else?" the man asked. "Names?"

"No names. There's a meetin' in two days. Late at night. They'll have another after that, if the Frenchie's still alive." Scully once more stretched out his hand. The coins hit his palm. "You want me to keep the Frenchie alive?"

"No, I can't see a need," the man replied conversationally. "But, I do want to know when you do it. In the event we must make it all tidy."

Scully nodded. "I'll be sure to contact you."

"You know where to leave a message."

Scully turned to answer him, and the man was gone.

Lord Jamison removed the old frieze coat he'd worn over his evening dress, walked up another alley, and emerged on to St. James Street, appearing as if he'd spent the night in more frivolous pursuits. Climbing the stairs to Brook's, he was greeted by the club's major domo. Jamison strolled casually through the rooms. There was no trace of the gentleman.

Jamison hoped this was the same man who Harry Marsh had been sent after. If only Harry had not died, they would have had their spy long before now. Jamison had narrowed the possible suspects down to someone in the Foreign Office. Aggravating, they'd been so close before losing track of the man. At least Jamison now knew where the French spies might come in. He'd have to write Rutherford, warning him.

Strolling into the library, Jamison made himself comfortable at a desk and pulled out a sheet of paper. Once he was done, he handed it to one of the servants. "See that goes out immediately."

The waiter bowed. "Right away, my lord."

Now, what was he going to do about the Frenchman? Jamison really couldn't allow him to be murdered.

Georges stood at the darkened cellar window of an elegant town house in Mayfair, watching.

"Are they still there?" the woman asked.

One of the two men ducked back into the shadows of the small square across the street. "Yes."

Fear laced her tone. "What do you think it means?"

"It means my dear cousin has tired of me." Georges stepped back from the window. "I need to leave soon. London is no longer safe for me."

"Georges, how do you know?"

"I feel it. How, *ma chérie*, do you think I've stayed alive this long? First the rabble, then Napoleon. I am one of the few true *aristos* left in France."

He ran the pad of his thumb over her jaw line, up to her bottom lip. "I cannot go back to my lodgings. I must find a new place to stay until I can arrange passage." His hand cupped the back of her head and held it while he kissed her ruthlessly. Her arms slid up to his shoulders and around his neck.

He broke the kiss. "*Chérie*, I must leave here now."

She pressed against him, rubbing like a wanton cat. "But where will you go?"

"I have a place no one knows of." Her mouth opened to ask another question. "No, it is better you have no information. Will you help me leave?"

She sighed. "Yes, I'll check the alley. Perhaps they have forgotten to watch it. At the worst, you can leave with a carter tomorrow."

Georges reached out to stroke her face. "Thank you."

She gave him a sultry smile. "You will, later."

The woman left his side, followed by the faint sound of a door opening. Georges glanced back to the man watching the house. How stupid of his masters to try to use Florian again. He'd lived under threat for five years. Georges could imagine the relief his cousin had felt when the Corsican was captured and exiled. He'd almost felt the same. Almost returned to court to demand his lands back. Then he'd heard the whispers and received the summons.

At the soft padding of slippered feet, he faced the door.

"It's safe," she said. "Here, I took one of the servants' cloaks. Until we meet again, my dear."

"*Oui,* until then." Georges kissed her swiftly. Once through the door, he turned his mind to his need to gather his few belongings and escape.

He walked quickly down the alley, toward the fringes of Polite Society and to another woman who would house him. He knocked twice at the servants' entrance, waited, then knocked three more times. The door opened, and he was pulled in by a girl.

"You want me to get the mistress?" she asked. "She's entertainin'."

"No, I do not wish to disturb her. Show me to a room, and I will speak with her in the morning."

The girl nodded and led him up the back stairs to a room on the second floor. "Best you stay here. Ain't no one going to be up this way. Should be water in the pitcher."

"Thank you. What is your name?"

"Meg." She gave what she obviously thought was a sultry smile as she eyed him up and down. "If you want, I can do for you. Won't cost you nothin'."

Georges shuddered inwardly. She couldn't be more than fifteen or sixteen, but had clearly been well used. He gave her his most charming smile and bowed. "I would love to take you up on your proposition." He dropped his voice to a seductive purr. "*Mais,* if your mistress wanted to visit, and I was unable to . . ."

Meg's lips turned down. "Guess you're right," she said, resigned. "Wouldn't do getting her upset with me. She said I ain't ready to do swells yet. Says I need to be more refined."

Georges smiled. "Then perhaps the next time you will be trained, and I will be available."

Meg smiled back. "I'll look forward to that."

She lit the candles in the room and left.

Slumping back against the door, he went to turn the key, but it wasn't there. He gazed around the chamber at the shabby elegance.

Ruby red bedcover and hangings. This room was clearly not used by their more important *clientèle*. Throwing back the duvet, he inspected the sheets. He'd slept in worse. At least there were no bugs. A decanter of brandy stood on a table. Walking over to it, he poured a large glass and tossed off half of it. By tomorrow he'd be out of London.

Chapter 6

November 8th, 1814, Kent

Anna paced the main hall floor of Marsh Hill while waiting for Rutherford. Finally she strode to the stables. Thunderer was saddled and waiting. The large gelding sidled up to her.

"You're right. We'll probably meet him on the way."

She walked him over to the mounting block and climbed up, before she heard the sound of a rider.

"Sorry I'm late," Rutherford said, as he reined in. "My house is in chaos. Althea was told she could make her come-out in the spring, and Mama just told me we are expecting a guest in less than two weeks, who will also make her bow to the *ton* at the same time."

Poor Rutherford. "Dear me." Anna choked back a giggle. "I think I almost feel sorry for you."

He scowled. "If this keeps up I may go off to my hunting lodge until the Season is under way."

That would be a very good idea. She was growing much too used to having him around. She urged Thunderer to a walk and started out of the stable yard. "I'm sorry to say, I think I'm going to make your day worse."

"Nothing you could do could make my day worse," he said

firmly. "The only thing that's got me through it so far is knowing I'd spend time with you," he said in an honest, matter-of-fact tone.

Anna tried to stop her heart from beating faster. "Rutherford, I don't think you've ever said anything half as nice to me before."

"Haven't I? I have some making up to do. Let's go."

Oh, no. She couldn't let herself be taken in by him. He might think he felt something for her, but it wouldn't survive his discovery that she was nothing like he thought she was.

They rode side by side toward the cliffs. Rutherford jumped down and caught her as she slid off her horse. A frisson shot through her, and she stopped breathing for a moment.

"Rutherford, I can't—this feeling, every time you touch me. You must stop."

"I know. Anna, I . . ."

"No, please don't say what you don't really mean."

His hands tightened on her waist, causing the fire to burn deeper. He did nothing else, and finally the warmth subsided enough for her to gather her scattered wits.

Anna glanced up and met his gaze. "Rutherford, I need to tell you something. Harry didn't die at Badajoz."

Rutherford closed his eyes for a moment. No lies, no prevarications. Only the truth for her. "I know. How did you find out?"

Anna leaned back and stared at him. "You know? How?"

He pulled her to him and touched his forehead with hers. He'd seen the look of hope in her eyes. This was going to be like killing Harry all over again. Only, this time, Rutherford had to do it. "Anna, Harry and I both worked for the Home Office. Harry was supposed to be on home duty. We were intelligencer officers. I came back from a mission to be told Harry had volunteered to go to France."

Rutherford turned her to face the channel. "He'd completed his mission, and the ship he was on went down in a storm during the crossing back to England. By the time I returned, your father had already been notified Harry had died in a regular unit. The lie was to match the tale he'd told all of you when he left."

Rutherford heaved a sigh and glanced at her. Would she shrink from him now, thinking him a man of no honor? "If anyone would have asked me, I'd have told them to tell you the truth. They didn't, and I was ordered not to say anything."

Anna shook her head. "But why? Why wouldn't they tell us the truth?"

He smiled grimly. "To save you the shame of knowing you had a spy in your family."

Anna's lips twisted in disgust. "That's—that's so stupid. As if any of us would care."

He wrapped his arms around her, welcoming her soft warmth. "I hoped you'd think that way. I wanted to tell you and your father. Then your mother said something once, about intelligence gathering, and I—I didn't know anymore how my news would be received. I was still involved in operations and couldn't take the chance. How did you discover Harry didn't die on the Peninsula?"

Anna leaned back against Rutherford. He relished the feel of her body against his. "Once the unit we thought Harry was in returned, Papa wrote the officer who'd supposedly sent the letter telling us about Badajoz. Papa wanted more information about Harry. You know, Papa has not been the same since we received the notice." A tear rolled down her cheek. "None of us have."

Rutherford rubbed her back like he had when she was a small child in need of comfort.

"The officer wrote, telling Papa he'd never heard of Harry and offered to help Papa find Harry's unit. Papa has dozens of letters from soldiers. No one knew Harry."

"No, they wouldn't have. We worked for a small department in the Home Office."

Anna glanced up. "You said his ship went down. How do you know he died?"

It was killing Rutherford to tell her all this. "Sweetheart, there were no survivors. No pieces of the ship found were larger than a plank. Harry was sailing from the tip of Brittany into Portsmouth."

She swayed; Rutherford caught her. Her voice caught on a sob. "Washed into the ocean."

"Yes. We searched for days, for anything."

"Please, you have to tell Papa." Anna turned and tugged on his coat. "He's planning to go to Town next week to try to find the truth."

He nodded. "I'll talk to him. Anna, are you all right?"

She sniffed, fighting not to give in to the tears. "I'll be fine. It is only—I feel as if I've lost him all over again."

Rutherford took his handkerchief out and blotted the corners of her eyes. "Do you want to go now or stay for a while longer?"

"Would you think me a coward if I wanted to put off going home?"

"No. We'll tell him when we return."

Anna and Rutherford walked along the cliffs, the wind whipping their warm cloaks around them. He told her about Harry's role during the war. When she asked about Rutherford's, the only thing he didn't tell her about was his current mission.

"I wish I would have known, Sebastian." She stopped to face him. "I'm so very proud of you. You took such risks."

"With Mama, the girls, and my other responsibilities"—he pressed his lips together—"it was the only way I could think of to serve and not be gone for months at a time."

Anna was quiet for several minutes. "That was important to you . . . serving?"

Rutherford glanced at her. "Yes."

Her gaze was intent, almost belligerent. "I think service is important as well."

What did that look mean? He shrugged it off and urged her forward. "I didn't tell you. I ran across Marcus on occasion."

"Did you? How interesting it must have all been."

They strolled back to the horses and returned to Marsh Hill shortly before the noon meal.

"Stay for luncheon please," Anna said. "We can talk to Papa after we eat."

Another conversation Rutherford was not looking forward to. He nodded. "If you wish."

Anna smiled. "Yes, and thank you. I feel as if I know my brother better. Why he did what he did."

Rutherford wanted nothing more than to drag her into his arms and kiss away all her pain. Instead, he followed her into the house and into the family dining room.

"Papa, I've invited Rutherford to dine with us."

Sir William smiled. "You know you're always welcome here."

Rutherford bowed. "Thank you, sir. It's a generous offer."

He, Anna, and Lady Tully made small talk until they'd finished eating. When Sir William stood to leave the room, Rutherford said, "Sir, I'd like to speak with you about Harry."

Sir William stilled and glanced at Anna.

"Please, Papa. Rutherford has some information I think you'll find interesting."

"Very well. My study?"

"Yes." Rutherford glanced over at Lady Tully. "My lady, if you wish to join us?"

She smiled. "Thank you, but no. I think this is a time for the three of you. I'll be here if there is anything you wish to discuss later."

Rutherford followed Anna and her father into the study and closed the door. Sir William indicated a chair, and Rutherford sat after Anna had taken a place next to her father.

"Sir William, I want to tell you that I'm glad you know Harry didn't die at Badajoz. Though I'm sorry to tell you, he did die, just much closer to home."

They spent the afternoon talking about Harry and his missions, at least what Rutherford knew of them.

"I still plan to visit Town next week," Sir William said. "If you'll give me the name of whom I need to see and a letter . . . I would like to see his service record."

"Yes, sir, I'm happy to do anything I can to help you." Rutherford had a week to try to talk Anna's father out of going. He didn't want to imagine how upset Jamison would be to have Sir William appear on his doorstep, as it were. "I think it's time for me to leave you. Anna, will you walk with me to the door?"

He searched her face. Fine lines crossed her forehead and settled between her eyes. Her mouth was pulled tight.

She rose. "Yes, of course. Papa, I'll see you later."

"Yes, my dear." Sir William held his hand out to Rutherford, who took it. "Thank you."

Anna and Rutherford walked out a side door. Before she could go farther, he said, "Anna, go rest for a while. You look exhausted."

She gazed up at him. "Yes, you're right. I do feel so weary."

Rutherford brought her closer and kissed the top of her head. "Sleep well. I'll see you in the morning."

The wheels of a carriage crunched on the drive. "You might want to take the back stairs," he said. "I think you have company."

Anna's eyes widened and rolled like a horse's. He laughed. The last time she'd done that her mother had lectured her on manners. "Go now, before they're inside."

Anna turned and went back into the house. Rutherford saw her staring at him out one of the stairwell windows, then walked over to where he could see Percy and his mother enter the house. He waited about five minutes longer before riding out the back way. There was no point in letting Percy and his mother know that Anna, the bane of Rutherford's life, was avoiding them.

At least she wasn't shunning him. After the way she had behaved at Charteries, he'd half expected it. His smug smile didn't last long before he was reminded that he loved her, and she for some reason didn't think they'd suit. How was he to convince her that she was the only woman he wanted to marry, and that what he felt was love and not only lust? If only women wouldn't make life so difficult.

Anna reached her bedchamber to find it blessedly empty. She removed her boots, stockings, and habit, carefully draping the former over a chair. She sat on the bed to lie down and stopped to remove her stays. As she slid between the sheets, her mind was in a whirl. *Rutherford and Harry, spies.* Harry lost at sea. How ironic. He'd always been such a strong swimmer and a good sailor. She prayed he hadn't suffered much.

Fresh tears flowed down her cheeks and on to the pillow. She'd been glad Rutherford had told them everything and that he'd been there for her. Ever since she could remember, he'd been a strong, solid presence in her life. Anna had wanted so badly for him to love her. Yet, now that she knew what he really wanted in a wife . . . Why couldn't he just leave her alone? Why was he so difficult?

Someone was talking to her. Lizzy. Anna opened her heavy lids. She must have drifted off to sleep.

"Miss," Lizzy said, "you need to eat before you go. You've slept clear through dinner. The master said not to wake you, but you've got that shipment tonight."

Anna rubbed her hands over her face. "Thank you for waking me."

She walked over to the basin to splash cold water on her face. That was much better. Lizzy dressed her and brought a tray. By the time Anna finished her meal, she was fully awake and ready to go.

When she got to the stable, Thunderer was ready, but Humphrey was not. "Humphrey, what's wrong?"

"It's me chops," he mumbled as if in pain.

She brought the lantern closer. "Let me see." His jaw was swollen as large as a small ball of yarn. "Here, open your mouth." Anna almost roiled at the smell of decay. "You need to go to the apothecary tomorrow, or you'll have even more problems. I'll be fine by myself until you're better."

Moments later, she quietly left on Thunderer. Once she'd cleared the immediate house area, she gave her horse his head. The air was cold and moist. Anna was thankful she'd dressed warmly. With any luck, Kev would have lit the fire in the old cottage Harry had used, and left to her. Otherwise, she'd have to change in the cold. She rode Thunderer into the stable built behind the cottage. "Here are some oats and water," she said. "I'll just be a few minutes."

The room glowed with the flickering of flames from the fireplace, but the only really warm area was right next to it. She quickly stripped off her habit and changed into breeches, shirt, and jacket, grabbing the warm frieze coat as she went back out to the barn where she switched out her sidesaddle for a regular one.

The stand of trees was not far, and it took only a few minutes to reach it. From there she could see everything and hear most of it. After tying her horse up in a wooded copse several yards back, she scrambled down the path to the beach.

Kev strode over to meet her. "Mr. Arnold, sir. We just got the first signal."

Anna nodded. "Wait for a few minutes after the second signal. If I see anything, I'll give a sign."

"Yes, sir."

She climbed up the rocky path and lay prone on the cliff's edge. When the second signal came, she scanned the beach and cliffs. After a few minutes, the smugglers took the boats out. She waited nervously until the vessels came back into sight and were beached.

Men seemed to mill around without purpose, but in no time at all the barrels were unloaded and secured to the carts. Once the crafts were empty, some of the gang pushed the boats back into the cove to take them to a dock on the outskirts of town. The rest of the smugglers helped move the carts to the wagon waiting at the end of the beach.

Anna searched the area again, looking for anyone who shouldn't be there. The idea of the gentleman from London made her anxious. A tingle ran down her shoulders, as if she were being watched. She shook herself and tried to relax. Maybe she was becoming too cautious. But Marshes weren't cautious; they were invincible. That's what Harry used to tell her when she'd been afraid of the dark at three and when she was facing her first Season at seventeen. This was the job Harry had left to her. She couldn't allow the burning on her back—Lord, it was as if someone were pressing down on her shoulders with a hot iron—to distract her. Anna struggled not to glance around.

The sooner she got the signal from Kev, the better she'd feel. There it was. She jumped to her feet and ran to Thunderer. Using a fallen log, she jumped onto her horse. Mounting in breeches was so much easier than mounting in a skirt. What would Rutherford think if he saw her now? Right now, he was only one of several problems—her father, the London gentleman, and Percy. If *he* persisted, she'd throw him into the fountain herself.

Anna cantered to the cottage, changed, rode home, and slipped silently up to her chamber where Lizzy waited.

Rutherford had arrived back at the Priory after talking with Sir William and had entered through a side door. He gave thanks none of his sisters or his mother was wandering the corridors and went directly to his study. With everything else going on, he'd neglected his estate work. By the time he needed to change for dinner, he was almost caught up. He glanced one last time at the correspondence and saw a rather grubby piece of paper, folded twice, but not sealed. He opened it.

Yr Lordship,
Delivrey tonite 1200 near cottage in woods. No closer than
trees.

No signature. Then again, he didn't really expect one. He remembered the cottage. He should have thought of it sooner. Harry had used it. Only a couple of miles beyond it stood a copse of trees on the cliff overlooking the beach, so he could watch from the thicket. The letter didn't say if the gang leader would be there. He scoffed—it was apparently easier to make an appointment with Prinny than with the head of the local smuggling gang.

Rutherford burned the note and went up to his chambers to change. "Robertson, I need to go out later this evening. I'll need dark clothing, nothing good as it might become dirty. See what you can put together."

"Like the old days, my lord?"

Rutherford grinned. "Very much like old times. I'll leave here at eleven thirty. Don't expect me back for at least an hour. With luck, I'll be longer." He had to admit, being on a mission again was exhilarating.

He walked down to the drawing room where he found his three sisters and his mother.

"All of you here?" he asked in surprise.

"Yes, Ruhy, isn't this grand?" Cecilia said. "We're all to practice our manners."

"Ah, well then. I must properly greet all of you ladies. You must first stand."

They all stood up, and one by one he bowed to them and brought a hand to his lips. A trio of giggles met his attempts at gallantry.

He gave them a pained expression. "When another gentleman does the same, try not to giggle at him."

His mother, Julia, Lady Rutherford, laughed as well. "Really, Rutherford, I do not know how I shall make these silly young girls into ladies."

Rutherford regarded his mother. A tallish, slender blonde with sparkling blue eyes, she was still beautiful. None of them really resembled her much in their coloring, but they had all got her height. He got on well with her most of the time, when she wasn't nagging him about marriage.

Of course, if he'd taken her advice and married when Anna first came out, he wouldn't be having the problems he had now. Not that she'd wanted him to marry Anna. His mother had set her sights much higher. He was brought out of his reverie by his butler, Griffin, announcing dinner.

Rutherford bowed to his mother and offered her his arm. She smiled and took it.

"My lady," he said.

Her eyes seemed to laugh as she inclined her head. "My lord."

He glanced at his sisters. "You will follow us in."

"But, Ruhy," Eloisa said, "I want you to take my arm too."

"The highest-ranking gentleman always escorts the highest-ranking lady."

"You mean there are rules about that as well?" Cecilia, the youngest, exclaimed in disgust. "I don't think I want a come-out. I'll just stay here."

"But Cece, you have to have one," Althea said gently. "How else will you find a husband?"

Cece pulled a face. "He'll just have to come find me here."

Rutherford's lips twitched, and he glanced at his mother.

"Perhaps she is a bit too young for this," Lady Rutherford conceded.

He agreed. "She might be happier staying in the nursery."

"You may be right."

Dinner passed with much merriment, but tea afterward proved to be too much for his youngest sisters. Their governess, Miss Jynkins, was called to fetch them.

"Jenny, you were right," Lady Rutherford said.

Miss Jynkins, a slender, jovial lady in her late forties, replied, "All in good time, my lady."

Rutherford bid them all a good evening and retired to his study until it was time to change for his outing. There was enough moonlight to make him take care that he wasn't seen.

He rode to the stand of trees and tied his horse up in the wood far enough back so that if he made any noise, it wouldn't be noticed. Creeping slowly up to the copse, Rutherford waited.

The silence was interrupted by the sound of another horse. Then there was silence again. He looked closely through the trees and saw a short, slender man nimbly drop to the ground and take the path to the beach.

Rutherford peered down. The man was talking to the smugglers. They all seemed to listen closely to what he had to say before he started back up the path. Rutherford moved back from his perch and hid.

Once the small man reached the top, he kept watch over the cliff. Rutherford remained perfectly still. Voices drifted up from the beach. He couldn't make out what they were saying from his position, but he'd wager a good deal the other man could hear everything. After almost an hour, the man nodded, got up, and slipped quietly into the darkness. The next sound Rutherford heard was a horse galloping away. A very efficient operation the smuggler's leader was running. Next time, Rutherford would arrange to meet the leader, whoever he was.

Chapter 7

November 9th, 1814, Bournemouth

Harry woke early to the sound of a carriage leaving the inn and hoped it was Miss Spencer-Jones. He felt a little guilty for not offering to accompany her at least part of the way to wherever she was going. Yet he told himself he had enough to worry about with his sketchy memory.

Still, he knew his lack of chivalry was going to come back to haunt him. He was soon washed and dressed. The tap was empty when he went down for breakfast. Harry's inner cavalier pushed him to eat hurriedly. He paid his shot and left. He might not see her coach. Harry hoped not, but at least he'd be behind it if they needed help again. He was beginning to think he wanted to get to Kent sooner rather than later. Anything to keep him out of the orbit of damsels in distress.

The day felt marginally colder than the previous one. Cold enough to cause him to stop at an inn to warm himself by mid-afternoon.

When Harry reached the Post House Inn at Southampton, an equipage that looked suspiciously like the one Miss Spencer-Jones and her companion were traveling in was in the yard.

He handed his horse to an ostler and grabbed the bags tied to his saddle.

"Ain't you the gentleman that helped us yesterday?" the coachman called.

Harry heaved a sigh, but managed a smile. "I am."

"Mighty glad for your help, we were," the coachman said. "Don't like being stranded on the side of the road with ladies. A mite too dangerous for my blood."

"Don't think of it. How long have you been here?" Harry asked.

"Oh, 'bout an hour I'd say. Miss says as how since they already have the bookings all the way to London, it wouldn't do not to stop. She and Mrs. Wickham are taking a walk. Miss ain't been in England before, so she's mighty curious about things."

Harry nodded and walked inside, handing his letter to the innkeeper.

"I'd give you the best room," the landlord said, "but I've a young lady in it. I've got one looking out over the harbor if you want it?"

Harry was just thankful for a room. "Yes, anything's fine. Thank you."

"Dinner's in an hour. I'll send some warm water up to you to wash the dust off. Let me know if you want a bath."

Harry accepted a bath for later that evening and followed one of the landlord's sons to his chamber. Maybe he'd take a walk as well. It had been a long time since he'd sat a horse for two days straight, and he was starting to feel it.

He'd washed, changed, and was about to exit the inn when a small voice nagged him. He turned back to the innkeeper. "A gentleman by the name of Reynolds hasn't checked in, has he?"

"No, that name don't sound familiar. What's he look like?"

"Shorter than me with lighter brown hair."

"He ain't here."

Harry rubbed his chin. "If he does show up, I'd appreciate it if you'd not allow him to stay here. He made himself a nuisance with the young lady yesterday. I wouldn't like to see it happen again."

"We're pretty full," the landlord replied, "and I don't like to see women bothered. I'm thinking he can find a place more to his taste."

Harry nodded. "Thank you."

He left the inn muttering to his inner knight, "I hope you're happy now."

After walking along the docks and back up into the town, he

took out the pocket watch he'd bought in Weymouth. Marcella used to tell him if he'd had something of his own, his memory would have returned. Unfortunately, he'd had nothing.

The farther he traveled from Guernsey, the more he felt he was leaving her far behind. Maybe he should go back. Then that voice, which he was becoming very tired of, told him to push on.

"You're damned persistent," he growled to himself. Ever since he'd left the Isle, he'd felt as if there were two people in his body. Two senses of consciousness in his brain. The one that had been with him for over two years now was cautious, and didn't want change. It wanted his wife and child. It wanted him to stay at their grave until he was old and died himself.

The other had been whispering to him since his memory had started to return, and it had come to the forefront during the passage to Weymouth. It was daring and chivalrous. It wanted to help unknown ladies, even flirt with them a little. It drove him on to a life that was still foreign to him.

He made his way back to the inn. The tap was almost full when he sat down to eat. Dinner consisted of a broth soup with mussels and a fish pie with cod and haddock. Carrots mixed with parsnips served as a remove. The landlord sent him a bottle of claret. There was fresh-baked bread, butter, and a gypsy tart for dessert. He savored every bit of it and lingered over the tart. He'd not had one in years.

The memory jerked him up. This was one of his favorites. *You see,* the voice said. *If you'd turned around, you wouldn't know you liked gypsy tart.* Harry put his head in his hands. Visions of the dark-haired girl flitted across his mind. He still didn't know who she was. Not a wife, he hoped. He left the room. His first foot was on the bottom tread when he heard a voice and wanted to groan.

"Mr. Marsh, how nice to see you here."

She must have asked the landlord his name. He was positive he hadn't given it to her. It was only the distant past he couldn't remember well.

Harry placed his foot back on the floor and turned. "Miss Spencer-Jones. I hope your trip today was pleasant."

"Oh, it was. The countryside here is so different."

That was his cue to ask why. "I would love to stay and talk, but I need to rest for my trip tomorrow."

"Then I'm sorry to bother you." She looked concerned. "Are you all right? I mean, do you need anything?"

Harry shook his head. "No, I just need time." He paused for a moment. Except for Marcella's family, he'd not talked with anyone about her. "You see, my wife died—" He'd been about to say a few months ago, but it wasn't. It was just shy of a year. "Several months ago. We lived with her family."

"I see. You must have loved her very much." Emma knitted her brow. He confused her. She didn't think she was conceited, but never had any man dismissed her so readily. She studied him closely. He was tall and very good-looking. His dark brown hair was not cut very fashionably and was too long. He wasn't that old. Laughter hadn't caused the lines bracketing his mouth, and his wonderful blue eyes were sad, haunted. Now she knew the reason. "I'm so sorry. I don't want to be a nuisance. I'm a very good listener. If you'd like to talk, that is."

Mr. Marsh seemed stricken. "Thank you for your offer. I–I just need to sleep."

Emma nodded. "I understand. Perhaps some other time."

"Perhaps." He turned and climbed the stairs.

Her eyes followed him, and she found herself blinking back tears. She did know how it felt to lose someone one loved. It had been two years since Adam died. Granted, they'd not yet married. They'd not even made love, though she'd tried to encourage him. Adam had wanted to wait until they were married.

Emma started to turn to go back into her private parlor, but that obnoxious Mr. Reynolds was asking someone for her. Instead she lightly ran up the stairs, straight into Mr. Marsh. He grabbed her and kept her from falling back down them.

His voice was deep and serious. "What is it?"

Her heart thudded, but she didn't know if it was that she didn't want to see Mr. Reynolds, or that Mr. Marsh was holding her so closely. "Mr. Reynolds. I heard him asking for me."

Mr. Marsh's voice was grim. "The landlord won't tell him you're here, but he might have seen your coach."

"How do you know the landlord won't tell him?" she asked, surprised.

Mr. Marsh flushed. "I had a talk with the innkeeper once I knew you were staying here."

"Did you?" She felt a fluttering in her chest. "How kind and how—how noble."

His flush deepened. "It was—it was the right thing for me to do. I don't deserve your thanks for such a small—"

"But you do," Emma interrupted. "Not many men would bother. Particularly for a lady they don't know and don't wish to know."

"It's not that I don't want to know you," Harry said. "It's—I have a lot on my mind."

She smiled. "You should go to bed. I'll go to my chamber, and maybe I'll see you later—some other time."

Not waiting for his reply, she walked swiftly to her room and then remembered her key was in the parlor. Could things get any worse? She'd look like an absolute pea-goose. She turned and found herself up against a muscled chest. Her breath left her, and she couldn't seem to get any more.

She straightened. "I am sorry. I seem to have left my key in my reticule in the parlor." Emma gazed into his eyes. They were smiling with amusement.

"Shall I go down and see if Mr. Reynolds is gone?"

"If you don't mind."

Mr. Marsh shook his head. "Not at all."

He came back a few minutes later with Mrs. Wickham in tow.

"Oh, there you are, my dear Miss Spencer-Jones. I'd been wondering . . ." Her eyes were wide with speculation.

Emma smiled tightly. "Yes, I daresay you have. I heard Mr. Reynolds and fled up here. It was not until I went to enter my room that I remembered my key was still in the parlor. Did you bring it?"

"Oh my, yes. Yes, indeed." Mrs. Wickham handed Emma her reticule.

"Thank you, Mrs. Wickham. I shall bid you a good night." Emma turned toward her chamber, unlocked the door, walked in, and leaned against the closed door until her heart slowed to a normal level. What was it about Mr. Marsh?

The fire had been stoked up and the drapes closed against the cold night air. Even with the warm clothing she'd bought, it was still cold. She wondered if she'd ever see her family's home in Jamaica again.

She'd been sent to England to find a husband. Not that it needed to be said. Why else would anyone come to a place as cold as this?

Part of her still missed her former betrothed, Adam, dreadfully. They'd grown up together and had always planned to marry. Then, a few weeks before the wedding, he had died.

Tears made steady progress down her cheeks.

Adam had been killed in a pirate attack. Marcus Finley had saved the ship, but Adam had already perished. Marcus had brought him home and helped Emma through the worst part. They'd spent so much time together, her parents had thought they'd make a match. Yet, while she'd spoken of Adam, Marcus had talked of Phoebe.

The silly man had even named his ship after her. He said it brought him luck. Emma wondered if Adam would still be alive if he'd named his ship after her. She'd cried for days after Marcus left. There was no one else to confide in, and she was so alone. She prayed with all her heart that Marcus had found his Phoebe and they were happy.

Yet now it was time to move on with her life. Would Harry Marsh be part of it?

Harry opened his chamber door, walked in, then slid to the floor. His mind and body warred. His chest tightened at the thought of Miss Spencer-Jones, and he'd felt stirrings in another area he'd thought dead. Her soft body, the scent she wore, one he couldn't place, stuck in his mind. When his hands had caught her, they'd almost made a trip down her body they didn't need to make. Maybe he'd just been without a woman for too long. He'd been keeping her at arm's length. Then she'd run into him this evening, twice. Guilt crept in and reminded him of Marcella.

Harry groaned as another voice said, *You can't make love to a dead woman, no matter how much you loved her.* Why couldn't he have just stayed on the island?

Because you're Harry Marsh, and Marshes are invincible. He closed his eyes. A child was crying and holding on to him. She had burnish curls and blue eyes. She pulled her lower lip with her teeth. Then she stopped weeping and nodded. "'Cause we're invincible."

"That's right, Anna. Keep saying that, and no monsters can get you."

Then a lovely girl in her late teens sat beside him in a garden. Tears sparkled in her eyes. The same eyes as the child's and the same dark hair. He held her trembling hand as she worried her lower lip and nodded. "Because Marshes are invincible."

"You'll be fine, Anna. Don't forget, I'll be there as well."

Anna. He had a sister. Not a wife, *a sister.*

November 9th, 1814, Marsh Hill, Kent

Anna was at the table with her breakfast plate and had poured a cup of tea when Rutherford walked in.

She blinked. "What would you like?"

"Tea and food?" He smiled, charmingly.

"Help yourself to the dishes on the sideboard." She waved her hand in the direction. "I'll serve you tea. Are you early, or am I late?"

"I'm early. I awoke at dawn, and rather than bothering my staff, I came here. I knew you'd be up. Besides, I rather like the idea of eating breakfast with you." He'd like the idea even more if he'd woken up with her. Anna blushed as if she'd heard him. "Where would you like to ride this morning?"

She tilted her head first one way, then the other. "Hmm, I don't know. Where would you like to go?"

He studied her face. "Not really fair turning the question back to me. I haven't ridden the beach in a while. What do you think?"

A smile dawned on her beautiful face and grew broad. "The beach it is."

Less than an hour later, they entered the shoreline from the opposite end of the one he was on last night. They walked their horses for a while, before nudging them faster, galloping down the beach. Rutherford tried to look for any changes since the last time he'd been here, but it was too long ago.

He hung back a little to watch Anna ride. A creature of nature. She infected him with the same desire to be free.

"Race," he called.

She urged Thunderer faster. Her horse was a good seventeen three hands. He'd been there when Harry had bought the horse for Anna and had tried to talk Harry out of giving such a large horse to his little sister. Harry had remained firm, saying Anna rode as well as either of them, and that she deserved the same type of horse. It occurred to Rutherford his friend had been right. Anna reached the end of the beach with Rutherford behind.

She turned, smiling. "Did you let me win?"

"No. You did have a head start though. I should have called the race when I was even with you."

Anna glanced narrowly at him, as if she didn't believe him.

"I was thinking about when Harry bought him for you."

"Ah. Did you approve?"

He smiled ruefully. "Not at the time. I can see now why he did it."

She grinned. "I'll let you race me back."

"You call the mark."

"Very well, on three. One, two, THREE!"

She took off at full pelt. It was all he could do to come in on her tail. They walked the heaving horses into the surf to cool them down and then back up the path to the cliffs

"I love it here," she said. "I love the wildness, the sea, the air. I love everything about it. I want to stay here forever."

As she stared out over the English Channel, the wind blew curling strands of hair loose from the knot on the back of her head. Her face was still flushed from riding. He wanted to say something, but his throat tightened. He tried to swallow and couldn't. *Ah, the ills that flesh is heir to.*

Anna glanced at him. "Don't you agree?"

He studied her as she considered him. "I do agree. I feel the same sense of freedom. I could never feel it anywhere else."

"I'm hungry. Do you have any money?"

His shoulders dropped and lightened. "Yes. I suppose it's only fair that I feed you now, since you fed me this morning."

"I'm afraid we will have to walk the horses to Thanport," she said.

"I have no other plans. Do you?"

She ducked her head and grinned. Two dimples creased her cheeks. "No."

"Lead on."

She turned Thunderer and waited for him to come beside her. Anna's forehead wrinkled. "It's funny. I've been thinking about Harry a lot lately. As if he's with me. I've not had that feeling since before he died."

Rutherford frowned. "Did you have that feeling before he left?"

Her face cleared. "Yes, I always knew. I can't explain it—I always sensed him. That was the reason, when the letter came saying he'd died, I didn't question it. I'd stopped feeling him. But lately, he seems to be with me again. Does that make sense?"

"I know twins feel that way. There's no reason I know of you couldn't have the same connection with Harry."

Anna worried her lip. "But what does it mean that I have it now? He's still dead."

"*That* I cannot explain, but I wouldn't let it worry you. You'll sort it out in the end."

Anna nodded. "Yes, I suppose you're right." She paused for a moment. "Do you still miss him?"

"Always. I'll never have another friend like he was. Marcus is close, but Harry was like a brother."

"Amid all your sisters?"

"Well, for years I was the only one. You know, Althea is more than fourteen years younger than I am. Then my mother had the other two. Of course, I'm sure there were mishaps."

"Childbirth is a difficult proposition," Anna said, thoughtfully. "My father says losing Harry was the last burden my mother could bear."

"Lady Marsh did seem rather agitated when you left London."

Anna nodded. "Mama lives in terror that something may happen to me. The problem is she's convinced herself that marriage will stop anything bad from occurring. Which, I have to say, makes no sense at all." Anna shook her head and continued, "What if I married someone who beats me? You can't say it doesn't take place. Look at poor Lady Henning. The dear woman is almost never in public, and when she is, she says she's run into a wall. Well, I can tell you, I know what being punched in the eye looks like. Yet, what is she to do, and where is she to go with the laws the way they are?"

Rutherford moved his horse over and placed a hand on her shoulder. "Are you afraid of that?"

Anna stuck her chin out. "No. I'd punch him first."

He let out a shout of laughter. "Did Harry teach you that as well?"

Anna grinned. "Yes. Do you think he'd have allowed me to enter Polite Society without teaching me how to hit a gentleman?"

Still laughing, Rutherford shook his head. "No, not Harry."

They were still grinning when they reached Thanport. Anna and Rutherford left the horses at the inn and walked to the shop.

"How many will you eat?" he asked.

"I'll start with one. You?"

"Since I cannot depend on you to share, I'll have two."

She ate all of hers and half of his second coffyn. "These are so good."

"I agree. He wiped her lips with his handkerchief. This wasn't at all the same as when he'd cleaned her mouth as a child. Now, he wanted to run his tongue over her lips and kiss them. "Would you like to walk around?"

"If you wouldn't mind, I'd like to go down to the pier."

He wanted to hold her hand, but settled for placing her hand on his arm. Once he resolved the problem with the smugglers, he'd devote all his attention to her and find out why she didn't think he wanted her.

Chapter 8

Anna and Rutherford arrived at Marsh Hill in time for tea and entered through the side door closest to the stables.

"I so hope Percy and his mother don't visit," Anna said.

Rutherford took her hand. "I'll be here if they do."

Unfortunately, when they strolled into the morning room, both Lady Blanchard and Percy were present. *Drat.* They should have checked the front of the house.

Anna assumed her London smile and greeted them.

Percy narrowed his eyes at Rutherford and tried to hide a scowl.

Rutherford, on the other hand, maintained a perfectly polite mien. The only indication that he intended to enjoy himself at Percy's expense was the slight upward curve of his lips.

Anna gave Rutherford a cup of tea and a plate with scones and small biscuits, then took a scone for herself.

He once more deflected Percy while she spoke with her aunt and Lady Blanchard.

When she'd had enough of listening to the two men snipe at each other, Anna went to the door that led to the garden. "Rutherford, come here, please."

Her back warmed as he stood behind her. "Do you see them? The first hellebores have bloomed. Let's take a closer look."

Rutherford's breath caressed her neck, and she suppressed a shiver of delight.

"Wonderful. I love hellebores."

Anna struggled not to laugh out loud and whispered, "Do you even know what they are?"

"I'm sure you'll show me," he answered in a low voice.

He opened the door and stood to one side, allowing her to pass.

"Here, I'll come with you," Percy said, rushing up to them. "Hellebores are my favorites."

"Only, Percy . . ."

"Rutherford, shush."

She glanced over her shoulder. "Come if you wish."

Rutherford twined Anna's arm in his as she led the two gentlemen over to a bush with orange leaves and said sweetly, "Percy, how do you like it?"

"A perfect example of the species," he replied haughtily.

To Anna's delight and amazement, Rutherford pointed to the real group of hellebores. "Percy, you're an idiot. Over there are hellebores."

Rutherford turned Anna to walk back toward the house.

Percy choked and sputtered, "What does it matter? I don't know why you are here, my lord, other than to make everyone's life more complicated."

Narrowing his eyes at Percy, Rutherford's voice was cold as winter. "Excuse me, but I don't believe I take your meaning."

"What I mean is that you are only interested in dallying with Miss Marsh, while I intend to marry her."

She couldn't believe he actually said it. "*You what?*"

"Well, I probably shouldn't have mentioned it in front of you. It is well known that you did not take in London, which is the reason you're still unmarried. . . ."

That was quite enough. Anna raised herself to her full height of a few inches over five feet and speared Percy with her gaze. "*I, not take?* Are you mad? I will have you know . . ."

"My dear, allow me." Rutherford tightened his grip on her arm. "Blanchard, you are out. Miss Marsh could have married at least ten times."

Percy jerked back as if struck.

Anna giggled. "Rutherford, you must remember this is England. I would not have been allowed to marry ten times. How do you know about the offers? I didn't tell anyone."

He smiled slowly. "Betting, my dear. It was entered on all the books. While you didn't say a word, your erstwhile swains were not so discreet."

Anna's eyes widened. "I had no idea."

"No, of course you didn't. Really not the thing to say to a lady. Wouldn't have mentioned it except for Blanchard here. I know there were more than ten. I just stopped counting."

A rush of affection for him infused her. "Rutherford, you kept track?"

His gaze was warm, and he seemed to see no one but her. "Well, of course I kept track," he said softly, and placed his hand over hers. "What do you take me for?"

Percy grabbed Anna's hand from Rutherford's arm.

Without a thought, she whirled, pulled him to her, and punched him in the face. Percy stumbled back into the fountain, landing in the cold water with a splash.

Rutherford smiled as she was wiping her hands. "Well done, my dear. A perfect flush hit."

Percy floundered for a few moments, before she said, "I suppose we should help him out."

"Not you," Rutherford said. "It would minimize the effect, and you might ruin that perfectly lovely gown. I'll do it. Though it goes sadly against the grain."

He reached out, grabbed Percy's flailing hand, and pulled him out of the fountain.

Percy, cold and angry, fixed his gaze on Anna. "When we are married, you will not do that."

Anna closed her eyes and struggled not to hit him again. "*We* are not going to marry. I don't know where you got such a ridiculous notion. I would rather be a spinster than marry you." She pointed to the door to the drawing room. "You are no longer welcome at Marsh Hill. Go. Now."

Dripping, Percy left.

Rutherford put his arms around her. "Allow me to congratulate you on a stellar performance."

Anna heaved a sigh. "Do you think he'll stop?"

"If he doesn't, either you or I will pummel him into the ground."

She brightened. "Yes, of course. What a grand idea."

Rutherford shook his head. "You're a bloodthirsty wench. Come, we need to go in. Are you ready to face them?"

"Yes, indeed. I want Lady Blanchard to know how badly her son behaved."

Though, when they entered the drawing room, Percy and his mother had already gone.

"Did Lord Rutherford really throw Percy into the fountain?" Aunt Lillian asked.

Anna stared at her in disbelief. "Is that what he said?"

Aunt Lillian's eyes grew wide. "Why, yes. Is that not what occurred?"

"I'll have you know that I put Percy in the fountain. Rutherford pulled him out. I wish now that he hadn't."

A slow smile dawned on Aunt Lillian's face.

"I will not allow Percy to visit again," Anna said. "Even if he is with his mother."

Her aunt's laugher filled the room. "Oh—oh—my dear. Of course not."

Anna's breath shortened with rage. She turned to Rutherford. "I cannot believe that—that coward, told his mother *you* punched him."

He rubbed her back. "I always thought he was a little weasel. What are you going to do about Percy's misperceptions concerning your marriage to him?"

Anna raised a brow. "Must I do anything?"

"Well, we know Lady Blanchard has been talking about it, and he's probably already spread it around the area that you are marrying him."

Anna scowled. "Then he'll look no how when it doesn't happen, won't he?"

Rutherford grinned. "He will indeed."

November 9th, 1814, London

Georges stayed at the brothel until late morning. He was lounging in a chair, reading, when "The Mistress," the nom de guerre of the French émigré operating the house, entered his room.

He allowed his gaze to roam the lush curves of her body as she walked toward him. "I thought you'd still be sleeping."

She'd been a street urchin when the revolution began. Her first protector had been a member of the inner council of revolutionaries. When the minister discarded her, Georges brought her to London to spy. She was an expert at obtaining information from gentlemen who worked in government offices.

Lowering her lids, she glanced at him. "I thought you might like to entertain me before you go."

"Ah, Désirée," Georges said. "How well you know me."

"Do I?" she asked. "Or do I just like the idea that a *marquis* must sell his body to me?"

Anger rose inside him. No whore spoke to him like that. He cupped the back of her head and smoothly brought her closer for a kiss. When she opened her mouth, he possessed it, tangling his tongue with hers. "Do you do this with everyone, or only with me?"

Sinking his hands in her hair, he pulled her back. "Answer."

"You. Only you."

She trembled as his hands roved her body and tweaked her already hard nipples.

"Tell me, Désirée, do your buds harden at a touch for another man?"

"No."

He grinned to himself as he spread her dressing gown open, exposing her nakedness, and reached between her legs. "Are you this wet for every man who has you?"

She moaned and spread her legs wider. "Never."

He slipped a finger inside her hot sheath. She rocked her hips in rhythm with his thrusts, responding just as he knew she would. Backing her against a wall, he released his hard member. Georges lifted her and brought her down sharply, impaling her on his shaft. "How many men can do this to you?"

He held her hard against the wall and thrust deep.

She screamed before she climaxed.

"Let us not have any doubt who has had whom in this little encounter." Georges lifted her off him, and she fell to her knees. "Take me in your mouth, and give me the pleasure I just gave you."

He groaned as her lips covered him. Holding her head to him, he pumped into her hot, wet mouth. When he finally found his release, he pushed her away. Désirée collapsed on to the floor. Georges took a cloth, wetting it in the basin, and wiped himself, then held out a hand to her and pulled her up. "Never forget, my sweet, *who* I am." She hung her head. "No, milord. I should not have said what I did." "I'm pleased we understand each other. I need my clothing and other items. Do you have someone you can send? They must be prudent."

"Yes, I shall send the boy. No one will notice him."

The night's sleep enabled Georges to think more clearly about his current problem. If he allowed Florian to chase him back to France, Georges would be seen as a failure, a disposable failure. Someone else would be sent over to finish what he did not. Still, he couldn't remain in London.

He knew the town of Thanport. He'd find a room nearby and monitor the meeting, or attend it, if Florian didn't. Georges's most pressing need was to quit London.

After Georges had eaten, a youth knocked on his door with Georges's portmanteaux and a small trunk. He sent the lad back out to buy a ticket for him on the mail coach to Dover. From there, he'd hire a horse and find his way to Thanport.

Désirée entered his room as he was repacking. He glanced briefly at her, took in the red silk robe she wore, and lifted a brow. "Yes?"

She licked her lips. "Please."

He smiled thinly. "Do the English not satisfy you, *ma chérie*? If you want more, you must tell me."

Her breathing shortened. "*Non.* They do not satisfy me."

"Come to me, Désirée."

She walked forward as if in a trance. Her chest heaved. Georges smiled. He kissed her and rocked his already hard shaft against her. Releasing his member, he turned her so that she faced the bed and slid it between her legs. "Bend over and spread your legs."

He was in her before she'd had time to obey. The bed was high, at her waist. Her hands gripped the satin bedcover. Georges cupped her breasts and played as he thrust into her. He tightened his hands around them and squeezed. "Tell me what you want."

Désirée groaned. Georges withdrew, flipped her over, then pulled her legs around his waist and entered her again. When she convulsed around him, he withdrew. "Your hand or your mouth. It makes no difference to me."

He never spilt his seed into a whore.

Désirée put her fingers around him. He spewed his come on to her stomach. Once he'd cleaned himself, he returned to his packing.

"Milord," Désirée asked, "how long will you be gone?"

He smiled charmingly. It would never do for her to know how desperate his circumstances were. Like a wild animal, she'd turn on him in an instant. "Not long. I'll visit when I return."

Désirée gave him a trembling smile. "I shall look forward to it."

"Call me a hackney. I'll need to go soon."

"Yes, milord." She pulled her robe together and left the room.

When the hackney pulled up to the mews behind the brothel, the boy came to get him. Georges loaded his luggage and gave the driver the direction. He arrived in time to catch the noon coach. He was one of seven passengers and made sure he had a place by the window.

The woman next to him was a buxom country woman, who said she'd been visiting her cousin. She held a large basket in her lap. Two men, who looked like clerks, sat across from him. He ignored the others, a man and woman dressed in black with a child. The conveyance wasn't particularly comfortable and it was over-crowded, but, for the moment, he was safe.

Florian left his club after luncheon and walked down the street to an alley. He stopped by a wall near the back corner of a building. After looking around, he removed a loose brick, took out a piece of paper, and shoved it in his pocket. With a glance up and down the alley, he rounded the back of the building and proceeded to the Foreign Office.

Once in the sanctuary of his bureau, he opened the note. Georges had given the thugs Florian had hired the slip. His face paled, and his heart began to race. His cousin would certainly know he was behind the men following him. Florian had to come up with a plausible excuse before their next meeting.

His mind blanked, then a vision of himself lying on the ground, blood pooling out around him pushed to the fore. He placed his trembling hands on his desk and tried to stop himself from shaking like blancmange. If he went ahead with the meeting in Thanport, maybe Georges wouldn't kill him.

Florian would have an excuse by then. A loud crack outside his window caused him to jump. He really wasn't feeling at all the thing today. He found a clerk and explained that he must have a touch of something and was going home. Florian retrieved his hat and sword stick, then left the building.

"There you are. Lord Florian Iswell, isn't it?"

Florian snapped his head up. "I beg your pardon?"

"I wanted to talk to you about a matter of some urgency," one of Lord Castlereagh's under-secretaries said.

Florian's stomach lurched. Had he been caught? If so, he may as well put a bullet in his head. "Yes, yes, of course. How may I assist you?"

The man took Florian's arm and turned him back toward the building. It turned out that the meeting was not nearly as painful as Florian had thought. By the time he made his escape an hour later, he'd discovered he was under consideration for a foreign posting, somewhere warm, he hoped.

Florian returned to his rooms and tried to set his mind to the problem of his cousin. Fortunately for his sanity, he'd received an invitation to a very select, impromptu party. Not the sort that would get him into trouble. Or where his indiscretions would be discovered. Only his French cousin knew Florian's tastes ran to young men, rather than young women.

Georges woke for the last time as the coach rumbled along the cobbled streets into Dover. It was past one o'clock in the morning. The driver gave him directions to a slightly better inn than the one that serviced the coach. Georges walked across the street and stood in a doorway before making his way to a tavern two blocks away.

The door was opened by a sleepy young man. "How can I help ye?"

"I need a room for the night."

The youth nodded. "We got room. Breakfast in the tap is included. If ye want a private parlor, it'll be more."

"Thank you. That will serve me."

Georges followed the man to a small chamber. While the young man built up a fire, Georges quickly unpacked a jacket and gave it to the man to be pressed. He almost asked for breakfast to be served in a private parlor, then thought better of it. His current resources were not unlimited, and he didn't know what he'd need in the coming days.

He pressed a coin in the younger man's hand and asked to be awoken in time to break his fast. Locking his door, he stripped quickly and got beneath the sheets. Georges had never killed a family member yet, but for Florian, he might make an exception.

Anna had never before been so thankful for country hours. Rutherford had joined them for dinner and tea, and she was still in her room by nine o'clock. Lizzy helped her out of her evening gown and in to bed until she had to dress again. The few months before Christmas were always the busiest for her smugglers.

She woke two hours later, scrambled into her habit, and slipped down the back stairs through the side door to the stables.

Humphrey's head was swathed in bandages. "Did the doctor remove it?"

"Yes, miss, he took out two. Warned me not to wait so long the next time. Said there was a woman he saw that let it go so long she died of the infection. Right glad I am you made me see him, miss. I'll be good enough tomorrow or the next day."

"You need to rest. There is no reason at all for you to worry about me."

"Master Harry . . ."

Anna sighed. "Humphrey, Master Harry is no longer here. I'll be fine."

Anna led Thunderer to the mounting block. Once on the large gelding's back, she turned him toward the meadow and the sea. After changing at the cottage, Anna arrived at the cliff with time to spare. She descended to the beach to wait.

Kev was the first to arrive. "We're going to be later than usual. Got word of a patrol."

"How'd that happen?"

"One of our men was in a tavern in Dover. He heard talk." Anna could just make out his grin. "They expect to be back in by midnight."

That was a relief. Harry had given her a contact in the event they were ever caught, but she'd never had to use it and didn't want to now. "Good. That won't put us off by much."

"I sent word to Lizzy that you'd be late."

Anna nodded. "Have you received the information for the next few shipments?"

"Yes, Mr. Arnold." Kev gave the dates for the next couple of weeks.

Once the men were assembled and the delivery signal given, Anna climbed back up the path.

She was in place when the ship answered. Focusing on the boats and the beach, she'd just started to relax when the hairs on her neck prickled and warmth spread across her shoulders. She fought not to squirm and look around. The two short blinks from a shuttered lantern indicating that they had possession of the cargo couldn't come soon enough.

Heat spread down her body. Why were they taking so long to get the shipment? She'd decided to go down to see what was wrong when she saw the flashes. Anna jumped up and ran. Thunderer went willingly, as if he too knew something was wrong. Anna looped his reins on the iron ring in the stable and ran to the cottage door. Her heart thudded as she shut the door and barred it.

Several minutes passed before her hands stopped shaking enough to undo the shirt buttons. She'd just donned her skirt when a horse trotted up to the front of the cottage. Grabbing her jacket and pistol, Anna breathed shallowly and waited until whoever it was left. The only noise was of the restless horse in front of the cottage, and the roaring of her heart in the ears. The window shutters were tight enough not to allow the low light from the fireplace to show through. Finally, the horse trotted off down the lane. Thank God whoever it was didn't think to look in the back, or he would have seen her horse.

She waited for another thirty minutes before making her way to the stable and back to the house. One more night alone. Humphrey would be well by the next delivery. The fear that someone else had been out there made her skin crawl. She shook herself and steadied her breathing. Now was not the time to lose her nerve.

Earlier that evening, Rutherford had arrived at Marsh Hill for dinner in time to see Anna descend the stairs. She wore a simple round gown in yellow cashmere, with pearls, and the need to kiss her had never been stronger. He took her hand and they entered the drawing room. Since Rutherford had told Sir William about Harry's death, the older man actually seemed more at peace.

He and Rutherford joined the ladies with their port after dinner, and the discussion turned to politics. Then Rutherford told them about his mother's attempts to include his younger sisters in Althea's lessons in deportment.

"I can see why it wouldn't be interesting to them," Anna said. "I think Cece's got the right idea though. Wouldn't it be nice if one could sit home and wait for her knight to arrive?"

He drove home wondering what Anna would do if he rode up dressed in a suit of armor and laughed ruefully. On one hand, they were getting along quite well. On the other, they were at a standstill. She frustrated every move he made to turn their friendship into more. He needed help and wished he had someone to talk to.

He'd received another note today. There was a delivery tonight. Another area in which he was making no progress.

Once again, he waited in the copse and watched as the small man monitored the beach and left. Rutherford decided to go to the cottage and look around, but saw nothing more than closed shutters and a little smoke coming up from the fireplace. Even in the dark, the yard appeared well tended. Apparently, Sir William had rented it to someone. Whoever was in there was probably in bed and asleep.

Rutherford rode back toward the Priory. If he didn't receive an invitation to meet the smuggler's leader soon, he'd introduce himself.

Chapter 9

The ship heaved and rolled wildly. A great crack rent the air as the main mast broke and fell, ripping sails and lines. The sharp tang of blood caught in his nose. Harry tried to pull one man out from under the mast, now lying on deck, then saw the large shard of wood sticking in the sailor's thigh. He was bleeding out and fast.

The deck lurched as the ship groaned and began to break apart. Harry was knocked overboard into the roiling waters. Men shouted and screamed, trying to escape the sinking ship. He swam as hard as he could away from the boat. The air was heavy, and the wind ripped through him as cold enveloped him. A sharp pain exploded in his head, and it all went black.

Harry woke gasping for breath. Beads of sweat ran down his forehead. He tossed and turned before finally settling, only to have more visions. This time of the girl, his sister, riding a large gray horse to a cottage.

He rubbed his face. There was so much he didn't remember. Perhaps that was the reason he clung to his memories of Marcella and the things he knew.

Unable to sleep any longer, Harry repacked his few belongings, before making his way to the taproom for breakfast. He took a seat at a corner table with a view of the stairs and the inn's yard. Not knowing what lay ahead, it was difficult to think beyond the day's journey. Tonight, he'd be at the Crown in Basingstoke.

About a half hour later, Miss Spencer-Jones emerged from the stairwell. She glanced at him and nodded without smiling, then left the inn with her companion. For some contrary reason, and even though he didn't feel like returning the gesture, Harry had wanted her to smile at him. He'd even begun to hope she'd be in Basingstoke as well. He gave himself a shake. There were more things to worry about than silken, gold curls and bright turquoise eyes. He paid his shot and was soon back on the post road. At least the ride gave him time to think.

Wrapped warmly in a sable-lined cloak with a fur rug over her lap and a hot brick under her feet, Emma leaned back against the squabs. She'd seen poor Mr. Marsh when she'd first come down the steps, his head in his hands. He looked weary, as if he was carrying a great burden. He must have loved his wife very much to still be so affected by her death.

Emma hoped he'd talk to her, but after her reaction last night, perhaps she should keep her distance. It wouldn't do any good to develop feelings for a man so in love with someone else. Even if the other woman was no longer alive. She wondered if he'd be in Basingstoke this evening and, if so, whether he'd be at the Crown.

She glanced up. Mrs. Wickham was chattering again. Actually, "again" was not accurate. The woman never stopped.

"My dear Miss Spencer-Jones, I've addressed you at least four times. You must be blue deviled. Are you still upset about leaving the West Indies? You shouldn't be, my dear. Truly, you will find England, and London in particular, most superior to anything you could find in the islands. Why, the shops on Bond and Bruton Streets are the envy of the world, and with your dear godmama bringing you out, well, I don't need to tell you how fortunate you are. I never had a Season. Dear me, no. My papa said it would be a waste of money since I was already promised to my dear Mr. Wickham."

A pained look passed briefly across her face. "So improvident. But there, I shan't refine too much on it. I have enough for my needs, and my sister is positively overjoyed that I'm finally coming home. . . ."

Emma nodded and made the appropriate sounds. She didn't

need to worry about making conversation. Mrs. Wickham was capable of carrying on a perfectly good discussion with herself. It was fortunate Emma was not susceptible to headaches, because she would surely have one by now if she were.

She closed her eyes and allowed the coach's movement to rock her. Maybe Mrs. Wickham would stop talking if she thought Emma was asleep. Not many more days now before they'd go their separate ways. Her mother had only paid for Mrs. Wickham to stay with her until her godmother met her at Grillon's Hotel in London.

". . . and won't you be so happy—Oh, are you asleep? Well, isn't it just like these young people these days. . . ."

Emma turned to snuggle in next to the side of the coach and hid a smile. Mrs. Wickham was still talking when the coach lurched to a stop, sending Emma sprawling off the seat. "What the dev—I mean whatever could it be?"

She knocked on the roof to get the coachman's attention. "Where are we?"

"We've just passed Winchester, miss."

Emma frowned. "Why have we stopped?"

"There's a wagon across the road."

"What sort of—Never mind." Emma pulled the window down and stuck her head out. "I can't see much from here. I'm coming out."

"No, miss, it may be a trap," the coachman said, too late. She'd already jumped lightly down from the conveyance and was walking toward the front. Two men emerged from the wood on one side of the road.

"Well, well, if it isn't Miss Spencer-Jones."

This was outside of enough. Why couldn't he just leave her alone? She turned and allowed her irritation to show. "Mr. Reynolds, *what* a surprise. I suppose you are responsible for this conveyance?"

"What a clever young lady you are." He leered at her. "Now, if you will please get in the cart, we may be on our way."

She tightened her lips. "Mr. Reynolds, I have no intention of going anywhere with you."

He smiled humorlessly. "Oh, but you will, my dear. Otherwise my friend here will shoot your coachman. You wouldn't want to be responsible for his death, would you?"

Emma was in no mood to put up with this. She smiled sweetly. "But Mr. Reynolds, I would not be the one responsible, you would."

He scowled. "Get in the wagon."

She quickly slanted her eyes at the coachman, who gave an imperceptible shake of his head. One hand was in sight, the other hidden.

"I have a better idea," she said. "Why don't you move the conveyance that you so unhelpfully left in the road, and I'll be on my way?"

"Hey there, you trying to bubble me?" Mr. Reynolds's accomplice asked. "Thought you said this bleached mort would be an easy mark. This here's a busy highway, and I ain't standing around all day. We'll be blocked at both ends. I ain't a badger, you see. I'm a rum diver. That wern't part of the deal. You just give me my balsam, and I'll be off."

Emma listened, fascinated by the man's speech. A piercing scream emanated from the coach. Mrs. Wickham had apparently stopped talking to herself.

The thug's eyes grew as round as pennies. "I'm piking." He climbed on his horse and left in a hurry.

Reynolds looked around and yelled at Mrs. Wickham to stop, which did no good at all. Then he pointed his pistol at the driver, who pulled out his long-barreled coach pistol.

"We seem to be at an impasse," Emma said, wrapping her fingers around the dagger in her pocket.

Reynolds moved to grab her arm.

She stepped back and made a sweeping movement with her hand, the blade barely visible.

Reynolds yelled, blood dripping from his arm, "What?"

"Miss Spencer-Jones, might I be of assistance?" an amused voice asked.

"Ah, Mr. Marsh, if you could help my coachman move the wagon"—she pointed to it—"we may be on our way."

A smiled played on his lips. "What would you like done with Mr. Reynolds?"

Emma studied Reynolds's scowling face. His pistol lay on the ground not far from his feet. "If the coachman will keep his weapon on him, and you can fetch his pistol, I believe we may allow him to leave."

Harry raised his brows.

Emma shrugged. "Yes, well, I don't have a great deal of time, and I do not wish to return for a trial. I doubt Mr. Reynolds will make another attempt."

Harry regarded her dubiously. "If that is what you want?"

"It is." She saw the concern in his countenance. Not many men would have honored her choice. "Thank you for not arguing."

Harry inclined his head. "Not at all."

The coachman, not waiting for Harry, scrambled down from the box and scooped up Reynolds's gun.

Emma held out her hand. "Give it to me, please."

The coachman hesitated, then handed it over.

"Thank you." She turned to Reynolds. "I am allowing you to leave. Do not try anything like this again. If there is a next time, I shall not hesitate to bring you before a magistrate. I'd have that arm looked at."

Reynolds scowled as if he wanted to say something, but instead mounted his horse and road off.

Harry pulled a face, as if just noticing the shrieks. He tilted his head toward the coach. "How long has she been doing that?"

Emma smiled broadly. "Long enough." She poked what she could of her head through the window. "Mrs. Wickham, they are gone."

She stopped screaming and looked at Emma in disbelief. "Gone? We are safe?"

"Yes, all is well. Mr. Marsh is here to help."

"Oh, oh, Mr. Marsh. What a kind man he is, so brave, so noble. Was it he who scared them away?"

Emma bit her lip. There was no point in explaining. "Indeed, Mrs. Wickham, and we shall soon be on our way."

Emma walked to the front of the coach to see the wagon being led off to the side. "What shall we do with the horses? We can't leave them here."

"Unhitch them and let them go," Harry said. "They'll find their way home. What will you do if Reynolds continues to accost you?"

That was not something she wanted to dwell upon. "As I told him, if he does it again, I shall be forced to seek out a magistrate. One would hope he has learned his lesson. I am not an easy target."

Something in Mr. Marsh's eyes changed. They looked softer as he returned her gaze. "No, you're not. You are an exceptionally talented woman."

"Thank you, Mr. Marsh." She turned to go back to the coach, then whirled back around. "Mr. Marsh, we'll be stopping for a light repast just a little ways up the road. Will you join us?"

He smiled. "Yes, I'd like that."

Emma's breath hitched. Such a wonderful smile. "Well then." Her voice was husky. "I'll just . . ." She waved a hand at the coach.

"Here, allow me." He put down the steps and handed her up. A shock raced through his hand. He glanced at her.

Miss Spencer-Jones's eyes were wide as she looked down at their hands, then back at him. "Oh, my."

Those two small words seem to explain the situation exactly. *Oh, my.* Now what was he to do?

She entered the coach and sat down. "If you don't mind riding next to us?"

"No, I don't mind at all." Harry mounted his horse.

He'd heard the screams and had expected to arrive to find a prostrate Miss Spencer-Jones. Instead he'd watched in appreciation as she skillfully wielded the dagger, cutting Reynolds, without batting an eye. Harry smiled to himself, then frowned and wondered what he was doing thinking about another woman.

By the time they reached the inn, he was in a state of indecision concerning his feelings. He dismounted and looked around for a groom. Seeing no one, he tied his horse up and went in search of a bucket of water. He found a small stable and a youth lying down on a bench.

"You there," Harry said. "I need some water, and there's a coach needing attention as well."

The lad jumped to his feet at the voice, then cast a doubtful eye at Harry and stopped.

"Well, come on now," Harry said impatiently. What the deuce was wrong with the boy? "We haven't got all day."

"Yes, sir," the boy said, still staring at him.

"Go."

The youth ran around to the front of the inn. Harry shook his head and followed. He made sure the stable boy was doing what he was supposed to before entering the inn.

"I'm sorry, miss," a middle-aged woman said. "We don't have a private parlor. If you don't mind eating in the common room?"

Emma inclined her head. "In fact, that suits me much better."

She turned the landlady's attention to Mrs. Wickham. "My companion must rest for a while. If you could take her to a bedchamber and see she is comfortable, perhaps she may dine there."

Mrs. Wickham nodded in agreement. "Yes, if you don't mind, my dear, dear, Miss Spencer-Jones. Maybe just a bowl of broth, and a bit of a rest, and I am sure I'll be fine to travel in an hour or so."

"Of course, Mrs. Wickham, an hour's respite will be just the thing. I have Mr. Marsh to keep me company. I'm sure there is nothing improper in us taking our luncheon in the common room."

"No indeed. Such a sweet inn."

Emma maintained her smile as the landlady led her companion up the stairs, then she closed her eyes.

Harry was grinning at her when she opened them. "Is Mrs. Wickham always like that?"

"Yes. A sillier woman I've never met. She talks incessantly and says nothing to the purpose."

"I did wonder," he said, "how the inn's being sweet made a difference in the propriety of dining with me."

"One of the many things I've heard her say that don't make a bit of sense to me," Emma replied. "The room looks fairly empty. Let's choose a table."

Harry selected one near the fireplace. "Will this do?"

"Thank you. I'm still not used to the cold. I daresay it will take me a while."

"Miss Spencer-Jones . . ."

"Please, call me Emma," she said. "After today, I think we can be on a Christian name basis."

"Then I insist you call me Harry."

"Very well, Harry it is. It suits you."

"I must be honest and tell you, I don't know if it fits me at all." He couldn't believe the strong urge he had to confide in her. "I'm having a slight problem with my memory."

Her steady blue gaze met his. She nodded.

Harry forged ahead. "I was in a shipwreck a couple of years back, and I've only recently started to remember my past."

"It happens," Emma said calmly. "Trauma seems to bring it on. Once you begin remembering, your memory will return faster. When you are once more surrounded by the familiar, more quickly still."

Harry glanced out the window, then back to her. "Part of the problem is I have not been around anything familiar. The clothes I was wearing didn't appear to belong to me, not even the boots. I had nothing from my past. It became a game to guess who I was." He paused and drew in a breath. "We figured out I must be a gentleman, because of my manners. A gentleman used to the country, and educated, but beyond that, nothing."

"I'll not be sorry for you," she said bracingly. "You will discover your life. And you had the rare opportunity to marry a woman you truly loved." Emma took his hand. "That, I will tell you, does not happen to everyone. I only wish I'd married Adam before he died. If I'd known—well, if I'd known how precious life was, there are so many things I'd do differently." She sighed. "But I can't rewrite my past. All I can do is look to my future."

The landlady came over to them, glanced at Harry, and addressed Emma. "Miss, we have a nice mushroom soup, a mutton pie, roasted lamb, some haricot vert tossed in butter, escalloped potatoes, and an apple tart for dessert."

Emma addressed Harry. "Mr. Marsh, do you have a preference?"

"Miss Spencer-Jones, I would prefer the roasted lamb over the mutton pie."

"We shall have the roasted lamb, and the rest."

The landlady eyed Harry again. It was all he could do to keep from scowling at her. "We would also like a bottle of claret if you have it."

The landlady huffed and walked off toward the back of the room.

"I do not understand why I'm receiving such looks here."

"Probably because of your clothes."

He glanced down at himself. "My clothes? What's wrong with them? They're warm and serviceable."

Emma giggled slightly. "But not fashionable. We must be close enough to London for people to take notice."

"Therefore, I am to be treated with gross impertinence due to my raiment?" Harry asked, offended.

She put her hand over her mouth and choked. "Yes, I believe so."

For two years, he had not worried about what he wore. "Then it behooves me to find a tailor and buy a couple of new rigs before I go home. But where?"

"I believe London will be the place to replenish your wardrobe. I am under orders to go to a Madame Lisette the minute I arrive. Are you traveling to London as well?"

He hadn't been. "I am now. Do you know someone who could direct me to a tailor?"

Emma leaned forward. "I have been reliably informed that the staff at Grillon's is very knowledgeable. I am sure they could help you."

"As no one knows I'm arriving home," Harry said, "and I don't wish to appear at the door looking beggarly, I suppose there is no harm in spending a few days in London. I don't know that I've ever been there, but if I have, it might jog my memory some more."

Emma sat back. Her eyes warmed as she looked at him. "I think that's a wonderful idea."

Harry reached across the table and covered her fingers. His palm tingled pleasantly at the touch. "Thank you. Other than my in-laws, I've not had another person with whom I could speak of this."

"I think we have the loss of a loved one in common. I wasn't married to Adam, but I'd known him all my life and loved him dearly."

A fragment of memory floated just out of reach. Harry suddenly tightened his hand on hers. "Say that again. Please."

Emma's eyes lit up. "I think we . . ."

"No, the second part."

"I wasn't married, but I'd known him all my life and loved . . ."

"Yes, there is something. Oh God, why can't I remember?" He ran a hand over his face. "She loved him, but was unhappy. Why?"

"Who, Harry?"

"My sister. I think. I've recently remembered that I have a sister. I–I recall her saying she'd love him all her life, but I don't know who." He sat back and pinched the bridge of his nose. "It's no use. I can't recollect."

Emma turned his hand in hers and tightened her grip. "You will remember. You must trust that you will."

The landlady and a servant brought their meal. Harry gave the landlady his most charming smile, and she snorted. When he glanced at Emma, she hid a laugh with her hand. His heart lightened. "I suppose I should get used to it until I'm able to buy new clothing."

Her eyes widened. "No, why should you? Anyone with eyes and a brain can see you're a gentleman."

"Thank you again."

"For what? Reminding you what you should already know?"

He sat back and stared at the fireplace. "Yes. I'm sorry."

Emma shook her head. "Harry, it will come. We have many shipwrecks in the islands. I've seen cases like yours before. Once you start remembering, your memories will come faster. Maybe in bits and pieces. Sometimes with a fragment of a sentence, but the more you recall, the more you will remember."

Harry closed his eyes. Her hand was strong and warm. Her voice reassuring. He gripped her hand like a lifeline. Calm and certainty amid his jumbled thoughts and emotions. He could remain here with her all day.

Then she let go.

"Let's eat. I still have to get to Basingstoke today."

Harry smiled. "That's where I'm going. The Crown?"

Emma smiled delightedly. "Yes, the Crown."

Chapter 10

Anna toyed with her food, taking a bite of egg. For the past two weeks, she'd spent at least part of every day with Rutherford. Frowning, she scowled at a piece of toast before biting into it. Something had changed. It wasn't only the stirring of the strange feeling in her body. She couldn't quite put her finger on what it was that seemed to be elementally different between them. Or was it only her? Still, as long as he held to his beliefs about what he wanted in a wife . . . She sighed and sipped her tea.

"You look to be in a brown study."

The deep drawl made her look up. "I am rather. There is something I'm having a problem with."

Rutherford walked into the breakfast room and took a cup, holding it out to her. Anna poured absently, then smothered the gasp as their hands met.

"Is it anything I can help with?"

She studied him as he took the chair next to hers. "Maybe."

Perhaps she should just tell him that she'd overheard him speaking with Marcus. What if he didn't truly regard her as an adult, capable of making her own decisions? She took another sip of tea. "When you think of me, do you think of me as a child?"

Rutherford had just taken a sip of tea and choked. He quickly brought his serviette to his mouth, before meeting her gaze. "No, I most certainly do not think of you as a child. I remember you as a little girl, but I think of you as a woman. Why?"

"Oh, no reason. I'm probably thinking too much." Anna speared another piece of egg and brought it to her mouth. His gaze was steady on her. Lately, when she was with him, all her senses were heightened. She had trouble not looking at his well-formed lips and wondering what they'd feel like pressed against hers. Anna gave herself an inward shake. As long as he wanted an obedient, complacent wife, just the thought of kissing him would take her down a slippery hill. She had no intention of allowing herself to be trapped into a marriage that would be unhappy.

Rutherford grunted as if he didn't believe her.

"I think it's something I need to settle for myself. I'm not sure anyone can help."

"Are you sure?" he asked. "I'm more than willing to try to assist you."

She shook her head slightly. "No, I'll either figure it out, or I won't."

"How soon will you be ready to go?"

"Give me a few moments to fetch my hat, and I'll be with you." She gracefully rose and left the room.

When *had* he stopped thinking of her as a child? Not too long ago, actually. When she'd refused to marry him, he'd had to take another look at her. He found the woman to be enticing indeed, and he'd fallen in love with her. It surprised him that he'd not expected it to happen. All thoughts of a marriage based on mutual liking to a woman he could easily manage had fled. If he could only make her see him as something more than a chum.

Rutherford walked into the main hall as Anna descended. His hands itched to hold her. He glanced around and realized they were alone. Someone should be here to chaperone, but they'd been alone in the breakfast room as well. *Damn.* Either no one was concerned about her, which he knew wasn't true, or they didn't view him as a threat to her virtue.

The devil. Neither she nor her family saw him as a man who wanted her. That would have to change. "Come on. We need to go," he growled.

She glanced up at him, looking confused. "Rutherford, what's happened? Why are you so angry?"

"I'll explain later." Much later, after he'd kissed her and run his hands over her perfect form. The thought of his lips on hers caused his body to harden. He took her hand and pulled her toward the door.

Anna struggled to keep up with him. "Rutherford, what are you doing? Why are you in such a hurry?"

"We need to go."

He reached the stable where her horse was ready and threw her on to the saddle. She gasped. His muscles bunched. Confounded woman. As soon as he had a handle on the smugglers, he'd deal with her.

Rutherford took her booted foot and placed it in the stirrup. Her leg trembled, and fire shot up his arm. He flung himself on to his horse and rode out of the stable yard. Anna followed and drew alongside him.

"Tell me what happened. Did one of the servants insult you?"

"Give me time. I'll explain in a while."

"Very well. I just don't understand."

He grimaced. No, of course she didn't. She really had no idea how he was feeling. That she was so oblivious to his feelings didn't calm him. They rode on through the forest, now almost bare of leaves, then on to the cliffs before he reined in.

"Anna, I have some things I must deal with, and afterward we need to talk. Until then"—he took a deep breath—"I don't want to say anything."

"If you're sure?"

"I am. Do you want to go into town again today?"

"Yes, I must. Lizzy and Aunt Lillian gave me commissions. I even have money today," she laughed.

His bad mood disappeared. At least he was the only man spending time with her. "I should allow you to pay for the coffyns, but I'm becoming rather used to being responsible for feeding you."

"I don't at all mind paying my fair share. . . ."

"No." He smiled. How to explain to her that he wanted to be responsible for her? He wanted to be the one she came to. "No, it's my pleasure."

Anna frowned. "Rutherford, you are acting very strangely today."

He shrugged.

"Well, if you're not going to explain, we may as well go."

They were leaving the inn's stable yard when Percy accosted them.

"Rutherford, I demand satisfaction."

Rutherford rolled his eyes. "Percy, I have no idea what you are talking about."

"You pushed me into the fountain."

"What?" The man was clearly delusional.

Anna stepped in between them, and stared up belligerently at Percy, then poked him in the chest hard enough for the man to step back. "Percy Blanchard, I put you in that fountain, and you know it. Don't blame it on Rutherford. Have you told the lie so many times you believe it yourself? Or are you not man enough to admit you were bested by a mere female? If you want satisfaction, I'll be happy to give it to you."

"Impossible, you couldn't have punched me that hard."

Her eyes glittered dangerously. "I'll do it again if you say another word or repeat your slander to anyone else."

She took Rutherford's arm and led them out of the yard. His lips curved up.

"Don't laugh. It's not funny." She scowled. "No wonder his mother doesn't allow him in London. He's out of his mind."

Rutherford tried not to chuckle, twined his arm with hers, and said gravely, "Thank you for defending my honor."

Anna glanced up at him with suspicion.

"Word of a Rutherford."

Her face relaxed, and she smiled a little. "Well, he ought not be telling such Banbury tales."

"No, but then again, he never was very brave, nor very smart."

"No, he wasn't."

Anna finished her shopping, and they indulged once again in coffyns.

"Will you come to the Priory for luncheon?"

Anna turned a wide-eyed gaze on him. "Do you think it wise? I mean, would your family get the wrong idea?"

"Hmm." His family might get the right idea. He'd have to drive his mother over to the Hill for tea. "I take your meaning. It's just that I have some work I should do, and I won't be able to dine with you."

He took her hands. "I enjoy the time we spend together."

Anna's eyes warmed. "I like our time as well. There will be other days, and I should really work with Papa on the Hill's accounts and alike. Shall we meet again in the morning?"

Rutherford tried to keep a pleasant expression on his face. "Yes."

They passed through the gates to Marsh Hill and galloped the last mile to the house. A groom came out to help her down and take her horse. Rutherford begrudged him the task and left.

He took the way through the meadows to the Priory. Once there, he gave orders that he was not to be disturbed, and ordered luncheon to be brought to his study. If he had to listen to talk of love matches at the table today, he'd go mad and might even throttle someone.

Anna reached her room, washed, and dressed in a light cashmere day gown. There was a note on her dressing table from Kev. The meeting with the London gentleman was set for midnight. She sat down at her desk and played with the feather of her quill before responding. She wanted Kev to bring the man to a different part of the beach from where their shipments arrived. She rang for Lizzy.

"Oh, miss, why didn't you call for me sooner? I'd have come to help you change."

"I didn't need help this time. Here, take this to Kev. I've made some changes."

Lizzy bobbed a curtsey and left. Anna went to her father's study. "Papa, I've come to help work on the accounts."

Her father's face brightened when she spoke.

"Here, I'll give you these." He pushed some of the ledgers from the stack toward the chair in which she sat and handed her a sharpened pen.

They spent the rest of the afternoon quietly working.

"I'm going to retire early this evening," she said.

Her father looked up briefly. "Very well, my dear, go and dress for dinner now."

Anna bent to kiss him on the cheek. "I'll see you in the drawing room. Don't forget."

He patted her hand. "I won't."

Anna reached her room and stared out the window. The incident with Percy still occupied her mind. She'd almost punched him, again. It wasn't Percy's knavery that had upset her as much as the threat to Rutherford. Not that Percy could best Rutherford in any match, just the thought was laughable, but Anna discovered she had an overpowering need to protect him.

She shook her head. Rutherford wasn't the only one hard to understand these days; she was as well. If only Phoebe were here to talk to.

Without Rutherford, dinner was a quiet affair. She excused herself from tea and went up to lie down. The late nights and early mornings were beginning to take their toll. She tried to will herself to sleep, yet her errant mind focused on Rutherford's face, his lips actually. She wondered what it would be like to kiss him, then frowned. She'd thought of that for years, yet something was missing, or rather something else was there now. Anna no longer wanted the chaste kisses she'd imagined before. She wanted something more. If she only knew what.

Lizzy woke her at half past ten. Anna was soon on Thunderer galloping toward the cottage. Once there, she scrambled into her men's clothing and hurried to the cliffs above the meeting spot. She planned to be there long before the gentleman arrived to keep an eye out for anyone else who might try to join them. She was sure Harry would approve of her caution.

A note arrived telling Rutherford about a meeting to be held that night. He decided to leave a little early and ride along the cliff toward the usual meeting place. Not far from his property line he saw the smuggler leader slip off his horse and tie the reins to a nearby tree.

Rutherford stopped as the man dropped to his stomach at the edge of the cliff, as if looking for someone. He moved closer to a large bush, taking cover. This was the third time Rutherford had seen him.

The man was rather short, with a slight frame. At first, Rutherford had thought he was a youth, but the confidence in the small man's steps, and the obvious respect the smugglers had for him, made Rutherford decide he was older. Tonight was the first time he'd seen him on this stretch of the cliff. Perhaps it was time to introduce himself to the mysterious man. It was time to find out what the smuggler knew about the possibility of French agents being brought into England.

Rutherford slid quietly from his horse and made his way over to the gang leader who was still watching the beach below. Rutherford was almost on the man when he looked swiftly around and jumped up to run.

Grabbing his shoulders, Rutherford lifted the man off the ground. Even for his size, he was light. His head jerked back in an attempt to make contact with Rutherford's nose. Rutherford cursed and dropped to the ground, landing on top of the smuggler.

"Try anything like that again," Rutherford growled, "and I'll put your lights out for you."

The small man was panting and squirming underneath Rutherford. He started to search for weapons and slowed when he reached the narrow waist swelling out into hips. He flipped the person face-up and found a band wrapped around the chest. Binding. A woman's breasts.

One light swipe across them told him he was right. A woman, not a man. The muffler hiding the lower part of her face loosened.

He pitched his voice low and gravelly. "Keep it up and you'll get more than you were expecting."

She tensed, and her body all but hummed with sensual tension. He answered.

Then his mind froze for a moment. Only one woman made him respond like that. *Damn it to hell.* It couldn't be. He pressed his face against the side of hers and breathed in. Lavender and mint. That explained his growing erection. What the devil was she doing here? And dressed like that?

He brought his urge to rail at her under control. Instead of scaring her, it would have the opposite effect. Different tactics were needed for Miss Anna Marsh. He touched the tip of his tongue to the outer whorl of her pretty ear and traced it, before moving his lips across the sensitive skin of her jaw. Nudging her head back, he found the pulse at the base of her throat. Finally, she sighed. *Not quite good enough.*

The muffler fell away. Rutherford took her face in his hands, grazing his lips against hers until she responded. His tongue caressed her mouth, encouraging her to open them. When she did, he entered. He moved one hand to her breast and rubbed lightly against her nipple. She moaned. He smiled through the kiss. This might end up working in his favor.

Anna could have sworn with frustration. The minute he'd touched her, the burning feeling coursing through her strengthened. When he ran his hands over her breasts, intense heat threatened to steal her wits. Her nipples hardened under his touch. *Sebastian.*

She wondered how long she could keep her identity from him. His low chuckle made her furious, and she struggled again. He'd told her he wanted to marry her, and here he was ready to do whatever to another woman.

Anna's heart beat faster as his lips reached her throat. When he kissed her, she thought nothing could be better; then his tongue moved against hers, and she thought she'd swoon. She tried to put her arms around him, but they were trapped under his body. It was as if he were possessing her. Thank God he didn't know who she was. To him she was just some female. *How dare he?*

"Anna, tell me what you're doing here," Rutherford whispered into her ear.

Drat. Well, the secret was out now. "How did you know it was me? I thought you were just kissing . . ."

He stared at her in disbelief. "You thought I'd kiss just any woman? What the hell do you take me for?"

She struggled to sit up, but his body weighed her down. "I haven't even given you leave to kiss me, and you're doing even more!"

"Harumph." He bent his head to kiss her again. "And I plan to continue."

"Sebastian!" She wiggled to get out from under him.

He groaned. "Anna. Be still. I'll let you up when you tell me what you're doing here. Until then . . ."

He moved his hand over her breast again, and an ache started between her legs. His mouth covered hers, and she opened to him. His tongue skated over her teeth, before caressing the inside of her mouth. She'd never imagined a kiss could be like this. He lifted his head.

"Why did you stop?"

"I thought you didn't want me to kiss you."

"That was when I thought you were kissing someone else."

Giving a short laugh, he said, "I suppose that, in a sort of convoluted way, that makes sense."

"I'm being perfectly logical." She twisted to try to free her hands.

He grimaced as if in pain. "Anna, don't move. Why are you here?"

Could it be he hadn't put it together? "If I tell you, you can't tell anyone else, and you must promise not to interfere."

"I promise not to tell. I won't promise not to interfere. This is a dangerous game you're playing, my love."

"I'm just doing what Harry did. There's really no danger."

Rutherford stilled, and his brows snapped together. "Are you telling me *you* took over from Harry when he left?"

"Of course I did. Who else could do it?" She struggled to get out from under him again. "I could ensure that only the proper goods were smuggled. You know, no people or information."

"How *did* you get in with the smugglers?"

"Harry introduced me before he left the last time."

Rutherford groaned. Only Harry Marsh would think allowing his younger sister to run a group of smugglers was a good idea. He'd need to get Anna out of this as soon as possible. She had no business dealing with smugglers.

"Kiss me again," Anna demanded. "You may touch me as well."

God, how things change in the dead of night. Rutherford kissed her and changed breasts, reveling in her moans each time he rubbed his finger across her nipple. "Who are you meeting tonight?"

"One of the gang was approached by a man wishing to smuggle wool to France. It doesn't make sense. I set the meeting so I could make out what he really wanted. I always arrive to these things at least an hour early, just to make sure it's not a trap."

What the hell had she gotten herself into? "I'm coming with you."

"Kiss me, and I'll think about it."

He supposed he could tie her up, though his marriage prospects wouldn't be very good afterward. "You'll not be able to think if I kiss you again."

"I will. I've had several thoughts already." Anna's chuckle was low and sultry. "Such as, I never knew how hard your body is."

If she only understood how hard.

"How can I refuse a challenge like that?" He crushed her mouth under his and plundered. *That,* for believing she could think while he was kissing her. Her body sunk into his. Her brain couldn't possibly be functioning. His barely was.

She pulled her arms out and pushed them under his coat. His muscles contracted as her hands roved, then held him closer. He pulled back from the kiss. "Well?"

Anna's breath came in short pants. "You're right. There was no use trying to think. What time is it?"

"We have more time. Are you going to let me come with you?" Better, at this juncture, to let her think she had a choice.

"If you stay hidden. I don't want to scare Kev. He's my chief man. By the by, what are you doing here?" she asked sharply as if her thoughts had finally coalesced.

Rutherford kissed her again, deeply, intending to steal her thoughts as he ran his hands over her body. He held her to him, reveled in her mouth, and fantasized about what it would be like to have her naked beneath him. To feel her soft skin rather than the rough muslin shirt and woolen jacket she wore. An urgency to possess her that he'd never felt for another woman shot through him. He had to have her. Even untutored, she was all he could want, but he'd need to stop soon. They must be ready for the meeting.

He slowly broke the kiss and watched her stare up at him, her desire clear.

"Come on," he said. "You need to get back into place. It wouldn't do for someone to happen along and see us like this. They might get the wrong idea."

"How could that happen? They wouldn't know who I am."

Rutherford smiled at her innocence. "They would recognize me, and you're dressed like a man, remember?"

"Oh." Her eyes grew wide.

He stood and helped her up, then kissed her again. "The next time I touch these"—he stroked her breasts again—"I don't want to do it through a band."

"Who says there will be a next time?" she asked haughtily. "This may have just been an aberration."

Ah. Miss Marsh of the London drawing rooms was trying to come back. "*This* was no aberration." He scowled.

Anna's eyes were wide and challenging. "No?"

"No," he growled as he reclaimed her lips.

Chapter 11

It took Anna several seconds to catch up with Rutherford as he re-possessed her mouth. Her tongue tangled with his, matching his fierceness with her own. A low growling emitted from him, and a strange shaft of pleasure shot down her body, causing a throbbing between her legs. Long moments passed after he'd stopped kissing and caressing her for Anna to get her senses back in order. Her breasts and lips were swollen and still yearned for him. She couldn't allow him to touch her again.

She shook herself and got back into position, peering over the cliff again. Kev arrived with the London gent. Scooting away from the edge, she scrambled to her feet.

Rutherford pulled her into his arms.

"They're here," she whispered. "I'll go down first. Stay back so they can't see you. Once you get to the bottom of the path, there is a small cave. You can hide there."

He nodded as she slipped away. Hunched over, she began her descent.

She pulled up her muffler, and stepped out from behind the lean-to on the rocky beach, staying far enough away so that the gentleman couldn't get a good look at her. "What we got here? Looks like a nob." Anna lowered her voice and spoke more in the vernacular.

"Ye got that right, sir," Kev said.

"Well, Mr. Nob, what ye want from us?" Anna asked. "It'd better be the truth, or I got nothin' to say to ye."

"I need to bring some people in," he replied.

Exactly what she'd thought. Anna narrowed her eyes. "Not the same story ye told before. What kind of people would they be?"

"Some French friends of mine."

"Frenchies?" Anna pretended to spit on the ground. "And why can't these *friends* use a packet?"

"That's not something I can discuss," he said. "Do we have a deal?"

"No," Anna replied.

"What do you mean no?" the man asked, offended. "I'm prepared to pay well for your services."

"Ye can't pay well enough to take care of me men and their families if we're caught."

"If you don't do as I ask," he said in an aristocratic drawl, "I'll make sure you are caught. You do know the penalty for treason?"

A chill crept up her neck. "Ye can try," Anna said in her best Harry imitation.

"I'll give you until tomorrow night to think about my offer." The man turned and sauntered back down the beach.

Anna pulled Kev to the side of the hut. "Follow him. I don't care where he goes. I need to know who he is. And Kev, don't let him see you. If anyone else is around, get them to help."

Rutherford remembered the cave, having hidden in it once while waiting for a ship to take him back into France. He had a good view of Anna and the two men, yet he could hear nothing they said.

He recognized Kev from the tavern. The other he guessed to be the London gentleman in question. Rutherford sat up and tried to get a better look. It was nothing she did, but he could tell Anna was agitated. Something was definitely wrong. He removed his pistol from the pocket of his greatcoat and watched until the other man left.

Kev shook his head. Anna said something. Kev took off after the gentleman, hanging back and hugging the side of the cliff.

"What did he want?" Rutherford asked as Anna slipped into the cave.

"He wants us to smuggle in his *French* friends. I knew this would happen. There has already been talk of getting Napoleon off Elba," she said a little shakily.

Rutherford's jaw dropped. "How do you know about that?"

"Rumors from the others across the way." She frowned. "He threatened to expose us and blame us for treason. S'bastian, I will not allow him to hurt my men. I'll have to . . ."

"What?"

She shook her head. "Nothing."

His heart contracted, then grew. He drew a ragged breath. She was not only the woman he loved and would make his wife, she was also the little girl who had called him Bastian before she could pronounce his name. The link to his whole life, and he had to get her out of this mess. "Come, we need to talk."

"Follow me." She turned and walked back to Thunderer. Rutherford started to throw her on to her horse, then realized she was riding astride. He cupped his hands to give her a boost, mounted his horse, and followed her to the cottage. She led him around back and showed him the stable.

Rutherford tied his horse to the iron ring in the wall. "Were you here yesterday evening?"

"Yes, why?" she asked suspiciously.

"I came by. I saw a little smoke from the chimney but nothing else."

She nodded. "I heard your horse."

"Anna, why didn't you tell me about this"—he waved his arm to encompass the cottage—"and the smugglers?"

"I promised Harry I'd not tell anyone." She grabbed Rutherford's hand and pulled. Once they were in the cottage with the door barred, Anna turned back to him. "Sebastian, what are you doing here?"

There was a mulish cast to her chin and mouth. One he knew well. If he didn't do something, and quickly, this was going to turn into a battle royal. He grabbed her waist, pulled her to him, and kissed her. His idea to make a plan burned to ashes as her lips set fire to his.

Rather than giving him a token resistance, she launched herself into the kiss. He groaned. Her hands clasped his face, and she tilted her head. Her tongue danced with his as if it had been waiting for this moment. He stroked her back and pulled her closer. She was on her tiptoes, trying to get closer.

"Oh, God, Anna," he mumbled into her mouth. "You'll be the death of me."

Anna chuckled.

"I thought you wanted to talk?"

Her voice was breathy. "No, you wanted to talk. I want answers."

His member hardened, and he held her tighter.

She sighed.

He began to caress a breast and found the band and glowered. "Take this thing off."

Anna responded as if cold water had been poured over her, and jumped back, eyes wide staring at him. Then her hand covered her forehead. "Oh, no, what am I doing?"

Strategic mistake. He'd gone too fast. He reached for her and caught the hands she waved at him to fend him off.

She jerked them away. "No." Tears misted her eyes. "This isn't right."

"What's not right about it? Anna, I want to marry you."

She clenched her teeth. "No, you do not. You want to marry a woman who is safe, and comfortable, and easy to manage. That's not me."

"Where did you get a daft idea like that?"

She threw her hands up and shouted, "I heard you tell Marcus!"

For the first time in his life, he wasn't sure what to say. His blood seemed to rush to his feet. "You heard . . ."

"Yes. Which is why we can't do any of this. I'll accept your assistance with the London gent, but after that"—her voice seemed to fail for a moment—"after that, you should stop coming to Marsh Hill."

He rubbed his face. This couldn't be happening. "Anna, I love you."

She shook her head slowly. "No, you love who you want me to be, not who I am."

What a mull. How was he to convince her he'd been wrong? "That's not true. Not any more. I want you, as you are."

"You're thirty-one years old." She put her hands on her hips. "You should know what you want in a wife. Even if you think you love me now, how do I know you won't change your mind, again?" She gave a small sob. "Sebastian, marriage is for life."

Not knowing what else to do, he drew her into his arms. His throat hurt so badly, he didn't know if he could speak. Yet, he had to say something. "Yes, marriage is forever. Give me a chance to show you that I won't change my mind."

She shook her head. "I don't know if I can." She lifted her tear-stained face to him. "It hurts too much."

His heart fell to his feet. He couldn't imagine his life without her. "Please don't give up on me that easily."

She stepped back, piercing him with a stern gaze. "How do you plan to convince me?"

If he didn't come up with something soon, the premonition he'd had in London of her walking out of his life would become reality. "We'll discuss the settlement agreements. I'll make sure you have a large enough allowance to do what you wish."

Anna crossed her arms across her chest and turned her back on him.

He raked a hand through his hair as his mind raced, searching for something. . . . "You may start helping me run the Priory."

She turned to him, her eyes wary. "What does that mean, exactly?"

"We'll go on as if we were married. Start making decisions about the estate together."

After the longest few moments of his life, she finally nodded. "Very well, but there will be no betrothal announcement. I've not accepted you yet."

"I understand." He put his arms around her again and rubbed her back until she leaned against him. "Do you love me, at least a little bit?"

Letting out a sigh, she replied, "If I didn't love you, I wouldn't even consider your suggestion."

Relief coursed through him. Perhaps getting her to accept him would be easier than he thought. He smiled and kissed the top of her head. "Then everything will be all right."

"Sebastian," she said sternly, "love does not conquer all."

"But, there is always luck with love."

He had a feeling changing her mind was not going to be easy. Though he held her, she didn't put her arms around him. After a while, he said, "Let's talk about spies and smugglers."

She nodded. "I'll tell you while I change."

Rutherford swallowed. *"Change?"*

She frowned at him as if he were an idiot. "I can't go home dressed like this." Making a twirling motion with her hand, she said, "You'll have to turn around."

He stifled a groan, but did as she asked.

"Why have you been following me?" Anna asked. "That is, I hope it's been you the past couple of nights."

"You remember I told you I worked as an intelligencer?"

"Yes."

Articles of clothing hit the floor. He started to look over his shoulder and stopped. "I was called back in to discover if any of the smuggling gangs are involved with or have been approached about bringing in spies. It took me over a week to find anyone who would agree to give me any information at all."

"One week?" Anna said, alarmed. "That's not long at all. I thought I was better protected than that."

One week was much too long as far as he was concerned. "The Priory owns the inn. Consequently, I threatened the innkeeper."

"What did he tell you?"

She shook out something that sounded like a skirt. He sucked in a breath. "Nothing. I started receiving notes telling me where to stand to watch the deliveries. I've been waiting for a meeting with you, apparently." He paused. "Which has been deuced difficult."

She heaved a sigh of relief. "That is rather the point. In a way, this solves my problem of the threat against my men. Though, I still feel the need to put an end to our London gentleman. He must have a government appointment of some sort to be able to make the threats he did."

"I suspect he works for either the Foreign or Home Office. Anna, this could get dangerous."

"You may turn around now," she said. "I understand the risk. What do you suggest I do when he comes back tomorrow?"

When he turned, his gaze dropped to her unbound breasts. "How would your men respond to an invitation to help the Home Office catch some spies?"

"I think they'd see it as a lark of the first order. Tomorrow night, I'll let him think he's frightened me and make the arrangements with him." She grinned wickedly. "Then I'll hold a meeting with the gang and explain that the Home Office needs our help. They'll want to be paid."

Jamison wasn't going to like that. "They won't do it for love of country?"

"They're not wealthy," she said, vexed. "Better if I can arrange for them to be remunerated by both the spy and the Home Office."

Suddenly, it struck him she knew exactly what she was doing. Nevertheless, he had to talk her out of remaining on this mission. He'd find someone else to take over the smugglers.

Rutherford chuckled. "You drive a hard bargain, Miss Marsh."

Anna walked toward him, her skirts swaying. "Did you think I wouldn't know how?"

He wrapped his arms around her. "No, I'm learning never to underestimate you."

Her jacket was still undone, and she was wearing stays. He prayed she wouldn't object to his touching her again. Anna moaned in delight when he moved his hands to cup her breasts. It was criminal for her to bind them. He tightened his hold and kissed her deeply. "That's so much better."

Reluctantly, he buttoned her jacket. "We'd better go. I'll escort you home."

"Oh, there's no need really," Anna replied airily.

"Yes, there is." He kissed her again. "One never knows when Percy will take to riding around the countryside in the middle of the night. He's just the sort of loose fish who would do such a thing."

Anna went off into a peel of laughter. "Very well, my lord, you may escort me home."

She waited while he banked the fire, then they walked around to the stable, and he switched her saddle. Rutherford kissed her lightly before he helped her on to Thunderer.

Anna smiled. "You know, I really can mount myself."

He gave her a strange look and grunted.

She probably shouldn't have allowed him to kiss and caress her, yet she couldn't seem to tell him to stop. Being in his arms was the most wonderful feeling she'd ever had. If it turned out it was only for a little while, at least she'd have her memories.

The moon had set, and they rode through the dark with the ease of long familiarity with the land. Over her objections, he helped her dismount in the stable yard. Humphrey led Thunderer away.

"You should go now," she said. "You need to get to your bed as well."

Rutherford took her arm. "First, I'll walk you to the side door."

Anna sighed. She should have known his protectiveness would increase with his commitment to her. "It's only a few feet away."

When they reached the door she turned to face him and put her hand against his lean cheek. "Good night."

Rutherford swooped to kiss her upturned face as his hands roamed her body as if he were claiming it. Anna shivered and trembled as small fires lit beneath her skin. She slid her arms around his neck, and she met him, tangling her tongue with his. Wanting to possess him as well. "Sebastian," she mumbled against his mouth.

"Have I ever told you I only like my name when you say it?"

She giggled softly. "I know you never scowl at me when I say it."

He broke the kiss and opened the door behind her. "It's late. Go to bed. I'll see you in the morning."

Anna took his face in her hands. "Good night." She kissed him one last time and walked in the door. They stared at each other before she shut it.

As she made her way up the stairs, peeking out each window on the way to the first floor corridor, she saw him watch her progress. Her body hummed with delight. She touched her still swollen lips. Her breasts were heavy and tight against the jacket of her habit.

Lizzy was dozing in a chair when she entered her room. "Lizzy, go on to bed."

Her maid opened her eyes and jumped. "Oh, miss, what time is it?"

"Later than usual. I'll be fine. Go to bed. We've had some developments. You won't need to wait up for me until we work things out."

Lizzy gazed at Anna. "Are you sure?"

"Of course. It will only be for a couple of weeks."

"All right, let me hang your habit up before it gets crushed."

"If you like." Anna removed the garment and handed it to her maid. Once Lizzy left, Anna gazed at her reflection in the mirror of her dressing table and frowned, trying not to allow herself to be hopeful. When Sebastian had told her he loved her, there was a rightness to it she hadn't expected. His kisses and caresses had thrilled her. Flames still simmered beneath her skin. She wondered how much more he'd show her while she made up her mind whether to marry him.

She unpinned her braids and wondered when Sebastian wanted to start sharing his work with her, and if he truly could do it.

November 11th, 1814, Marsh Hill, Kent

Rutherford woke determined to bring Anna around to his way of thinking as soon as possible. He'd start today by inviting her to luncheon at the Priory, after which they could work on the accounts. He sent a message to Anna, then spent most of the morning getting his account books in an order easy for her to follow, before driving to fetch her.

"Good afternoon." He took her hand and brought it to his lips.

She smiled. "How are you doing today?"

"Better than yesterday." He returned her smile. "I've brought my curricle. Would you like to drive?"

Her eyes, which had been a little guarded, started to sparkle. "Your grays?"

He bowed. "Naturally. What else?"

"I'd love to."

Sitting back, he watched her expertly handle his pair, who weren't the easiest beasts to manage. "You haven't lost any of your skill."

She slipped a quick glance his way before returning her attention to the horses. "Thank you. I had good teachers."

Both he and Harry had taught her to drive. Rather than keeping an eye on his team, he perused Anna. She wore a bronze velvet carriage gown, trimmed with dark brown and cream, under a spencer in the same colors. Her hat, made of all three colors to match, had a large feather that curled down and caressed her chin. She'd never looked lovelier. It was as if she was growing more beautiful each day.

His body responded to her each time their legs touched. He wanted more than anything to take her in his arms, but not while she was tooling his carriage. The horses might object. "Turn south at the next crossroad."

Anna nodded and expertly feathered the curve.

"Well done."

She grinned. "I so wish Mama would allow me to have my own carriage."

"You'll have one soon enough."

She glanced sharply at him, then back to the horses. "What do you mean?"

He stared straight ahead, and said as casually as he could, "I can't have Lady Rutherford being driven all over London, when her dearest friend has a high perched phaeton. Can I?"

"My lord, are you trying to bribe me?"

"Would it work?" He raised a hopeful brow.

"No."

"I didn't think so. No, not a bribe then, a statement of fact. Any whip as good as you ought to have your own carriage."

Anna blushed. "Are we going anywhere in particular?"

"Is there somewhere you'd like to go?"

Anna tilted her head. "When do we have to be at the Priory?"

Rutherford sat up. "I'd forgotten." He took out his watch. "Now."

"Left at the next lane?"

"Yes, then straight for a few miles. You'll see the turn."

"Do you know," she said, "this is one of the few times I've not ridden to the Priory?"

"Yes, I suppose it is. We—you, Harry, and I—were always on horseback."

"Sebastian, if we marry, do you think your mother will be happy?"

If? There was no if *about it. When.* "I've already told her I will choose my own wife."

"Mama, who is your goddaughter?" Cece asked.

"She is the daughter of a very old friend of mine who married a younger son of the Duke of Queensbury." Julia Rutherford glanced up from her embroidery frame. "She must be, oh, around four or five and twenty, which is not a great age where she lives. I've been assured that, despite being raised in such a remote place, she has all the accomplishments and will know how to go on."

Julia glanced at her three daughters, who were assembled in the morning room before luncheon and bursting with curiosity over their houseguest and, Julia hoped, her future daughter-in-law. "The poor dear was betrothed to a man who died, but I'm told she is over her grief and willing to make a good match."

"Where does she live?" asked Eloisa.

"In the West Indies."

"Mama?"

"Yes, Cece."

"Will we like her?"

"I trust we will all like her. If she is anything like her mother, she will be a very modest and biddable lady. I expect to receive a message any day now that she's arrived in London. After which, I intend to post up to Town to fetch her." She looked meaningfully at them. "It is my wish that Rutherford be taken with her."

"Yes, Mama," her daughters said in unison.

Finally she could arrange a match for her recalcitrant son that was worthy of him.

"Mama?" Cece asked again. "What is her name?"

Julia set aside her tambour. "Her name is Miss Emeline Spencer-Jones."

Chapter 12

Anna drove with a flourish into the drive leading to the Priory. "Sebastian, thank you. This has been so much fun. Whether we marry or not, I do want a carriage of my own."

"I knew you would."

She smiled and chuckled lightly.

His hand slid around her shoulders and down her back.

She fought to stay focused on the horses. His touch was warm and sent tremors through her. "More bribes?"

"More promises."

"I see." She'd reached the stable yard, bringing the curricle to a halt.

Rutherford jumped down and came around to help her. He held out his hand. Anna placed her much smaller one in his. His long, strong fingers clasped hers tightly and seemed to absorb the tremors streaking up her arm.

"Let's go through the side door," Rutherford said. "I'll show you my study, and afterward we'll find everyone else."

The room, situated at the back of the house, was large and airy. French windows, flanked by long windows, led to the terrace. The study had two fireplaces, one at each end. His desk was placed close to one of them.

A seating area filled one part of the space, and bookshelves lined the walls. "I love it."

He stood behind her with his hands on her shoulders. "It's my favorite room."

Anna turned in a circle admiring the space. "I can see why. What a comfortable place to work."

"I thought we could buy a partner's desk and toil together."

She bit her lip. He was going too fast. "Please, don't try to rush my decision. Let's wait for a little while."

"I want to make you happy. I know you and Phoebe have discussed any number of improvements that should be made on major estates. You shall have a free hand."

His gaze was earnest. Her fear was that it wouldn't last. "Will I? Are you sure you're able to allow it?"

"I'm not going to tell you we won't have disagreements. You and I are both strong-willed. But I know you. You will always do what's best for our family and the Priory."

Tears misted her eyes, and she blinked them back. "Sebastian."

She reached up and brought his head down. She touched his lips gently.

He chuckled wryly. "It's taken me a while. Please marry me."

She pulled back a little. "Why ask again so soon?"

His gaze heated. "To give me a reason to beat up Percy."

She burst into laughter. "Sebastian!"

"What? Not a good answer?" He shrugged. "Ah well, it was worth a try."

"I'll give you that." He'd probably propose many more times until she said yes. "Let's find your family. You know, as much time as I've spent with you, I don't know them well at all."

Rutherford glanced down. "You're right. The girls are all young, and our mothers are not particularly close."

"Is anyone close to my mother now? She's been so difficult since Harry died. She's so rarely at the Hill anymore. I don't know how Papa puts up with it."

He held her closer. "He loves her."

She shook her head. "Yes. Even though it was arranged, they did fall in love."

He drew her in his arms again. "Is that the reason you said love can't overcome all?"

When Anna glanced at him, he looked different somehow. "You're very wise all of a sudden."

He gazed down at her. "Perhaps I finally understand what's important."

Anna put her arms around his neck. "Sebastian. We must both be sure this is what we want."

He kissed the tip of her nose and asked, "What time do you want to meet with our spy this evening?"

Anna hoped the change of subject meant he agreed with her continuing to lead the gang. If not, they would have even more problems. "The meeting is at midnight," she replied. "We should be there at least an hour ahead of time. I don't trust him."

He kissed her ear and whispered, "For good reason. If he'll betray his country, he'll betray anything. Did Harry teach you how to shoot?"

She met his gaze. "Yes, do you want me to bring my pistol?"

Rutherford searched her face. "I want you to start carrying it everywhere."

Startled, she asked, "Do you really think it necessary?"

"I'm taking no chances with you." He crushed her in his embrace. His lips took hers. She gave, and he took more. His tongue explored her mouth as if to learn every crevice. Anna met him and challenged him, staking her own claim.

When they pulled apart, Rutherford caressed her cheek and jaw. His hand roved down her back. Anna stroked his in return. When he cupped her bottom and pulled her close, she did the same, copying everything he did. Anna matched him move for move until wetness pooled between her legs, and his muscles bunched and hardened under her palm. She'd never realized how strong he was.

When he finally stopped and lifted his head, his heart was pounding and his leather breeches were uncomfortably tight. Rutherford placed a hand on her swollen breast. Anna made a mewing noise and pressed into him.

His voice sounded harsh, even to him. "Anna, my love, we need to stop this. Now."

Her tone was breathy and warm against his ear. "Where are you leading me?"

"To me, my love. Only to me."

A knock sounded on the door. "My lord, are you in there?"

They quickly moved apart. "Yes," he called.

"Luncheon is served, my lord."

"Please have a place set next to me for Miss Marsh. She will be joining us."

"Yes, my lord." The voice sounded baffled.

"Well, my dear, shall we go beard my family?"

"I suppose we'd better."

He took her hand, and they walked into the dining room. Waving the footman off, Rutherford pulled out the chair on his left for Anna. His mother sat at the foot of the shortened table. His three sisters were spaced between them.

"Mama, you remember Miss Marsh?"

His mother was clearly not happy to see Anna and hesitated before rising to greet her. Perhaps he should have waited until she'd agreed to marry him before bringing her here.

"How are you, my dear?" Mama asked in a strained voice.

Rutherford fixed his stare on his mother. What the devil was wrong with her?

She smiled politely. "Lovely you could join us."

Anna curtseyed. "Thank you, my lady. I am delighted."

He introduced his sisters, who stared at her with open mouths. "Make your curtseys," he said gruffly. "Where are your manners? Do you want her to think you have none?"

Cece looked at him, wide-eyed. "But, Ruhy, why is she here?"

His mother put a finger over her mouth and tried to get his youngest sister's attention. Long used to his mother's machinations, he asked Cece, "Why do you ask?"

With perfect candor, his sister said, "Well, you never invite ladies here, and Mama said she was trying to arrange a match with Miss-Miss—" She turned to her mother, whose face was now bright red. "What was her name?"

"Miss Spencer-Jones," Althea hissed.

Cece smiled. "Thank you. That's right. Miss Spencer-Jones."

Rutherford stared grimly at his mother.

She had a wan smile on her face.

"Thank you, Cece," he said. "You'd be well advised to keep that type of information to yourself. You will be seeing a great deal more of Miss Marsh than you've been used to in the past." He glanced at his mother. "I expect her to be welcomed."

Anna smiled at his sisters and greeted them warmly.

"Mama, I'd like a word with you after luncheon."

Anna pinched him and whispered, "Don't. We have not even agreed to marry yet."

She might not have agreed yet, but she would. He whispered back, "My love, she has meddled enough. Her goddaughter will be here for some time. She cannot be allowed to wreak havoc with us."

Anna firmed her chin. "You must do what you think best."

Rutherford's smile was only for her. "Please trust me to do as I see fit."

"Of course, she is your mother."

"True, but I've seen how well you handle your own. Go on here as you would."

Anna gave him a small shake of her head as he held out a chair for her. Under the incredulous gazes of his sisters, and the rather sickly look on his mother's face, he took her hand and kissed it.

"We're in for it now," she whispered.

"As usual, you're probably right."

Eloisa opened her mouth, and Rutherford silenced her. "I will answer one question from each of you."

Griffin leaned over. "My lord, if you'd like us to serve the family and withdraw?"

"No, not at all," Rutherford said. "This will all be public soon enough." He indicated to the impatient Eloisa that she could speak.

"Ruhy, what's going on?"

"I am doing my best to convince Miss Marsh to marry me, but she has not accepted me yet."

Eloisa drew her brows together. She had something of Sebastian's look when he was younger, and Anna knew that the interrogation was coming.

"Why?"

Rutherford raised a brow. "Why? Because I love her, and I wish to marry her."

"Has she said yes yet?" Cece asked.

"No. I'm working on that now."

The rest of the meal continued in near silence. When they were finished, he sent the children back to their studies. "Mother, later we need to speak."

"Of course," she said, and left the room.

He'd be damned if he'd allow his mother to berate Anna or stop him from marrying her.

* * *

Anna watched Lady Rutherford go. Did she not realize how angry she was making Rutherford and what would happen if they wed? It would be horrible to live in a house where his mother disliked her so. As Anna and Sebastian entered the study, his anger was palpable.

"Sebastian." Anna put her hand on his arm. "It will be fine."

"What in blazes is she thinking of, trying to match me with a woman I don't even know? She's out of control."

"Ever since your father died, she's wanted you to wed. It's as if she's in a race with time."

"That, and she wants me to marry up, but you are the only woman I wish to spend the rest of my life with." He pulled her closer. "Anna, tell me you won't allow my mother to sway your decision."

Anna searched his strong, lean face. Sebastian's jaw had firmed, and his gaze bore into her. "No, I won't allow Lady Rutherford to influence me. I may not be a duke's granddaughter, but I daresay the Marshes have been around at least as long as the Rutherfords."

Sebastian smiled. "Indeed."

She stood on tiptoe and gently touched her lips to his. "Now, for the ledgers."

He opened the first one and started to explain what it was. She stopped him. "These are the tenant accounts."

"How did you know?" he said, staring at her.

"I've been keeping the books at the Hill for several years now." She sat and reviewed the columns. "Have you visited Holkham Hall in Norfolk?"

He drew his brows together. "Yes, though I've not instituted many of the changes yet."

"You should. It is amazing the difference it can make." He nodded, and she went back to the figures. "I don't understand why your yields aren't greater."

"What do you mean?"

"These fields"—she pointed at one of the family names—"are right next to ours and about the same size. I know your tenant, Mr. Milkin. He works just as hard as his neighbor on the Hill's land. Yet he produces twenty percent less, probably because part of the field is prone to flood. If you'd build a better irrigation system, it would help not only him, but the tenant on the other side as well."

Sebastian took out a rolled up map and placed it on top of the ledgers. "Show me where the problem is."

She traced her finger down one side of the plan to where a stream frequently overflowed its banks.

"You should have the same difficulty."

"We did, until we built up a berm to contain the water."

"I had no idea you were so involved in the farming."

That didn't surprise her. What did he really know about her now? "After Harry died, Papa took no interest in anything, and Mama was gone. It was up to me." She frowned and glanced at Sebastian. "What did you think I'd been doing?"

"From the way you behave in Town, I had assumed you were interested in fashion, the latest novels, and parties."

He was partially right. "I do like those things, but I have broader interests as well. Just as I hope your concerns extend past gaming, entertainments, and your clubs."

He shook his head. "Perhaps I don't know you as well as I thought I did."

Anna heaved a sigh. "That is the reason I've been so concerned you truly don't want me as a wife after all. Two years can make a great deal of difference. I've been trying to show you."

The sun had shifted so it was now shining in directly through the windows. For a moment, his chiseled face looked more careworn, then he smiled. Anna's heart wanted to melt. Sometimes she wished she weren't so different from other young women. Yet, there was too much at stake for her to let her love for him take the lead.

He placed his hands on her shoulders. "If I'd known you were so talented, I would never have said what I did to Marcus."

Anna shook her head. "Why?"

"Because then I would have wanted a wife who could help with all the estate management." He caught her gaze and held it. "Anna, I just want *you*. In all your guises."

She searched his face. If only she could be positive he knew what he wanted. "Sebastian, are you sure?"

He drew her up and kissed her. "I've never been more certain of anything in my life."

"Rutherford, you wished to speak with me," Lady Rutherford said from the corridor.

He groaned. "I'll put her off. What I have to say to her won't take long any way."

Striding to the door he opened it. His mother looked in, and her smile faded when she saw Anna.

"Mother, how can I help you?"

Lady Rutherford's lips pursed tightly. "What are you doing alone with Miss Marsh?"

"We are going over the accounts. If we are going to marry, she has a right to see how things are run."

Lady Rutherford's complexion seemed to pale. "Indeed. Being in a closed room alone with Miss Marsh is not a good example to set for your sisters."

Sebastian's countenance darkened. "Very well. We shall take a ride." He reached out his hand for Anna. "Miss Marsh?"

"Yes, of course." The proprieties could have been met by keeping the door open. Anna wondered if there was something else going on. Other than Lady Rutherford's dislike of her.

Chapter 13

Anna and Sebastian returned to the stables, where he ordered the carriage to be made ready.

"Do you want to drive?" he asked tersely, handing her into the carriage.

She'd rarely seen him so angry. Lady Rutherford didn't have any sense at all when dealing with her son. "Not if you need to."

He climbed in and took the ribbons. Rutherford whipped the horses up and headed for the gate. He was silent for several minutes as he rounded the corner on to the main road.

Anna watched him in his frustration. "Where are we going?"

"To the cottage, if you have no objection."

"No, none at all." Perhaps they could finish their conversation. She held on to the side of the curricle and watched as the woods and brown meadows swiftly passed by.

He pulled the curricle behind the building. They watered the horses and fed them oats. "Come." He took her hand.

When Anna entered the cottage, her breath came out in a puff.

"I'll build the fire up." She glanced down at the small stack of wood. "We'll need more kindling. There is a pile on the side of the house."

He nodded and left. Opening the shutters, she was thankful the windows were glass. At least the sun would make the cottage feel warmer.

A search through the cupboards unearthed tea, mugs, and sugar. Rutherford returned with an armful of kindling. Once the fire roared and popped to life, she filled the old iron kettle, placed it on the fireplace crane, and swung it over the flames.

"Well, now we should be warm soon." Anna turned to find herself in Sebastian's arms and laughed. "I don't quite think this was what your mother had in mind when she wouldn't allow us in your study alone."

He grinned wickedly. "If she knew about this place, she'd have played gooseberry herself."

Anna wondered how her skin could thrill to his touch through all her clothes. His body was so large and warm. She could barely reach all the way around him as she burrowed her hands under his coat. Even if it all came to naught, there was no reason she couldn't take some joy in being with him.

"I wish it weren't so blasted cold in here," he said.

His palm traveled lower over her, leaving a trail of tingling warmth, and she gasped in response. "I'm not cold."

Rutherford chuckled.

He unbuttoned her pelisse and loosened the scarf. Chilly air hit the back of her neck. "Oh, that is freezing."

Removing her hat, he placed it carefully on the table before feathering light kisses on her neck. Anna's skin flushed, and she was warm again. The heat moved to her jaw, his lips firm but soft. The next thing she knew, the back of her knees hit the bed, and she toppled on to it with Sebastian half covering her. His arm circled her and shifted them farther on to the mattress.

"Anna, I love you."

Sebastian unbuttoned the front of her gown and unlaced her stays. His hands cupped her breasts, and he buried his head in them. When he took one nipple into his mouth, she arched and cried with pleasure.

It might be wrong, but she wanted this. Streaks of intense pleasure coursed through her as she responded to his caresses. She could barely think, but she had so many questions. How could he make her feel like this? How did he know what to do? And if this was what a man and a woman did together, how could any woman not like it? Her body ached and wanted more. She twisted and moaned and finally got her hands under his jacket.

Drat. She'd forgotten to take off her gloves. "Sebastian, I want to touch you."

"Umm, do as you wish." He moved to the other breast.

"I still have my gloves on." Her heart pulsed, and fire flooded her body. She could barely get the words out. "I can't take them off while you're doing that."

"Let me see." He lifted up and quickly removed her gloves. "Now, where was I?"

Anna tugged at his shirt, and it wouldn't budge. She settled for rubbing her palms over the soft linen of his shirt. His skin burned beneath her hands. When she ran her fingers over his muscles, they tightened.

He groaned and attended to her breasts with renewed vigor, before laying claim to her mouth. She rubbed greedily up and down his back, reveling in the feeling. "Sebastian, is it always like this? So wonderful?"

"Only with you. If I do something you don't like, tell me and I'll stop."

Want him to stop? Her heart raced, and the breath to answer wouldn't come. Cold air drifted up her legs. His hand touched the back of her knee before moving to her inner thigh. She shuddered. Soon he touched her curls and rubbed the place that ached so much. He seemed to know just what to do.

She arched up and tried to put her legs around him. "Oh, Sebastian, that feels so good."

He chuckled. "Wait just a moment, and it will feel even better."

One finger slid into her, and little shudders ran through her. He removed it and filled her again. His mouth came down hard on hers. His tongue caressed and sucked hers, causing an inferno. She couldn't think or breathe. If he kept this up, she was going to explode. It was as if it was a warm summer day and she was in an eddy being carried out to sea. She trembled as warm waves of bliss washed over her. Her heart filled with love for him. If only all this could last.

Rutherford held her gently to him, nuzzling her hair and placing soft kisses on her head.

"Did you like what I did?"

For a moment, all she could do was smile, but something was wrong. "Sebastian, what about you? Is there something I should do?"

"No, I'm fine." His inner beast roared at him to take her up on her offer. He shoved it away. Not yet. He didn't mind using seduction to help her choose him, but he'd not go further than this until she said yes.

"But I *want* to do something."

Of course she did; she wouldn't be Anna if she didn't. "No, sweetheart. There is nothing you can do for me unless you agree to marry me."

She frowned, and he was reminded how stubborn she could be.

"That is not fair." She narrowed her eyes. "Are you saying that just so I'll accept you?"

Is that what she really thought, or was she just angry? "No. Unless you wish to be compromised into wedding me, I cannot allow this to go any further."

Anna stared up at the ceiling, gnawing on her bottom lip. "I suppose in this case, you know best."

He wouldn't hear that much when they married. "Thank you."

"What time is it?"

"Time to take you home."

She turned to him, her voice deeper, sultry. "Not yet. Kiss me again."

The desire in her eyes nearly undid him. He shouldn't have introduced her to this much passion until they were betrothed. He knew her too well. There'd be no going back.

He kissed her slowly, exploring her mouth and savoring her sweet taste. "Now, Miss Marsh, we need to leave. Or my mother won't be the only one wanting to chaperone us."

After getting up, Rutherford held out his hand to help her. He retied her stays and buttoned her dress, while Anna tidied her hair.

"Where are my gloves?" She glanced around. "Oh, here's one."

He handed her the other and helped her into her pelisse and cloak before running an expert eye over her. "You'll pass inspection as long as no one looks too closely."

Anna's eyes widened, and she looked down at herself. "What do you mean?"

He ran the pad of his thumb lightly over her lips. "They're swollen, and you have the look of a well-pleasured lady."

She blushed, something she didn't do nearly often enough.

Walking over to the fireplace, he banked the fire. "That will keep it at least a little warm in here for tonight."

Anna closed the shutters, and they made their way to the carriage. He kissed her one last time before helping her up to the seat. "You drive."

She took the ribbons, expertly threading them around her fingers. "Thank you, my lord."

It would be all he could do to keep her from racing forward physically. Her passion for life was mirrored in her passion for him. It boded well for their future, but it was going to kill him until she agreed to marry.

He sat back against the seat, and a movement near the woods caught his eye. He turned as a man on horseback rode away. Who the hell was that? From now on, Rutherford needed to ensure that Anna never came here alone.

They dined at Marsh Hill, and he returned home after tea was served.

His mother was waiting for him when he entered the Priory.

"Rutherford, I think we should probably have a talk."

"I agree. Griffin, please light the candles in my study." He took his mother's elbow and followed his butler.

Lady Rutherford took a seat in front of his desk. Nervously, she clasped and unclasped her hands. Once Griffin left, Rutherford took his place at the desk, allowing the silence to stretch.

Finally, she said, "I–I find I was at fault for telling the girls about my hopes for you and my goddaughter. Though, if you would have taken me a little into your confidence, none of what occurred at luncheon today would have happened."

He'd not allow her to talk him round. If she thought she'd drive a wedge between Anna and him, she was very much mistaken. "Madam, you are well aware of my feelings when it comes to your match-making attempts."

He poured a glass of brandy and took a swallow. "I've told you on more than one occasion to leave the matter of my wife to me. I have known since before Miss Marsh's come-out that I intended to marry her. However, she was young and needed to mature. I've no objection to your goddaughter's visiting or to your sponsoring her for the Season, so long as you understand you must look to another gentleman to wed her."

Setting his glass down, he fixed her with a hard stare. "As soon as Anna has accepted me, I shall expect you to do your duty and begin handing over the household reins to her."

"Yes, of course," his mother said stiffly, gazing at her hands.

He softened his voice a little. "Mama, I don't want to send you off to the dower-house, but if I must, I will. Get rid of your notions of arranging an advantageous marriage for me and come to know your future daughter-in-law. I think you'll like her."

Mama inclined her head and left the room.

He sat back in his chair, toying with his pen. Had Anna actually changed that much or was it him? She had a great deal more countenance now, though that was probably to have been expected. Anna had always been lively and not only cared about others, particularly those less fortunate, but stood up for her beliefs. It was one of the many things he loved about her. In fact, it shouldn't have surprised him that she had Radical leanings. Now that he thought about it, it was too bad a woman as intelligent as Anna couldn't vote. Frustrated, he pitched the pen across the desk. Perhaps the better question was when had he become such a damned prig?

Rutherford reached across to retrieve his pen. A letter he'd not noticed there earlier was propped up against the standish. He picked it up and looked at the seal. Jamison. It was dated three days ago and informed him about the meeting between a suspected traitor and a French spy. Rutherford took out a piece of foolscap and penned a missive in return.

The 11th of November, 1814
Dear Lord Jamison,
I am in receipt of your letter concerning our friends. I have made the contacts you wished me to make and have received an offer of help. There is a little matter of remuneration for their services. Please tell me what I may offer. Initial negotiations with our friends will be held this evening. I will immediately inform you of the arrival date of any goods.
Yr. Obedient Servant,
R.

Rutherford folded and sealed the missive, then rang for Griffin.

"Yes, my lord?"

"See that this letter goes out by express post. If I receive any more correspondence from Lord Jamison, I wish to be notified immediately, no matter where I am."

Griffin bowed and took the letter. "Yes, my lord. Will there be anything else?"

"Yes, her ladyship is expecting a visitor. Keep me informed as to when the lady is arriving."

"Yes, my lord, and may I say that the household is happy with your choice of Miss Marsh? We look forward to being able to felicitate you."

Rutherford smiled wryly. "Whenever she accepts me."

Griffin bowed again. "Miss Marsh has the reputation of being a bit strong-willed and a determined young lady. The dependents of the Hill think the better of her for it."

"Made changes there, has she?"

"Yes, my lord."

"Very well, Griffin. Tell the staff I'll look forward to their good wishes."

Griffin bowed and left Rutherford to his musings. No, the essential parts of Anna hadn't changed. He'd become a dry stick.

He thought back to this afternoon and groaned. Her breasts were fabulous; he could have feasted on them all night. Her legs were strong from riding and her skin like softest silk. Her lush red lips drove him to madness. Suddenly sitting became uncomfortable. *Damn.* This was getting him nowhere. All he could do was prove to Anna that he really wasn't a dead bore.

He frowned as he remembered the horseman. Rutherford glanced at the clock. It was time to change to meet Anna and their spy. Shortly before eleven o'clock, he rode quietly into the stable yard at Marsh Hill. Anna sat on Thunderer, talking with Humphrey, who nodded when he saw Rutherford.

"Good evening, my lord."

"Good evening to you, Humphrey."

Anna's horse sidled, eager to be off. He understood her need to serve her country and Harry's memory, but her involvement in the smuggling gang had to stop. It was not a part she could play as Lady Rutherford.

He was the magistrate after all.

* * *

Anna walked into the cottage, glad it was warmer than usual. Going to the cupboard, she unlocked it and removed her male clothing.

Rutherford strode in and a chill hit the back of her neck. "Close the door. You're letting the cold air in."

Once the door clicked shut, she removed her skirt, boots, and stays. When she started to bind her breasts, he stopped her.

His voice was low and seductive. "Not yet."

Reaching around her, he brought his palms up under her bosoms, holding them, kneading softly.

Anna leaned back against his chest. "They're too large."

"Never." His breath caressed her ear. "They're perfect. They fill my hands beautifully."

Anna looked down as he brushed his thumbs against her nipples. The fire in her leapt even hotter than before. His hands were so dark against her skin. Each covered over half of her bosom. She didn't recognize the sultry voice as her own. "They do seem to fit well."

"Someday, I'll hold you like this, then bend you over and take you."

Anna's breath quickened. Oh, this talk was so wrong. "Will I like it?

One hand skated down her stomach and covered her damp curls. His fingers pressed in over the thin muslin of her chemise. She leaned back farther and opened her legs. She loved how he touched her. She choked down the pain that started in her throat. She'd not think of this ending. Not unless she had to.

His low chuckle tickled her ear. "Do you like this?"

She licked her lips and swallowed. Before this afternoon, she would never have believed anything could feel so good. "Yes, oh, yes."

"Then you'll like the other."

She tried to press on his fingers and wanted more. "When will you take me?"

His lips and tongue ran lightly over her jaw and down the side of her neck. One strong arm wrapped around her, holding her breasts as his hand continued to stroke between her legs.

She wanted to swoon with pleasure, but then she'd miss what Sebastian was doing. New aches and desires only he could relieve coursed through her, and the throbbing between her legs increased. Why didn't he put her out of her misery? Her hips moved of their own accord, telling him what she wanted.

"I'll take you when you say you'll be mine. Not before."

She could have wept with frustration. "That's blackmail!"

He sat down on the bed, taking her with him. His legs stretched out, and he propped his upper body on the pillows. She lolled back, enjoying the feelings as his fingers slid into her, thrusting.

"Watch, my love."

Anna lifted her heavy head to do what he asked. Her legs were splayed open over his, and his hand pumped between them. Sebastian kissed her again, and she exploded, contracting around his still thrusting fingers until she lay limp on him.

The room was warm enough, and he was like a hot chair beneath her. He held her close, keeping her warm. If only they didn't have to go back out. After several minutes, she tried to get up, but had no purchase.

He lifted her and put her on her feet. To think she'd lived for so long without knowing about what joy a man could give a woman. There must be something she could do for him even if she couldn't marry him. She'd have to find a way to discover what it was.

Sebastian and Anna made their way down to the beach, keeping out of sight until she saw Kev.

"Mr. Arnold, what's he doin' here?"

"Kev, we need to talk," Anna said. "The Home Office knows about the spies. They've agreed to pay us to help catch them. Lord Rutherford is their representative."

Kev let out a low whistle. "That so? Well, I'll be. Helpin' the Home Office."

Rutherford couldn't stop his lips from twitching. "Umm, yes, Mr. Arnold will negotiate the sum to be paid to you."

Anna nodded in confirmation and added, "We will also demand a large payment from the French."

Kev grinned. "That's a good deal."

"Call a meeting for two nights from now." Anna frowned at him. "Don't look happy tonight. I want the nob to think we're not pleased about bringing in his Frenchies."

Kev wiped the smile from his face and did a credible job of glowering.

The moment the signal came that the traitor was approaching, Rutherford hid on one side of the shed and listened while Anna bargained with the gentleman. Strong-willed indeed. She was able to fleece the turncoat for more than Rutherford had thought possible.

Kev was grinning from ear to ear when he and Anna came back to Rutherford. "Best bargainer I ever seen, even better than the other Mr. Arnold."

Anna was smiling as well. She was having so much fun. Rutherford wondered how he was ever going to put an end to her smuggling activities. Lady Rutherford, the smuggler, he thought drily. That would never do.

"Kev," Anna said, "were you able to find out where he's staying?"

"No, but we got someone on a horse to follow him tonight." Kev frowned. "There's somethin' else you might want t'know. Sam was in the village last night and saw another swell waitin' for our gent. The nob didn't look none too happy too about it."

"Perhaps our London gentleman is being blackmailed," Rutherford suggested. He turned to Anna. "Come, we need to go home."

She nodded. "Kev, tell everyone to be careful. We cannot afford any mistakes."

"I will. You be safe. 'Night, your lordship."

Anna walked up the path with Rutherford close behind. When she reached the top, she glanced over at him. "You're not really going to take me home now, are you?"

"Yes. I'll change your saddle while you get into your habit. Leave the fire banked."

"But I want to do something for you," she insisted.

"When you decide to say yes, you can do something for me." Rutherford put his arms around her and kissed her soundly. "I'm fine."

His inner beast raised its head and roared, *You're not fine. Take what she's offering.* Rutherford ignored it. "A couple of weeks isn't that long to wait." *What!* "In the grand scheme of things, that is."

Anna glanced up at him with unease in her eyes. "It may take longer than that. I'm quite serious about my concerns."

"I know you are. Take all the time you need." He pressed his forehead to hers. "I shouldn't have let you go as far as you did, and I shouldn't have done what I did tonight."

"No." She shook her head. "I wanted you to touch me. I like what you do."

"I know you do. That's the reason it's so hard for me to stop." He heaved a sigh. He'd never wanted a woman like he did Anna. "If Harry were here, he'd have my head." Not to mention another part of Rutherford's anatomy.

Anna scowled. "Everyone keeps saying what Harry would do. He's dead. I need to make my own choices now."

Rutherford stifled a groan. She really didn't understand what would happen if anyone found out. They reined their horses in at the cottage. "Anna, please go and change."

The ride to Marsh Hill was made in silence. Rutherford had known her since her birth. Anna was never that quiet unless she was plotting mischief. By the time they rode in, he'd just about talked himself into not touching her again until she agreed to be his wife.

Though how he was going to keep his hands off her when he needed her so much was a question he'd yet to answer. He stayed on his horse as she slid down. "May I join you for breakfast?"

"Yes." She smiled. "Good night, Sebastian."

"Good night, my love."

If he got her to say she'd have him, he'd be able to keep her away from smugglers and spies alike. Though, short of compromising her, which he'd not do, he didn't know how to bring her up to scratch.

Chapter 14

November 11th, 1814, Grillon's Hotel, London

Harry awoke to the sounds of traffic and street vendors. He stayed still for several minutes, absorbing the noises. They seemed familiar, comfortable. How much time had he spent in London? The only thing to do was find out.

Once he'd washed and dressed, he knocked on Emma's parlor door where he was to meet her and her companion for breakfast.

Mrs. Wickham opened it. "Oh, my, good morning, Mr. Marsh. I do hope you slept well. I never sleep well in a new place and all the hustle and bustle here in London. I barely closed my eyes."

Harry bowed. "Good morning, Mrs. Wickham. Is Miss Spencer-Jones not up yet?"

"Oh, heavens, yes. You cannot keep that young lady down. She went to the hotel office to have some letters posted and obtain directions to the modiste."

Emma sailed into the room, followed by their breakfast. "Good morning." She smiled at him. "I have directions to the most popular men's shops, in the event you needed them." She handed him a slip of paper.

Harry returned her smile, hoping he'd recognize some of the names. "Schultz, Weston. Weston. I used to go there, I think. And Hoby for shoes. Thank you."

She blushed slightly. "We'd better break our fast. There is so much to do today."

After they'd finished, Harry asked, "Where will you go first?"

"To Madame Lisette's, the modiste. You?"

Harry shrugged. "It's a toss-up. I don't know which I need more, clothes or boots."

"Why don't you choose the one closest? Here, I have a map."

Emma took the City plan out of her pocket and spread it out. "Hoby is on the corner of Piccadilly and St. James Street, and Weston, at 27 Old Bond Street. They're both very close, but I think Weston has the edge. What do you think?"

Harry studied the map and glanced at her intent face. "I agree. Weston's it is. Where on this map do you go?"

"Right here." She pointed to a place on Bruton Street. "Our way is a little farther. We've been advised to take a hackney. The hotel's arranging one that will stay with us until we've finished, as well as a footman. Would you like to meet us back here for luncheon?"

Harry grinned. "Will you be done by then?"

"One must eat after all." Her eyes twinkled. "I can always go back out later, if I wish."

Harry searched her face. "Be careful. You don't know that Reynolds may not be around."

"Thank you," she said quietly, then rallied. "You should be off. We can't go anywhere of import until you have the proper clothing."

"Yes, you're right. I'll see you later." Harry stood and took his leave.

Once downstairs, he strode out of the hotel and turned right. A few minutes later, he walked into Weston's and, seeing the clerk, prepared to wait patiently. However, when the salesman pointedly refused to even acknowledge Harry's presence, his indignation started to rise. "Good morning, I am in dire need of new clothing. I think you may have my measurements on file."

The man looked Harry up and down before sniffing. "I hardly think Mr. Weston would have served *you*."

That was more impertinence than Harry was willing to stand. In a cold voice, he said, "My name is Mr. Harry Marsh. Go check. No, better yet, bring Mr. Weston here."

The clerk hurried away and came back with a shortish older man wearing a pair of spectacles. "May I help you . . . Mr. Marsh, is it really you? *But we'd heard you were dead.*"

"I had an accident," Harry said, chagrined. "To tell you the truth, I don't remember everything. I knew how to get here though."

"As well you should, sir. I've been dressing you since you came upon the Town. Freddy, what are you standing there for? Get me my measuring tape." Weston turned back to Harry. "I apologize. When I heard you'd died, I didn't keep your sizes."

The tailor eyed what Harry was wearing. "Dear me, yes. You are in need of new clothes. Leave it to me. I shall have at least evening wear ready for you today, so that you may dine at your club. Are you at Marsh House?"

"No, I'm at Grillon's for the time being. After I have new suits and shoes and alike, I'll be off to Kent." He lowered his voice. "I did have a valet, didn't I?"

Mr. Weston nodded emphatically. "Of course, and he was very good. You don't remember him at all?"

Harry pulled a face and shook his head. "No, and I suppose after all this time, he's found a new position."

Weston stared at Harry for a long time before answering. "He has. You need a hairstylist as well. I know of a very good man. I'll contact him. He might be available today."

The whole time the tailor talked, he took Harry's measurements. "There. You will want to visit Mr. Hoby next. If you come back here afterward, I should have something ready for you to try."

Harry thanked Weston before making his way over to Hoby's. He entered the shop to find two other gentlemen being fitted. One of the men stared at him for so long Harry started to feel uncomfortable. He raised a brow. "May I help you?"

"Harry, is that you?"

He narrowed his eyes as a piece of memory eluded him, then with great relief, said, "Huntley."

Harry's throat tightened, and he had the unnerving feeling he was going to weep. "Huntley," he repeated.

Gervais, Earl of Huntley, stood and clasped Harry's hand. "Where have you been, and why are you dressed like that?"

"It's a long story. I was shipwrecked and lost my memory. I-I've just recently begun to get it back. I was just over at Weston's. He said everyone thinks I'm dead."

"Yes, the *Gazette* listed you as dying in Badajoz."

Harry shook his head, trying to clear it. "If I was ever on the Peninsula, I don't remember it. Of course, I don't recall a whole lot yet."

A clerk tried in vain to get their attention until another gentleman spoke up. "I am Featherton. If you're here to get boots, you need to let this man measure you."

"Of course." Harry expected to receive the same dubious looks from the clerk here and was surprised when he did not.

"Mr. Marsh, I don't know if you remember me, but you helped me get my apprenticeship here."

Harry tried to recollect and couldn't. "I'm sorry."

"No matter." The man smiled. "I heard you tell Lord Huntley you'd lost your memory." He looked at Harry's boots. "I take it you'll need everything?"

Harry was relieved. "Yes. Do you know what I usually wear?"

"Of course. I'll take your measurements and bring out a few styles of which you might approve."

Harry waited while a drawing of his foot was made. A face flashed in his mind. The girl, his sister, again. He'd spent a good deal of time thinking about her. His friend would know if he was right as to who she is. "Huntley, I have a sister. Anna is her name, isn't it?"

Huntley raised his quizzing glass and peered at him. "You really did lose your memory. Yes. Her name is Anna. You and she were . . . are very close." Huntley grinned. "When she was first out, you growled at anyone who tried to dance with her. Until she took you to task, that is. She was in Town until she went to Finley's wedding. You probably won't remember him. He was at school with us, but got sent off to the West Indies not long after he came down from Oxford."

Huntley paused for a moment. "Do you remember Lady Phoebe Stanhope?" Harry shook his head. "Finley married her. Sad thing though, his older brother died just after the wedding. Finley is Evesham now. Lady Phoebe and Anna are great friends."

"Is my sister—Anna—is she married?" Harry asked, almost afraid to hear the answer.

"No, though Rutherford's making a push in that direction. You'll remember him. You and he were best of friends all your lives."

Huntley's eyes lit with mirth. "She'll lead him a pretty dance before she agrees to wed."

Harry wished he did recall. Was Rutherford the one she loved? "Is he tall, as tall as me with darker hair?"

"That sounds like Rutherford." Huntley paused before asking, "Who knows you're here?"

"No one. I only remembered my last name a few weeks ago. It took me a little longer to remember where I lived. I'm just here, in London, to replenish my wardrobe before I go to Kent."

Huntley thought for a moment. "Let's say we go over to Marsh House. You may have something there to wear. I don't know who's left, but there should be a caretaker."

The clerk came out with some shoe and boot styles for Harry's approval. He made his selections. As they walked out the door, he said to Huntley and Mr. Featherton, who was following along, "I have to go by Weston's. Do you mind?"

"No, not at all. Featherton, we're not doing anything this morning, are we?"

"Nothing at all," he replied amiably. "Happy to help."

"Here, Harry," Huntley said. "See if you can find Marsh House. I'll set you straight if you can't."

Harry grinned widely, happy to have at least one friend who he remembered. Whether he could find his house was another matter. "First Weston's."

He retraced his way back to the tailor's shop with Huntley and Featherton. Harry's shoulders and heart lightened. Ever since he'd met Emma, his life had begun to take shape. Much of it was still out of reach, yet for the first time, he was convinced his memory would fully return.

Once he reached the tailor's, Harry was fitted and told to come back later that afternoon.

After a couple of false starts, he found his family's London town house on Green Street. He took a deep breath and walked up the stairs, thankful the knocker was still on the door. A tall, gaunt, elderly gentleman opened the door and gaped at Harry for several moments before tears flowed down his cheeks.

"Master Harry." He turned toward the inside and called, "Mrs. Minton, come quick. You'll not believe who's here."

A plump, middle-aged woman with crimped gray curls hurried

to the door. "Mr. Minton, what is all this about? You yelling in a gentleman's establishment, of all things." She glanced in the direction Minton pointed. Her eyes grew as wide as saucers, and she fell upon Harry.

"Oh, Master Harry. My dear, dear boy. You're not dead."

Harry put his arms around her. "No, Minny, I'm not dead. May we come in?"

Mrs. Minton wiped her eyes on her apron and led them into a parlor. "We're just covering everything up. Your mama's just left to visit some friend." Disapproval colored her tone. "Miss Anna's gone home already. You sit right here, and I'll bring tea. Cook just made scones. Oh, won't she be so happy to see you!"

Memories flooded back. Snatching freshly baked scones. Cook scolding, but never telling his mother. He frowned. Something wasn't right.

Huntley patted Harry's back. "Do you want us to leave you?"

He almost panicked. "No, you'll need to tell me what's still in fashion. I've been gone for a long time."

"Can't leave him to the servants crying all over him," Featherton said sagely. "Wouldn't be right. We'll do our duty and have tea, then take a look at his clothes. See what he can still use. Where're you staying, Marsh?"

"I'm at Grillon's." Suddenly he needed to talk to Emma. "What time is it? I really must buy a watch, if I don't have one here."

"Harry, calm down." Huntley squeezed his shoulder. "It's only half past ten."

"Yes, it's just so–so much. I have an appointment at one o'clock for luncheon."

Minny came back with Cook, who promptly fainted.

"Well," Minny said, as if she'd been insulted. "I am sure I have never seen her do *that* before. Mr. Minton, please fetch me some water." She searched in her pocket and came out with a small box.

"What is that?" Harry asked.

"Smelling salts. Bring her right around." Minny passed them under Cook's nose.

Her eyes opened, and she sat straight up. "Mrs. Minton, I saw a ghost."

"No, no, Cook. It really is Mr. Harry."

Cook, after gawking at him for some time, burst into tears.

"Grillon's it is," Huntley said in Harry's ear.

Harry walked over, helped Cook up, and braced himself to be set upon. Cook wrapped her arms around him and cried on to his coat.

"It's all right. I'm here now." He patted her back. "What's this I hear about scones?"

"Oh, yes, yes, scones. I'll get them straight away."

The Mintons left as well and closed the door behind them. Harry laughed weakly. "At least I know I was well liked."

"They're not going to want you staying at a hotel," Huntley said seriously.

"I know, but I need time to sort this all out, and I can't do that when they're hovering over me. No matter how much I appreciate the sentiment."

Minton entered with a tray. "Here you are, Mr. Harry. Will you be staying here?" he asked hopefully.

Harry's heart tightened. "Minton, I lost my memory, and it's just starting to come back. I didn't even remember my sister's name until just recently. I barely found my way here. I'd like nothing better than to stay." He paused. "But I have to go home. I would dislike it immensely if word got there before I did. Please understand."

Minton tapped the side of his nose. "You tell me what you need, and I'll try to keep Mrs. Minton and Cook out of the way."

"Thank you," Harry said, relieved. "I must go over my clothes, if there are any here, and I need to find transportation to Kent. I've been on horseback for the past week." He grinned wryly. "As soon I can pull together my kit, I'll be off."

"If you don't mind," Minton said, "Mr. Harry, I won't tell the women you're not staying here until you've gone."

Harry was grateful for Minton's understanding. "That would probably be for the best. I also need to find a valet."

"I know of an excellent valet looking for a new position," Mr. Featherton mused. "My man told me about him. Thing is, I can't remember his name."

"Mr. Farley, your old valet, will be happy to hear of your return," Minton said. "He was done up good when news of your death came. Said you were the best gentleman he'd ever dressed."

Mr. Featherton lifted his head. "Farley you say? Damn me if that isn't the name of the valet my man told me about." Featherton turned to Harry. "Maybe he'd like to come back to you."

"Well, it wouldn't hurt to ask. How do I find him?"

"Leave it to me, Mr. Harry," Minton said cheerfully. "I know how to contact him. I'm sure he'd be happy to go through your wardrobe as well."

"Good, that's good." Thankfully, everything seemed to be falling into place. "Minton, how often was I in London? Could I have left something I valued here?"

"Until your death," Minton said, "we were all in London a great deal. Your room has been left as it was. Other than to clean it, her ladyship wouldn't allow anyone to touch your room. Finish your tea and have a look."

"Thank you." Harry poured tea and bit into a scone. Light, buttery, and with a hint of sweetness. Heaven.

He passed them to Featherton and Huntley, then ate two more. "I used to steal these."

Huntley bit into his. "I don't blame you. I'd pilfer them too. Do you think she'd leave you? I'd pay her a fortune just for these. I'd even let her cry on my neck cloth."

Harry chuckled.

Featherton drank the last of his tea. "Are we ready to brave your old clothes? Don't want to keep going around Town in that rig." He raised his quizzing glass and shuddered. "Might give people the wrong impression."

Harry wasn't quite sure what impression that would be, but the more people who saw him here, the faster word would get to Marsh Hill. He must get home soon.

Chapter 15

Harry, Huntley, and Featherton stood before the open doors of Harry's wardrobe. They'd already opened the drawers and glanced through them. Featherton cast a knowledgeable eye over the clothes. "I'll tell you what. I'll take out everything useful and place it on the bed. If your valet comes back, he can have another look. The important thing is you have a good number of shirts, cravats, breeches, and pantaloons."

They spent the next hour discussing, discarding, and keeping. By the time they were done, Harry had a large stack on the bed and an even larger pile on the floor.

He found his jewelry box and dumped the contents on a desk. Harry picked up a gold signet ring. "Is this mine?"

Huntley spread the items apart. "Yes, you used to wear it on your ring finger. See here, a watch."

Harry picked it up and opened it. "A picture."

Huntley laughed. "I told you, you were close to your sister. Anna probably gave it to you."

It was the girl from his dreams. "Is this a good likeness?"

Huntley studied it more closely. "I don't think so. It doesn't capture her. It's a pretty girl, but doesn't show the spark of life she has. She's older now. I'm sure it was done when she came out."

They rummaged through more of Harry's things, finding quizzing glasses, fobs, and a couple of snuff boxes. "I'll keep the watch and the ring with me. The rest, I'll go through when I know what it is."

There was a sharp knock on the door before it opened. He turned and immediately recognized the man standing just inside the room. "Farley."

"Mr. Marsh," Farley bowed. "May I express my delight at seeing you once again among the living?"

Harry shook himself and smiled widely. "Farley, how glad I am to see you. Did Minton send for you? Yes, of course he did. You'll know about my little problem, then."

Harry flushed when Farley grimaced.

"I understand you are staying at Grillon's. I will arrange to have anything suitable sent over. We must have our hair cut as well. In the meantime, allow me to dress you in something more befitting your station."

Huntley took Featherton's arm. "Harry, we'll meet you downstairs. I give you fair warning, I plan to try to convince your cook to rule over my kitchens."

Harry gave a bark of laughter. "Good luck with that. I'll be down shortly." Once they'd gone, he turned his attention to Farley. "What can I wear and what can I not?"

Farley took out a pair of knit pantaloons. "These are still in fashion. Let's see how much you've changed."

Harry stripped off his clothes, donning the items his valet handed him. When Farley handed Harry a cravat, he deftly wound the long, two-foot-wide length of linen around his neck and arranged it.

"Perfect." Farley held a coat and helped Harry into it. "A little tight. You've grown broader in the shoulders. If you'll just take a seat, I'll get your boots."

His valet dove into the wardrobe and emerged with a dusty but serviceable pair of Hessians. Farley cleaned them and brought them to a high shine. Once on Harry's feet, the boots fit perfectly. Harry studied himself in the mirror. Other than his hair being too long, *this* was what he was supposed to look like. "Thank you, Farley. If you decide to come back to me . . ."

"Mr. Marsh, I shall meet you at Grillon's this afternoon."

Harry's lips tilted up. "I am dining with a lady and her companion this evening."

"You will be presentable, sir."

Harry's throat tightened with emotion. "Thank you."

Farley bowed, and Harry went downstairs, feeling much more the thing. He grinned at Huntley's look of amazement when he entered the room. "Amazing what a good valet can do."

"Harry, you look like yourself again."

"I think so. Walk with me to Grillon's. I wouldn't want to cut anyone I should know."

Huntley nodded. "Would you like to go to Brook's this evening?"

"Thank you, but I have dinner plans, and I don't want word to get back to my parents before I arrive. Good Lord, I can't forget horses. I need to see what's here."

They left out the back gate to the mews. Harry entered the stable and perused the horses slowly, not yet seeing what he wanted.

Suddenly, a horse started kicking his stable.

"Here ye devil, stop! He's dead I tell ye," a man yelled. "Why will ye not believe it? You're a damn stubborn horse. Wi not a bit of sense in ye."

Devil, a black with white socks. *"Devil,"* Harry called.

"Don't know who ye are, or what you're about, but stop. The wee laddy's been out o'his head the past week. The master should a sold him."

Harry rushed forward and grabbed the large black gelding before he could trample the stall. The horse snorted and nuzzled him. "Hey, watch my rig, it's the best I've had in years. You're a devil, you know that."

The horse nodded and quieted. Harry turned to the stable master. "You're Arch, aren't you?"

The older man stared at him. Harry supposed a great deal of that would occur.

"Mr. Harry? Yer supposed to be dead."

"So I understand." He grinned. "I'm sorry to inconvenience you, but I need to go to Kent, and I've been sitting a horse for the past week. Can you help me?"

Arch seemed glad to be allowed to carry on as usual.

"We've got your curricle and your roans. No one's used the carriage since ye left. Miss Anna wanted to drive it, but her ladyship wouldn't ever let the pur lassie."

Harry raised a brow in inquiry.

"Got real protective over Miss Anna after you died."

"I take it that's been a bone between them?"

"Aye, it has. You know what Miss Anna is."

Harry wasn't sure whether he did or not. His sister seemed to be a termagant. "I'll need a coach for Farley and my baggage as well. You can send Devil with the baggage coach. I've got a hack stabled at the hotel. Please fetch it and bring it here."

"Aye, sir, I'll get it all ready for ye. When will ye be leavin'?"

"Early morning the day after tomorrow. Can you bring it all to Grillon's?"

"Aye, Mr. Harry. I'll do that, and I'd like to say welcome back."

"Thank you, Arch. It's good to be back." Harry rejoined Huntley and Featherton.

So much had happened today, he really needed to be alone for a while, and he wanted to speak with Emma. "My horses and carriages are still here. Even Devil."

Huntley opened his mouth to speak and hesitated.

"Go on," Harry said.

"I don't wish to add to your troubles, but you'll hear about it in any event. Your death caused a rift between your parents. Your mother refused to get rid of anything of yours. Your father gave up his seat in Parliament and buried himself in Kent."

Harry studied his friend's face. "My sister?"

"She goes between the two. I don't think she lets anyone know how she feels." Huntley grinned. "She's like you, Harry, only better-looking."

Harry wished he knew what that meant, but was afraid to ask.

He invited Huntley and Featherton to Grillon's for dinner the following evening. On their way to the hotel, Harry saw a few people who knew him and was happy to have recognized their faces, even if he'd forgotten their names. Once he said farewell to his friends, Harry took the stairs two at a time to the first floor.

When he knocked, Emma opened the door and gasped. "Harry?"

He smiled broadly as he walked into the room. "Weston remembered me, and I ran into an old friend at Hoby's. . . ." He felt like a child eager to tell his news and related everything he'd learned.

Emma took his hand in her much smaller one. "Harry, this is wonderful. I'm sorry about your parents, but maybe, with your return, they can work it out. I look forward to meeting your sister. I think I'd like her."

He smiled ruefully. "I'd been thinking she sounds a little hot at hand. Huntley told me she was like me. Now I don't know what to think."

Emma laughed musically. "You'll meet her soon enough. How old is she?"

"I forgot to ask. She must be close to her majority."

Emma's eyes glowed softly with understanding. He had to get his memory back soon. That was the only way he could suggest courting her.

A smile tugged at Emma's lips. "Harry, how well you look, dressed like a gentleman."

He smacked his head with his hand. "I'll have to go back down and arrange a room for Farley, my valet."

She tugged the bell pull. "How fortunate it was that he didn't like his new position."

"I agree. I recognized him straight away." Harry led her to the table that had already been set for luncheon. "Tell me how your shopping went."

"Oh, Madame Lisette is a wonder. She's having some gowns sent round today, and I have another fitting tomorrow. Harry, I've bought so many gloves, hats, and other things, I almost feel decadent. We don't have the same selection in Kingston." She speared a piece of chicken. "I've been assured I'll use them all. I sent a note to my godmama this morning. I don't know how far away from London she lives."

"What is her direction?"

"Well, that's just it. The only address I have is her London house. I was told that if she was not still in Town, the note would be forwarded to her."

"I planned to depart in two days. If you wish, I shall remain until your godmother arrives."

She gazed at him, her eyes a bit sad. "As much as I enjoy your company, I don't wish to hold you up. You are remembering so many more things." She covered his hand with hers. "It's important you go home."

Even though he'd been saying the same thing, he was disappointed to have it repeated back to him. "I've invited two friends to dine with us tomorrow evening. I hope you don't mind."

Emma smiled softly. "No, how could I? I'm happy to meet your friends."

They'd almost finished eating when he asked, "Where is Mrs. Wickham?"

She grinned. "Shopping fagged her. She'll join us at dinner."

A knock sounded on the open door. "Come in."

One of the hotel managers entered. "Miss Spencer-Jones, you called?"

"Yes. Mr. Marsh's valet is joining him, and he'll need a chamber."

The man bowed. "Of course. I will arrange it immediately."

After he'd left, Harry grinned. "Thank you."

"It was the least I could do."

Harry wanted to take her in his arms. He took her hands instead. "I should go now. I'll see you this evening."

Emma nodded. "I'll see you then."

Farley arrived that afternoon with the hairdresser and Harry's trunks, which had been found after a search of the attic.

Once Harry's hair had been cut into a more fashionable style, Farley stood back, pleased. "I must say, sir, I am glad to be back."

"Yes, Farley, as am I." Harry couldn't wait for Emma's reaction.

Emma passed a hand over her eyes. She was so happy for Harry, yet wondered if his newfound knowledge would be the very thing that separated them. He was such a good man, kind, generous. She always had a feeling she was protected when he was near.

But more than that, he had a good sense of humor and cared deeply about his family. Emma was sure he'd have his pick of the *ton's* ladies. Women who were a part of his world—not an interloper seeking entrance.

She was falling in love with him. Why did it have to happen now? With a man who didn't even know himself yet? Maybe it was good he'd leave before she did. It would give her time to start forgetting him.

November 12th, 1814, Kent, the Pelican Inn, between Dover and Thanport

Georges lounged on a chair next to Florian's bed, waiting for his cousin to awaken. After Florian's first meeting with the smuggler's leader, Georges had followed Florian and had no problem convincing the landlord to give him a key to Florian's room.

"Florian, *mon cousin*, I must speak with you."

Florian's eyelids flickered.

Georges grinned and clapped his hands loudly, causing his cousin to sit up with a start. "Ah, I'm glad to see you are among the living again."

"How—how did you get in here?" Florian asked, backing up against the headboard.

"Your innkeeper is, how shall I say it? Very obliging."

Florian glanced around the room as if looking for a way out. His hand went to the table next to the bed and groped. "What do you want?"

Georges had already made sure there were no weapons at hand. He smiled coldly. "We have a date for our first arrivals. Have you made the arrangements with the smugglers?"

"Yes, of course. There is just the matter of payment."

"How much?" Georges asked sharply.

"One thousand pounds." Florian inched farther away. "Half to be paid before the delivery and half after."

"One thousand pounds?" Georges had to remember to keep his voice down. "Are you mad?"

"I-I bargained him down from two," Florian said sulkily. "They're taking a very large risk."

Georges jumped up and paced the small room. "Is there a chance to lower the payment?"

Florian shook his head. "No. They want the first five hundred before their boats put out to pick up the packages and the second five as they're coming in. If we don't pay them, their leader swears he'll dump the cargo. The people won't last three minutes in the water at this time of year."

"Merde." Georges continued pacing. "Could you not have used your superiority?"

"No," Florian said almost proudly. "They are Englishmen. Not just any member of the aristocracy can threaten them."

"What about a noble in the area?" Georges asked. "Surely they would listen to someone they know."

"There is only one peer in the immediate vicinity."

"Is there any way to recruit this man?"

"Approach him if you wish," Florian sneered. "His best friend died at Badajoz."

"He has no weaknesses? A sister to exploit?"

"None of his sisters are out. He's wealthy and has no vices that could be used for our purposes."

"Bien," Georges said fatalistically. His chief would not like spending so much money, but there was nothing he could do. "Thus we pay these low-bred English. The cargo will come on the fifteenth. We shall prepare for the arrival at eleven thirty that evening."

Florian inclined his head. "I'll send word."

"You will do more than that," Georges said in a threatening tone. Florian needed to be kept afraid. "We need two large coaches and reliable drivers. You'll guarantee their safe arrival at the house where you'll take them."

Florian blanched. "But—I've never done that before."

"Then you shall learn, quickly."

Chapter 16

November 12th, 1814, Marsh Hill, Kent

Anna awoke early, but rather than rising, she stayed and thought over what had occurred yesterday with Sebastian. She'd been prepared for a battle over the accounts, and had been pleasantly surprised when he had actually listened to her. She wasn't totally convinced, but it was a good start. She did believe he loved her. If only she was naive enough to believe that was enough, she'd be the happiest lady in England. They were certainly attracted to each other physically. *That* hadn't been at all what she'd expected. There was a stark difference between the chaste kisses she had imagined before and the heated ones that made her toes curl. Love for him sunk deep into her bones and swirled in her mind. If only she could bring herself to just accept him, perhaps her dreams would come true after all. Yet that wasn't the answer, and she knew it. Phoebe was right. With Sebastian, Anna had to be sure.

Her thoughts slid back to the cottage and the pleasure he'd showed her, while taking none for himself. That was something she could explore before she had to make a final decision. There must be some way she could please him. She frowned. Although well educated in many subjects, she was still woefully ignorant concerning what happened between a man and a woman. *Harry's book.*

Anna jumped up and went to her desk where she'd hidden it. The book was extremely illuminating. It had not only drawings, which she hoped were accurate, but directions as well. Most of the portrayals depicted the "act" itself; however, a few showed other forms of intimacy.

She stopped flipping the pages when she found a picture of a woman kneeling before a man, his member in her mouth. Anna read the instructions and smiled. Though the words made a small attempt to be clinical, she was growing warmer by the minute. She turned back to the other pictures of men and women joined together. That must be what Sebastian wouldn't do with her before she agreed to marry him.

"Oh, my. That sounds nice." Her breasts swelled as she thought of him touching her that way, and she grew damp between her legs. Anna turned the pages, pausing at some of them and tilting her head. Could it really be done like that? Sebastian would know.

There was no point in waiting any longer. Despite what he'd said about waiting, today she'd give him pleasure.

Rutherford was awakened by a shriek. When Robertson opened the bed hangings, Rutherford raised a brow.

"My lord, it appears a fox has got in amongst the hens."

"That answers my first question."

Doors slammed, and his two youngest sisters dashed into his chamber. He closed his eyes. "I will speak to you at breakfast. Now leave."

Small feet shuffled back out. "Robertson, I believe there is more afoot than chickens."

Rutherford rose and dressed, then sent a note to Anna begging her forgiveness and saying that he'd be by as soon as he could. He descended the stairs to the breakfast room where he found his sisters and his mother at the table. After taking his seat and a cup of tea, he surveyed his family. "What is going on?"

Eloisa jumped in. "Mama received a note. . . ."

"Enough, if Mama received the letter, she shall explain."

His mother raised her chin. "I received a letter from my goddaughter. She is at Grillon's. I shall post to London immediately."

He took another sip of tea. "I bid you a good journey. However, I fail to understand why that should cause my bedchamber to be invaded."

He cast a quelling glance at Cece, who'd begun to giggle.

His mother didn't meet his eyes, and said, "I said I'd take Althea, and the other two wanted to come as well."

"How long will you be away?"

"Not long at all. I should return in a couple of days."

The idea of any of his family running off to London or anywhere else without him right now caused him to shake his head. "Not today."

"What do you mean, not today?"

"I really do not think I'm being obtuse," he said decisively. "Unless you wish to travel on Sunday, write the lady and explain that you'll arrive Monday afternoon. I'll expect you to return the following day. The girls will remain here."

A cacophony of voices rent the air.

His mother, one of the few persons who knew of Sebastian's spying activities, raised an inquiring brow.

He nodded. She didn't need to know the details, only that it was unwise for his sisters to be running around England.

"Quiet, or you will all go to your rooms." Rutherford waited for the noise to stop and said to his mother, "Indeed. Things are a little interesting at the present. If your goddaughter has a companion, I suggest you not go at all."

His mother pressed her lips together. "My goddaughter's companion does not travel with her beyond London. Well, then, I must travel on Sunday. I shall leave alone on the morrow after church."

"I'll send outriders with you."

"Will you tell me all of it?"

"Yes, afterward." When they had the French spies in hand.

She inclined her head. "Very well, then."

A footman entered and handed Rutherford a note.

Dearest Sebastian,
I shall meet you at the cottage.

Yours,

A

"What the devil?" He'd forgotten to tell Anna about the man near the cottage. "Get my horse," he bellowed to the footman.

Rutherford fixed each of his sisters with a stern look. "I must go. We shall continue this discussion when I return."

His horse was being brought out as he entered the stables. After swinging himself up, he took off at a gallop.

By the time Anna reached the stables, Humphrey had her horse ready. He stopped her as she led Thunderer to the mounting block. "Where's his lordship?"

"I'm meeting him. I'll not be alone for long."

Humphrey's chin firmed. "I told him and Mr. Harry that you'd not go out by yerself."

"Humphrey, truly," she said in her best wheedling tone, "I'll only be alone for a little while. Lord Rutherford will be with me soon."

The groom grumbled, but in the end Anna got her way. She rode off, smiling in anticipation. The morning was warmer than usual, and the sun shone. She stabled Thunderer at the cottage and walked around to the door.

After opening the shutters, she was busy building up the fire when she heard a horse. The door opened, and she stood to greet Sebastian, but Percy was there instead.

She edged back against the fireplace, being careful not to show she was alarmed. Surely she could handle Percy. "What are you doing here? No, don't bother telling me. *Get out.* I have nothing to say to you."

Percy advanced into the room. "But I have something to say to you. As long as you're playing Rutherford's whore, you may do for me as well. After all, what's another when you've already had one?"

His features contorted into a lewd smile. A ripple of terror ran down her spine, and the hairs on her neck stood up, but she daren't allow him to see how frightened she really was.

"You have no idea what you're saying. *Get. Out. Now.*" Anna narrowed her eyes menacingly and took a shallow breath as she reached behind her, grabbing the fireplace poker.

Percy sauntered toward her. "Anna, my dear, I'm a man just like Rutherford . . . or is it his wealth you find so attractive?"

She moved behind the table, hiding the iron rod in her skirts. "Percy, I'm warning you. You don't know what you're saying. Leave."

He laughed like a madman. "You think he's going to marry you, but he won't. Not after you've warmed his bed."

Anna prayed Sebastian would get here soon, but until he did, she was on her own. She clenched her jaw. "You always were an idiot."

Percy lunged over the table to grab her. Anna swung the poker down hard on his shoulder, jumping aside to hit him again. Screaming, he started after her, but stumbled over a chair. Anna raised the rod again. "The next hit goes to your head."

Percy scrambled to his feet and fled out the still-open door, straight into Sebastian. He grabbed Percy and drove his fist into the sapskull's face. There was a satisfying crunch. Blood shot out from Percy's nose and it was off at an angle.

Sebastian turned to Anna. "Close the door and stay inside."

She quickly closed the door, ran to the window, and opened it.

"Go anywhere near her again, Blanchard," Sebastian snarled as he punched Percy in the stomach, "and I'll kill you."

A whoosh of air left Percy, and he fell to the ground. But instead of staying down, like a sensible man, he got up and did what Anna thought had to be the stupidest thing in the world. He spoke.

"I'll be here when you're done with her. . . ."

Rutherford hit him again. This time, Percy stayed on the ground, moaning.

Still furious, Sebastian untied Percy's horse and wacked it on its rump. "You can walk home."

There was blood everywhere, mostly on Percy. Anna couldn't help but be thrilled that Sebastian had dealt so handily with the idiot. Of course, now she had another problem. The chance of someone's finding out about what she and Sebastian had been doing just increased tremendously.

After Percy had been gone for a few minutes, the cottage door slammed open. Sebastian dragged her into his arms, crushing his lips to hers. A frisson of excitement coursed through her, and Anna returned his kiss hungrily.

"God, Anna, you scared me to death. I don't know what I'd do if anything happened to you." He held her back, searching her face. "Anna, are you all right?"

"I'm fine." Sebastian looked as if he was about to argue. "Really, there's nothing wrong with me. I'm glad you pummeled Percy. He deserved it, broken nose and all."

He stared at the ceiling for a moment before gazing at her again. "My love, it's not just Percy. We need to talk."

"Perhaps he won't say anything," she said, praying Sebastian would agree, yet knowing he wouldn't.

"Anna"—though he frowned, his voice was gentle—"do you want to put your reputation in Percy's hands?"

If only she could think her way out of this mess, but not one idea floated through her brain. She shook her head. "No."

"Anna, marry me, please. Let me protect and cherish you."

"Sebastian, I . . ."

He placed a finger over her lips. "I know you don't love me yet, but I'll do everything I can to be the man you want me to be."

Her chest ached so badly, she could barely draw a breath. "Oh, don't you see? I do love you. I've loved you most of my life, but I need to make sure we will be happy together."

He sat on a chair and pulled her on to his lap, holding her to him. "Anna, life doesn't issue guarantees. I realize I've been a bit overbearing lately."

She nodded and gave a small chuckle. "Stodgy."

"Yes, but that's probably due to the fact that I haven't had a strong woman to manage me."

She had never expected to hear that from Sebastian. She leaned back and gazed at him. "We still have a great deal to resolve."

He smiled. "I promise you, we'll do it together. Miss Marsh, will you do me the honor of being my wife and baroness?"

Tears misted her eyes. "Yes, my lord, I will."

Sebastian kissed her slowly. When he opened his lips, she ran her tongue over his teeth, capturing his mouth. Sliding her hands under his greatcoat, she pushed it down over his arms.

"Anna, what are you doing?"

"Taking this off." She slid off his lap and pulled him up. "Trust me."

After she'd dispensed with his coat, she unbuttoned his jacket, pulling it down from his shoulders, kissing him on his jaw, as he'd done to her.

He was too tall for her to kneel while he stood. "Hmm, how to do this? Sit please."

Sebastian did as she asked, but it was clear he had no idea what she'd planned.

Kneeling, Anna unbuttoned the fall of his buckskin breeches.

His fully erect shaft sprung up to greet her. She took it lightly in her hands and lowered her mouth over it.

"Oh God, Anna," he moaned. His fingers winnowed through her hair, loosening the pins in her tresses.

He tasted salty and musky. She whirled her tongue and sucked. Other than his hands in her hair, he was still. She lifted her head. "Am I doing this right? I read the instructions."

Rutherford groaned. "You're doing it perfectly."

She bent back down to him.

After a few moments, he jerked. *"Wait—what instructions?"*

Anna gazed up at him. "I found a book. I think it was Harry's."

"Where?" Sebastian asked, as if in anguish. "Where did you find it?"

Anna grinned. "At Marsh House, in the library. I wanted to do something for you." She bent her head again.

The book. He'd been there when Harry had bought it. God, there'd be no stopping her now. "Come." Rutherford helped her up and kissed her gently.

She tugged on his shirt and cravat.

Capturing her hands, he said, "Slowly. This is not an act to be rushed."

His lips teased hers to answer as he gradually moved her back toward the bed. He unbuttoned her jacket, running his palms over her breasts, enjoying her sharp intake of breath.

Her skirt made a swoosh as it fell. He lightly grazed her body with his hands, savoring her curves and the panting noises she made. He lingered at her buttocks. She rocked into him. Anna's moan made him even harder. He laughed when his breeches dropped. It was a good thing they were already at the bed, or he'd have been hobbled.

"I want your shirt off." She pushed it up. He pulled it over his head. Her hands were touching and exploring his chest and back. No other woman's touch had ever heated him like Anna's. His shaft was harder than it had ever been and being rubbed by the soft muslin of her chemise.

When they were both naked, Rutherford swept Anna up in his arms and placed her on the bed. "I love you, Anna Marsh."

She was exquisite. Slowly he placed soft kisses down her neck and over her soft, creamy breasts. Stopping at each one to nibble and sup. He licked her taut belly. One he hoped would soon hold his child.

He'd known her for so long, but had never truly seen her before now. She was his to love and protect. Marcus was right, when a man truly loved a woman, there was no sacrifice in saying it.

Sebastian shouldered her legs apart and licked her already wet curls. When she arched her hips, he held her down, entering her with his tongue. She tasted like sweet honey and the sea.

Rutherford placed two fingers into her hot, wet sheath. Anna sobbed, urging him deeper. She cried out in pleasure as she contracted around him.

"I want to make love to you," he whispered.

Her eyes opened and gazed into his. "That's what I want. I want you to make me yours."

"Banns tomorrow?" he asked.

She nodded. "Yes. Banns tomorrow."

Though he'd never taken a virgin, he'd heard enough about it. It killed him that he'd have to cause her any injury. "This will hurt, but only once."

She nodded. "I'll be all right."

He entered her as slowly as he could. She was so tight, but there was no resistance. Her legs were lean and muscled. Sebastian stopped when she tensed. "Anna?"

"I'm fine. Go ahead."

She took deep breaths. When she relaxed, he buried himself into her, then withdrew and entered her again. Using long, slow strokes, he brought her to a frenzy. She shattered, bringing him with her. He pressed deeper to prolong her orgasm, hoping to give her more pleasure than pain.

Rutherford gathered her to him. His throat ached. He knew he'd never truly made love before now. With Anna, everything was different, deeper, better. "You're mine now, forever."

"And you're mine." She cuddled closer as he pulled the blanket over them. "I'm so happy. I never knew it would be like this."

Anna pressed her head against Sebastian's chest to feel the deep rumble when he spoke.

"No, nor did I." He stroked her hair. "I wish we could stay here all afternoon, but we need to talk to our families and find the vicar."

Turning her head, she found his nipples and licked one. "What would we do, if we stayed?"

He breathed in sharply. "With any luck, I'll show you tomorrow."

"Shall I bring the book?" Anna asked.

Sebastian's chest turned into a quake as he broke into laughter. "If it's the same book I think it is . . . Yes. Right now, we need to dress."

Anna stayed under the covers and watched him as he donned his clothes. She loved his broad chest, covered with soft dark curls that reached down to his member. His stomach was flat and his thighs all muscle.

He was so strong, yet he'd held her so tenderly. "You're beautiful. Like one of the Greek statues."

Sebastian grinned. "One with a head, I hope."

Anna laughed. "And a face."

"Your turn."

Once she was dressed, they searched for the hairpins that had fallen out. She took out the rest of them and shook out her hair to rewind it into a knot.

Sebastian came up behind her. "Tomorrow, I'm taking all the pins out. I love how your hair curls around your shoulders and down your back."

Anna's contentment spread. Perhaps she would enjoy being married to him. If only she'd been allowed to make the decision herself, rather than having it forced on her, everything would be perfect.

After Sebastian banked the fire, they left the cottage. "Do you think Percy will be a problem again?"

His smile left him. "If Blanchard is smart, he won't. Unfortunately, I place no dependence on his intelligence."

When she landed on Thunderer, Anna cried out in pain.

Sebastian looked at her sharply. "Does it hurt?"

"A little," she replied. The pain receded a bit, but the ride home was not going to be pleasant.

"Drat, we need to find a carriage for you." His brows drew together, and he looked up at the sky. It's almost noon. Let's go to the Hill. You can change, and I'll ask your father if we may use his gig." Sebastian's gaze came back to her. "I must have rocks in my head. If you'd like, I'll procure a special license. We can marry as soon as I get it."

He was not going to rush her. Besides, she wanted what was left of her family there. "No. We cannot. My mother's not here."

She smiled when he smothered a curse.

"You're right, and my mother is making a trip to Town to fetch her goddaughter."

"Sebastian, let's go. We can't make any firm decisions until we discuss it with our families."

They rode slowly into the stable yard. She smiled gratefully at him when he lifted her down and helped her to the door.

"I'll have Ledster put me in a parlor," Sebastian said. "I assume you want us to meet your father together."

Anna nodded. "I'll be as quick as I can. If anyone asks why we want the gig, we'll tell them I fell off my horse."

Sebastian snorted. "When was the last time you fell off a horse?"

Anna grimaced. "A long time ago. Think of something else if you can."

She kissed him quickly and tried to hurry up the stairs, but found she was a little stiff.

Lizzy was in her room when Anna walked in. "How fast can you get a bath ready?"

"There's usually warm water in the kitchen. I'll have one set up in a few minutes."

"Thank you. You may wish me happy. Lord Rutherford and I are to marry."

"Oh, miss." Lizzy hugged her. "I'm so happy for you. I'll get that bath right away."

A half an hour later, Anna, dressed in a bronze carriage gown, opened the door to the small front parlor. "Ledster is dying of curiosity."

"How can you tell?" Sebastian asked. "I've never seen him change his expression."

"It's the way he's hovering. Come, my father is in his study."

They walked hand in hand down the corridor. Anna knocked on the door and entered. "Papa?"

Next to her, Sebastian bowed. "Sir William." He turned to Anna, and asked, "I think I ought to go first, don't you?"

Anna waved an arm. "Oh, very well. Do your duty."

Sir William glanced at them and sat back in his chair with a smug smile.

"Sir, I'd like to ask for Anna's hand in marriage."

"Just the news I wanted to hear," he said. "I've been expecting this since you returned. Anna, tug the bell pull. We shall celebrate."

Ledster opened the door before Anna finished the first pull. "Yes, Sir William?"

"Please ask Lady Tully to attend to me and bring champagne. Lord Rutherford and Miss Anna are marrying."

"Wonderful news, sir," Ledster said and left.

"What will you wager," Anna narrowed her eyes, "he was waiting outside the door?"

"Not a farthing," her father replied. "I'd be surprised if his ear wasn't at the key-hole. Rutherford, I suppose you'll want to discuss the settlements?"

He sat on the sofa with Anna. "Anna and I have already discussed them. I'd be obliged to you if you would arrange to have all her property put into a trust for her benefit." Sebastian grinned at her. "She and I still need to decide what her allowance will be and how much will be set aside for daughters and younger sons. If you'll give me a list of any other items you'd like us to consider, we'll make time for it."

A footman brought the champagne. After handing a glass to Anna, Sebastian took a sip. "We'd like to have the banns read tomorrow, so we must chase down the vicar today and, of course, inform my mother."

"Papa," Anna said firmly. "Please write Mother. She must be here for my wedding."

The happy sparkle left her father's eyes.

"Yes, of course. I'll write her immediately."

Aunt Lillian entered the room just ahead of Cook, Ledster, and the housekeeper, Mrs. Ledster.

"I told you he was excited," Anna said quietly to Rutherford. "Hmm."

"What have we here?" her aunt asked, smiling broadly.

"We're going to have a wedding," Papa responded.

Aunt Lillian embraced Anna and Sebastian. "I am so happy for the two of you."

Ledster, his wife, and Cook hugged Anna and sobbed. Anna did her best not to laugh at the expression of dismay on Sebastian's face when he thought they'd embrace him as well. Instead, the women bobbed curtseys and wished him happy.

"Sir, may we use your gig?" Sebastian asked Papa. "Anna didn't want to meet with the vicar and my mother in her habit, and there is not enough time to ride home and bring my curricle."

She gave him a sidelong glance, and whispered, "Well done."

"Yes, of course." Papa glanced from her to Sebastian. "When is the wedding?"

"As soon as possible after the last banns are read," Sebastian replied hopefully.

Anna nodded. That would give her mother time to arrive, and give Sebastian and her time to work out any of their differences.

Papa pulled his date book toward him. "The thirtieth of November. I suppose Lady Rutherford will want to hold a ball in your honor?"

Sebastian's jaw tightened. "I would say that is extremely likely."

"Good." Papa said. "Let us have a bite to eat before I send you on your way."

"I believe luncheon will be ready shortly," Ledster offered.

As they discussed what the settlements should include, it was clear to Anna that Sebastian had been giving them a good deal of thought. He'd come a long way since that day at Charteries. Perhaps her dreams really would come true.

Once they'd finished eating, he said, "If you are ready, my love, we need to be off."

She rose and gave him her hand. "I'm ready."

All except for telling his mother. Anna was not looking forward to seeing Lady Rutherford.

Chapter 17

Rutherford placed Anna's fur cloak around her shoulders and handed her into the gig. Humphrey spread a warm rug over her legs. Swathed in a shawl, spencer, cloak, and with a warm brick at her feet, she looked snug indeed. Dark curls escaped charmingly from under her velvet hat.

Rutherford handed Anna her muff. "I hope you don't get too cold," he said solicitously, and smiled.

Anna fetched a sigh and looked upward. "Heaven forbid I should become chilled. Let's hunt down the vicar. With any luck at all, he'll be at home."

But when they arrived at the vicarage, the housekeeper told them he was out. Rutherford and Anna finally caught up with the man at the inn.

Rutherford jumped down from the carriage. "Stay here, I'll bring him out."

Anna nodded. "By the time you unwrap me and hand me down, I daresay you could have him here."

He grinned. "I'll be back shortly."

He found the vicar in the common room playing chess. "Mr. Thompson, I'd like a moment of your time."

The man glanced up from his game. "Yes, of course, my lord. What can I do for you?"

Rutherford motioned with his head for Mr. Thompson to step

outside. The vicar excused himself and followed Rutherford, who told him about the wedding as they walked outside.

Mr. Thompson bowed to Anna. "Ah, Miss Marsh, Lord Rutherford tells me I am to wish you happy."

Anna smiled and held out her hand. "Yes, if you wouldn't mind."

"Reading the banns would be my pleasure. I'm delighted we'll be able to keep you in our little area of Kent."

To Rutherford's surprise, Anna went on to discuss some parish issues with the vicar before they left. How in the devil did she keep up with it all?

Rutherford climbed back into the carriage. "Correct me if I am wrong, my love, but you *have* been in London until recently."

"I have been back for over two weeks, and I correspond with him regularly. Someone must keep up with the parish doings. If not me, who?"

Who indeed. Anna apparently had her fingers in more pies than he knew about. "I would have thought my mother might be the proper person," he said grimly. "It is, after all, my living, and she is currently the most senior lady."

"I will not speak poorly of your mother, Sebastian. It just happened to fall to me, and as we are to marry, it is no great matter."

Rutherford gave a bark of laughter. "Thompson was right. I made a good choice."

Anna's eyes lit up. "Did he say that?"

Rutherford glanced at her again. She really was remarkable. "He did indeed. At the risk of increasing your good opinion of yourself, I'll tell you my staff is delighted at the prospect of you becoming their mistress."

Anna patted his arm. "It's all as it should be."

"Yes, it is." Rutherford couldn't believe his luck. Despite her being forced into the betrothal, it was working out better than he'd expected.

He stopped the carriage in front of the Priory's portico and hoped his previous discussion with his mother had done the job. He lifted Anna down and took her arm. As they reached the top step, his butler opened the door.

"Griffin, you may gather the staff in the hall. I'll need no more than twenty minutes with her ladyship and my sisters."

He bowed. "Yes, my lord. They are all in the morning room. May I bring champagne?"

"Yes, please," Anna said. "Lemonade and some cakes as well, if you please."

"Yes, my—Miss."

At least his staff was treating his betrothed as they should. Rutherford walked into the morning room with Anna beside him. "Mother, girls. It is my pleasure to inform you Miss Marsh has, finally, agreed to be my wife."

His announcement was greeted with open-mouthed silence.

His mother put her tea-cup down with a snap.

Eloisa, who'd been taking a sip, spewed out the liquid and frantically began to mop it from her gown. Cece dropped her untouched biscuit, and Althea started to smile before she glanced at her mother and went still.

His mother rose and glided forward to Anna. "I am very happy for you both, my dear. I know you will make Rutherford a good wife."

Once the girls rushed forward, he was not happy to see his mother retreat to the other end of the room.

"Ruhy, what does this mean?" Cece asked.

He stooped down. "This, my pet, means you will have a new sister. Once we marry, Anna will come to live with us."

Only because he couldn't think of a good reason for her to move in before the wedding.

Cece glanced up with wide eyes at Anna, who smiled and gracefully stooped.

"I do hope you'll like my living here," she said.

Cece looked at him, and he nodded. "Yes, we will like that quite well. Do you know how to play games?"

Anna smiled mischievously. "I know quite a few games. I'll have to see which ones you already know."

Eloisa impatiently pulled her younger sister away. "I shall quite like having you here. It will make Ruhy happy." Eloisa lowered her voice to a conspiratorial whisper. "He's much easier to get along with when he's happy. He's a gentleman, you see."

Anna's lips tipped up. "Yes, indeed, I quite understand your point. I shall do my best to see he is always cheerful."

Eloisa nodded. "Yes, I think you will. You love him a lot, don't you?"

"Yes, I love him a lot."

Rutherford helped Anna rise. Althea came forward a bit shyly. "I wish you happy and—and I'm glad you will join our family."

Anna nodded graciously. "Thank you, Althea."

Griffin came in with the refreshments.

"Ooh, champagne. May I have some?" Eloisa asked.

Wanting to include her in all the decisions from the start, Rutherford glanced at Anna.

She nodded. "Yes, you may have a taste."

He handed his glass to Eloisa. She took a small sip and made a face. "I don't like it."

"There is lemonade if you prefer," Anna said, "and some cakes."

"Ruhy, I want to try," Cece said.

He held the glass for her.

After taking a sip, she made a face and shuddered before smiling. "That's good."

"You may have lemonade as well," he said.

"Me next." Althea smiled shyly. "I always seem to be behind my younger sisters."

"It's no bad thing to be a little cautious," Anna murmured.

Althea smiled gratefully at Anna and took the glass Rutherford handed her.

Taking one sip and then another, his sister said, "I do like this."

Rutherford gave Althea a glass of her own. "Don't like it too much."

She threw a questioning glance at Anna.

"You'll want to limit yourself to two glasses at a party," she explained. "Better yet, drink lemonade or orgeat or, of course, tea. A lady should never be seen to be the least bit tipsy."

"Anna, will you be in London for my come-out?"

"Yes, of course. Rutherford and I will both be there."

"I'm glad," Althea said.

"I daresay, you will think me a dry stick before the end of the Season," Anna responded.

Althea laughed.

Rutherford wanted nothing more than to take Anna into his arms. She'd fit into his family very well.

His mother drifted back over to them. "When is the wedding to be?"

"On the thirtieth," he responded. "The banns will be read to-morrow."

"I see." Her tone was so dry one could strike a match on it. "How long have you known this?"

"Anna accepted me this morning. There is no reason you cannot leave for Town after the service." He turned to his betrothed. "My mother's received word her goddaughter is here, and she must fetch her."

Anna smiled politely. "You'll be bringing out two ladies next Season?"

"Yes," Lady Rutherford said. "Althea and Miss Spencer-Jones. Her grandfather is a duke."

Anna's smile tightened.

"Mother," Rutherford said warningly.

"I didn't mean anything by it. I suppose . . . Well, it doesn't matter. I have every intention of having her make a brilliant match."

"My lord?" Griffin asked.

Rutherford turned. "Are they ready?"

"Yes, my lord."

He looked over his shoulder at his mother. "I am introducing Anna to the staff."

"Of course you are." His mother left the room.

Anna raised a brow. "Oh my."

"I've already told her, if she cannot behave, she'll have to move to the dower-house. We used to get along well. I don't know what's happened recently." Her behavior toward Anna could not be allowed to continue. He supposed another talk with his mother was in order, but he was at a loss as to what to say.

Althea spoke up. "She had her heart set on someone called Lady Phoebe."

Rutherford almost rolled his eyes. "Let me tell all of you. Lady Phoebe is the only woman who has ever knocked me down with one punch. Even if she'd been interested, I would not have married her."

He watched disgustedly as his sisters and his betrothed went into whoops.

Anna recovered first, though her voice still trembled with mirth.

"Phoebe told me that you said you couldn't marry a lady who had a better right than yours. Oh my." Anna fanned herself with her hand. "Shall we go see the staff?"

"Yes, let's."

She placed her hand on his arm and glided by his side. From behind, his sisters chattered to each other.

"I wonder if she can teach me to walk like that?"

"She's really very pretty. Beautiful even."

"Shush, they can hear you."

"Oh, Althea, who cares? She'll hear a lot more when she comes to live with us."

"Mama doesn't want her to marry Ruhy."

"Shush. You'll hurt her feelings."

Rutherford bent to whisper, "I told you they were embarrassing."

"Yes." Anna grinned. "But very kind-hearted."

"My mother will either come around or leave."

Anna pressed her lips together. "Sebastian."

"Please." He hoped his sisters hadn't heard. "Only you are allowed to use my name. It wouldn't do to encourage them."

Anna stopped. "I don't understand. Why is that?"

"Because when you say it, it's musical, and I love it."

"That has me at *point non plus*."

He relished the moment. He probably wasn't going to win many arguments with her.

When they reached the main hall, the servants were lined up according to rank. Anna greeted them one by one. Rutherford was astonished that she knew most of them by name. His chest puffed out, like that of a bantam cock, as he followed her down the line.

"Miss Marsh," Mrs. Thurston, his housekeeper said, "if you'd like to inspect the house before your wedding, I'd be happy to take you round."

"My mother leaves for London tomorrow," Rutherford whispered. "Monday would be a good day."

"Mrs. Thurston, is Monday convenient?"

The housekeeper smiled broadly. "Yes, miss. I'll have everything ready."

After promising to inspect the kitchen as well, Anna and Rutherford decided to take a turn around the garden.

Her lips formed a thin line. "I cannot help but hope your mother accepts me."

"For years, she's wanted me to marry higher," he said. "Then she became fixated on Phoebe. I didn't have the heart to tell her I'd no interest in Phoebe."

Anna turned to him. "Never?"

He glanced at her. "No, never. It was always you, but you were so young, and then Harry died. We seemed to drift apart."

Anna stared ahead. "I was desolate when you didn't offer for me my first Season. I couldn't understand why you didn't want me."

He drew her into his arms, needing to assuage the long ago hurt. "My heart, Harry was frantic over you. He was ready to fight anyone who came around, and, due to your age, he would have taken it as the worst sort of betrayal."

She took a hand from her muff and reached out to him. "What's important is that we have each other now." She chewed her bottom lip. "I shall leave your mother to you."

Sunday, November 13th, 1814, St. Clement's Church, Thanport, Kent

Rutherford escorted Anna into the church, followed by his mother, sisters, Sir William, and Lady Tully. They all sat in the Rutherford pew. He was pleased to note his senior staff was present and as many of the lower members of his household as could be there.

He cast a warning glance at Percy, seated with his mother. The man looked like a gang of thugs had beat him. If Percy said a word, Rutherford would cut the fool down where he stood and carry Anna off to London to marry by special license. He almost wished for the excuse.

He appraised his own family. His sisters were behaving, and his mother appeared resigned.

The banns were read before the service began. After the service had ended, Rutherford and Anna stood outside the small church, besieged by people wishing them happy.

"That went well, don't you think?" Anna asked.

"Yes, though I half-way expected Percy to make an objection."

"On what grounds?" she asked. "Besides, he wouldn't dare. If you didn't kill him, I would."

He grinned. "You're fierce."

"Yes, well, I do not like anyone threatening my family."

"It's one of the things I admire about you."

Anna was quiet for a few minutes. "I wonder when my mother will arrive."

Rutherford put his hand over hers. "Don't worry about it. At least *she'll* be happy we're marrying."

"Yes. She's wanted us to wed for a long time. It's as if she thinks she'll get Harry back if we do. Sebastian, he's been on my mind so much lately. I wish I knew why."

"Maybe because you've only recently learned the truth of his death."

"No, it's something else. A strange feeling as if he's trying to get my attention." She shook her head. "I wonder what it means."

Chapter 18

"Harry," Emma said, "a letter from my godmama arrived last night. She's arriving today."

Harry's throat tightened. "That's wonderful." Wonderful was not what he felt. He tried to keep his face still as she searched it. He knew last evening when they dined with his friends he was falling in love with her. Yet, his guilt over his dead wife and his uncertainty about himself kept him silent. "Did she give you an idea of when?"

"Late. She doesn't like traveling on Sunday, but there is a family matter to which she needs to attend. I hope I'm not a burden."

Harry rose from the table. "How could you be anything but a joy?"

Her troubled heart was reflected in her eyes. He wished he could reassure her. "When you have an address, send word here, to the hotel. I'll do the same."

Not knowing what the circumstances were with her godmother, or if she'd change her mind after he left, Harry didn't want to press his address on her. He was pleased when the tension left her lovely face.

"Yes, I'll do that."

He took her hands. "Emma, I do want you to write. Though it may take a while to sort out my life."

She glanced away. "Mrs. Wickham and I are attending the service at St. George's church. She is all a-flutter to show it to me."

"I'll escort you, if you'd like."

Her smile was back, but he thought it was a little forced. He almost couldn't bear to leave her.

"Thank you. I'd enjoy your company."

Harry saw her eyes moisten. His voice strangled. "Don't cry, please."

He wanted to take her in his arms, to follow her to where she'd be living, anything but let her go.

Emma blinked back the tears. "No, I won't. Harry, I'll wait to hear from you."

Mrs. Wickham entered full of cheer. Emma turned her back to the door and walked over to the window as Harry turned to greet her companion.

"Mr. Marsh, has Miss Spencer-Jones told you she'll leave on Monday? Oh, but of course she has. I've written my sister to tell her I shall quit London on the same day. When do you depart?"

"I'll go after church services and dinner." He'd need to send a message to Arch about his change of plans.

"Oh, my, so soon." Mrs. Wickham looked disheartened. "Well, perhaps we will see you when the Season begins. My sister is bringing out her eldest daughter."

Harry smiled amiably. "I shall look forward to it. I'm sorry, but I must go. My valet needs to speak with me."

Mrs. Wickham curtseyed and smiled at him. "So fortunate, Mr. Marsh, that you discovered you are a gentleman of means."

"Yes, indeed," Harry replied. "Miss Spencer-Jones?"

"I'll walk you to the door," Emma said. "I am reliably informed we have an hour before the service at St George's begins."

"I shall come for you." He took her hand and placed a lingering kiss on it.

She gazed up at him. "I shall wait."

Harry bowed and left her standing at the door, a tense smile on her face. At twenty before the hour, he thought of going to her parlor, but decided against it. If the opportunity presented itself, Harry was sure he'd not be able to resist kissing her. That wouldn't be fair to her, not until he knew himself better and knew what he could offer. Instead, he sent a message to her to meet him in the hotel lobby.

Her face lit when she saw him. He returned her smile, and then Mrs. Wickham appeared. They walked the few blocks to St George's. Though he did not see many people he knew, there were some. He'd need to go home quickly.

"That was a very good sermon, I thought," Mrs. Wickham said as they made their way back to the hotel after the service.

Harry paid little attention to her. The back of his neck prickled, and he searched for the reason. Reynolds lurked near a corner. "Emma, keep your eyes ahead. Reynolds is here."

"Oh, no. I'd hoped he'd cease following me."

"Apparently not. I'll stay as long as I can. You must remain inside after I leave."

She nodded. "Yes, but I have some things I need to collect in the morning."

"Send a messenger. I'll arrange for extra outriders to accompany you to your godmother's house. You can tell her your father required them."

"I will, Harry. Thank you."

"One more thing. I'll leave from the alley behind the hotel. That way, he'll think I'm still here."

Emma's gaze met his. He hated to leave her, but he had to go home before the news that he wasn't dead preceded his arrival. He'd seen too many people now. "I know you are well able to take care of yourself, but please, for my sake, because I cannot be here with you, take care."

She pressed her lips together and nodded. "I will."

He had to believe they'd meet again. He needed to see her. Harry tightened his grip on her hand. "Thank you. I'll come to you as soon as I'm able."

"I know you will." She closed her eyes for a moment, and when she opened them, they brimmed with tears. "Harry, I'll miss you."

It was all he could do not to drag her into his arms. Reaching out, he caressed her cheek with one finger. "I'll miss you as well."

That afternoon, Emma went with him to the back door of the hotel. He held her hand until he was forced to release it.

Farley gave Harry directions to his home. They were different than the directions to the cottage he remembered.

"Farley, there is someplace I need to stop first. Go to Marsh Hill, and wait until I come."

"We'll be at the gate," Farley said.

"That will do." Harry started his horses. Once he reached the first of the large posting houses, he'd see if his father still stationed his cattle on the road.

Sunday, November 13th, the cottage, Kent

After church and Sunday dinner with his family, Sebastian and Anna each got picnic baskets from their cooks and drove to the cottage. She'd told her father she planned to spend the rest of the day and evening with her betrothed. Papa would have assumed she meant at the Priory.

Sebastian's lips touched hers, and she responded eagerly. Anna had brought the book and insisted they try the positions one by one. Each time they made love, he asked if she was all right, and she assured him she was. She might not be able to walk on the morrow, but right now, she was wonderful. Everything was what she'd hoped it would be.

Anna lay beneath him, her skin dewed. His large body half covered her, and his breath came in short pants. She writhed and cried out as she reached for the sun to engulf her. She held him tightly. Just a few short weeks ago, the idea that she'd be like this with him had never entered her mind. She laughed at her naivety. She hadn't even known what the pictures in the book meant. A burble of laughter rose within her.

"What are you giggling about?" He shifted her. The hair of his chest rubbed tantalizingly against her nipples.

"Did you say something?" How she loved his chest.

"Anna, where are you?" he asked good-naturedly.

She hadn't seen him laugh and smile this much in years.

"I'm here with you in a way I never knew existed before," she said, before drifting into a satisfied sleep.

When she awoke, it was dark. The shutters were closed, and the cottage warm. Sebastian kissed her and rose, putting more wood on the fire.

"Are you sore yet?" he asked, with concern.

Anna moved, and muscles she hadn't known she possessed ached. "Maybe."

"Eat."

Anna opened her mouth, and he gently placed a morsel of cheese between her lips. She chewed, savoring the taste. "Once we're married, how often will we be able to be alone like this?"

"We'll have to make time," Sebastian said. "Here, drink some wine."

She pushed herself up on to the pillows. "I could stay here forever."

He chuckled deeply. "I love you more than I thought I could love another being. You were right to make me wait."

She smiled at him and licked the corner of his lips. "I love you. You were right not to marry me when I was seventeen. What time is it?"

"Past eight o'clock." Rutherford suddenly lifted his head and canted it toward the door. "Did you hear that?"

A carriage. "Yes." Anna sat up. "Who would be out here at this time of night? You don't think it's Percy, do you?"

"Not even he's that stupid."

What if it was the London gent? "What do you want to do?"

"With the fireplace going, we can't very well pretend we're not here. Get dressed."

Anna took her chemise and stays from him. Thank goodness stays were one of the front-lacing ones. She donned her gown. It seemed so long since she'd been dressed. Being with him naked seemed the most natural thing in the world.

Rutherford buttoned her gown before going to the door. Anna hurried to stand beside him when he opened the door. A large man got down from a curricle.

Anna's heart stopped. *Harry?* It couldn't be. *But it was.* Tears of joy sprang to her eyes. "*Harry, oh, Harry! Thank God!*"

Heedless of her bare feet, she ran out the door and flung herself at him. Her brother enveloped her in arms as strong as Sebastian's, but completely different. "Harry. Where have you been? We—we all thought you were dead. Sebastian, come look, it's Harry."

Sebastian walked forward and clasped her brother's shoulder. His voice was gruff. "Thank God. Thank God. You're alive."

* * *

Rutherford and Anna. *At the cottage?* A red fog came over Harry. There was only one thing to do with a woman at the cottage. He put her aside and roared, *"Anna, stay there!"*

He knocked Rutherford's arm off his shoulder. "What the hell are you doing here?"

Not waiting for an answer, Harry aimed his fist at his former friend's jaw. Rutherford ducked. The coward didn't even try to hit him back. "You'll meet me for this, you rogue."

Anna screamed and grabbed Harry's arm. He tried to shake her off as he went after Rutherford again. "I'll deal with you later," he shouted and addressed Rutherford. "You, fight like a man."

Harry lunged at Rutherford.

Anna yelled something.

Rutherford's face flushed, and he brought up his fists.

She let go of Harry and ran around to step in front of Rutherford. *"Harry, Sebastian, stop right now!* Harry, listen to me. Sebastian and I are getting married."

Rutherford tried to move her aside, but she turned on him. "Don't you dare hit him, and no one is meeting anyone." Her chest heaved as she narrowed her eyes at both of them. "Calm down, both of you."

"Anna, get away from him," Harry growled.

"No. I will not have my brother and my *affianced husband* fighting."

Harry stepped back, feeling like he'd been doused with cold water. "Husband?"

"Affianced husband. The banns were read today. We will marry in two weeks."

He glanced at Rutherford. "Is she telling the truth?"

Anna scowled. "Of course I am."

"Yes, she's telling the truth. I'd marry her sooner if she'd let me."

Harry rubbed his forehead. He'd be damned if he was going to apologize. His body trembled, but the rush of anger was starting to fade.

Anna grabbed his hand, tugging. "Come inside. We have food and wine. You must be hungry."

He allowed her to drag him into the room and sat in the chair she pulled out facing the fireplace. Harry dropped his now throbbing head in his hands. Her fingers squeezed his shoulder.

"Harry, where have you been?"

He lowered his hands and gazed at her. Huntley was right. The picture didn't do her justice. Anna's cheeks were still flushed, and there was a mulish cast to her chin. The gaze that searched his face had a maturity that hadn't been there before. She'd grown up, and he'd missed it. His heart clenched hard.

Anna studied him for a few moments. "Harry?"

"I lost my memory. I'm just now getting it back."

Anna glanced at Sebastian. "Tea. The water is hot."

He nodded.

"Well, you obviously remember me."

"You were one of my first memories, but I didn't know until recently you were my sister." He stopped, unable to continue.

She knelt beside him. "What do you remember? Start from the beginning."

He told them about the ship, about his wife and baby. Tears started in his eyes.

Anna blinked back her own tears and grabbed his hand. "Go on."

"It was months after her death when I finally remembered my last name and even longer before I knew where I lived. My father-in-law said I could stay there, but encouraged me to find my life. And—and here I am."

Anna didn't wipe the tears streaming down her cheeks.

"I ran into Huntley in London. He helped me. My clothes were not quite up to snuff. Farley came back. Devil knew me right away. I came from London as quickly as I could."

Sebastian placed a cup in front of Harry. "Your father discovered you hadn't died at Badajoz. The Home Office had been told you went down in a shipwreck. Therefore, I told your father and Anna. Harry, you are the only one to have survived."

Harry shook his head. "I don't understand Badajoz."

"Do you remember your job?" Rutherford asked.

"No."

"You and I are Intelligencer intelligence Officers for the Home Office," Sebastian said. "We wanted to do something to help the war cause, but neither of us could leave England for any length of time due to our responsibilities."

Sebastian pushed the cup into Harry's hands. "You took a job in

France whilst I was away. It was only to have been for six months. You hadn't told your family exactly where you'd gone. They just knew it was something for the government, so Jamison decided to let it out that you'd died at Badajoz. The time periods matched."

"Jamison?" Anna asked.

Sebastian frowned. "Yes, why?"

Anna poured a cup of tea. "That's the name of my contact."

"Your contact?" He stared at her. "What do you mean?"

She shrugged. "I didn't tell you because it was supposed to be a secret."

Sebastian closed his eyes. "Would you like to tell me about it now?"

She looked from Harry's curious gaze to Rutherford's not quite patient one. "Well," she said, "when Harry left me in charge of the smuggling gang . . ." When Harry jumped, Anna stopped. He didn't say anything so she went on. "I was to report any problems I couldn't handle to this Lord Jamison. Harry gave me the codes."

Sebastian fixed Harry with a gimlet eye. "Harry Marsh, you are the most irresponsible person I know, to have put a nineteen-year-old in charge of a smuggling gang."

Harry rubbed a hand over his face.

"You weren't irresponsible," Anna declared. "You trained me. You knew I could do it. Marshes are invincible."

He glanced at her. "Marshes are invincible. I taught you that."

"Yes." Anna hurried back to him. "Do you remember?"

Harry took a sip of the tea. It was too sweet. Was it made for shock or because he used to drink it that way? He regarded Anna. "I remember a young child sitting on my lap—you. Then I remember you, older. We were in a garden."

She nodded her head. "Yes, I was seventeen. Mama decided I was old enough to come out. I was scared. It's what you said to me before I left."

"Huntley said I wouldn't let anyone near you," Harry mused.

Anna grinned ruefully. "No, not until we had it out."

He glanced at the rumpled bed, then at Rutherford, and frowned.

"No, I didn't start courting Anna until later. I was helping you keep the wolves at bay," he assured Harry.

Harry's voice tensed. "When did all this begin?"

"We decided to marry just recently. The banns were read today,"

Anna reminded him. "Harry, he . . . we didn't . . . Sebastian wouldn't . . . not until I agreed to marry him. We've loved each other for a long time. There were just problems we needed to work out."

Anna turned her gaze to Rutherford and back to Harry. "Let us take you home. Papa will want to see you."

She started to laugh, and Harry thought she was going to have vapors.

"Sebastian, oh dear, I'm not nearly as eligible as you thought, and you won't get the cottage now that Harry has returned."

Her betrothed smiled. "Your wealth never mattered to me."

Harry watched as his friend wrapped his arms around Anna.

"You are every bit as eligible, and now I have my best friend back." Rutherford stopped. "Sweetheart, you need to put your hair up before we go."

"I suppose it wouldn't do for anyone to suspect."

Rutherford raised a brow. "I'd get my wedding faster."

Harry frowned. Rutherford was right. "An excellent idea. In fact, you should marry as soon as possible."

Anna searched for the pins and deftly wound her hair into a knot. "No."

"What do you mean no?" Harry scowled.

"Don't snarl at me. We cannot marry until Mama is here."

He closed his eyes for a moment. "Huntley said she and Papa had been having problems. She's not in London. Where else would she be but here?"

Anna put on her hat. "At a house party."

Harry took a large drink of tea. "Maybe you'd better tell me what's going on before we go."

Anna stared at him for a few moments. "Mama wouldn't believe you were dead and insisted on keeping everything as it was. She wouldn't even allow me to drive your curricle because you hadn't given me permission before you left. I think she just became over-protective."

Harry shook his head, trying to make sense of what she'd said. "That wasn't very fair. You're a devilish fine whip."

Anna smiled gently. "Let me finish. Papa became obsessed with your death. He wrote everyone he could think of your death. Mama is rarely here these days, and Papa won't go to London. Though he's ready to go to the Home Office and demand the truth, even though Sebastian already told Papa everything he knew."

Harry was still for several moments. The crackle of the fire filled the silence. "Jamison wouldn't have liked that."

"Have you remembered something?" Sebastian asked.

Like pieces of a puzzle, the scenario started falling into place. "There was an Englishman in the Foreign Office working for the French. He was being paid in gold coins. I went over to find the courier and intercept him. When I delivered the payment to the gentleman, we'd have him."

Harry rubbed his forehead as it all came back to him. "Everything was going well until the blow. The ship hit something, and all hell broke loose. I helped as much as I could before I was knocked overboard. The next thing I remember is being on the beach."

He raised his head and stared at Anna. "I left you in charge of my smuggling gang?"

"Sebastian was gone. Who else could you trust?"

Harry rubbed his face again. He'd clearly almost walked in on his best friend and his sister making love, and they wanted to talk about the smuggling gang. Were they trying to divert his attention from what they were doing? He clenched his jaw. "I don't understand why we're discussing them now."

Anna stamped her foot. "Because we've been approached about bringing in French spies. Sebastian . . ."

Harry interrupted. "She was always the only person who could call you that."

Rutherford grinned. "She still is."

"Will you listen?" Anna asked impatiently. "Sebastian was called back to find out if there were any spies trying to come in. We found out about each other accidentally, and now we're working together."

Harry regarded Rutherford, who coughed.

"Working with her," he said, "has always been easier than working against her. You have no idea how glad I am you're back."

Anna looked from Harry to Sebastian. "Oh, no you don't. You're not cutting me out. Harry can take over the gang again after we catch the spies."

Harry laughed, softly at first then with great gawps. "Lady

Rutherford, smuggling gang leader. Anna, have you forgotten Rutherford is the magistrate?"

Anna dropped her jaw and turned to her intended. "You never said a word."

"You might not have accepted me."

Harry laughed even harder.

Rutherford scowled. "By the way, Harry, you want to know why we're here? She found your book."

Wiping his eyes, another memory niggled. Harry quickly sobered, hoping he was wrong. "Which book?"

His friend raised a supercilious brow.

Damn. So much for wishful thinking. "*That* book?"

"*Yes.*"

"*Oh good God.*" Now he really didn't want to know what had been going on.

Chapter 19

They were almost at Marsh Hill when Harry remembered he'd forgotten to congratulate his sister and Rutherford. "I don't think I wished you happy. I am glad for you. I was just a little taken aback at first."

"Harry," Anna said.

"No, little one, I'm not going to interfere. You're an adult and a betrothed woman." Even if she was his little sister, he couldn't very well complain when he'd bedded Marcella every chance he got, before and after they'd married. He'd not be a hypocrite, nor would he rock the fragile boat they were all on. "Rutherford, how did your mother take the news?"

"About as I expected she would," he said drily. "She already had another match in mind before I told her I planned to marry Anna."

Unfortunately, that wasn't a surprise. Lady Rutherford had never liked the Marsh family.

When they reached the gate, the traveling coach was pulled up to the side of the drive. "It's Farley," Harry said. "I told him to wait for me."

The coach started forward. Harry waited for Anna and Rutherford. "I forgot to tell you about my greeting at Marsh House. Minton cried, Mrs. Minton attached herself to me, and Cook fell over in a faint."

Anna gave a whoop of laughter. "Well, don't expect it to be much better here. Harry, we've all missed you so much."

"Wish I could say the same. I didn't remember even *you* until a week or so ago. I hope my arrival doesn't give anyone apoplexy."

"I'll go in and prepare Papa," Anna said. "You two sort everything else out."

"That's probably a good idea," Harry replied.

When they'd brought the carriages to a halt, Harry jumped down and helped Anna descend. After she ran inside, lights started illuminating the windows. He glanced at Rutherford. "How has she been?"

"Anna is the one who's held the family together," he replied. "She is the perfect lady in London and a hoyden here. Except for several months after your death, when we sort of propped each other up, I'm afraid I wasn't much help. I knew she wanted to marry, and I kept putting it off."

"What changed?" Harry asked.

"Lady Phoebe Stanhope and Lord Marcus Finley married."

"Huntley mentioned that, but I'd no memory of them at the time. That's a match I wouldn't have thought to make."

Rutherford grinned wryly. "You weren't the only one. Finley was determined it would be her or no one, but that's a story for later."

"You were still hiding behind Lady Phoebe's skirts?"

Rutherford nodded. "Yes. Though after I saw how happy Marcus was, I felt as if I was missing something. Of course, I also thought Anna would immediately fall in with my desires."

"Huntley said she'd lead you a merry dance."

"He was right." Rutherford paused for a bit as if deciding what to say next. "There were some concerns we needed to address. Your little sister drives a hard bargain."

Harry was getting a very good idea how shrewd his sister was. "For some reason, that doesn't surprise me."

Rutherford nudged Harry. "Sir William."

Harry followed the direction Rutherford pointed. Anna held his father's arm as they stood on the front steps of the house, then walked toward him.

Tears stung Harry's eyelids, and he slowly went to meet his sire. "Papa," he said, hugging his father.

"Anna told me a little of what happened," Papa said. "Why didn't you send word?"

"There were so many things I didn't remember. I needed time. By the time I reached London, the memories started coming faster. Then I ran into Rutherford and Anna this evening, and they flooded back."

"Sebastian, come with me." Anna held out her hand. "Humphrey will take the gigs. Mrs. Ledster is making Harry's room ready, and I need to speak with Cook." She whispered, "Papa won't want you to see him cry."

"Should I leave?"

"No, no one wants you to leave." She glanced at Harry and Papa. "They need a little time alone."

Harry ran the gambit of hugs and kisses, before finally reaching the manor house stairs. Anna led them into the dining room, where a cold collation was being set out.

"Cook is heating up some soup as well," Anna said as they took their places.

"Aunt Lillian?" Harry asked the elegant lady before him.

Tears glistened in her eyes, and she hugged him. "Yes, Harry. I'm overjoyed to see you home and in good health."

He glanced at Anna, wondering why their Aunt Lillian was there. She mouthed, "I'll tell you later."

"I don't understand the reason we have all the staff in here," Lillian said briskly.

"No, let them stay," Harry said. "Anna and Rutherford have heard most of my tale, but I'd rather relate it only once more."

Leaving out the part about his work, he merely said he had been on his way home from France. He told them about Marcella and how she'd nursed him back to health, giving silent thanks that his memory hadn't returned while she was still alive. As accepting as his family was and as good and kind as she'd been, she would never have felt comfortable in the more rarefied world of the *ton*.

After they'd eaten, and he'd once again been welcomed home, Harry, his family, and Rutherford repaired to his father's study where he related his mission to his father.

"What happened to the gold?" Rutherford asked.

Harry uttered a short laugh. "I still have it. Or most of it. It's what I've been living on. I think you know almost everything now."

He debated for only a few moments before telling them about Emma. "I met a lady traveling up to London. She's from the West Indies and knows Marcus Finley. Once she's settled, she'll write Grillon's with her direction." He paused. "I plan to go see her."

"Harry." Anna's eyes had popped open when he'd mentioned Emma. "Tell us more about this lady."

He smiled, but shook his head. "Not yet, little one."

She fidgeted in her chair like she used to when she was young. "But, Harry . . ."

The clock chimed one o'clock.

He yawned. "I'm for bed. It's been a long week and an even longer day."

He added his entreaties to those of his father and Anna's that Rutherford spend the night with them. Anna left to have a room made up for him and send a note to the Priory.

Harry wondered briefly where she would sleep tonight and decided he didn't need to know. He'd promised himself he wouldn't interfere. He wondered what Rutherford thought about Anna's involvement with the smugglers.

November 14th, 1814, Marsh Hill, Kent

Rutherford listened as Anna slid almost silently through the connecting doors into the chamber she'd assigned to him. The one on the opposite side of a parlor from her room in the children's wing. She appeared almost ghostly in a long flowing night rail. Her dark chestnut curls trailed over her shoulders to her waist. His fingers tingled as he looked forward to spearing them through her long, silky hair again. She slowly drew her gown over her head and tossed it onto a chair. Rutherford threw the covers back to welcome her as she climbed in on her hands and knees, cat-like in her grace. She touched her lips to his.

"Take me again." Her voice was soft, low, and sultry.

Rutherford groaned. He could be ten times as tired as he was now and still not be able to resist her. "How do you want it?" he breathed into her ear.

"Any way you choose."

He lay on his side, turning her back to his chest, and entered her. She drew a breath, and he covered her mouth, remembering her lusty cries. "Sweetheart, we're not in the cottage. You'll have to be quiet."

Anna nodded.

"Do you want me to remove my hand?"

She shook her head.

Rutherford plunged into her soft warmth, then bent her forward so he could go deeper. Her body became almost rigid before she gave herself over to the delight. Anna grabbed his hand and held it fast against her mouth when she screamed.

He took all she could give him before he fractured. He cupped one perfect breast and drew her closer to him.

"Sebastian, I'm so happy. Life is almost perfect now."

He nuzzled her hair, breathing in the fresh scent of the sea. "Yes."

Perfect, now that Harry wasn't trying to kill Rutherford, and he had his best friend back. He should feel guilty about keeping Anna here in his bed, but she *had* come to him.

Her voice interrupted his musings. "I wonder what the lady he met is like."

Rutherford chuckled quietly. "I'm sure you'll find out sooner than he wants to tell you."

He traced her lips with his thumb. She was smiling. Harry had no idea how formidable his little sister had become in his absence. "Good night, my love."

Anna twisted to kiss him. "Good night. I love you."

Rutherford awoke just before dawn to Anna rocking against him. He grew hard and slipped into her wet heat. Her sounds were soft and breathy and a low keening noise emitted from her as she came for him.

He tightened his hold on her, and they slept until a knock on the connecting door woke them.

"Miss, you'd best come out now."

"I'll be right there, Lizzy."

Rutherford rolled her over to face him. "I hope she's discreet."

"She's Kev's sister. Kiss me, I have to go."

"Kev's sister?"

"I'll explain later." Anna touched her lips to his, and the desire to keep her almost overwhelmed him. She threw on her nightgown.

"I'll see you at breakfast." Anna smiled and blew him a kiss.

Rutherford watched her close the door and sent a prayer of

thanks for last night. He could hardly wait for the wedding. He wanted to spend the rest of his life waking up with her.

The door from the corridor opened, and Robertson entered his room. Rutherford would have to tell his valet to start knocking.

He met Anna in the breakfast room and took in the large amount of eggs, ham, and toast on her plate. "No kippers?"

"No, I don't like them." Anna waved her fork to indicate he was to take the seat next to her.

He pointed at her plate. "Are you always this famished in the morning?"

She wrinkled her forehead a little. "I've always had a good appetite, though I'm not sure when I was last this ravenous."

"If I have anything to say about it," he said as he walked to the sideboard, "you'll be this hungry a great deal of the time."

"What do you mean?"

He grinned. "I shall join you in a large breakfast. With men, it's not so noticeable."

She drew her brows together.

"My love, it's from our activities."

A smile dawned on her face. Anna was sipping tea when Harry joined them.

"Now that we're all here," Rutherford said, "I'll tell you about the note I received from Jamison. He's sending down helpers as soon as we notify him of the date the shipment's arriving."

Anna set down her cup. "We probably won't receive much advance warning."

"No doubt you're correct." Rutherford nodded. "I'll mention that to Jamison. It would be a shame if they don't get here in time to partake in the fun."

"I'll stand watch, as usual," Anna said. "With the two of you and the smugglers, I don't see any reason you cannot take them yourselves, if need be."

"My love, I'd prefer you not be alone." Hell, she'd better not be there at all. "There's the second man to think about, and we don't know what his roll is. He may decide to observe as well."

Anna gazed at him for a long moment, worrying her plump bottom lip. Finally, she said, "I won't argue with you, Sebastian. Though, remember, they won't have advance notice of *where* the shipment is arriving. I'll have the signals given as before, just prior to our readiness to accept delivery."

"I suggest Rutherford stay with you," Harry said. "Except for Kev, the smugglers don't know he's involved, and it might be a good idea to keep it like that."

"And it will get you back in with the gang," Anna said thoughtfully. "Sebastian, what do you think?"

"I agree." He grinned. "I'd rather keep watch over you than a smuggler. If anything were to happen . . ."

She patted his hand, and her eyes twinkled with excitement. "This is quite like old times, with the three of us together. What shall we do today?"

"I have to go back to the Priory and check on my sisters. With Mother away for a few days, they need to be reminded they're still being watched."

"Didn't you ask her to come straight back?"

"I did, but she had a friend she wanted to visit in Town."

"I'm supposed to meet with your housekeeper today," Anna said.

"That's right. I'd forgotten. You can get to know my sisters better as well."

"Where is Lady Rutherford?" Harry asked curiously.

"Gone to fetch a young lady. Some granddaughter of a duke. Do you want to come with us?"

Harry shook his head. "No, I'll visit with Papa for a while. How long do you think you'll be?"

"Most of the morning," Anna said.

"Can you meet me at the cottage after luncheon?"

She smiled. "I think we can manage that."

Rutherford raised a brow. "Carriage or horses?"

Anna gave him a chagrined look. "We'll ride over to the Priory. If need be, we can take your curricle."

After she left, he turned to Harry. "Percy Blanchard has become something of a problem."

Harry sipped his tea. "I remember Percy as somewhat of a man milliner. What did he do?"

Rutherford told him about Lady Blanchard's telling anyone who would listen that Anna had no choice but to marry Percy and of

Percy's attempted assault on Anna at the cottage. "He was watching her. It's the only way he could have found her alone. Fortunately, she had sent a message to me before she left."

Harry's face had hardened. "I don't know whether to be pleased about Anna's intrepidity, or find Blanchard and kill him."

"I already gave him quite a beating," Rutherford said. "You're welcome to do it as well."

"Let's see what he does," Harry replied. "Now that he knows she is marrying you, he might give it up."

"I wish I could be as sure as you," Rutherford said as he poured more tea. "Tell me about the lady you met?"

Harry gave a bark of laughter. "What is it about betrothed men that makes all of you want to help your fellows follow the same path?"

Rutherford sobered. "Is it too soon for you?"

"It's not so much that as I want to know who I am first." Harry ran a hand over his face. "Until then, I'm not in a position to offer marriage again."

Anna glided back into the room. "You two look serious. What are you discussing?"

Rutherford stood and put his arm around her. She was his now, and he didn't care who saw him. "Marriage. Harry, we'll see you in a few hours."

Harry bussed Anna on the cheek. "I used to tell you to be good."

"You can still tell me to be good." Anna reached up to return his kiss. "I'll see you soon."

"Wait," he said. "It just occurred to me that in two weeks I'll lose you."

Anna glanced at the ceiling. "Harry, I'll be right down the road, and you'll have Sebastian as a brother."

"We'll keep a room for you," Rutherford teased.

"That's a promise I'll make sure you'll keep," Harry retorted.

Rutherford caught up to Anna in the corridor leading to the side door and hooked his arm around her waist. "I love you."

Anna stopped. "And I you. More than I ever knew. It's a different feeling than I thought it would be."

He bent his head and kissed her. "I know what you mean. This has been very much of a revelation."

Anna tilted her head. "I wonder if Harry is really interested in the lady he met."

"Match-making already?"

"I just want him to be happy."

Rutherford touched his lips tenderly to hers. "As do I. I want our children to play together."

She placed her hands on his cheeks and opened her mouth to his questing tongue. "That's what I want as well."

Lifting his head, he scoffed. "What you are going to do is scandalize the servants."

Wistfully, Harry watched his sister and Rutherford leave the room and wondered if he could have the partnership they had. He thought of Emma. Whether she'd like it here, living with his mother and father, or if they'd have to buy a property nearby. His father had other estates, but now that Harry had found his family again, he wanted to be close to them.

In taking up the threads of his life, Harry realized he'd changed, yet how much was as yet unknown. Whether this was his personality, or if he was now a combination of the man he'd been for the past two years and the man he was before his memory loss, or . . . *Damn.*

There was the problem of his parents as well. The troubles they were having, because of him, had begun to gnaw. Had he been selfish in accepting the last mission?

"I'd have thought Anna and Rutherford would be down."

His father's statement brought Harry out of his reverie. He grinned. "They've been and gone to check on Rutherford's sisters. Lady Rutherford is in London for a few days."

"You know," Papa said as he took a plate, "I would never say anything to Anna or Rutherford, but I am concerned about how Lady Rutherford will get along with your sister."

Harry sipped his tea. "I've always thought it strange how she and Mama never got along. Whereas you and old Lord Rutherford were great friends, as are Rutherford and I." Harry shook his head. "Anna's become a strong woman, and, in Rutherford, she'll have a husband who supports her. She'll be fine."

Harry's father took a seat. "She's not much like your mother."

"No. Huntley said she was like me. I didn't understand it at the time, but now I do."

"She is very like your grandmamma," Lillian said from the doorway. "It's a shame Mama died before you could know her well. Both of you take after her. Anna is lucky to have found her match." Lillian took a plate and nodded toward Papa. "Your father told me to leave Anna alone and she'd bring it about."

Harry laughed lightly. "She does seem to get what she wants."

"I will say that for her." Lillian raised her brows in a question. "Harry, dear, what do *you* want?"

"Right now," he replied, "I want to get to know myself. Part of me is still in a fog." He paused. "Then I want what Anna and Rutherford have."

"Would you consider standing for Parliament in the next election?" his father asked. "I don't really want to go back, and the man who took my place is not well thought of. I'd like to keep the seat in the family."

Harry cocked his head and stared at the wall. It would give him an occupation beyond the estate, and he'd always been interested in politics. "Yes, I'd like to stand, if the party will have me. Will you try to hide my memory loss?"

"No. You just have to show it's affected nothing else," his father said firmly. "It would be better if you marry. You cannot be considered for any senior positions without a wife."

"I see," Harry mused. "If all goes well, I just may be able to accommodate you."

He wondered how long it would take before he saw Emma again.

Chapter 20

Later that evening, Anna laughed so hard she had a stitch in her side, and Aunt Lillian had tears in her eyes. They were playing charades in the drawing room. Cece was bouncing around trying to make them understand who she was.

Earlier that day, Anna had begged off the house inspection so she and Sebastian could spend more time with Harry. They'd gone into town, and Harry had been mobbed by people welcoming him home. She was happier and more content than she'd been in years. Her brother and her betrothed had come to some sort of understanding. She'd half expected Sebastian to resist her plans to continue working with the smugglers. She was glad he hadn't. It would have been a serious problem for her.

Sebastian agreed with her suggestion to bring the girls and their governess to the Hill until Lady Rutherford returned. They'd dined *en famille* and played games after dinner. Together, the men kept the girls well entertained.

Althea came to sit beside her and said in her quiet way, "I've never seen my brother act so silly."

Anna put her arm around her. "It's been a long time. Harry and Sebastian were my protectors and my fun-makers when I was a child. Once, when Percy Blanchard hurt my feelings, Sebastian threw him into the fountain."

"Why do you call him that?"

Anna shrugged. "I've always called him by his first name. Although for years, it was Bastian. I couldn't pronounce it properly, you see."

"We never have fun like this at the Priory," Althea said wistfully.

Anna hugged her. "We'll have to see what we can do about that."

She broke into laughter as Harry scooped Cece up and carried her horsy-back around the room.

Althea glanced up. "I think I'm going to like having you live with us."

Anna hugged her tighter. "I know I'm going to like living with you."

The next thing she knew, Sebastian lifted her in his arms. Anna shrieked like a child and turned to see Harry lift Althea up.

Anna put her arms around Rutherford's neck and kissed him. "We need to get them to bed."

"We need to get to bed," he retorted.

"Hmm." She smiled and glanced at her father and aunt. "Not for a while yet."

Harry and Sebastian chased the two younger girls up the stairs to their room. Althea chose to walk sedately next to Anna.

"I know my sisters have already asked, but when did you decide you wanted to marry Ruhy?"

"Oh, I have wanted to marry him since I was a child and had an idea of what marriage was." Anna stopped for a moment. "Yet it was something else entirely, a spark, a fire that neither of us could ignore. That's what changed everything." Anna took Althea's arm and continued to the corridor. "My dearest friend, Phoebe, told me about it. When you feel a sparkle, well, maybe more of a jolt—as if someone takes your breath away each and every time he touches you—that is the man you should look at more closely."

"My mama is only concerned with title and money," Althea said.

"Enough money to live on is not to be dismissed lightly. Title"—Anna shrugged lightly—"I would not have married without love. You go to bed, and I'll see you in the morning."

Althea kissed Anna's cheek. "Good night, Anna."

"Good night, Althea."

Anna kissed Cece and Eloisa good night as well.

"That was fun tonight," Eloisa said.

"I'm glad you had a good time."

"I never knew Ruhy could be so much fun," Cece added.

"We'll have to convince Harry to visit often," Anna said as she drew the covers up over the younger girls. "Sebastian is always funnier when he's with Harry. Good night."

Anna returned to the drawing room just as her father and aunt decided to retire. After wishing them a good night, she joined her brother and her betrothed.

Sebastian held his hand out to her. She took it and sat next to him. "I'm so glad the girls had a good time. It's strange to think you've never played with them. You two played with me all the time."

Rutherford rubbed his chin. "Playing wasn't encouraged at the Priory. Something we'll have to change."

"Yes, we will." She turned to Harry. "You, my brother, must visit often. We can't have little girls growing up without knowing how to play."

"And our children." Rutherford took her hand.

Anna met his molten silver gaze. "And our children."

"It's late. You two should be in bed as well," Harry said.

Sebastian lifted her in his arms. "Harry, good night."

Anna hung her head back to see him. "Good night, Harry."

He laughed. "Good night to the both of you."

Rutherford dropped her off at her room and went to his own. "How long will you be?"

Anna pursed her lips. "Give me about twenty minutes. Lizzy needs to comb my hair and braid it."

He reached up and curled one loose strand around his finger. "Leave it. I want to take it down."

Anna smiled softly and shook her head. "Will you really comb it?"

His eyes softened. "Yes."

"Very well."

Sebastian started down the corridor and stopped. "Have you heard from your mother?"

"Goodness, what made you think of that now?"

He shrugged his shoulders. "Thinking of mine, probably."

"Papa has," Anna said. "She's over the moon about our betrothal and on her way here. Of course, she doesn't know about Harry."

Sebastian came back to her and wrapped her in his arms.

"Papa sent a courier immediately after we told him, and she

replied immediately. He received the note while we were out today."
Anna couldn't stop her brows from knitting. "I don't know how
long it will take her to arrive. Oh, Sebastian, I hope they'll be able
to mend their marriage."

He touched his forehead to hers. "You know she wasn't always
this way."

"No. She changed so much when she received the news of
Harry's death. Papa as well." She pressed her lips together.

Sebastian gathered Anna to him. "I hope they can forgive each
other. I think they were very much in love."

Anna nodded. "Yes, they were." She stood on her tiptoes and
kissed him. "The hard part is that they each feel betrayed by the
other. I'll see you in a bit."

She couldn't imagine starting a marriage without love. How
hard it must have been for her parents.

Lizzy was ready to help her change. Once Anna was in her
nightgown, Lizzy waited.

"I'm leaving it up tonight," Anna said airily.

Lizzy's eyes grew round.

Anna wrinkled her forehead and looked everywhere but at her
maid. "Yes, well, if he enjoys combing it, there is one less thing for
you to worry about."

Lizzy grabbed her hands and jigged. "Miss, it's so nice to see
him in love with you. Everyone's talking about it."

"Oh, no." Anna closed her eyes for a moment. "That is just the
sort of thing that will set Lady Rutherford's teeth on edge."

Lizzy shrugged. "But you'll be Lady Rutherford soon."

"Well, that is true. Still, I do not want to be in my mother-in-
law's black book."

"Miss Anna. You were in her book when Lord Rutherford decided to marry you. There's not a thing you can do about it."

Anna sighed. "I'll see you in the morning."

Lizzy smiled broadly and left the room.

Anna picked up her comb and the bowl for her hairpins and
walked through the parlor to Sebastian. He stood naked, staring out
the window. She marveled at his body. All hard muscle and long
lines.

Dark curls covered his chest and ran down to his groin. His shaft began to rise as he turned to greet her. *All muscle and all mine.* Anna couldn't keep a wicked smile from her face as she sat down at the dressing table and waited.

Sebastian strode over to her and bent to kiss her neck.

"No, you said you wanted to take care of my hair. You must do that first."

Silently, he removed the pins and placed them in the bowl. Then he took the comb from her hand and began at the ends, deftly working up to her crown. Anna reveled in his touch.

"Do I have to braid it? I love your hair when it's down."

Their gazes met in the mirror. Contentment and love filled her. "No. If you want my hair down, down it will stay."

Sebastian lifted her up and carried her to the bed. "You're my love and my life. I don't know what I'd do if anything happened to you."

He unbuttoned her nightgown and pushed it open, revealing her breasts. The air was cold, but her breasts heated, wanting his touch. He cupped them and weighed them as if trying to decide what to do, then like a feather, his lips grazed one nipple. Desire thrummed through her and wet heat pooled between her legs. She panted, wanting him to take her, fill her. He moved to the other breast, pushing her gown over her hips. Anna swallowed, her voice sounding harsh. "Take me now."

"Not yet.

"But I'm ready."

"Umm." One hand moved down to her curls.

Anna widened her legs and rocked, encouraging him to enter her. He slipped one finger inside. She uttered a breathy cry. Her skin flushed. Just as she could feel her release, he stopped. "Sebastian!"

"You'll have to wait."

Anna opened her mouth to protest, and he brought his hard lips down upon hers, his tongue surging into her mouth. When she moved to wrap her arms around him, Sebastian captured both her hands in one of his and raised them over her head. His mouth left hers and placed soft kisses on her jaw and neck. She tried to open her legs but he'd trapped them. She wiggled desperately.

Sebastian chuckled deeply and moved to her breasts. Flames shot through her as his mouth wandered over her stomach and nestled between her legs. With her hands now free, she tried to urge him up. He licked, and she grabbed the sheets and arched into him as he played.

Anna thought she'd die of need before he was finished. "Oh, now," she pleaded. He rose up and entered her slowly, then withdrew.

"Keep your eyes open. I want to watch you."

"Now, Sebastian, now. Please."

She tried to grab him, anything to make him enter her more fully. He captured her mouth at the same time as he plunged into her sheath. Flames engulfed her. She wrapped her legs around him, urging and pushing. When she opened her eyes, his gray ones, dark with silver around them, bore into her.

"Stay with me, love."

He teased her over and over again, bringing her to the crest and taking her back down again. Anna sobbed, wanting release.

He pumped into her again, then twice more. "Now."

Their wet bodies trembled. His mouth covered hers. When she gave herself over to the inferno, he tumbled in after her.

Rutherford collapsed to her side and drew her to him. His fingers lightly pushed back the damp curls clinging to her face. Anna's chest heaved as she gasped for air.

He knew he'd pushed her. He'd exposed his heart and soul to her, if she could but see it. He'd never expected the depth of feeling he had for Anna or the vulnerability that came with it.

"Are you all right?" He propped her up and held a glass of wine to her lips. "I wanted to show you how I feel, how much I love and need you."

Anna's breathing gradually slowed. She sipped the wine and gazed up at him, her beautiful blue eyes dark with passion. "You did." She reached up to touch his face. "And I'm glad. We've changed again, haven't we? I mean this was even deeper than before."

"Yes."

"Do your chambers at the Priory have a bathing room? If you intend to do this again, we'll need one."

His laugh started deep in his chest.

She placed her glass on the night table. "Remember, my love, we must be quiet." She drew him into a searing kiss.

Holding her close to him, he stroked Anna's hair. He'd do anything to protect her and prayed he wouldn't lose her in the process.

November 15th, 1814, Marsh Hill, Kent

"Miss, you need to wake up."

Anna groaned and snuggled closer to Rutherford. He held her to him for another moment. Soon she'd be with him always. "You'd better go."

"How long until we're married?"

His deep chuckle rumbled in his chest.

"One last kiss."

"You're insatiable."

"I'm a wanton—look at me with no clothes and in your bed. I don't even want to know what my hair looks like."

Rutherford held her away from him. Her large eyes were luminous. Her body was still slightly flushed and her hair wild. Anna was the most sensual creature he'd ever seen, and she was his.

"You are a delectable houri. Go before I start something we don't have time to finish."

A sensuous smile played on her lips, and she raised her eyes to him. God, she took his breath away. More than anything, he wanted her beneath him.

"Miss!" Lizzy's impatient call broke the spell.

She sighed. "Coming, Lizzy."

Anna kissed him quickly and reached for her gown. "I'll see you at breakfast."

Another knock, this time from the door to the corridor. "My lord, may I come in?"

"In a minute, Robertson." Rutherford glanced at Anna and rolled his eyes. "This is as bad as the Park during the Grand Strut."

Anna grinned and pressed two fingers to his lips. He kissed them, and she disappeared through the door to the parlor.

A half hour later, he descended to the breakfast room to find Harry eating and entertaining Rutherford's two youngest sisters. "Good morning."

"Good morning, Ruhy." Eloisa giggled. "Harry was just telling us about the time you climbed the trellises and they fell down."

Rutherford smiled and glanced at Harry. "Your father whipped us both for that."

Harry's eyes twinkled as he took a sip of tea. "Yes, not for climbing the trellises, but for allowing Anna to do it as well."

Rutherford filled his plate and sat across from Harry. "I remember. She had scratches all over her, and her dress was ruined."

"Good morning," Anna said. "Whose dress was ruined?"

Rutherford glanced at her. "Yours. Do you remember when the trellises came down?"

She smiled brilliantly. "Oh, yes. Mama was so angry. She was sure I'd be scarred, and Papa punished you both."

Harry gave a bark of laughter. "And you cried as if you were the one being beaten."

Anna's eyes shone with delight. "I was so sorry for the both of you."

"Rutherford promised to replace your dress and Harry to take care of your scratches," Sir William said from the door.

Cece and Eloisa went into whoops.

"Oh, my," Anna said, wiping her eyes. "We had such fun."

"Speak for yourself." Harry's brow furrowed, but his eyes danced. "I couldn't sit for days afterward."

"What has got all of you going?" Lillian asked as she entered the room with Althea.

Anna glanced up. "Oh, we were reminiscing about things we did when we were children."

Sir William took his place at the head of the table. "What are you planning for today?"

Harry shot Rutherford a look. "There are some things I'd like to discuss with Anna and Rutherford, if you two have the time?"

Anna glanced at Rutherford. "We don't have anything planned, do we?"

He studied Harry. "No, we're at your disposal."

Sir William took the cup of tea Anna handed him. "Rutherford, you are all welcome to remain here, if you'd like. I'm finding it pleasant having the sound of children in the house again."

"Thank you, Sir William. I think we'd all enjoy staying here."

Rutherford wondered how happy his future father-in-law would be if he knew where Anna was sleeping.

Rutherford glanced at his sisters. "Wouldn't we?"

The girls all nodded their heads vigorously.

Anna ate her last bite and finished her tea. "Harry, where do you want to go?"

Harry raised a brow.

Anna nodded. "Ah, yes, of course."

Rutherford glanced at Harry. Apparently, Sir William didn't know about Harry's use of the cottage. "Anna, would you like to ride or take the carriage?"

"Ride. I'll change and be right down."

Rutherford watched her leave before giving his attention to his sisters. "Girls, we'll be gone most of the morning. You have your lessons and, if you're good, we'll play games in the afternoon."

Althea cast a stern glance at both her sisters. "We promise. Don't we?"

"Yes, Althea."

She sat up straighter. "We shall look forward to your return."

Rutherford and Harry bid them good day and walked to the stables.

"What's this about?" Rutherford asked.

"I've been thinking. I have all or most all of my memories, but I'm confused about some things. I think you and Anna will be able to help me."

"Of course, we're happy to do what we can."

Anna joined them a short while after the horses were saddled, and they set off, not slowing until they reined in at the cottage.

After helping her down, Rutherford held Anna in his arms for a few moments, enjoying her soft, warm body against his before they turned to their horses.

When he entered the cottage, it was in a shambles. Furniture broken, the feather mattress torn apart, and crockery smashed. "Anna, you don't want to come in here."

She scuttled under his arm. "*Oh, no!* Who . . . ? *Percy.*"

"That would be my guess." Rutherford moved aside for Harry to enter.

Harry stopped at the door and surveyed the damage to his cottage. "I'll kill him."

"There's nothing to do but clean it up." Anna pursed her lips. "Other than our having to replace some of the furniture and crockery, it can all be repaired. Let's see what we can save."

At the end of an hour, they'd set aside what they could and had a pile to burn.

"Look at the bright side." She smiled widely. "You men can make a large fire, and I shall go shopping."

"I'll have the carpenter replace some of the furniture." Harry said.

"The Priory carpenter can help as well."

"Let's build the fire." Anna carried out the blankets that had escaped Percy's destruction for them to sit on.

Rutherford went to get the saddles. Anna placed a hand on Harry's arm. "We'll make it right again. There is nothing that cannot be replaced."

He covered her hand. "You're right."

Once Rutherford returned, they made themselves comfortable.

When he drew Anna to him and placed an arm around her shoulders, Harry knew how large the hole in his heart was. He wanted Emma there.

"Harry, what is it you wanted to discuss?" Rutherford asked.

Harry pulled a face. "I need to know who I am. Not just my name, but what kind of person I am. After I lost my memory, I was fairly quiet. My wife helped me. She made me laugh, but there was always a sadness inside me." He paused and stared into the fire for several moments, trying to gather his thoughts. "Am I making sense?"

Anna leaned toward him. "You didn't put yourself forward and take charge. Is that it?"

"Well, yes, I suppose. Then on the trip to London, there were circumstances where it was clear to me that I wasn't being treated with the respect that some part of me was accustomed to. What I want to know is, am I more like my old self now?"

Rutherford stared at him. "You've always taken command or tried to." He grinned. "Even though some thought you reckless, you never really had a devil-may-care attitude. I think that was because of Anna."

Harry studied her, grasping for a memory that tried to elude him. "I always took care of you."

Anna's lips pressed into a tight smile. "From the time I was a baby. You sang to me. You helped me learn to walk. So many different things. When I was sick, I'd cry for you."

Rutherford tightened his grip on her and handed her his handkerchief.

"Yes, I remember," Harry said slowly. Images ran through his mind. He turned his gaze on Rutherford. "You helped, when you were there."

Rutherford raised his brows. "Well, I didn't have much choice. Not only were you my best friend, you were my closest neighbor. Unless I wanted to stay at home, which I assure you I did not, I had to help you. I half expected you to take her back to school with you, the one time she cried so much."

Anna's eyes opened wide. "When was that? I don't remember it."

Harry laughed. "You were three. It was at the end of the long break. Mama thought it would be best if I left without telling you, but I couldn't do it. You clung and screamed so when anyone tried to take you from me."

Harry shook his head and laughed some more, then glanced at Rutherford. "And you said, 'For God's sake, Harry. There'll be the devil to pay if we're late. Get her nurse and take her with you. We'll figure out how to manage when we get there.' "

"As I don't have any memories of Eton, I take it Mama and Nurse were able to pry me from you."

"Yes, still crying. I felt like the most horrible person in the world leaving you. Nurse wrote and told me you finally calmed, though for weeks you asked for me. She said she read you all my letters and made some up as well."

"I remember her reading your letters to me. It made me want to learn to write so you could read mine."

The more stories they told, the more images came to him. Not only him taking care of Anna, but during her first Season when she stopped him from making a cake of himself with a young woman. "What I don't understand is how I could have forgotten you or Rutherford."

"Harry, you said you had nothing of your own," Anna said. "Not even your boots. You'd nothing to grasp on to that was yours. Then, maybe, when you fell in love, you didn't want to remember."

Harry thought about what she'd said. "You may be right. On my way here, especially in London, I realized Marcella would have been very uncomfortable with—with all of this." He shook his head. "To think I might never have come home."

Anna leaned over and touched his hands. "You are back with us now. I'm very sorry you lost your wife and child. I would have loved to have met anyone who cared for you."

"It seems as if she were part of another life. My father-in-law was right. It was—is time for me to move on and claim my life. Tell me about you two."

They glanced at each other and smiled. Harry had never seen either of them so happy. More and more he wanted the same joy and contentment.

They told him how they'd helped each other after his death and about Phoebe and Marcus.

"I think I told you, Emma knows him. He brought back to her the body of her betrothed," Harry said. "She thinks very well of Marcus."

By the time the fire burned low enough to put out, Anna and Rutherford had offered to help find his Emma.

As they mounted their horses, Harry said, "Show me where you meet with the gentleman and where the deliveries are arriving now. You're changing locations?"

"Yes," Anna said. "Just as you told me."

Harry glanced at Rutherford, who was shaking his head. "What is it?"

Rutherford frowned and tilted his head slightly toward Anna. "I'll tell you later."

First they rode over to the stand of trees. Anna and Rutherford remained on their horses while Harry walked around the area. "It's a good site. Well done."

He remounted, and they cantered to the cliff over the shed. His little sister had been a good leader. "Anna, I have no complaints at all."

Rutherford gave him an unholy smile. "You should have heard her bargain for payment. Your smugglers are being paid not only by the French, but by the Home Office as well." He paused. "One thousand pounds from each."

Harry gave a low whistle. "I didn't teach you that."

Anna gave him a look. "I do have talents of my own."

They rode home in the direction of the cottage.

Still far enough away not to have been heard, Anna pointed to a horse standing riderless in the front. "Look!"

Harry motioned for them all to stop and glanced at Anna. "Stay on Thunderer."

She pressed her lips together.

"Anna, please. If anything were to happen, you can get away and find help."

She sighed. "Very well."

He and Rutherford dismounted and tied their reins to a tree. They skirted around the side of the cottage and looked in. Percy was trying to smash what they'd saved. Harry's anger rose faster than it ever had in his life. He roared and rushed through the front door. Grabbing the other man, Harry drove his fist into his nose, before throwing him against the wall.

Percy fell to the floor, staring at Harry as if he'd seen a ghost.

"You bloody prig. You'll pay for all the damage to this cottage, either in coin or with your bones."

Percy's nose was again off to the side of his face. Blood ran down his cravat and shirt. "You can't prove I did anything."

"He's really not very intelligent," Rutherford said.

Turning back to the miscreant, Harry smiled. "Blanchard, you'd think you'd been beaten enough. You won't get very far thinking that what you did can't be proven. In case you've forgotten, Rutherford is the magistrate."

Glancing around the room, Rutherford said in a hard voice, "Marsh wasn't the only one to see you trying to destroy what's here. I saw you too. Because your family is well thought of, I let you go before. That was a mistake."

Rutherford found some rope and continued, "You will be placed in a cell at the inn, and a hearing will be held. Unless you agree to transportation, you'll hang."

"You won't do that. I'll tell everyone I saw you and Anna. . . ."

"What did you call her?" Harry asked with a deadly calm. Feral terror entered Blanchard's eyes.

"M-M-Miss Marsh."

Harry kept his eyes on Percy. "I'd rather just kill him now," Harry said amiably. "He's more trouble than he's worth. We can dump him at sea."

"I suppose that would make it neater all around." Rutherford nodded. "The Blanchards won't have to be troubled with a scandal, and we won't have to worry about your sister, my affianced *wife*. The idiot doesn't seem to take warnings at all."

Percy's head swung back and forth between them. "No, no, please! I'll do anything you ask. Please don't kill me or-or send me away."

Harry fixed him with a hard stare. "Why should we believe you?"

"I-I didn't give my word before. I-I'll give it now."

Rutherford raised a brow. "You'll sign a sworn statement that you caused the damage to this cottage and tried to accost Miss Marsh, soon to be Lady Rutherford. And you will make monetary reparations for the damages done?"

"Y-y-yes, anything."

"You will not go within two lengths of Miss Marsh, nor will you cause anyone else to do so on your behalf."

"Y-Yes."

"Harry?" Rutherford asked.

Harry waited for a few long minutes, making sure Blanchard was convinced it'd be die or be transported. "Very well, subject to my sister's approval."

"I'll speak to her. If she agrees, Percy, you will come with us to the Priory."

Rutherford left to talk with Anna, and Harry gave Percy a hard look. "You're very lucky I don't kill you for even thinking about laying a finger on my sister. If you violate the terms of your release, your statement shall be used to transport you, if you're still alive, that is."

Blanchard shook like a blancmange. "I understand."

"Good. Now tell me what the devil you thought you were doing."

Chapter 21

Harry had asked Anna to stay on Thunderer, but had said nothing about her remaining in the trees. She moved her horse to the outside of the door so that she could listen and see in.

"Mama blamed me for not convincing M-Miss Marsh to marry me. I-I thought if I could show her I was man enough . . ."

A low growl emitted from her brother. "True men don't attack females, and they don't destroy the possessions of others. Do you honestly think she'd jilt Rutherford for you? She's planned to marry him for years, and he her."

Percy hung his head.

Sebastian, who'd joined her, had a pained expression on his face.

Percy had to be the stupidest man she'd ever met, and there was no excuse for his behavior, still Anna couldn't hurt Lady Blanchard. "Very well."

Sebastian strode back into the cottage. "She'll agree."

She didn't know who was angrier, Harry or her betrothed. They tied Percy onto his horse, and Harry took the reins. Sebastian led the way as they rode to the back of the Priory and entered through the French windows from the terrace to his study.

Anna wrote the statement out in her best copperplate. Sebastian and Percy signed it. Harry acted as witness.

After Percy left, Anna sighed. "I wish I knew what got into him."

"His mother." Harry tightened his lips. "He's not evil, just weak."

Anna bit her lip. "Will you truly transport him if he doesn't behave?"

"No," Harry said cheerfully. "He'll be dead."

She stopped herself from rolling her eyes. *Men.*

Anna, Sebastian, and Harry returned to Marsh Hill in time for luncheon. After they'd eaten, Harry and Sebastian took the girls outside and played chasing games, then hoops. At Lillian's behest, Anna stayed in the morning room to make lists for the wedding.

She hadn't got very far when she shoved them aside. "I wonder if Harry's being back will help the problem between Mama and Papa."

Lillian frowned. "I wish I could tell you. When a couple is passionate and they fight, it can end very badly. If she hadn't left as she did, I think they could have got over it. There is now such a rift."

"And to make matters worse, at least for Papa, Mama was right. Harry was alive. If we'd been told he went down between Brittany and England, I know they would have searched for him, longer than the government did."

Lillian reached out to pat Anna's hand. "My dear, I know you want to help, but your parents must work it out for themselves. There is really nothing you can do."

"Yes, I suppose you're right." She looked up at the clock and opened the door to the garden. "Sebastian, Harry, you need to bring the children in now."

A discussion of some sort went on between her brother and her betrothed. The two youngest got on the men's backs.

Anna smiled and said to herself, "Enjoy it. You'll be grown soon enough."

After she changed, she found Sebastian waiting for her in the parlor between their rooms. He had a bottle of wine.

"In a perfect world"—he handed her a glass of wine and kissed her—"this is how we'd begin every evening."

Anna took a sip. "Thank you. Perhaps we should make this a tradition."

He nodded. "What do you have planned for tomorrow?"

"I need to meet with your housekeeper."

He grimaced. "It's not that I normally notice the way the house looks. Yet since I've been here with the girls, I've realized the Priory could use some work."

"What do you mean?" Anna asked.

Sebastian shook his head. "I can't explain it. You'll have to take a look."

November 16th, 1814, the Priory

Anna and Sebastian rode over to the Priory right after breakfast. His housekeeper, Mrs. Thurston, took them on a tour of the house.

Mrs. Thurston grimly pointed out the shabby, moth-eaten hangings. "It's true that we've not entertained here in many a year. . . ."

Anna understood. It was still no reason not to keep up the house. The only rooms that didn't need renovation were the morning room, drawing room, and Lady Rutherford's apartments.

The housekeeper took copious notes. "I'll have these copied for you, miss."

"Thank you. I look forward to them."

"You won't," Mrs. Thurston said. "But you'll get them any way."

Anna chuckled lightly. "You're probably right."

"While you're getting bad news," the housekeeper said, "you may as well go through the kitchen and cellars. If you'd like, I'll make a list of linens to be replaced."

"Yes, please do," Anna replied. "Ask Cook to attend me, if you will."

"Yes, miss, my pleasure."

Things were very wrong here. It was not as if Sebastian didn't have the funds to keep up this place and several more. Anna turned to him, opened her mouth, and shut it again. "We need to go to your study."

He nodded and led the way. Anna walked in and waited until he closed the door. "Why does Mrs. Thurston not have the authorization to replace items such as the sheets or towels? It is a much more efficient method of ensuring they're taken care of."

Sebastian looked abashed. "I quite frankly have not taken much notice."

"Unfortunately, that doesn't surprise me. Men usually don't, until they stick a foot through the sheets," she said with exasperation. "I propose a trip to a fabric warehouse I know of to replace the hangings." Anna paced the room. "We can take Althea. She needs the experience. In fact, this is a good time to involve her in everything she'll need to learn, if she hasn't already, to hold house. What is your budget for the household expenses?"

He shrugged.

She furrowed her brows. "Sebastian, when was the last time those books were reviewed?"

"My love, I've left all that to my mother."

Anna pinched the bridge of her nose. "This is so irksome. Lady Rutherford already doesn't like me. It will seem to her that I've intruded and taken over without the least bit of delicacy."

"Come here."

She walked into his arms.

"I'll take responsibility," he said. "Tell me what needs to be done, and I shall order it."

"I need to review the household books and make a new budget."

Sebastian kissed her wrinkled forehead and smoothed it lightly with his thumb.

Anna sighed and tilted her head back. He found her lips, and she slid her hands from his chest to his neck as a warm tremor shot through her. Would it always be like this? She pressed against him, as he brushed her already furled nipples.

"Sebastian?"

"Yes." His eyes were warm silver.

"Will we always want each other?"

His voice was rough. "I'm not a soothsayer, but I hope so."

Warmth pooled between her legs, her heartbeat increased, and his hard shaft pressed against her. Anna reached down and stroked the bulge in his breeches. His groan rumbled through her.

Oh, God, she needed him. "How and where?"

He backed her up to the wall and rucked her skirts up.

"Wait." Anna unbuttoned his fall, releasing his already hard member.

Sebastian lifted her. "Wrap your legs around me."

When he entered her, she moaned and held on tightly as he thrust deeply into her. Her tension grew with each stroke. Just before she cried out, he captured her lips, drinking in her cry. Warmth filled her as he released his seed.

Sebastian carried her over to the sofa and held her on his lap. Using his handkerchief, he cleaned her.

Anna was in a warm stupor until a knock on the door made her jump. "Oh, no."

Warmth flooded her face as she hopped off his lap and shook out her skirts, hoping they weren't too mussed.

Sebastian, showing none of her perturbation, stood and made himself presentable again.

He looked over at her and raised a brow.

Anna pressed her hands to her cheeks. Good, they were cooling. "Yes, I'm ready."

"Come," he called.

The Priory's cook, Mrs. Pippin, a short, rotund woman with silver curls under a mop cap entered the room. "My lord, Mrs. Thurston said you might want to see me."

"Indeed, I am showing Miss Marsh around the house and making a list of items that need to be looked into."

She bobbed a curtsey to Anna. "It will be my pleasure, miss."

Rutherford stood back as Anna grabbed her notebook and followed his cook into the corridor and down the stairs to the kitchen."

"It's not as fancy as what you've got at Marsh Hill," Mrs. Pippin said.

"Indeed?" Anna was startled by the remark, then remembered that Mrs. Pippin's niece worked at the Hill. "Why don't you tell his lordship what the differences are?"

Cook stood before her old-fashioned open fireplaces. "This for one. Mrs. Kramer at the Hill has one of the new closed stoves. Makes it much nicer . . ."

Anna licked the tip of her pencil and made notes as Rutherford nodded and agreed with everything his cook suggested.

After Anna and Sebastian were finished, they thanked Mrs. Pippin and made their way back to the main hall.

Rutherford's expression was grim. "Griffin, please bring the household accounts to me in my study."

Griffin bowed and left.

Rutherford closed the door. "What the devil has my mother been doing if not seeing to the house?"

Anna shrugged lightly. "Not every woman knows how to hold house."

"No, I suppose not." He rubbed his cheek. "What are we going to do?"

"We'll make it right. I only wish I could find a way to do it without upsetting your mother."

Griffin entered with the books and placed them on the desk.

"Thank you. You may leave us and close the door." Rutherford moved a chair closer for Anna. "You look at those while I look at the estate accounts."

An hour later, she leaned back in her chair and rubbed her neck. "I'll take you up on the partner's desk."

"We'll look for one when we go to Dover." He pointed at the accounts. "What did you find?"

"I think the amount budgeted is too small. I have a larger one at the Hill, though it is a much smaller residence. Still, that is not the reason there's been no refurbishment." Anna sighed. "Other than for food and wine and alike, none of the money was spent on the house. With the sole exception of new drapes in your mother's chambers, it's gone elsewhere."

Rutherford frowned. "Where?"

"According to this"—she pointed to the account books—"your mother bought ten ells of silk, hats, shoes, some jewelry. The list goes on. She's been using the household account to dress herself."

He shook his head. "That doesn't make sense. She has a more than adequate jointure. I pay for all her living expenses and those of the girls."

Anna shook her head. She certainly hadn't expected to find what she did and wasn't at all pleased about it. "I don't know, my love. I wonder if that is one of the reasons she's not happy with you marrying me."

"I don't understand it at all." He glanced at the mantel clock. "It is almost four o'clock. We need to go back to the Hill. If we get an early start in the morning, you'll be able to meet all the tenants."

They rode across the fields and entered the stable yard of the Hill to see a coach being brought around from the front of the house.

"Mama's home." Anna slid off Thunderer and strode to the side door. Sebastian followed. She walked into the front hall to see her mother crying and hugging Harry. Her father stood off to the side gazing hopefully at his wife.

When she would have gone to Papa, Sebastian stayed her. "It's their marriage. Just as what we have will be ours. I know you do not want to choose between them."

Anna nodded slightly. "You're right."

Several minutes passed before Lady Marsh could let go of Harry. When she did, her gaze moved to her husband.

"William." There was a hitch in her soft voice.

"Lucilla, I'm sorry. I was wrong."

Her mother held out her hand to her husband. "I never should have left as I did."

He embraced her.

Tears pricked Anna's eyes. She smiled up at Sebastian, and he drew her closer.

Harry joined them. "Do you think we should play least in sight?"

"We can change and meet in my parlor." Anna gazed at her parents. "Are the children still upstairs?"

"I believe so."

She turned, and they walked down the corridor to the back stairs. Many of the servants peeped into the front hall and then ducked out of sight. There was a hum of activity.

Ledster asked Anna if Cook should hold back dinner.

"Push it back a half an hour, and send a dinner tray up to the children." She thought for a moment. "Better yet, have them meet us in my parlor. I'll ring when they are ready for dinner."

"Yes, miss." He bowed and left.

Anna kissed Sebastian lightly on his lips before entering her room where Lizzy waited.

"Is it true? Her ladyship is back?" Lizzy asked.

Anna smiled. "Yes, she is. I hope everything will be all right again. I couldn't have received a better wedding present. My brother and my mother back here at the Hill. Oh, drat, hand me a handkerchief." Taking it from Lizzy, Anna chuckled wetly and wiped her eyes. "My nose will be red."

"Here, miss, splash your face and it will be fine. How was your visit to the Priory?"

Anna told her most of what they'd found, leaving out the part about Lady Rutherford's personal purchases.

Lizzy rolled her eyes. "Well, they are happy as grigs to be getting you."

Anna sobered. "More talk?"

Lizzy's eyes widened. "How could there not be? The two most important families in the area? And everyone knowing how you took care of everything while your mama and Mr. Harry were gone." She nodded. "The tenants are doing a jig to meet you. You mark my words, there'll be more talk when you start making changes."

Anna made a face. There was no hiding anything in the country. Especially when there were so many relations between the Hill's servants and the Priory's.

She quickly changed and was waiting in the parlor when Sebastian arrived.

He strode to her and wrapped his arms around her. "My love, do you know I hate your being out of my sight?"

Anna chuckled. "Do you know how much I enjoy hearing you say that?"

"Come now, you two. You've still got sometime yet until you're married."

They turned as one to greet Harry.

"I'm not going to be happy when my mother returns," Sebastian said. "I wish she'd stay away until the wedding."

Anna opened her eyes wide. "Sebastian, I know you don't always agree with her, and there are problems, but that's not a nice thing to say."

"I wish it," he said, unrepentantly. "Because once she is returned, I've no excuse to remain here."

Anna frowned. "You're right. She'll insist you return with the girls."

"I do feel for the both of you," Harry said with specious sympathy. "What a sad pair you are."

Anna punched playfully at him. "It's nothing to laugh at."

"No, you misunderstand. I lived in the same house as Marcella. I *do* know how you feel. It's not the same, but you can still use the cottage."

Sebastian glanced at her brother, startled. "What brought this about?"

"I remembered something else." Harry looked at Anna. "You've loved him for years."

Her throat tightened. "Yes."

Harry smiled. "I'm glad to finally see you happy. You weren't before."

Anna struggled to hold back her tears. "No, I wasn't."

Sebastian turned her face to his. "Because of me?"

She touched his cheek. "Yes, but it's fine now."

Anna hugged Harry. "Well, I for one am very glad you understand. I hated it when I thought you and Sebastian were going to fight."

"Ah, yes, well, it was quite a shock at first, and it didn't help that you were much younger when I left" Harry glanced at Sebastian. "After I had time to think about it, I knew you wouldn't hurt her."

Sebastian grabbed Harry's hand and patted him on the back. "No, I wouldn't," Sebastian said gruffly, slipping his arm around Anna.

"I'm glad that's settled." She sighed. "Now we only have Mama and Papa to worry about."

Harry poured glasses of wine for them all. "I think they'll be fine."

High voices were heard in the corridor, and the door bust open. "What's going on?" Cece asked.

"Is Mama home?" Eloisa added.

Althea shook her head. "No, if Mama was home we'd have to leave. What has happened?"

Chapter 22

Rutherford glanced at his sisters. "Lady Marsh has arrived, and we wanted to give her and Sir William time to themselves."

Cece scrunched her face. "I don't understand. Why?"

Rutherford decided this was the perfect time to teach his younger sisters a little about couples. "Because they are married and need time to be alone."

Cece wrinkled her nose. "Ugh."

Althea grinned. "When Anna comes to live with us, we will need to give Ruhy and Anna time to themselves as well."

Rutherford raised a brow, and Althea raised one back.

He wondered if he should insist she not be presented until the following year, when she would indeed be old enough to marry. From the corner of his eye, he saw Anna put a hand to her mouth and turn away, a sure sign she was laughing. "Yes, we will wish to be alone at times."

Cece narrowed her eyes. "Are you going to kiss her?"

He glanced at Anna, then Harry. Both of their shoulders shook with amusement. "Anna, my love."

She turned back toward him. Her eyes danced with merriment. "Yes, my love."

Anna wasn't helping. He fought the smile hovering around his mouth. Harry apparently lost the battle, because he began to laugh loudly.

"I don't see what's so funny," Cece pouted.

Anna schooled her expression. "Come here, sweetie."

Cece walked slowly to her.

Anna put her arm around Cece's shoulder. "Betrothed people and married people kiss. It's normal."

The child's eyes grew wide. "Do you have to?"

Anna slowly nodded a couple of times, and said gravely, "Yes. It's obligatory."

"Yeew, I'm not ever going to get betrothed."

Rutherford was about to contradict his sister, when he caught Anna's warning look. "That's a very good idea just now."

Anna smiled approvingly. "Tonight, you'll dine in the schoolroom. Tomorrow evening, you'll dine with us again."

Cece grumbled and was led away by her two older sisters. Althea looked back with a very grown-up look on her face as they left the room. "That's it," Rutherford growled. "She is not coming out next Season."

Anna wrapped her arms around him. "If it were left to you, she wouldn't come out at all. The Season is several months away. We can make a final decision later."

Harry slapped Rutherford's back. "You'll have to get over it sooner or later. Remember, I'm letting you sleep with my sister."

Anna blushed a perfect scarlet. *"Harry."*

"You'll figure out a way to pay me back."

Rutherford chuckled and folded her in his arms. "We both need to pay him back."

They were informed dinner was ready and that Sir William and Lady Marsh would dine in their rooms, and Lady Tully in her's. Other than breakfast, Rutherford couldn't remember a time when the three of them had dined alone. "Harry, when do you want to begin searching for your Emma?"

"I've yet to receive her direction."

Anna drew her brows together. "Maybe we can contact Grillon's and ask who came to fetch her."

"That is a possibility. She expected her godmother the day I departed. I wouldn't have left her otherwise. On her way to London, a man by the name of Reynolds tried to abduct her."

Anna's eyes lit with amusement. "Oh, Harry, did you vanquish him?"

He laughed lightly. "No, Emma did."

Anna clapped her hands. "Even better. I think I'll like her very much."

He took a sip of wine. "Yes, I think you will. I wish I'd hear from her. I'm getting worried."

November 17th, 1814, Grillon's Hotel, London

Emma stood staring out the window of Lady Rutherford's elegantly furnished parlor. Cream and gold mixed with greens and blues. She missed Harry already, and the sooner she could get an address, the sooner she'd see him, but she had quickly learned Lady Rutherford was not to be rushed.

Though she never took Emma with her, her godmother seemed to need an extraordinary amount of time to visit with friends. Her godmother had taken Emma to the theater one evening and to the British Museum the other day. But Emma's gowns, shoes, and accessories were ready, and she didn't wish to dally in London.

At least Mr. Reynolds was no longer a problem. He'd tried to find her room, had got lost, and had entered the chamber of another lady. The shrieks from down the hall had been loud enough to garner a crowd. Mr. Reynolds had been taken off by a constable, who said the bailiff had been searching for Reynolds. Apparently, he was now in debtor's prison.

The weather was holding, yet one of the older guests had said it would soon change.

"Did your chaperone go off safely?" Lady Rutherford asked.

"Yes, my lady."

Mrs. Wickham's relatives had sent money for her to take the mail coach. A circumstance about which she was none too happy.

"Emeline, or Emma, though Emeline is such a lovely name, we shall have a wonderful time. I thought you might be well suited to my son, but he is recently betrothed." Lady Rutherford frowned. "A mere baronet's daughter. Although, she *is* a great heiress and took very well during her Seasons."

Clearly, Lady Rutherford did not like her future daughter-in-law.

Emma didn't need to look back to see the dissatisfaction on her godmama's face. "She is a lucky lady."

"Yes, yes, she is." Lady Rutherford smiled tightly. "We shall look much higher for you, my dear."

Emma closed her eyes. A vision of Harry floated before her. She wondered how he was, if his family embraced him or scorned him for being a spy. She gave thanks to her father for giving her the power to control whom she'd marry.

"I'll have the ballroom at Rutherford House re-decorated. You and Althea, my daughter, will be introduced together, and I shall give a ball in your honor."

"Thank you, my lady. That's very kind of you." All Emma wanted was an address so that she could write Harry.

November 17th, 1814, a coastal village in Kent

Seven days had passed and another six remained until his sweet packages arrived. Georges moved each night, arranging to arrive at yet another inn each day after breakfast. He'd heard from Désirée; the shipment was still on schedule.

Georges thought of bringing her to him. He needed some sort of release, but it would be too dangerous. No one could know where he was. He ate in yet another common room. The serving maid was friendly and gave him a good view of her breasts as she asked if he'd like anything else. He considered taking her up on her offer, but thought better of it. He couldn't afford the complications. He'd wait until he was safe, at least safe enough.

He hated this hiding and waiting, but it would be worth it to have his lands and his title back. Then he could approach the Honorable Miss Charlotte Marling. She looked like, what did the English call it? Ah, an ice princess. But he'd sensed a hunger in her. He'd school her like he'd schooled Désirée. Except the lovely Charlotte would be his personal courtesan.

November 18th, 1814, Marsh Hill, Kent

Anna woke in Sebastian's arms. He snored softly in her ear. She pressed back against him, and his almost flaccid member awoke. She sighed happily. This was an addiction. He was an addiction. His shaft grew hard against her. She hoped he'd soon waken. Or perhaps, she could take him while he slept. Maybe the book would have something. Sebastian's hand traveled from her waist to her breast. The ache between her legs grew as he played with her nipple. She pushed back against him in encouragement. When he thrust forward, Anna moaned.

He rolled her on to her stomach, shoved a pillow under her hips, and trapped her legs. When he mounted her from behind, Anna cried out with anticipation into the mattress and tried to touch the flames she knew would come, but he slowed. She moved her hips in frustration. He chuckled, held her legs tightly against him and thrust into her. She had no purchase and couldn't move.

Finally, her tension rose, and she trembled as bliss enveloped her. He groaned and collapsed, bringing her close to him.

He kissed her. "My heart and my life are in your hands."

A light tap came on the door. "Miss, you've got to come now."

He held her close one last time. "You need to go."

She closed her eyes and burrowed against him. "I know."

Anna groaned as she lifted the covers and slipped out of bed to pull her nightgown over her head and shrug into her wrapper, before disappearing through the door.

The breakfast room was empty when she and Sebastian arrived.

"Do you want to stay here or shall we meet your new tenants?" he asked.

"*My* new tenants?" She handed him a cup of tea. "I like the sound of that."

They ate in companionable silence until Harry arrived. "Good morning. What are you doing today?"

Anna turned. "Good morning. We are going round to Rutherford's tenants."

"Take your time," Harry said. "I'll entertain the girls after their lessons."

Anna stood. "Thank you."

"Have you seen either Mama or Papa?" he asked.

"No. I'm beginning to wonder if we're ever going to see our parents again." Anna turned to Sebastian. "I'll meet you at the stable."

"I take it all went well yesterday?" Harry asked.

"That depends," Rutherford responded dryly. "If you're asking whether the staff likes Anna, the answer is yes. All went well."

"Then what?"

"My mother. It appears she's been using the household account to replenish her wardrobe. What I do not understand is the reason she's doing it."

Harry finished making his breakfast selections and poured a cup of tea. "What will you do?"

"I don't know. I don't know if she'll accept Anna, and I am not in favor of Althea's coming out so early." Rutherford sat back shaking his head. "I can't put my finger on any one thing, but something is not right."

"Do you know how long her pilfering the household account has gone on?"

Rutherford sat back in his chair. "No. We only looked at the accounts for this quarter. We'll need to look further back."

He stood and walked to the door. "Thank you for looking after the girls."

"My pleasure. Let me know what you find and if you need help."

"As always."

Rutherford and Humphrey brought the horses out as Anna crossed the yard.

"Just in time." He threw her on to Thunderer. "Harry suggested we look back further in the accounts. If you don't mind, I'd like to do it this afternoon."

"If we have the time. Like you, I want to know what we are dealing with."

"Come then, my love." He spurred his horse forward.

The Priory's acreage was large. Even so, they managed to visit all of his tenants and take notes.

They arrived back at the house in mid-afternoon. As he and Anna had not eaten since breakfast, he ordered a nuncheon.

"Your steward, Mr. Stanley, has been doing a good job." Anna said. "There are not many complaints and not much to do." She glanced up from her list. "Though there are some enlargements of the tenants' houses to make, and there is a definite need for a school."

He'd noticed the same problems and agreed. "Do you think the Hill might be interested in a combined school?"

"I don't know why not." Anna sat back. "I can't think why we didn't think of it before. We might be able to have the younger children in the building we're currently in and build another one."

234 • *Ella Quinn*

Rutherford glanced at her. How could he have been so blind not to have noticed all she'd done at Marsh Hill? Even his steward was following her lead.

If he could just convince her to let Harry take over the smugglers before the spies were brought in, he'd be happier. If she didn't agree, he'd have to take measures to stop her involvement.

A knock sounded on the study door. Griffin entered and announced that their meal would be served shortly.

"Griffin," Rutherford said, "please have the household accounts for the past year brought to my study."

"Yes, my lord."

"A wine, my love?" he asked as they entered the drawing room.

"Yes, thank you. Don't you want to eat while we work?"

He handed her a glass. "No, I don't want to get into that habit. I'd like my sisters to join us for meals, if you don't mind."

"Not at all. Shall we make a deal that we'll always dine with the children when we don't have company?"

"Does Harry count?"

Anna's dimple popped out. "No, of course not. Nor his Emma, when we find her."

Rutherford stopped in the middle of taking a sip of wine. "That sounds much more interesting than trying to figure out what my mother is doing."

A knock came on the door. "My lord, Miss Marsh, your nuncheon is served."

Anna smiled. "Thank you, Griffin." She turned to Rutherford. "Shall we go?"

He put her hand on his arm, and they walked across the corridor into the family dining room. "Sit next to me."

They had a leek and cod pie with sautéed carrots and parsnips, and a salad of greens from the succession houses.

"This is really very well done." Anna signaled for a footman. "Please convey my compliments to Mrs. Pippin."

The corners of Rutherford's lips turned up. "She'll be your devoted slave for that. I can't remember the last time any of us sent her a compliment."

"You, my love, need to treat your servants better."

He covered her hand with his. "You're a breath of fresh air."

She met his gaze, and he raised her hand to kiss.

"Yes, well, let us get on with the more unpleasant work." She stood to push back her own chair, only to find a footman doing it for her. "Thank you. What is your name?"

"Joe, my lady—I mean, miss."

Anna bestowed a smile on him. "Thank you, Joe."

Rutherford took her hand, and they walked to the study. "Which time periods do you want?"

"How far back are we going?"

"When I think of the condition of the drapes, I'd say years, but probably only the past twelve-month."

Anna tilted her head. "I'll take the first two quarters of this year."

"Why those months?" he asked, perplexed.

"Your mother will have been preparing for the Season, and when it comes to that, I daresay I know more about what is required than you do. I seem to remember she only buys her clothing in London."

Rutherford responded slowly. "Yes, of course."

He handed her the books. An hour later, he called for refreshments. After two hours, he closed his ledgers. "I can't make anything out of it."

Anna was munching on a biscuit. "What would have occurred late last spring?"

He sat back in his chair. "Nothing much in England, but the last two battles of the war we fought were Orthez and Toulouse."

She didn't know what that would have had to do with the spending. Shaking her head thoughtfully, she said, "I don't know what it was, but that was when the accounts were depleted. Your mother didn't do much refurbishing here, and there was a great deal of money in the bank. Then over a few months' period, it was spent."

"On what?" he asked perplexed.

"That's just it." Anna shrugged. "The entries for this house don't make sense. She was in London during that time. It's as if she made them up out of whole cloth. I know you don't want to hear this, but you'll have to discuss the expenditures with your mother."

"I'll send a letter to Hoare's and tell them she is no longer authorized to draw on any of the Priory's accounts."

Anna frowned. "Do you think you should take such a drastic step?"

"Sweetheart, what would you have me do? The letter probably won't arrive until she's back."

"Yes, well then. You must do as you think best."

"But?"

She raised one slender shoulder. "I don't know. I thought you might want to speak with her first."

He closed his eyes briefly. "Very well. I'll wait until she returns."

"I think you've made a good decision." Anna smiled softly.

"I hope so," Sebastian said, chagrined. "I don't want her to run through all the money currently in the bank."

There must be some way to accomplish what Sebastian wanted without hurting his mother. "You'll have to add me to the household account soon any way. Open a new one and have any sums left over transferred."

"Now that's a good idea." He sat up and reached for a sheet of paper. "I'll write the letter and have it executed on the date of our marriage."

Anna glanced at the clock. "Yes. If we leave now, we won't be late for dinner with Harry and the girls. Shall we go?"

Less than thirty minutes later, they'd reached the Hill, and Sebastian lifted her down, holding her for several moments.

"I must change," Anna said.

"Where shall I meet you?"

"Find Harry, and I'll find you." She strode off to the side door.

"She's someat, ain't she?"

Rutherford turned to see Humphrey sitting on an old stool mending a harness. "She is indeed," Rutherford replied. "You'll miss her?"

"Oh, aye, that we will." The groom took a stitch. "But ain't no use her stayin' here. Her ladyship's back, and Mr. Harry will marry someday. She's got to find her own life. She'll do ye good at the Priory."

Rutherford smiled. "She will at that."

He changed for dinner and found Harry in the morning room. It was the place he remembered best from his childhood, cozy and warm, with cream walls and soft yellow hangings. "Have your parents made an appearance?"

Harry grinned. "Not yet. Have you figured out what your mother's doing?"

"No, but we're closer. Anna discovered the date things started going wrong. She thinks I'll have to talk with her. That, I can tell you, it's not a discussion I'm looking forward to."

Harry glanced at him. "I don't blame you."

Rutherford moved over to the window and decided to voice a concern that had been bothering him. "It occurs to me, I may leave this earth sooner than Anna."

Harry's brows lowered. "What's brought this on?"

Rutherford shook himself. "I don't know. Thinking about my parents. My father was so much older than my mother, and they didn't have the same type of marriage your parents did."

"How could you expect them to?" Harry asked. "Your father was probably twenty or more years older than your mother. They didn't even like being in the same room together for more than a few minutes at a time. That's probably why there's such a gap between you and Althea."

Rutherford frowned. "It certainly wasn't due to the types of problems your mother had."

"Lord, no," Harry laughed. "You'd have thought the sun had come up for the first time the day Anna was born."

Nodding, Rutherford said, "I remember. So different than Althea's welcome, or the others'. My father barely acknowledged the girls. I guess he only wanted boys. I want so much more for Anna and me."

"Don't let it bother you." Harry walked over to him and slapped his shoulder. "You and Anna will have an excellent marriage."

"Of course, you're right." Rutherford glanced at the lawn and could imagine children running. "Do you remember the games we played out there?"

"We'll do so again with our children."

After dinner, when tea was brought, Althea sat beside Anna.

"You do know how to serve?" Anna asked his sister.

"I've seen it done, but I've never actually poured," Althea said.

"There is no time like the present to learn."

He watched as Anna made gentle corrections while Althea poured. "There, well done."

"Do you really think so?" His sister colored with pleasure.

"Of course." Anna smiled. "We'll have to bring you up to snuff before you come out."

Althea glanced at Rutherford and frowned. "I wonder why Mama never thought to teach me any of this."

"A very good question." He wondered why as well. What had his mother been up to?

Chapter 23

"Did you tell me you'd already visited Madame Lisette?" Lady Rutherford asked.

Emma took a breath and turned to face her godmother. She was very tired of the delay in London. She tried to keep the irritation from her voice. "Yes, I have everything I shall need until we return for the Season."

Lady Rutherford beamed. "Excellent. I imagine we'll do some entertaining, though, to be sure, there are not many young men to interest you in our area."

Emma gave her godmama the smile Lady Rutherford expected. "I really think I should just become used to being in England. It's all so different and large."

Emma hadn't spent an hour in Lady Rutherford's company before Emma had decided not to tell her godmother about Harry. No gentleman less than a viscount would interest Lady Rutherford. She was a bundle of contradictions. At times she could be warm and caring, and then the next minute, was so distracted she appeared shallow and vapid. Emma didn't quite know how she was to spend several months in the woman's company. What Emma needed urgently was an address for Harry. "If you could give me the direction to your home, I will write my mama."

"Oh, there is no need," Lady Rutherford replied airily. "I already wrote telling her you had arrived. By the time she receives the letter, you will be at my town house, which is the address she has."

"Yes, Godmama." Emma tried not to sigh. "When shall we leave for your home?"

"Well, I would like to stay for a few more days in London." She sighed. "Though I suppose I should go home. With the wedding coming up . . ."

"We can leave today. I don't have anything else I need to accomplish and, after traveling so much, I would like to be settled for a bit."

Lady Rutherford formed a *moue*. "No, dearest, tomorrow at the earliest. Are you sure you don't mind leaving the metropolis so soon after your arrival?"

For the first time since Emma had said farewell to Mrs. Wickham, Emma's smile was genuine. "Not at all. As I said, I'd like to be still for a while. I'm sure I shall visit all the sights in London upon my return."

"Good. Have you hired a dresser?"

Not another delay. "No, I've been using the services of one of the maids."

"You really do need a dresser," her godmother said. "We must remain until you've hired one."

Emma tightened her lips at this latest attempt to remain in London. "The maid is really very experienced. Perhaps she would agree to stay with me."

"You can always try, my dear," Lady Rutherford said doubtfully.

"Please excuse me." Emma walked out of the room and ran down the corridor to the bell pull in her chambers. In less than five minutes, a young woman with straw-colored hair appeared.

Emma took her hands. "Molly, I like your work very well. Would you entertain the idea of becoming my dresser?"

The young woman gave Emma a toothy grin. "Oh, miss, I'd like it ever so much. Are you sure? I ain't fancy."

"You do a good job. As long as you are honest with me, we'll have no problems. I'll ask if Lady Rutherford's dresser can school you."

The maid nodded. "I'm honest. When my mistress died, the recommendation she gave me got me this job, and I'll do my best to learn."

Emma sighed with relief. "Can you be ready to leave in the morning? We are traveling to the country and shall be there until the Season. I've been given to understand it is a quiet place."

Molly grinned. "I'm not Town-bred. I don't mind it here in London, but it'll be nice to get away for a while."

Emma nodded. "Good. Gather your things and pack mine. I'll inform the hotel you've decided to stay with me."

"Let me get them to bring the trunks."

Emma returned to her godmother's room. Smoothing her skirts, she took a couple of deep breaths before knocking on the door and entering. "It's done. Molly will come with me. We'll be ready in the morning. Is there anything you'd like me to do for you?"

"Oh, so soon?" Lady Rutherford's eyes widened. "Well, then, yes, my dear Emma, could you have the coach readied?"

Emma curtseyed. "Yes, Godmama."

After Emma returned to her room, she rang the bell pull for a steward. "Please tell Lady Rutherford's coachman we will depart in the morning. I'd like breakfast served at eight o'clock."

"Yes, miss."

Emma pressed a coin into his hand.

He smiled. "I'll do it right away, miss."

Closing the door, she took the few steps to the desk chair and sat with her head in her hands. How could her parents have thought she'd be happy here? London was so unlike Kingston. Life was so much more complicated here.

Yesterday, when she had visited the bank in the City, they'd been shocked to see her, even though she knew her father had written them before she left, *and* she had her own letter.

Not knowing what she would need, or where the nearest banking facilities would be, because she'd not been apprised of her destination, Emma had drawn a sizable amount.

The bank manager had insisted a clerk accompany her back to the hotel until she told him she had a footman with her.

She refused to be a charge on her hostess, resolving not to owe Lady Rutherford anything when she left to join Harry. Emma had no doubt she loved him. He was caring, protective, and he made her laugh. Harry Marsh was the only bright spot in this, so far, cold and dismal land.

The next morning, Emma joined her godmother for breakfast at eight o'clock sharp. "My lady, won't you be happy to be home?"

Lady Rutherford looked at Emma blankly. "Oh, oh, yes, of course. Please pass the jam, my dear."

Emma wanted to frown, but maintained her countenance, saying brightly, "Thank you so much for agreeing to sponsor me."

Lady Rutherford took a sip of tea. "It is all my pleasure, my dear. I appreciate your taking charge of the arrangements. I'm really not at all good at that."

Emma smiled politely. "Thank you."

She devoutly hoped Lady Rutherford did not like the plodding pace that Mrs. Wickham enjoyed. Then again, if it were not for the slow speed of their travel, she would never have met Harry.

The sooner she discovered the direction of Lady Rutherford's home, the sooner Emma could write him. "I have the coach ordered to leave in a half an hour."

"Yes, dear. As you wish," Lady Rutherford said. "I know you'll be happy to stop traveling."

Emma finished her tea. "I'll see you downstairs."

Lady Rutherford put her cup down.

Emma met with the senior Rutherford coachman, Dobbins, while the trunks were being loaded. "How long will it take us?"

"His lordship keeps horses stabled on the road," he replied. "His lordship's horses be sixteen mile tits. I'll get you there in about six hours. Maybe sooner. Her ladyship don't mind traveling fast."

Lady Rutherford, her dresser, and Molly appeared at the door.

"Wonderful." Emma smiled. "We shall be on our way."

Dobbins handed Emma into the coach, and she took her place next to Lady Rutherford. "I think we are ready to go, Godmama."

Lady Rutherford slept most of the way, waking only for a light meal and tea. Enjoying the silence, Emma read.

They arrived at the Priory in mid-afternoon to be informed that Lord Rutherford would not be back until the morrow and that all the Miss Rutherfords were with him.

Lady Rutherford frowned. "I might have known how it would be."

Emma smiled politely and was happy to go to her room rather than listen to her godmama complain about her son and future daughter-in-law.

By five o'clock, it was dark. Emma walked around the chambers she'd been given and glanced out the windows, seeing nothing but the reflection of the room. She wondered where Harry was and how far away. She found paper, pen, ink, and wafers and sat down to write a letter to him.

November 19th, 1814, Marsh Hill, Kent

Doors slamming, shushing, and the sound of feet running down the corridor woke Rutherford. Beside him, Anna sat up.

He grumbled sleepily. "What the devil are they doing?"

"Anna, are you up?" Cece's penetrating voice carried down the corridor.

"Shush. Go down to breakfast," either Althea or Eloisa said. Right now, he couldn't be sure.

"That's a good idea. All of you girls go down before you wake everyone," Lizzy said. "I'll send Miss Anna down in a while."

Lizzy must be outside Anna's room.

"Come here." Rutherford pulled Anna back down.

"Miss, you need to come."

He groaned. "So much for that."

Twenty minutes later, Rutherford held Anna's hand as they walked into the breakfast room. They were the last ones to arrive. His sisters were entertaining Sir William and Lady Marsh. This was what he wanted to accomplish at the Priory. Happy, smiling faces of his family at the breakfast table.

Harry sat back in a chair. "It's about time you two showed up."

Rutherford looked down to see Anna blush. "Tell me what you want to eat, my love."

"Just eggs and toast. I'll pour your tea." She took a seat next to Harry. "Mama, Papa, good morning."

Her mother smiled. "Good morning, my dear. It's so nice to have the family back together again."

"I take it that everything's—all right?"

"Yes, we just needed some time alone," Lady Marsh said. "Thank you for giving it to us."

Rutherford took a seat next to Anna and glanced at his sisters. "Would one of you like to tell me what you were doing this morning making enough noise to wake the dead?"

Cece gave a good imitation of his scowl. "When are we going to Dover?"

"*Are* you going with us?" Anna asked.

Cece nodded her head. "Harry said we were all going."

Anna glanced at her brother. "Ah, I see. When did you tell them that?"

Harry grinned. "Last night, I promised them if they were good, we'd take them with us."

Anna put her hand on Rutherford's arm. "There's your answer."

She glanced at Cece. "We shall plan to leave in an hour. If you've finished, go on and change."

Once the girls made their noisy way up the stairs, Anna turned to Harry. "Have you considered how we are going to keep track of the two youngest in the warehouse?"

"You aren't," he said. "Whilst you are shopping, I've decided to take them around town. We'll meet for luncheon at the Ship. I've reserved a private parlor."

Anna reached over and kissed him. "You are truly the best of brothers."

Lady Marsh looked up. "It's so nice to see the three of you together again. Lord Rutherford, I am extremely happy that you and Anna have decied to marry. I'm also very pleased you and your sisters are visiting for a few days."

"Thank you, my lady, and for allowing us to stay."

Anna glanced around the room. "Where is Aunt Lillian?"

"I'm here, my dear. If you're going out, I'll say good-bye. I'm leaving today, but I shall return for your wedding."

After they wished her aunt a good trip home, it was decided Harry would ride in the coach with the girls. Rutherford would take Anna in his curricle.

Just over an hour later, they rumbled over the cobblestone streets of Dover and into the yard of the Ship, a century-old posting house near the center of town. Harry walked off with Eloisa in one hand and Cece, skipping, in the other.

Rutherford accompanied Anna and Althea to the warehouse, located a short distance down the busy high street. "Anna, I'll see you at the inn."

She grinned. "Are you sure you don't wish to help select fabrics?"

He lifted his quizzing glass and surveyed the racks against the walls and the numerous tables set up in the room. "No, my dear. I'll leave that to you."

"Very well. I'll see you later at the Ship."

He left them to shop, making his way back to the inn. Opening the solid oak door, he strode through the heavy curtain hung to keep the cold out. "I'm here to see Mr. Smythe," he said to the landlord.

"Yes, sir, please follow me."

They walked down a corridor from which Rutherford could see a workroom and the kitchen, then up the narrow backstairs to a parlor. The landlord opened the door, and Rutherford stepped in. The room was a fair size, but had no decoration save a few paintings on the wall. It was probably used for a card room. He waited until the sound of footsteps receded before raising a brow and regarding the elegant gentleman lounging at a table set in the center of the chamber.

The weak winter sun poured through small windows. "Smythe, a very English name, *Monsieur le Marquis*."

"Indeed. I fear England is rubbing off on me." He kicked a chair out from the table. "Please, sit."

Rutherford took a seat. "A little far afield from your usual haunts, aren't you?"

The gentleman motioned to the decanter of wine. Rutherford nodded, and the gentleman poured a glass. "London has become inhospitable for me."

Rutherford smiled thinly. "I heard arrangements had been made to dispose of you. Family can be the very devil. You should at least try to get along with your relations."

"Ah, my dear Rutherford, how well you know me."

Rutherford picked up the glass and took a sip. Nothing to complain about there. "Who are you whoring for this time?"

The other man assumed a slightly pained expression. "You wrong me, Rutherford. I am merely trying to protect what is mine."

Leaning back in his chair, Rutherford stretched out his legs, crossing one booted foot over the other. He twirled his wine glass and watched the liquid briefly coat the sides. "What is it you want?"

"You English," the man complained. "Always wanting to get straight to the point."

Rutherford set the glass down with a snap. "I don't have all day.

My betrothed is shopping nearby, and we are to meet here when she's done."

"Ah, yes, I did read you have become *engagé à* the lovely Miss Marsh. I felicitate you for making such a conquest."

"Cut line, Georges, and tell me what you want, or I'm leaving, and Jamison can send someone else to play games with you."

Georges sat up, all hints of languor gone. "There is going to be a delivery from France next week that you may want to consider intercepting."

Rutherford controlled his countenance. "A human delivery?"

"Yes, you could say that."

Finally, word about the spies. "When?"

"Early morning on the twenty-fourth," Georges replied.

He never did anything for nothing. "What do you want from this?"

Leaning back in his chair again, Georges studied his glass, before saying, "I merely wish to take one of the packages with me."

"And do what precisely with it?" Rutherford asked, all his suspicions roused.

"That is personal." Georges's gaze bored into him with an intensity Rutherford had rarely seen the man exhibit. "Will you agree?"

Rutherford pretended to consider the information. "I'll have to tell Jamison."

"But, of course. I would expect nothing less from the so loyal and proper Baron Rutherford."

Rutherford glanced down at his glass and thought of Anna. "Who knows, were I in your position, to protect my family, I might play the same game you are."

Georges smiled wryly. "No, no, Rutherford. Of a certainty, you would always remain faithful. I do not wish to think of you otherwise."

Rutherford tossed off his wine and stood. "How will we know which package is yours?"

"You cannot mistake her. She will not belong with the rest."

"Very well. I'll send word."

Georges rose as well. "It may take me a few days to respond."

"I understand. Stay safe." Rutherford held out his hand, and Georges clasped it.

"You as well. These are troubled times."

Leaving out the back door of the inn, Rutherford strode down the mews into a side street, making his way to the opposite side of the road in front of the Ship. Several minutes later, a sailor walked past and dropped a folded paper. Rutherford placed his foot over it. When he was sure the sailor wasn't followed, he picked it up and opened it. *Anchor.*

He strolled toward the docks, taking his time as if he had nothing better to do, slowly heading for the Anchor Tavern, a small run-down inn on a side street off the wharf. After spending a few minutes perusing the ships, he entered the tavern and asked for Mr. Brown.

Rutherford supposed if he had to meet anyone else today, the man would be called Jones.

Once again, he followed the landlord up a back staircase to a small, seedy parlor. He was greeted by a large man with fair hair. He shook Jamison's hand.

"What did Georges say?"

"They're arriving on Thursday, the twenty-fourth. He wants to keep one of them," Rutherford replied.

"Indeed?" Jamison said. "I don't know if I like the sound of that."

"Knowing our dear Monsieur le Marquis, he wouldn't have contacted us if it wasn't important that he take the person he has in mind. It's the only way we'll get his help."

"Very well. I'll send the other men in the day before."

"That would make me feel better." Rutherford grinned. "By the way, I ascertained who Harry left in charge of the gang."

Jamison raised a brow.

"Miss Marsh."

"*Miss Marsh?* Your intended?" Jamison's jaw dropped open.

"Yes," Rutherford said ruefully. "You may imagine my surprise when I made the discovery."

Jamison gave a bark of laughter.

As long as Rutherford was being free with his information, he might as well tell Jamison everything. "By the way, Harry's back."

Jamison stopped laughing and frowned. "Where the devil has he been?"

"On Guernsey. Lost his memory. He's fine now."

"Guernsey! To think he was so close, and we never had any

idea." Jamison shook his head. "He was a lucky dog to have survived."

"Indeed."

"Do you think he'd like to come back to work?" Jamison asked.

"You can ask, but I don't think his plans lie in that direction. He's thinking of running for Parliament."

"His father's seat?"

"What else?" Rutherford stood. "I must go. I'm engaged to meet Miss Marsh and my sister for luncheon."

Jamison shook his hand. "Good luck. I'll send word when the team I send is in place."

Rutherford nodded and left the room.

Again, he went out the back, circled around, and waited before taking a circuitous route back to the high street, where he visited a furniture maker before walking back to the Ship.

Rutherford was the first to arrive. A little while later, Harry came in with Eloisa and Cece. His sisters' cheeks were pink, and they looked wind-blown. Eloisa presented a much neater picture than Cece, whose braids were undone and whose hands and skirts were smudged with black. "What on earth happened to you?"

Harry laughed and pulled Cece around to re-braid her hair. "She wanted to get a better look at a gull and tripped. I don't know if the dress is ruined or not."

By the time Harry was finished, Cece was at least presentable, and her hands were clean.

"Harry," Eloisa said, "how do you know how to braid hair?"

"I used to braid my sister's."

"Oooh." She glanced at Rutherford.

"She was always messy."

Anna glided in, looking precise as a pin. "Oh, good, you're all here. I'm famished."

Althea trailed behind her, tucking loose curls back under her hat. "I don't know how Anna does it. She went everywhere I did, and there's not a hair out of place."

An image of Anna's wild hair first thing in the morning crossed Rutherford's mind. He smiled. "Althea, you'll have to have Anna teach you. I assure you, she wasn't always like that."

A knock came, and three servants entered carrying large trays.

Their little party did a good job of disposing of the bread, meats, cheeses, a large portion of venison pie, sides of brussels sprouts with shallots and chestnuts, as well as copious amounts of lemonade, and small jam-filled tarts.

Cece finished a lemon curd tart and swallowed. "I think you should bring us to Dover more often."

Eloisa nodded her head. "Me too."

Rutherford shook his head at the amount of food his sisters had consumed, then turned to Anna. "Did you buy everything you needed?"

"Most of it. I'm afraid the coach will be rather full on the way back. I had them wrap the materials by room." She glanced at the girls. "You won't mind sitting on packages, will you?"

"Will I be high enough to see out the window?" Eloisa asked.

"Why, yes, I think that can be arranged."

Harry narrowed his eyes. "I'm not sitting on parcels."

Anna's eyes sparkled. "No, you'll have them under your feet."

"I want to go see." Cece jumped down off the books on her chair.

They all trouped out to the carriage. Rutherford quite frankly thought Anna had been exaggerating, until he saw how tightly the coach was packed. "Do I have any money left?"

Anna's eyes widened. "I don't know, my lord. How much did you have to begin with?"

Rutherford considered his affianced wife. "How hard of a bargain did you drive?"

"You know, it is so vulgar to speak of bargains. I shall only say we shall always buy from Plum's."

"That good?"

"Hmm."

Harry, who'd stayed behind to pay the shot, joined them.

"You've been in a very good mood today," Anna said to him. "Exceptionally good. What's the occasion?"

"I took your advice and wrote to Grillon's. I should have an answer by Monday."

Anna squeezed his arm. "Oh, Harry, that's wonderful! I hope we meet her soon."

Chapter 24

Emma woke to sun streaming through her window. She'd been so tired the previous night, she'd barely looked at her room. It was pleasant enough. Though Lady Rutherford was not much of a housewife. The drapes needed replacing, and numerous other small items popped out. Emma wondered what the new Lady Rutherford would be like. She rose when Molly came in with her wash water.

"Miss, I'll have a bath set up before dinner."

"Thank you. How are you being treated?"

"It's fine. I've heard a great deal about Lord Rutherford's intended. People here seem to think she'll make a lot of changes. She lives not too far away. All the children and Lord Rutherford are staying with her family right now. Seems like her brother's recently returned."

Emma nodded.

"We're all expected at church this morning. It's to be the second reading of the banns."

"Yes, of course. Please get out the Parisian green cashmere gown with the wool spencer. I'll wear my dark brown cloak."

"Which hat, miss?"

"The poked one with the gathered silk."

Dressed in a simple wool morning dress, Emma descended the

stairs and asked directions to the breakfast room. She ate alone and returned to her room to dress. Forty-five minutes later, she was in a coach with Lady Rutherford being driven to Thanport.

The church was a lovely old stone Norman building. Unfortunately, the service had already begun when she and Lady Rutherford arrived. Emma was truly grateful that, due to the brim of her hat, she could not see if people stared at them for being so late. She followed her godmother to a pew where a fashionably dressed, dark-haired gentleman and three girls were seated. He opened the door for them.

The girls moved to allow Emma and their mother places on the benches. Emma shivered and was thankful to see warming boxes for their feet.

"I'm happy to see you here, Mother," Lord Rutherford whispered, and nodded to Emma.

The girls smiled at her. Emma smiled politely in return. How awkward this all was. She was tempted to look around, but the walls surrounding the pew were so high, she could only see the vicar.

Once the service ended, the children piled out of the box. Emma had her back to the door, retrieving her prayer book, when she heard a familiar deep voice.

"Are you still planning to take your dinner with us today?"

She turned so quickly she almost tripped. Her heart stilled as joy burbled up inside her. Standing before her was Harry, in a discussion with a beautiful dark-haired lady and Lord Rutherford. The only problem was Harry had his back to her. How was she to attract his attention?

Lady Rutherford, impatient to leave, took Emma's arm and steered her down the aisle toward the doors. *Drat.* Even if he looked, he wouldn't recognize her.

"Well, my dear," Lady Rutherford said, "I'm very sorry, but we will be joining Sir William and Lady Marsh for dinner today. I had hoped to have a quiet family dinner at the Priory."

Emma's heart thumped wildly, and she tried to keep her voice from trembling. "Is that Lord Rutherford's betrothed's family?"

Her godmother sighed. "Yes."

Emma grew impatient with the slow moving crowd in front of her. "The one in which the son has recently returned?"

Lady Rutherford patted her hand. "Yes. I'm not at all sure what happened. It was reported that he'd died on the Peninsula some-where. To think of the *Gazette* making such an error."

Emma's stomach tightened. "Will we go there directly?"

"As soon as we've had a word with Mr. Thompson. I think the sermon was particularly good today."

By then, they'd reached the vicar. Emma thanked him for a excellent sermon and stood next to her godmother while Lady Ruther-ford talked. It seemed like an age before Emma was in the carriage again. Her stomach did a flip at the prospect of meeting Harry again.

Thankfully, her trembling hands were hidden in her muff. How much more had he remembered, and would he still want to see her?

The trip seemed to take forever, but finally, they turned on to a tree-lined drive. When they stopped in front of a large manor house, a footman helped her down, and a butler took her cloak and hat. Emma gazed around the large, light-filled hall. What a homey place.

"Emma, come along, dear."

She followed Lady Rutherford to a drawing room, where a tall, broad-shouldered gentleman and a small, slender lady waited to greet them. Lady Rutherford made the introductions.

Sir William bowed. "We are very happy to have you visiting us, Miss Spencer-Jones."

"We are indeed." Lady Marsh warmly welcomed her. "We'll have to introduce you to our daughter and son."

Emma curtseyed. "Thank you. I'm very happy to be here. I haven't seen much of your county, but it seems very nice."

"You'll have to take a ride to the cliffs," Lady Marsh said. "They are quite famous."

"I'd like to see the Channel." Emma replied. Would Harry notice her? She hoped it wouldn't be awkward. "I'll have to see about buy-ing a hack."

A large presence suddenly loomed behind her. Her back grew warm from his heat. Emma's breathing shortened. She made herself smile. For good or bad, now she'd know.

"Miss Spencer-Jones?"

Emma turned and gazed up into Harry's impossibly blue eyes. Her heart skipped. He was grinning. "Harry."

"It looks as if I won't need to worry about receiving an answer from Grillon's after all."

"No." Her heart raced so quickly, she couldn't speak. He was here, and he still wanted her.

He took her trembling hand. "Come. Let me introduce you to my sister. I understand you've already met Rutherford." He lowered his voice. "Are you all right?"

"Yes, oh, yes." Better than all right. "I'm perfect."

"By the way, I have to tell you, I'm not at all fond of the hat you were wearing."

"No?" Emma asked, confused. "Why is that? It's supposed to be all the crack."

"No, don't get me wrong," Harry said. "It's very fetching. However, I wasn't able to recognize you in it. Thankfully, we'd already made arrangements for you to dine with us."

"I'd wondered how long it would be before you'd know I was here."

He gave a short laugh. "It might have been a while. Lady Rutherford referred to you only as a duke's granddaughter. I only told Rutherford and Anna your name was Emma. You will have noticed, Lady Rutherford is not enamored of the notion of my sister's marriage to her son."

"I'll tell you she doesn't try to hide it either," Emma said. "I wasn't in her ladyship's company for an hour before I knew she didn't like the match. She is looking forward to my making a brilliant one."

Harry frowned. "Harumph."

Emma summoned up her courage, and said softly, "But perhaps."

He gazed down at her, his eyes warm. "Yes, perhaps."

His response warmed her. "I can see your family loves having you back."

"Yes. My father wants me to run for Parliament in the next election."

"Harry, I think that's fascinating."

The room was long, and he'd stopped them half-way between the parents and his sister and Rutherford. "Emma, we need to talk. Will you walk with me after dinner?"

"Of course I will."

He squeezed her hand. "Thank you. My sister, Anna, is very excited to meet you. She and Rutherford were going to help me search for you."

Emma trilled with light laughter and covered her mouth. "And all the time I was coming to you."

Harry glanced down at her. "Why didn't you write?"

She gave an aggravated sigh. "I didn't know where we were going until I arrived. Lady Rutherford refused to give me the direction."

As he and Emma reached his sister and Lord Rutherford, Harry said, "My search is over before it began."

Miss Marsh's eyes opened wide, and she held out her hands in greeting. "You're Emma?"

"Yes, I am." She took the outstretched hands. "I am so glad to meet you."

Miss Marsh's eyes were the same color as Harry's, and her gaze was welcoming. "Thank you for helping Harry."

Emma blushed. "Miss Marsh, I really didn't do that much. He was bound to have remembered once he was back in a familiar setting."

"Please, call me Anna."

Emma smiled. This was the type of greeting she'd hoped for. "Then you must call me Emma."

Lord Rutherford bowed. "We're very pleased you're here."

"As I am to be here, my lord."

"I would be honored if you'd address me as Rutherford," he said.

"In that case, you must call me Emma."

"How are you settling in at the Priory?" he asked.

"I really haven't spent much time there, and it's dark so early here. I'd like to walk around the house and grounds."

"Why don't we go to the Priory after dinner?" Harry suggested. "I can show you the gardens."

"Very well, if that is what you wish." Emma wondered what he would say, and desperately wanted it to be something she wanted to hear.

The meal was excellent and everyone, with the exception of Lady Rutherford, had plenty to say. Lady Rutherford continually glanced at Anna and Rutherford. Emma was thankful her god-mother hadn't yet seen her interest in Harry.

After almost a week spent in Harry's company, Emma knew she had fallen in love with him. A different love than she'd had with her deceased betrothed, more mature. As much as she wanted to race ahead, Harry needed time. The question was, how much time would he need?

"Miss Spencer-Jones."

She looked around to find Miss Rutherford addressing her.

"Please call me Emma."

The girl blushed. "Thank you. I am Althea. May I ask you a question?"

"Of course."

"How long of a trip was it from the West Indies?"

"It took us two months. Because of the season, we sailed north before crossing. Then I spent a week traveling from Weymouth to London." Emma laughed as she answered more questions from the girls.

"That's enough," Rutherford said. "She's staying with us. You may bombard her with your queries later."

"Harry told us you know Lord Marcus Finley," Anna said. "He's the Earl of Evesham now."

"Yes, I've known him for years. Marcus was a good friend. How sad for him that his brother died, even if it was expected. When did it happen?"

Rutherford pressed his lips together. "He died immediately after the wedding."

Curious, Emma asked, "Married? Tell me, did he find his Lady Phoebe?"

"Oh, yes, that's who he married," Anna said. "The wedding was a few weeks ago. Rutherford stood up with him."

"Wonderful!" She was so happy for Marcus. "Do you know, years ago he named his ship after Lady Phoebe? We all wondered what would happen if they didn't marry. It's very bad luck to change a ship's name."

"He must have been very sure of himself," Anna said. "What a surprise that must have been for Phoebe." Anna grinned. "They took the boat to France on their wedding trip. I know he hadn't told her the name before they left."

Harry placed his hand over Emma's. "I didn't remember it at the time, but Marcus, Rutherford, and I were all at Eton and Oxford together."

They finished eating and got the carriages organized. Emma turned to her godmother. "I've been asked to accompany the others back to the Priory."

"You go, dear," Lady Rutherford said. "It is good for you to be around younger people. I shall wait for the girls to be ready and take my coach. I have some household matters I need to deal with this afternoon. Please ask them all to stay for tea."

"Yes, ma'am. I'll be happy to relay your invitation." There was something distinctly off about Lady Rutherford, but Emma didn't know her well enough to know what it could be. "Are you quite all right, my lady?"

Lady Rutherford patted Emma's hand. "Yes, child, I'm fine. I just have something on my mind."

"Very well, I'll see you later." Emma swept a curtsey and joined the others in front of the house.

They made a merry party as they traveled to the Priory. Harry, Rutherford, and Anna decided to have a curricle race on the only stretch of road wide enough to accommodate them.

Emma held on to her hat and the carriage. Anna drove Rutherford's carriage and won by a small margin. Even though Harry lost, he bragged about his sister. It was the most fun Emma had had in months.

When he helped her down, his face had the same warm expression she'd seen during their last day in London. Then, it had been mixed with uncertainty. Now, it was not. For no reason she could think of, her throat became dry. "Harry, I . . ."

He squeezed her hand. "Not here."

Emma swallowed and nodded curtly. "Yes, of course."

Harry led her into the main hall where Anna and Rutherford were discussing window hangings.

"When do you think they'll be ready?" Rutherford asked.

"Mrs. Thurston assured me there are two seamstresses working on them. We'll replace them in order of room importance. I have also discussed with her the need to keep all the chambers in good condition."

"I want your rooms done first," Rutherford said.

"In that case, my lord, you will have to see to it. You know perfectly well . . ."

"Yes, I know."

Emma turned to Harry, and said in a low voice, "I am a very nosy person. What's going on?"

He turned her away from the others. "He took Anna to inspect the house, and all was not as it should have been. We went to Dover yesterday and bought fabric. Rutherford was embarrassed to have Anna see in what poor shape the house was in and wants everything shipshape as soon as possible." Harry glanced briefly at his sister and her betrothed. "They've agreed to make several changes. The problem is Lady Rutherford. Anna wants to try to get along with Rutherford's mother, so all the orders must come from him."

Emma worried her lip. "I agree with Anna. Lady Rutherford would not take modifications coming from Anna well at all. I have to say, I noticed the problem in the chamber I was given. Harry, I don't understand what she has against Anna."

He shrugged. "Rank. Anna's portion is large enough, even with my return from the dead, and our family is old and well thought of."

Emma was startled. Even in the West Indies, most of the estates were tied up. "So the estate is not entailed?"

"No." He laughed and his eyes crinkled at the corners. "She was a great heiress for a few years."

Emma's brows rose and drew together. "But, you said it is a matter of rank? Is that the reason I was only known as a granddaughter of a duke?"

He raised his hand and dropped it again. "Yes. Rutherford's mother thought to make a match with you and him. Of course, he'd already decided on Anna. Or I should say, they'd decided on each other."

What a very sad family. "Do you know, in a way I feel sorry for Lady Rutherford."

Harry's lips tightened.

Emma put her hand on his arm. "Something is very wrong. I sensed it in London and even more so here."

His expression grew serious. "Do you have any idea what it could be?"

She sighed. "No, none at all."

* * *

The two couples walked in the gardens. They skirted the fountain and the formal rose garden, making their way to the folly and around the lake, then went back toward the house. Harry steered Emma toward an arbor. He'd been thinking about her for two weeks and was almost sure he was in love. A different love than with Marcella, one in which they both knew who they were.

Harry and Emma both spoke at once.

She blushed. "You go first."

"I wanted to say, I'm glad you're here. You?"

"I'm glad you're here." She gazed up at him. "Tell me, have all your memories returned?"

"Yes." His lips twisted into a remorseful smile. "I also discovered my true manner is not what it was on Guernsey."

"Does that bother you?" she asked.

"A little. I wish I could have been who I really am with Marcella." He closed his eyes and opened them to find concern in Emma's face. "Then again, I'm not sure she would have wanted me as I am."

Emma's brow creased. "I don't understand."

Harry wasn't quite sure how to explain it. "How would you have described me when we first met?"

Her eyes widened. "You were a little shy, self-effacing"—she smiled up at him—"and very kind. You kissed my hand."

Harry grinned at the memory. "That isn't who I am."

Emma's smiled deepened. "Oh, I don't know. You're still very kind. Harry, I knew you for who you were the first time you saved me from Reynolds. Even more so when you didn't understand why the landlady wouldn't take orders from you."

"And you told me I needed new clothes. All of which led me to finding myself."

"That was bound to have happened."

"Yes, but you made it happen sooner."

She tensed, and he didn't know why. "What's wrong?"

"I don't want your—regard for helping you. I would have done it for anyone. I want . . . I want you to . . ." She shook her head, broke from him, and moved away.

Did she really think he cared about her because of her help? "Emma, I don't want any misunderstandings between us. I've had enough of that." In two strides he was with her, turning her to him.

"I think I'm falling in love with you, but not because you helped me. Because of who *you* are. If you don't feel the same, tell me." He searched her face. "You came all this way for a Season. To have your pick of the *ton*. I don't want to be the one who takes that away from you."

Tears pricked the back of her eyes. "Harry, I am in love with you. I knew it that last day in London. I don't need to be a single woman to have my first Season." She blinked and straightened her shoulders. "I could be a married woman and enjoy it with my husband."

Emma stopped and waited for him to respond.

He took her hands. "If you can be patient for just a little while longer?"

"Of course." She glanced up at him searchingly. "We should spend the time learning about each other and talking about what kind of marriage we want. I have to tell you, sometimes I'm not the easiest woman to get along with."

His lips quirked up. "If you'll recall, I saw you chase off Reynolds and his accomplice."

She blushed. "Yes, well. It had to be done, and I didn't know you'd be there to help."

"Would you have liked me to help?"

She smiled slowly. What a question. "What woman does not dream of being rescued by a handsome knight?"

She lowered her gaze from his eyes to his lips. They were behind a hedge, and she was sure no one could see them. "Harry?"

"Yes." He drew her closer and bent his head.

Emma closed her eyes as his lips touched hers and firmed. He licked tentatively across the seam of her lips. She opened her mouth and met his tongue with hers. Heat welled as they began a slow dance. He tasted so male. She had no other words. His hands seared her back through her cloak and gown. Emma's breath quickened and need—long denied—welled up in her. It had been years since she'd been kissed. But Adam's kisses hadn't been like this. It was as if Harry wanted to possess her. He tilted his head deepening their kiss, and her thoughts dissolved like the foam on a receding wave.

Harry stifled a groan and thanked God that kissing Emma was not at all like kissing Marcella. Emma met him stroke for stroke, her kisses as greedy as his. Her body softened as he stroked her back. Then her arms came up around his neck, and she pressed herself to him.

He hardened, and something inside him swelled and crowed. When he lifted his head, Emma placed her hands on his cheeks and her forehead against his. Harry wanted her so badly, but a small voice of reason pushed through. This marriage would be different than his last. He'd wait until they were married before he made love to her.

She kissed his chin. "I think we need a plan."

Harry blinked. "A plan?" How had she had the wits to go from that kiss to a plan?

"Yes, all successful endeavors begin with a strategy."

"And how do we go about this? What would it entail?"

"Well, it would involve our individual goals and how we can join them. We should make a list."

He regarded her serious mien. "Very well, we'll do it."

Emma nodded. "Good."

Harry bent his head and kissed her again. She yielded her mouth and sighed when he claimed it. A much different marriage. One he was looking forward to. He might not need much more time at all.

"Harry, Emma. Where are you?" a high voice called.

Emma started to giggle. "Courtship here might be a bit more interesting than I'd anticipated."

He shook his head. "Yes. I've been teaching them the games I used to play as a child."

Her eyes sparkled. "I see. I hope they don't regard me as an interloper."

Harry grinned. "We may have to have a talk with them."

"Cece, come back here now," an older voice said.

"But I want to find Harry. . . ." The voice trailed off.

He heard a cough and looked around to see Rutherford and Anna, both smiling at them.

"I take it we should go in?" Harry asked.

Rutherford's smile deepened. "Yes, it's almost time for tea."

Harry looked down to see Emma blushing.

"Are we to wish you happy?" Anna asked.

Harry closed his eyes and took a breath. "Not yet. We need a little more time."

When he opened his eyes, his sister's gaze was full of disbelief. "Umhm. Shall we go?" she asked. "Or would you like more time?"

"When did you become such an incorrigible little minx?" Harry asked.

"She always was." Rutherford put his arm around her. "She's just older now."

"Anna, would you like to go in?" Emma tilted her head toward Harry. "The men can trade insults while you and I get to know each other."

Harry allowed her to slip from his arms and walk off with his sister.

"It's just as well," Rutherford said. "There is something I have to tell you about the smuggling shipment." He told Harry about the meetings with Jamison and Georges. "This is getting too dangerous, and there are too many people playing. I do not want Anna involved."

Harry stared at him for several moments. He hoped Rutherford's protectiveness was not going to drive a wedge between him and Anna. "I understand, but I think you need to discuss it with her."

"I'll tell her the shipment was canceled."

Harry raised his brows. "Not the best plan you've ever had. What do you think she'll do when she discovers you lied to her?"

Rutherford was still for a moment and swallowed. "She cannot find out."

"I'll have no part in deceiving her, but I won't betray you either."

Anna waited until they were far enough from the gentlemen before she ventured her question. "What are the two of you waiting for?"

"We haven't known each other long at all," Emma said. "We need to thrash out what we each want from a marriage, and Harry still needs time."

"Have you discussed where you'll live?"

"No, not yet. I'd have no trouble living with your parents, if that's what he wants. In fact, I'd prefer it. I come from a very large, close family, and I miss the noise and confusion."

"Goodness, you don't mean to tell me you all lived together?"

Emma smiled. "There is one main house. My eldest brother, his wife, and their children live there with my parents and younger sisters. My married brothers have smaller houses on the property, but mostly we all come together for meals."

Anna shook her head. "It sounds like a village unto itself."

Emma grinned. "That is a good way to put it. We're very organized, I'll tell you."

"You'd have to be. Living so far away from everything and with so many family members. How do the younger ones live?"

"Do you mean my younger brothers?"

"Yes."

"They each have professions. One is a shipbuilder and the other a lawyer. The latter hopes to become the representative to the court. To be able to address Parliament."

"I am flabbergasted it all works so well."

"We don't always get along. There can be pretty serious disagreements." Emma laughed again. "But my parents always maintain that once the fight is over, the parties must remain friends." Her eyes became misty. "Then the rum is brought out, and we all discuss the problem. What's important is that we come to a resolution and the trouble is not allowed to fester and become poisonous."

Anna was amazed by the difference. "How I wish we could do more of that in England."

"Well, Jamaica is small, and we all need to stick together."

"Even if you haven't announced a decision, I am delighted you'll be my sister. You must tell Harry everything you've told me, if you haven't already."

Emma took her hands. "Thank you, for everything. You're so kind to me."

"Even more, I understand how important it will be for you and Harry to discuss your views, but I don't think you'll have the trouble with him that I had with Rutherford. It took him forever to come to the point, then more time to agree to my terms."

Emma's laugh was light and tinkling. "Do I dare ask?"

"I want to have an equal partnership. I've done a lot of reading on the rights of women, and my dearest friend was raised with those ideas. I'm very pleased that Rutherford has come to understand I take those issues seriously. Particularly, one venture I took over from Harry. Though we haven't discussed it, he's raised no objections. I could not have agreed to marry him otherwise."

Chapter 25

November 20th, 1814, a coastal village, Kent

Georges paced his room, raking his hand through his hair. He prayed that Jamison would take his offer. He still had trouble believing what he'd been told. At first he'd thought it wasn't possible. There must be a mistake. Madeleine, Demoiselle du Beaune, would never agree to be a whore.

The idea revolted him in a way he could not have imagined before. *Aristos* were, as a whole, demeaned for being what they were. Yet, before his death, her father had been careful, and the family had retained all their lands and houses. What had happened?

Georges muttered to himself. "I'll have to ensure that the English authorities never touch her."

A cold hand gripped his heart.

Once, in a distant world, he'd loved her, and their fathers had discussed a match. Then the horror came, and his father had been murdered. Georges had taken his mother and sisters to England. He had made a deal with the devil. As long as he could keep his family safe, anything he did would be worth it, and now he had Madeleine to worry about as well. He tried to shut out the memory of her.

In a land of dark hair and eyes, her coloring was unusual. She, like her mother, had silvery blond hair. Eyes that were icy blue. She was the most perfectly beautiful woman he'd ever seen. A clear sign that God, much as a good gambler would, had a hand in everything. But she'd lost. How? And how could he protect her from further degradation?

His hands covered his face as he thought back over all the disappointments of his life. He had to save her.

November 20th, 1814, Calais, France

Her head high, Madeleine stood before one of the men responsible for sending her to England to whore. He sniffed as if he disliked his job, but his lust-filled gaze roved down her body and back up again. He was a disgusting pig.

"Mademoiselle, do you come here of your own will?"

Madeleine bit her tongue before she responded. "Yes, and I have the necessary requirements. I know that I must be a virgin on the night the English gentleman takes me."

The man before her scowled.

She hid a triumphant smile. Then he smashed her into the wall. "Remember who your masters are. You are a whore. Expect to be treated as one."

Madeleine trembled in horror as one hand grabbed her breast and squeezed. She clenched her teeth. Never show pain, never show anything. She kept her thoughts on Genevieve, her younger sister, only thirteen. She'd agreed to do this to save Genevieve. Her mother had wept bitterly when they'd taken Madeleine away.

"You're a cold bitch," the pig spat.

Madeleine gazed over his shoulder, refusing to meet his eyes. She'd give him no excuse to hurt her. "Yes."

He took her back to her room, but before he shoved her in, she asked, "When?"

"In a day or so. Watch your precious virginity. We must save it for an important man."

She let out a breath. The pig knew and was no real threat. He only wanted to scare her. Thankfully, she'd been allotted a private chamber and her maid, rather than the overcrowded room the other women shared.

If only her father had not been such a blind idiot, trusting Napoleon's advisor, Fouché. If Papa had got them out of France before he had died, her family's life would have been so much different. Instead, he'd left them to fend for themselves, and the pigs had been ready to take a thirteen-year-old girl to whore.

November 21st, Marsh Hill, Kent

Anna woke heavy-eyed. It was still dark. She'd tossed and turned most of the night, and, despite her warm feather bed and duvet, she was cold. There was no large, slumbering male next to her, radiating heat.

Her body hummed with desire. A desire that wasn't going to be satisfied this morning. Love-making was a drug, and she'd had a steady diet of it for the past week. But that was only part of it. She missed Sebastian. Missed the way he held her close to him and the funny things he'd say in the morning. She'd been surrounded by love her whole life. Yet, she had never known a love like this. So deep it hurt at times.

Frustrated, Anna threw off her covers and rang for Lizzy. Her maid opened her door a second later.

"How did you get here so quickly?" Anna asked.

"Lord Rutherford is downstairs." Lizzy grinned. "He said to get you up and dressed."

"Get my habit out."

"Miss, he said to tell you he's got his gig."

"Oh, very well, my brown wool carriage gown." Anna washed her face and brushed her teeth. Lizzy quickly dressed her, then Anna sat impatiently as Lizzy wound her hair into a simple knot.

"Miss, do be still," Lizzy said. "I can't get these pins in with you jumping around the way you are. By the look on his face, he's not going anywhere without you."

Anna let out a sigh and tried to be calm.

"There. Here are your gloves, muff, and cloak. Be off with you."

"Thank you, Lizzy. If anyone asks, I'm out for a drive. I'll be back later today."

"Yes, miss."

Anna strode rapidly down the corridor. When she reached the top of the staircase, Sebastian glanced up. He had dark circles beneath his eyes. He looked like she felt, tired and annoyed.

She joined him, and they strode to his carriage. The air between them crackled with sensual tension. Neither of them spoke until he brought the carriage to a halt in front of the cottage.

Anna hopped down. "I'll go in and stoke the fire."

"Here, take these. I'll bring in the rest."

She turned to see him holding some sacks. "What are they?"

"Provisions. I raided my larder."

Her tension drained, and she smiled. "Hurry."

He nodded. "I will."

Opening the door, she glanced around. Harry had been working on the cottage, cleaning it up and refurbishing it. It was even better than before. She soon had a blaze in the fireplace and emptied the sacks. Bread, cheese, ham, tea, sugar, and a jug of milk.

Anna went to the pump and brought in a bucket of water. Sebastian strode in as she refilled the old iron kettle and swung the crane over the fire.

He set his bundles down and unpacked them. Plates, mugs, cutlery, candlesticks, and candles. After he helped her set everything out, he spread a large down duvet over the bed and slipped back outside.

When he returned, he set the bar on the door. "Come to me. I didn't sleep a wink last night."

His arms closed around her.

"No, neither did I." Anna breathed in his unique scent, male and sea. "By our wedding date, I'm going to look like a hag."

"Tired?"

"Yes, and cranky."

"Give me a minute." He walked to the fireplace, filled a warming-pan with coals, then ran it between the sheets. "Let me help you."

Sebastian took her cloak and unlaced her gown.

She shivered as the warm wool fell off her shoulders.

"Cold?"

"A little." She finished undressing and got in the bed and held the covers up to her chin.

He climbed in next to her. "If I didn't think I'd have been taken for a thief, I would have come to you last night."

Anna snuggled next to him. "I missed you so much. I don't know how I'm going to stay sane for the next week."

Sebastian held her closer. "I don't know either. Kiss me."

The kiss began as a simple acknowledgment of their love and rapidly spun out of control. His hands lit fires under her skin and a desperate need throbbed between her legs. His body tensed as she stroked him; evidence of his desire rose.

Sebastian moved over her. She spread her legs in silent welcome and moaned as he filled her. "You've made me an addict."

"Have I?" His voice was tense.

Anna opened her eyes to gaze at his face. Never soft, it now had the look of hewn granite. His eyes were closed. The rising tension roiling through her body ripped her thoughts away. Waves of pleasure made her feel as if she were falling.

She heard her own moans and sobs as if from a distance. Then one large wave swept her away and Sebastian cried out, collapsing next to her. When had this act, their joining, become a meeting of their souls? She wanted to tell him, but Morpheus pulled at her.

Rutherford listened to her soft breathing. He'd thought his love for her couldn't grow deeper, but he had been wrong. Every time they mated, he felt more exposed, more vulnerable. The need to protect her settled over him more intensely.

What would Anna do when she found out he'd betrayed her by not telling her when the shipment would arrive? He could only pray their love was strong enough to survive the discovery. He shoved his fear aside and settled into sleep.

When he awoke, the cottage was warm. Anna was still asleep, a soft, warm bundle curled against him. He slid from the bed and began to pile food on the plates and make tea.

"Sebastian?"

"I'm right here. Are you hungry?"

"Mmm . . . very."

Once he set the tea to brew, he went back to her. She was still sleepy, but her eyes no longer looked bruised. "Come, my love, and eat. You need your strength."

A slow, siren-like smile graced her lips. Anna held her arms out to him. Sebastian gathered her up, wrapped her in a blanket, and carried her to the table.

She helped herself to some of the cheese and munched contentedly until her tea was ready. "Are we going to do this every day until the wedding?"

"Would that we could." He handed her a mug of steaming tea

with milk and sugar. "Do you think your parents will allow you to disappear every day?" Sebastian cut the bread.

Anna wrinkled her nose. "I might be able to tell them we have work to do at the Priory." She frowned. "No, chances are, they'd send a note over about something and be told I wasn't there."

She glanced around. "What time is it?"

Rutherford pulled his pocket watch from his waistcoat on the chair. "Just after one o'clock. We slept for a long time."

She took a large slice of ham. "No wonder I'm so hungry. We'll have to leave soon."

He would much rather have stayed here with Anna, but nodded.

Suddenly, her face fell, and her voice hitched. "Oh, Sebastian, I don't want to go back."

Anna looked very close to tears, and he hoped she wasn't going to cry. "We'll think of something, my love. I promise you we will."

Harry's rooms overlooked the stable yard. He woke to the sounds of wheels. Muffled voices conversed, and several minutes later the carriage left. He lay in bed staring at the hangings. For months after Marcella died, he had dreamt of her. When his memory started to return, his nighttime wanderings ranged from the ship to his sister, but his dead wife had always had a place. He knew he couldn't re-marry while she still filled his unconscious mind. It would, in some way, be disloyal to his future wife.

After he had left London, he'd not remembered his dreams. Last night he had imagined he was making love to a woman. In his vision, Harry had expected it to be Marcella. But when he'd looked at her face, it was Emma. This was the sign he'd been waiting for. The sign that he was now free to go on with his life, a new life with Emma.

Harry spent the morning with his father going over accounts. Shortly before lunch, his mother knocked on the door.

"Do either of you know where Anna is?"

"She's with Rutherford," Harry said. "They left early this morning."

Mama frowned. "I need to discuss the wedding with her."

"She'll probably be back for tea." He chuckled. "Though don't be shocked if Rutherford is in tow."

"They really shouldn't live in each other's pockets," his mother said disapprovingly. "People will talk."

"Mother," Harry responded, "they'll be married in eight days."

"Of course they will," Mama retorted, "but this type of thing doesn't last forever. Once they return to Town, I am sure Lord Rutherford will want to spend time at his clubs and at other events not suitable for ladies. I do not wish to see Anna hurt when he is no longer dancing attendance on her."

His mother was so studiously not looking at his father that Harry quickly glanced at Papa, who'd not lifted his head.

"Things are very different when in the country," Mama said.

"I see. We'll all just have to let them work it out."

She turned to leave. "When you see your sister, please tell her I'd like to speak with her."

"Of course."

Harry watched the door close and thought for half a minute of inserting himself into his parents' business, then rejected the idea. Whatever mistakes his parents had made were no bread and butter of his, though he did wonder what had happened as Mama always seemed to prefer Town. Nevertheless, Harry was sure they wouldn't appreciate his interference.

Aside from that, he had his own problems. He'd never been allowed to run tame at the Priory as Rutherford had at Marsh Hill. If he and Emma weren't to set up Lady Rutherford's back, he'd need an excuse to call there. And the only one he could think of was to visit Rutherford.

"Papa, I'll be back in a few minutes."

Harry left the study and went to the stables in search of Humphrey. "I need a message sent to the cottage. Anna must come home now."

"I'll see to it," Humphrey said.

Harry returned to the study until tea was announced. When he entered the morning room, Rutherford and Anna were just sitting down. Mama poured.

"Lord Rutherford, how nice you could join us." She handed him a cup.

"Thank you, my lady."

Turning to Anna, Mama said, "My dear, we need to discuss the plans for your wedding."

Anna stared at their mother for several moments. "We only want our families and perhaps a few close friends."

Mama frowned. "My dear, I think you'll regret not having a large wedding."

Anna stood and walked to stand behind Rutherford's chair. He took her hand. "No, Mama. What I would regret is having dozens of guests to worry about. Please understand."

Her mother's mouth formed a thin line. "If that is what you wish."

Anna went to her and hugged her. "Thank you, Mama."

"You need to go to the Priory," Harry said after his mother left.

Rutherford raised a brow. "Why?"

Harry grinned. "To give me an excuse to be there."

"I see." Rutherford glanced at Anna. "We can go now, and you may dine with us."

Anna nodded. "Lizzy and Robertson can bring our evening costumes over in the carriage. Harry, you'll have to take your curricle."

He furrowed his brow for a moment. "Ah, yes, of course. Hard to ride in evening kit."

When he reached the Priory, a maid told him Miss Spencer-Jones was in the back parlor. Emma glanced up when he opened the door, setting aside the book she'd been reading. Harry entered the room.

She rose and walked into his arms. "I wondered if you'd ever arrive."

"I had to send a message to Rutherford."

"Where was he?"

"With Anna. He came to Marsh Hill early this morning. Before six o'clock."

Her eyes widened. "What on earth were they doing up?"

"I've no desire to talk about my sister and my best friend. I want to kiss you."

She met his gaze and placed her hands around his neck. "Then kiss me."

Harry swooped and captured her lips. Emma met each slow, sinuous stroke of his tongue with one of her own. His hands moved from her back to her sides. Harry's thumbs lightly flickered over her nipples and made circling motions. Emma arched into him. He swallowed her moan with a kiss. She stood on tiptoe, rubbing against his already hard member. He pulled her closer to him, wanting her nearer, needing to possess her. She was making his resolution to not bed her until after they were married much harder.

Harry groaned and, without breaking the kiss, maneuvered them to the door, locking it. Her nipples were tight buds. The fabric of her gown strained as he gently kneaded. One of her hands reached under his jacket and caressed his back, her fingers pressing into his muscles. He unlaced her bodice. He couldn't let this go too far. If he could just touch her silky skin, that would be enough. It had to be enough.

Emma stopped to rid herself of her sleeves and let the gown fall to her waist. His groin tightened. She was so lovely, and he wanted her. Just a taste, that was all. Her short stays were the next piece of clothing to fall. Picking her up, he carried her to the sofa, settling her in his lap. His eyes feasted on her perfect, creamy mounds topped with dark pink nipples. Harry nudged her chin back, kissing her jaw and throat. He made his way down to where one nipple called to him. Through the thin muslin of her chemise, he taunted it with his tongue, then drew it into his mouth and sucked.

Emma cried out softly and pressed closer to him. The sensation was so exquisite she could barely breathe. He blew on the nipple and ran his thumb over it again before going on to the other breast.

She'd had to beg Adam for each kiss and every caress. He had been so concerned they'd be caught. Harry's mouth claimed hers again. Her whole body throbbed with need and desire. What would he do if she asked for . . . "More."

His chest rumbled with his chuckle. "More? Your wish is my command."

Had she really said it out loud?

He untied the ribbon and drew her chemise down, exposing her breasts. He teased them with his fingers, then his tongue.

"How much more?"

"I don't know. I've not been this far. I thought I'd leave it to you."

He grunted, then tended to her again. One hand skated over the skirts of her gown between her legs and rubbed. He kissed her as she opened her lips to cry. A jolt of pleasure coursed through her.

Oh, this was every bit as good as she'd heard it was. Harry held her tightly. Soon her sense of propriety, that had so conveniently deserted her, made itself known. Loath as she was to leave his arms, she sat up. "Help me dress. We cannot be caught in a locked room."

"Yes, it would cause just the trouble I'm trying to avoid." He stood her on the floor and laced her gown up. Taking quick strides to the door he unlocked it, glanced out into the corridor, then closed it again.

He was back to her in an instant and took her hands. "I love you."

She smiled a little. "I love you as well. I thought about us a great deal and how happy I could be to spend my life with you."

"Emma, what do you want from a marriage?"

"I made a list."

Harry laughed. "Will you let me see it?"

Emma went to the desk. "I was working on it here." She picked up a sheet of paper and handed it to him.

Harry read it, then looked at her in surprise. "Love, trust, friendship, honesty, loyalty."

She smiled a little nervously. "If we have those things, everything else will follow."

Harry folded the list and put it aside. "Emma Spencer-Jones, I promise you love, trust, friendship, honesty, and loyalty. Will you be my wife, my friend, and my lover?"

She wanted to throw her arms around him and say yes, but she had to ask, "Harry, are you sure? If this is about what just happened, I-I don't want you to rush."

"No, I made the decision this morning." He paused for a moment. "It may sound silly, but I was waiting for a sign, and it came."

"If you're sure, then yes, I'd like nothing better than to marry you, Harry Marsh."

He pulled her into his arms and kissed her. "When do you want to tell Lady Rutherford?"

Chapter 26

Julia Rutherford paced her parlor. If only she had a little more time. She glanced down again at the empty space on her desk where she'd left the household ledgers before she'd gone to London. Rutherford had them. She knew it.

He'd be furious with her, and she couldn't blame him. Even if she'd taken the money for a good reason, it was still wrong of her. She tugged the bell pull. A footman answered. "Is his lordship at home?"

"Yes, my lady. He's in his study."

Julia took a deep breath. Better to get it over with. A few minutes later, when she reached out to knock on the door, her hand shook. He'd soon know everything.

"Come," he called.

She made herself smile and entered. "My dear, there is something I need to tell . . ." She flinched at the sight of Anna sitting next to her son. "What is Miss Marsh doing in here?"

Rutherford raised a brow. "We're going over all the accounts. Anna needs to be familiar with them."

This was worse than Julia had thought. That her future daughter-in-law should know as well. She couldn't keep herself from stuttering. "Oh . . . oh . . . yes . . . of course."

Rutherford stood. "What did you want to see me about?"

Anna started to rise.

"No, stay where you are, my love." His brows lowered.

"Are you sure?" Miss Marsh said. "I mean . . ."

"Yes, please stay."

She eased back into her chair.

"Mother." He indicated a chair facing the desk.

It took all her bravery not to run out. She folded her hands in her lap and tried to calm herself. "It's about the household accounts. I've been using them—I've spent the money on myself."

His lips thinned to a line. "We know. What we can't figure out is why. You have a generous jointure."

Heat rose in her face, and she glanced quickly at Miss Marsh. Her expression of unruffled interest hadn't changed. Julia addressed her son. "I've been supporting someone. A man. He-he was injured in the war and didn't receive the pension he was to have got. He's been very ill." Her voice faded.

"Go on." Rutherford's face had grown hard, harder than she ever remembered it.

Flustered, she continued. "There were court expenses and lawyer's fees and medical bills as well as the rooms. I couldn't afford it all and my personal expenses as well."

His voice was wintry. "What is this man to you?"

Tears filled her eyes, and she blinked, trying not to cry. After her husband died, she had thought never to hear that tone again.

Miss Marsh came to her. "Sebastian, that's enough. Leave us for a few minutes. Please."

He gave a disgusted snort, but did as she asked. Once the door was closed, Miss Marsh pulled a chair over to Julia, handed her a handkerchief, and took one of her hands, chaffing it. "I know you haven't always liked me. But, I think telling me will be easier than telling Sebastian."

Lady Rutherford wiped her eyes. "You have to understand, I never meant to hurt anyone."

Miss Marsh nodded.

Julia took a shaky breath. Not able to meet the younger woman's eyes, Julia focused on the fire, blue flames mixed with red, yellow, and orange. "Years ago when I was first out, I fell in love. John was a third son of an impoverished peer. My father wanted more for me, and when John asked for my hand, Father refused to even consider him." Her throat tightened. "We discussed running away to marry, but John was in the army, and his commander knew my father. It would have been disastrous. Lord Rutherford offered, and my father accepted for me. I-I was devastated, and I suppose foolish. Rutherford was so much older. I talked John into—well . . ."

Miss Marsh squeezed her hand. "I understand."

"T-thank you. I didn't know then that things could be"—Julia lifted her head and stared out the window—"could be faked. And I was too stupid to stay quiet. I hated the idea that I would have to live my life with someone other than John." Julia closed her eyes. "That I would have to give myself to another man. After Lord Rutherford and I married, I told him." She met Miss Marsh's steady, non-condemnatory gaze. "I wanted him to leave me alone, you see. He was furious and said and did hurtful things. He said I owed him an heir. He didn't touch me until he was sure I wasn't breeding. After that, he demanded I do my duty until he got me with his child. You don't know how happy I was when Sebastian was born. His father never came to me after that."

"Did John come back?" Miss Marsh asked.

Julia nodded. This was easier than she'd expected it to be, and she needed to tell someone. "Yes, he was posted in London for several years before the war. Old Lord Rutherford didn't know. I was discreet. I only went to my husband when necessary. My deception worked until the last time I was with child. By that time, he was incapable and . . ."

She broke down into tears.

"Yes," Miss Marsh said. "I do not think the girls or anyone else will be helped by that knowledge. I take it that was when he was struck down by apoplexy?"

"No, his apoplexy came just before then. At least his illness is not on my conscience."

Miss Marsh frowned. "The old Lord Rutherford provided for your daughters?"

"No. That as well as my jointure was in the marriage settlement." Julia glanced at Miss Marsh. "We all knew unless I died in childbirth, I'd outlive him by many years."

"John is now in London, I take it." Miss Marsh said.

"Yes. I lied to him as well. He doesn't know I've been the one supporting him. He wouldn't have allowed it." Julia swallowed. "You would not have wanted to see the slum he was living in when

I found him. He'll begin receiving his pension soon, and his health is much better." She had never thought she'd be thankful for Miss Marsh. It had been easier to talk to her than to her son. Sebastian's hard face looked so much like his father's.

Miss Marsh was quiet for several minutes. "How long have you been supporting him?"

"Over a year."

"My lady, do you and John still wish to marry?"

"Yes, but he won't do it if he cannot support me."

Miss Marsh worried her lip. "Does your jointure end if you re-marry?"

Julia glanced up. What was Miss Marsh thinking? "No, I have it for life."

She stood and shook out her skirts. "I have an idea. If you agree, I'll talk to Sebastian. I suggest you and John marry and live in the dower-house so you're not separated from your daughters. You know, as the children's guardian, Sebastian won't allow you to re-move them from the Priory. John will have his pension to help sup-port you."

"What about Emma?"

Miss Marsh smiled. "If need be, I'll sponsor her. I would like to put off bringing Althea out until the following year. Sebastian thinks she's too young."

"If you're sure you don't mind?" This type of understanding was not at all what Julia had expected from Miss Marsh. Sebastian had indeed made a good choice.

Miss Marsh smiled warmly. "Not at all. If this is what you want."

Julia dried her tears and straightened her shoulders. "Yes, I think it will answer."

"Let me help you to your chamber, and I'll speak with Sebastian."

She stood and turned to Miss Marsh. "Thank you," Julia said shakily. "I am sorry I've not welcomed you as I ought to have. It— it wasn't that I didn't like *you*."

Julia held the handkerchief to her mouth, forcing back another sob. "I couldn't bear to see you or your family. Your family had everything I wanted and could never have."

Miss Marsh hugged Julia and smiled. "There's still time for you. Come, once you are in your room, I'll send your dresser to you."

Anna accompanied Lady Rutherford to her chambers, then returned to the study where Sebastian awaited her.

"Well?" he asked.

She rubbed her forehead and prayed he'd understand. "In some ways it's complicated and in others so simple. Tell me, what do you know about your parents' marriage?"

He drew his brows together. "She was never happy. I couldn't understand why. She had everything."

"Except love."

"Did she want it?"

"Your mother was in love with a young man in the army. Her father wouldn't let her marry him and arranged a marriage with your father. She and the young man . . ." Anna waved her hand.

"I understand."

"After they married, she told your father."

Rutherford ran his hands over his face. "Oh, God."

"My feelings precisely. Your father kept her here until she was pregnant with you. Sebastian, he almost never touched her again. Except when she performed as a wife, she's been faithful to the man she loved as a young lady."

He stared at her, comprehension dawning in his face. "The girls aren't my father's?"

"No. Apparently when she discovered she was breeding, she'd go to your father. Except for the last time when he'd already had apoplexy."

Sebastian stared out at the lawn. "He died shortly afterward. I wonder if he even knew she was pregnant. Still, he never paid attention to the girls. Any affection he had was lavished on me, and it wasn't all that much." Sebastian turned back to her. "I never thought—I never understood my mother. I don't know what to do."

Anna continued. "I do not know, and I didn't want to ask her. Your mother's lover's name is John. He was badly injured. All her money and the household funds have gone to take care of him. He doesn't know she's supporting him. He doesn't know about the girls either." Anna paused and fixed her gaze on Sebastian. "I suggested to your mother that she and John marry and live in the dower-house. The country has got to be better for him than London." Anna hoped she was getting through to Sebastian and that he'd go along with her plan. "Sweetheart, your mother heard he'd come back and searched for him. She found him in a slum."

Rutherford held his hand out to Anna. She went to him. Cupping the back of his neck to bring his head down to hers, she touched his forehead with hers. "She told me the only reason she didn't like my family was because we had everything she never would. I told her it wasn't too late for her. Please don't make my words a lie."

He shook his head. "I cannot imagine my mother in a slum."

Anna chuckled lightly. "Well, it may not have been as bad as we think. Though it was probably worse than Bloomsbury."

His shoulder shook as a small laugh escaped him. "Yes. You know, my love, I'm curious about him."

"As am I. Your mother also agreed that Althea will not come out this Season."

He kissed her. "You drive a hard bargain."

"My love, Althea is just not ready," Anna said. "Your mother spent the last year helping John and ignoring her daughter's domestic education." Anna sighed. "Even if Althea wanted to marry, she doesn't have the skills to run a house. She's beautiful. She could make a very good match, but that comes with responsibilities."

Rutherford grimaced. "I don't dispute you at all. I just dread telling her."

Anna reached up to smooth his brow. "I'll explain it to her."

He bent his head to kiss her and a knock sounded on the door. "Who is it?"

"It's us," Harry answered.

Rutherford sighed. "Come in then."

Harry and Emma walked in hand in hand.

Anna smiled. "How can we help you?"

Harry's eyes twinkled for a moment, and then he frowned. "We've decided to marry and don't know how to tell Lady Rutherford."

Anna hugged Emma and her brother. "I'm so happy for you. I'll tell her. I don't think you need to worry. Lady Rutherford has agreed that I will be in charge of Emma."

Emma's mouth dropped open. "O-oh, my."

Harry gave a bark of laughter, and Rutherford poured brandy for them and sherry for Anna and Emma.

Anna sat on the sofa. "When do you want to wed?"

Harry glanced at Emma. "As soon as possible?"

She nodded. "Yes. There is no reason to wait."

"Harry, tug the bell pull," Sebastian said, as he went to his desk and pulled a piece of paper toward him, then scribbled a short missive.

When Griffin answered the call, Sebastian handed him the sealed letter. "Have this taken to Dover for the mail. It needs to go out tonight."

Anna widened her eyes. "What was that?"

"That is going to bring a special license." Sebastian grinned.

She smiled broadly. "Ah, I see."

Emma frowned. "Well, I'm glad you understand. I do not at all."

"A special license will allow you to marry without the banns being read." Sebastian turned to Anna. "How would you like to share our wedding with Harry and Emma?"

How clever of Sebastian to think of it. "I'd love it. What could be better? Emma, do you mind?"

Emma beamed with delight. "No, it's a wonderful idea. We can help each other with the preparations."

"Yes, and stand up with each other." Anna was really looking forward to having Emma in the family.

Everything was going so well. Almost too well. She and Sebastian had worked out their problems, Lady Rutherford would finally be with John, and Harry was returned and happy. She glanced at the clock. "Oh, no, look at the time. We must change."

She took Emma's arm. "I am so glad to finally have a sister."

"I think we shall make a good time of it," Emma said as they walked out the door.

Harry turned to Rutherford. "I guess we'd better change as well. What was all that about your mother?"

Rutherford took a large sip of brandy. This was not something he wanted to discuss, even with Harry. "It is a long story and not mine to tell."

He shrugged. "As long as it allows me to marry Emma, I don't care."

Rutherford put his glass on the desk and slapped his friend on the back. "That, my friend, it will do."

Harry raised a brow. "To whom did you send the letter?"

Rutherford grinned. "I'll tell you later."

Within the hour, he met with his mother in the drawing room.

She was a little pale and trembled when she met his gaze. "I—I don't know how to begin."

He took her hand, searching for something to say that would not make matters worse. "Anna explained it."

"I do like her," his mother said. "She'll make you a very good wife."

He'd better tell her the rest now. "Mother, Harry and Emma have decided to marry."

His mother's eyes widened. "They only just met."

"No, not really. They traveled up from Weymouth together." He stuck his head out the door and called over a footman. "Please ask Miss Marsh and the others to come in. Bring champagne."

Anna entered first with Emma and Harry behind her. Emma glanced at Rutherford's mother. "I take it he told you?"

She smiled. "Oh, my dear, are you sure?"

A smile hovered around Emma's lips. "Yes, my lady. I am very sure."

Lady Rutherford took her hands. "Well then. Everything seems to be working out for all of us. Rutherford, if you don't mind, I shall leave for London tomorrow. We'll be back for the wedding." She turned to Anna. "You know what you want. Do you mind my deserting you like this?"

Anna's eyes sparkled. "No, not at all. I'll manage. You do what you need to. Bring him back with you."

"Thank you." His mother swallowed. "Please, call me Julia. I am delighted Rutherford had the good sense to fall in love with you."

His betrothed's eyes softened. "Thank you. Your good wishes mean a great deal to me."

"I guess this means we'll all move back to Marsh Hill." Rutherford watched Anna as she put it together.

"Of course, Emma cannot possibly remain here whilst Julia is in London. There is no reason you can't come tonight. I'll send a note." Anna turned her gaze to his mother. "Do you mind?"

She shook her head. "No, my dear, not at all. It will make my departure much easier, not having to deal with the girls in the morning."

Anna wrote a missive and handed it to Rutherford. "I think this will do it. Have Miss Madison join us."

Rutherford handed the note to Griffin and asked him to have the governess attend to him. He turned to Anna and raised a brow. "Room distributions." She grinned. "It's time to pay our debt to Harry."

"I'm sure he'll be happy."

A few minutes later, Miss Jynkins entered.

"Dear Jenny," Anna said, "we are all moving back to Marsh Hill. I am so sorry to put you to the trouble."

"It is no problem at all. However, I shall not tell the girls until we are ready to leave. I am sure you understand."

"Indeed. Have their clothes and whatnot packed while they eat dinner," Anna said. "Lord Rutherford shall send some maids to help. You may leave with the children as soon as you are ready. We'll be along later."

Harry whispered to Emma, "They'll be so ecstatic, we'll have trouble putting them to bed tonight."

Rutherford and Anna saw her brother and his betrothed off immediately after dinner, as he and Anna were getting ready to leave, Rutherford turned to his mother. "Mama, I'm sorry."

She shook her head. "None of it was your doing, my dear."

He took her hands and held them, wanting to make it better for her. "Be that as it may, I hope you will now find your happiness."

She blinked her eyes rapidly. "Thank you. I'll take my time returning. All of you seem to like it at Marsh Hill."

Rutherford grinned. "Yes."

His mother gave a sob and tried to turn away, but he held her. "It wasn't your fault. Now that I have Anna, I couldn't imagine being forced to marry another."

She raised her head. "Thank you. I never meant to hurt anyone."

The back of his throat was sore. "Be back by the twenty-ninth, will you?"

"Yes, of course. Could you see to the dower-house?"

"We'll look at what needs to be done. Do you need funds?"

"I could use a couple of hundred pounds."

"Wait here. I'll write you a draft." He strode off and returned a few minutes later. "Here you are."

She hugged him. "Sebastian, love her."

"I do, Mama."

Tears rolled down her cheeks. "I am happy for you." She fled up the stairs.

Anna turned to him. "Is she all right?"

"I think so."

Anna worried her lip. "She's held so much in for so long."

"I would say I wish I'd known, but I don't know if that's true."

Anna put her hands on his shoulders and gazed up at him. "It would have placed you in an untenable position."

He kissed her forehead. "You're right. I'm glad you were here today. I don't think I could have . . ."

She gave him a smile. "Tomorrow, we need to see to the dower-house."

When they arrived at Marsh Hill, Jenny had the girls ready for bed. Once they were tucked in for the night, the couples spent some time in Anna's parlor before retiring.

Harry hugged Anna. "Thank you for your help today."

Her eyes grew misty. "That's what sisters are for. Good night to the both of you." When they left, she turned to Rutherford. "I'll not be long."

A short while later, Rutherford held up the covers as Anna slid into bed and settled back against him. "What a wonderful day this has been."

Mostly due to Anna's efforts, it had not turned into a disaster. "Certainly much better than I expected it to be."

She shuddered. "The thought of giving myself to another man repulses me. Your mother is much braver than I would have been."

He held her closer. "I tried to imagine what I'd feel if I'd not been allowed to marry you." He shifted over her, to see her face. "Anna, I'd kill any man who hurt you in any way or tried to come between us."

The problem with her being involved in the smuggling mission flashed into his mind. What if the man was him?

Chapter 27

Rutherford's arms were around Anna when he woke. She slept boneless against him. His chest tightened when he thought of losing her and her trust. He'd been feeling more and more uneasy about not telling Anna about the shipment. It didn't help that Harry wasn't on his side. Still Rutherford couldn't risk her safety.

Anna stretched against him and mumbled. "What is it?"

"Nothing."

"You're tense."

"Just a bad dream. Go back to sleep."

Lizzy's voice came through the door. "Miss, it's time to leave."

Rutherford pushed aside the hangings with a silent curse. Daylight. He must have fallen back to sleep. "Anna, wake up."

"No."

He pushed the covers back, and she cuddled into him. "Come, my love."

She opened her eyes.

He smiled as Anna pouted, something she so seldom did, and shrugged into her wrapper.

"One week?"

"One week."

Less than an hour later, Anna grinned as she gazed around the table. Breakfast with his sisters was a noisy affair.

Sir William raised his quizzing glass and said, "I suppose someone will eventually tell me why we have all of the Priory here."

Harry glanced at Anna, who replied, "Papa, Lady Rutherford needed to visit a sick friend in Town, and it would not have been proper for Miss Spencer-Jones to remain at the Priory."

"Ah well," Papa said. "You know I always enjoy the children."

"Mama joining us?" Harry asked.

Sir William glanced around as if just discovering his wife was not there. "She should be."

Harry motioned for a footman. "See where Lady Marsh is."

"Yes, sir."

A few minutes later, Lady Marsh entered the room. "My dear, you wanted me?"

Harry said. "I wanted to tell everyone at the same time. Miss Spencer-Jones has agreed to be my wife."

Lady Marsh's jaw dropped. "Isn't this a little sudden?"

Harry grinned. "What you don't know is that we met as I was traveling to London. She helped me get my memory back."

"Well, then. How wonderful." Mama hugged him and then Emma. "I wish you both very happy. Have you decided on a date?"

"If the special license arrives in time, we plan to marry at the same time as Anna and Rutherford."

"We have a lot to consider," she said, and then said not another word.

"Mama, Emma is used to living with a large family," Harry said.

"Of course you'll live with us," Sir William said as he accepted another cup of tea. "Where else would you live?" He addressed Anna, "My dear, you need to decide what you want to take with you to the Priory. We can have it all packed and carted over."

"I'll make a list today." Anna finished eating and rose to leave. "Rutherford?"

He rose. "Yes, I'll join you."

Miss Jynkins took the girls up to the schoolroom, and the two couples walked up to Anna's parlor.

"That was strange," Anna said. "I wish I knew what was going on between Mama and Papa. I thought they'd worked everything out."

"If your mother is concerned, I'll try to take over...." Emma said.

Harry shook his head. "No, it can't be that. She's let Anna run the house since before I left."

"Better than fighting the inevitable," Rutherford said under his breath.

"Did you say something, my love?"

"Me? No, not a word. I was just thinking."

"I say we leave it to them and go on as we wish." Anna frowned and turned to Harry. "What has Papa been working on lately?"

"I'm not sure. He's received a number of letters, but he hasn't discussed them with me."

Anna shrugged. "What do we want to do today?"

"Why don't you take Emma around the Hill and get her acquainted with the staff," Harry suggested, "I'll do some estate work and see if I can figure out what Papa's about. Rutherford?"

"There are a few matters I need to attend to. Do you wish to meet for luncheon here or at the Priory?"

"Let's meet at the Priory," Anna said. "Afterward, we can show Emma around town and you"—she looked pointedly at Harry—"can tell the vicar you are marrying. Give me just a moment and I'll be back. Emma, you'll find a pad and pencil in the desk."

Anna walked into her bedchamber. "Lizzy?"

"Yes, miss?"

"Have you heard anything from Kev? We should know about the shipment by now."

"Not a word. I'll check on it today."

"Thank you. Oh, I almost forgot to tell you. Harry is marrying Miss Spencer-Jones."

"How in the world did that happen?" her maid exclaimed.

Anna told her about Harry and Emma's trip to London.

"Oh, miss, that's so romantic."

She laughed. "I think you're a romantic. I'm taking Emma around this morning as she'll be taking over my duties. Lizzy, please make a list of what needs to go to the Priory."

When Anna walked back into the parlor, Rutherford drew her into his arms. "I needed to kiss you before I leave."

She tilted her head up. "I'm ready."

He smiled. "You only think you are."

Sebastian captured her lips and laid siege to her senses. He tasted fresh, with just a hint of tea. Her body was flush against his; she moaned. The exciting, now familiar need shot through her body. She wanted him. He lifted her with one hand under her bottom. And stopped.

"What?" Anna asked. Her body trembled with unfulfilled need.

"Someone's coming."

Sebastian slipped into his room as one of the tweenies entered.

Rutherford found Harry in the main hall. "What is it?"

"Are you still determined to keep the shipment a secret from Anna?"

"Yes. I'm too afraid she'll be injured."

"I understand you want to keep her safe," Harry said. "But what if she finds out and shows up?"

Rutherford stopped walking. The possibility of Anna's just appearing while the delivery was being made was too horrible to think of. His mind went blank.

Harry raised his brows. "It could happen, you know. She's not at all stupid."

Passing a hand over his eyes, Rutherford groaned. "I didn't even think of that."

"I'll see you later." Harry strode down the side corridor.

Rutherford drove his curricle to the Priory. There were no good choices. How best to protect her?

When he reached his office, a letter sat conspicuously on the table. Who now? Rutherford picked it up and looked at the seal. Jamison. No postage. It had to have come by special messenger. He broke it open and spread the paper out on the desk. Help was on the way. They'd arrive in Dover tonight, five men and coaches for the packages. Rutherford opened the door, asked the footman to summon Griffin, and closed the door. A minute later it opened. "Yes, my lord?"

He held up the letter. "When did this arrive?"

"Just now, my lord. I was preparing to send it to Marsh Hill."

"Miss Spencer-Jones and Mr. and Miss Marsh will join me for luncheon."

"Very well, my lord. Does Cook know you are expecting guests?"

"No, please tell her. Give Cook my apologies as well."

Griffin bowed and left.

Rutherford attempted to work, but couldn't get his mind off Anna. He walked to the French windows and gazed out over the terrace and park. Something gave him an ominous feeling about his betrothed, as if he were about to step into the fens without a guide.

Harry was right. Anna wasn't stupid, and she *was* a managing sort of woman. What were the odds she'd forget to ask about the shipment? No, that was a wager he'd refuse if someone else offered it. Then the question became what to do if she accused him of trying to keep it a secret?

Damn Harry Marsh for putting him in this position.

Shortly after noon, Anna breezed into his study, bringing a cold, fresh scent with her. But the smile on her lips didn't reach her eyes.

He drew his brows together. "Is there something on your mind?"

Anna tilted her head and met his eyes. Her pretty lips formed a *moue.* "Well, I hadn't heard anything about the shipment, so I had Lizzy ask Kev. He'd sent a message to Harry two days ago. I don't know why Harry didn't tell me." She opened her eyes wide. "Do you know?"

Before Rutherford could answer, she looked down at her hands, then back at him again. "It wouldn't have anything to do with you trying to protect me?"

There was a shrewd look in her wide blue eyes.

He hadn't expected such a direct attack. "Yes. Anna, I can't let you risk yourself and possibly our child. You could be breeding."

"Even if I was, I'm not going to be down on the beach. I'll be safe where I always am."

Her jaw clenched as she started to pace the length of the room, her skirts kicking up with each step. Her hands balled into fists. He had to make her understand.

"Do you remember," she said in a raw voice, "when you told me you needed to serve?"

He nodded, curtly. "What does this have to do with that?"

"This was my only way to serve. Not only my country, but my brother's memory." When he didn't answer, she continued. "Do you think only men feel that need?"

Why was she being so difficult? "Anna, it's not the same. Ladies serve by caring for their families."

"Men have families as well. Some women need more. I needed more." Her tone softened. "I've worked with these men for over two years. They trust me. How would you feel if you were taken off a mission before the end? Don't you see? I have to finish this."

Sebastian attacked his hair. Nothing mattered but her safety. "No. It's too dangerous. You're mine, and you'll do what I tell you to."

The minute the words were out of his mouth, he knew he'd made a serious mistake. Anna's jaw dropped, then snapped shut. She stared at him like he'd betrayed her. By pretending to go along with the plan, had he? Did it matter? She was angry, but that wouldn't last. The most important thing was Anna's protection, even from herself if need be. This mission had become too dangerous for her to be involved.

Her chest rose and fell with barely suppressed fury. Then her expression changed from anger to determination. She briefly closed her eyes and gave a small shake of her head. "I'm sorry you feel that way. I find we do not suit, my lord." She turned and walked to the door. "Good-bye, Sebastian."

"Anna, wait! What if you're breeding?"

When she glanced back at him, her face was deadly calm. The same as when she'd negotiated with the spy. "I'll let you know. I plan to leave in a couple of days. Don't try to follow me."

The door shut with a click behind her.

He wanted to run after her, but his feet wouldn't move. Sinking down on to a chair, he groaned. "Oh, God. What have I done?"

Damn himself for being a stupid prig. All he'd wanted to do was keep her safe, and now she was threatening to run off, who knows where. Despite what she said, he had to find her. Make her see reason. Make her marry him.

Harry burst through the door. "What's going on? I just saw Anna walk out the front door. She said the wedding is off."

"She says she's leaving." How could Rutherford face his best friend or her family?

"The devil she did," Harry roared. "What if she's carrying your child?"

Rutherford shook his head. For the first time in his life, he was lost. "I don't know what to do." He bit down hard on his inner lip to keep the tears at bay. "Harry, how do I get her back?"

"Grovel. And you'd better do a damn good job of it."

* * *

Anna reached the stables and started to saddle Thunderer. She could barely see through the blur of tears. Just when she had everything she'd ever wanted in life, it had all fallen apart, like a sand castle on the beach. Thank God she'd found out before they married.

She was at the end of a lane when she found herself on the way to the cottage. At least she'd be alone there. Her family, Mama especially, would not be happy about her decision. Still, she was one and twenty with her own funds. She needed to go someplace far away, perhaps Italy. She sobbed again. She'd miss her family, but if she remained here, she'd have to marry Sebastian, and she couldn't live with being ordered around. If he was trying to stop her from doing what she had done for over two years, what else would he forbid? For her, life was more than just home and family. She couldn't tie herself to a man who couldn't accept that.

By the time she led Thunderer around to the back of the cottage, she'd stopped crying. A list, she needed to make a list. After building up the fire, she took a notebook and pencil from her pocket, but nothing came, no ideas, no plans, just misery. If only she didn't love him so much.

Sometime later, Anna was sitting at the table, staring into the fire, when the door slammed open.

Sebastian stood in the entryway looking every bit a warrior. His face was flushed, and his chest heaved when he drew a breath and growled, "You're not leaving me."

"Get out. I'll do as I please. You don't own me!" Rage coursed through her. Anger at him for his betrayal and at herself for loving him, despite everything. She clenched her fists, wanting to pummel him for destroying it all.

His eyes were molten silver as he glared at her, as if he'd like to throttle her.

"You're right. I don't own you. Even when we're married, I won't own you."

"Didn't you hear me?" She tried to keep the tears from her voice. "We are not going to wed. I'm leaving England."

He muttered something under his breath. "I'll follow you."

She threw her hands up and said through clenched teeth, "No, you will not."

"You can't stop me." He strode over to her, his face fierce and resolute. "I'll spend the rest of my life making a fool of myself dogging your footsteps around Europe or anyplace else you decide to go. I'll sleep outside your door."

"You say that now, but no one loves another that much." It was a lie. She loved him every bit that much. He was so close his legs were touching her knees, but his hands remained by his sides. The air between them crackled. Oh, how she wanted to believe him.

"I love you more than that." He lifted her to her feet, wrapping his arms around her. "I was wrong for saying what I did. My only excuse is that I love you. If something were to happen to you, my life wouldn't be worth living."

"I can't live the life you want me to." No, she couldn't let him talk her round. "I'd suffocate and die."

His arms were so strong, and her body heated, wanting him.

"I just wanted to keep you safe."

He was so frustrating. "Sebastian, life is a risk. Women die all the time in childbirth. Will you keep me safe from that as well?"

A look of anguish passed over his face. "Anna, I'm sorry. When it comes to you, some primitive beast comes out. I just want to protect you."

"I want to defend you too. It's part of being in love, but that doesn't mean I'd stop you from being yourself."

He let out a breath. "You're right. I didn't think of it like that."

She'd been gradually sinking into him. Reveling in his heat. His palms stroked her back, and he started nibbling her neck. "I don't know. I've no guarantee you won't try to control me after we're married."

"We'll put it in the marriage settlement. Wife is allowed to tell husband to go to the devil when he acts like a prig."

"Who will decide when husband is being a prig?" His hand cupped her breast. She moaned.

"Wife is at all times in charge of determining husband's state of mind." He cupped her derrière, drawing her closer to him.

"I don't know." His engorged member rode against her. She bit her lip to keep from moaning again.

"I'll frame a copy and hang it on the wall." Cool air swirled around her legs as he rucked her skirts higher.

"I may need more convincing." His fingers skated over the sensitive part behind her knee and kept going higher to the apex of her thighs. He stroked. That felt so good. Any minute now, she was going to melt.

"Hmm." He lifted her on to the table, spreading her legs with his body. His shaft hovered near her entrance, making her quiver with anticipation.

"What about, wife is always right?"

"Always?" She wanted him so badly her whole body ached with need.

"For the rest of our lives." She wrapped her legs around him, and he entered her.

"Yes," she moaned.

"Yes, to this?" He plunged into her, again. "Or yes to us?"

Anna clung to him, panting. "Yes to both."

"You drive a hard bargain."

"You knew that." God, it was amazing she could speak.

Sebastian thrust into her again. She clamped her legs tighter as his hands steadied her back. She pulled his head down to her, sucking and biting his earlobe. Then she kissed him, thrusting her tongue into his mouth, taking him as he took her. She'd never get enough of this man. Even when he was being a dry stick, he was hers.

She came fast and hard, like fireworks exploding.

Chapter 28

November 23rd, 1814, Dover, Kent

The next day, Rutherford handed Anna into the coach, as Harry assisted Emma before the men climbed in. Anna and Emma had decided they'd take the coach to Dover, explaining that if they did much shopping, it would be easier to carry their purchases home. Rutherford suspected it was to keep Emma warm. Anna said that her future sister-in-law had frozen the previous afternoon when they went to Thanport.

Yesterday had been a close call, but in less than a week, Anna would be his, forever. Rutherford had never thought he'd look forward to being leg-shackled, yet here he was, counting the minutes. The coaches pulled into the inn's yard.

"I received a missive from Jamison yesterday. I'll have to meet with the men."

Anna nodded. "Look for us when you're done."

Rutherford lifted her hands and kissed them. "I will."

He waited while they walked over to the main shopping street, before turning toward the docks and the Sloop, a dockside tavern. As agreed, his associates were waiting for him in a private parlor in the back of the inn.

"My friend." An elegant man, a little shorter than Rutherford, stood to greet him.

He glanced over the five men. He knew the first man and another one who stared out the window. "No names, I take it?"

"No. We, of course, have assigned names for each other. Just so that we don't become confused."

Rutherford nodded slightly. "Indeed. Do any of you have a document for me?"

The elegant man grinned. "Is it for you?"

Yes, he would have read the betrothal announcement. "No, a friend of mine."

The man took a packet out of his pocket. "Here you are."

"Thank you for bringing it."

The elegant man bowed.

"Now then, you know the assignment." Rutherford took out a hand-drawn map and spread it on a rough table in the center of the room. "These are the directions to where I'll meet you. It's about a half an hour horse ride from here, longer in a carriage, and not difficult to find."

He let the men study the map before saying, "We expect the shipment to arrive around three in the morning. Be at the meeting place no later than one thirty. I'll go over the details at that time. I'd advise you to get as much sleep today as you can. I expect it will be a long night."

He turned and walked out of the inn and circled round to the docks, still busy with ships and sailors. After waiting for about twenty minutes, he made his way to the shopping district.

Harry leaned against the outside wall of a large fabric store, looking bored.

Rutherford grinned. "New gowns?"

His friend grimaced. "I'm not sure. I think it may have more to do with petticoats."

Rutherford's smile deepened. The only interest Harry ever had in women's fashion was how to unfasten it. "Where do you need to go after this?"

Harry's discontent deepened. "I must buy Emma a ring. We don't have anything suitable in the family jewelry."

The thought occurred to Rutherford that he wanted a ring for Anna as well. Something not tainted with his family's unhappy marital past. "Why don't I wait here, and you can go to the jewelers?"

Harry pushed himself away from the wall with a sigh of relief. "Thank you."

"I'll meet you there." Rutherford strolled into the store and found the ladies looking at flannel. "What is that for?"

"Petticoats."

"I thought Harry was joking."

"No. Poor Emma has been so cold. We are discussing the merits of wool over flannel."

"Get both," Rutherford said.

"That is a very good idea. Emma, you can wear the flannel under the wool, if you'd like."

Rutherford rubbed his cheek. "How many, er, petticoats do you plan on wearing?" He knew some ladies wore up to five. He'd never found more than two on Anna. "Or is that an indelicate question?"

They laughed.

"It depends how cold I am," Emma said. "Very well, I shall take the wool and the flannel."

"Do you have much more shopping to do?" Rutherford asked.

"We are almost done. Why?"

"Harry is waiting for us down the street."

Anna took Rutherford's arm. "I must say, you are much better to have with one when shopping than my brother. At least you're helpful."

He grinned. "I aim to please."

Anna's light laughter floated musically through the air.

He could listen to that sound forever. "Come, let's tell the clerk and brave the cold to the next shop."

Rutherford took her arm and drew her away. "Are you making any purchases, my love?"

"Me? No. I have everything I need."

"Do you?" All ladies could find something to buy.

Anna smiled. "Yes. I shall receive a rather large package from Madame Lisette soon. We should stop at the post office whilst we are here to see if it's in."

"Ah, that explains it."

"Why?" she asked with a curious look. "Do you wish to buy me something?"

"Yes, now that you mention it, and I will." He glanced at the clerk who was wrapping Emma's purchases. "Please have that sent to the Ship." He held an arm out to both of them. "Ladies? Let us see if we can find something more interesting to buy."

Rutherford stopped at the door of the local jeweler. "It is not Rundell and Bridge's, but I'd match our man against them any day."

Anna considered her question.

"You, my love, need a ring," he said as he ushered them into the store.

"Oh, I thought you'd have one," she said.

"Nothing I consider suitable."

"This is going to cost you a great deal more than wool, my lord." She swept into the shop.

Harry's brows were creased as he frowned over a tray in front of him. Emma went to him and glanced down. "What are you trying to decide?"

He glanced up at her. "You need a ring. Church won't marry us without one."

"May I help," she asked tentatively, "or would you rather do this yourself?"

His face relaxed. "You may help, if you'd like."

Emma bent over the tray. She picked up a ring, finely wrought in gold. "I like this."

"Do you? Are you sure you'd not like something with sapphires or rubies? That was what I was trying to decide. Which you'd like better."

"Well, maybe for a necklace or a bracelet, but not for a ring."

"That was easier than I expected." He called to the clerk. "We'll take this one, and you may show me something else." Harry studied her. "Emeralds, I think."

Rutherford hid his laugh. Bending his head, he whispered, "Don't you dare tell me you want plain gold."

She whispered, "No, I prefer rubies."

"Of course, my love. Your taste is always exquisite."

Rutherford selected a gold ring set with rubies and small diamonds, and then spoke in low tones with the clerk and the jeweler.

Anna and Emma had their ring sizes taken. The jeweler promised the rings would be done in short order, and the couples left to walk to the Ship where the landlord showed them to his best private parlor.

By the time they'd finished luncheon, the packages from the jewelers and the fabric shop had been delivered. Harry made a show of slipping the ring on Emma's right hand. "The next time I put this on you, it will be in church."

Emma smiled, but her eyes were suspiciously damp.

Rutherford turned to Anna. "Your turn."

He took the ring from the box and slipped it on over her knuckle. "I want this ring to symbolize a new beginning for the Rutherfords."

Shortly after one o'clock the next morning, Anna, Sebastian, and Harry rode through the cold, dark night. Only a sliver of moonlight betrayed their progress. They reined in at the back of the cottage. Harry saw to the horses as Anna and Sebastian hurried inside.

Sebastian got out Anna's men's clothing while she stripped off her riding habit. He'd told Anna and Harry about the meeting with the other men before they left the Hill.

For some reason unknown to Anna, her mother had decided to stay up talking to her. Finally, Anna's yawning had convinced Mama she needed to retire. Just in case Mama decided to check up on Anna, Emma had volunteered to sleep in Anna's bed.

Rutherford picked up the clothes she'd cast aside in her haste, folding them and storing them in the bin. Harry came in and helped her braid her hair.

"I hear them," Sebastian said.

Anna slapped her hat over her braids, pulled it down, and held out her hand. "The muffler."

Harry gave it to her. She wrapped it around her neck and donned her thick wool coat and gloves. "Done."

Sebastian glanced back at her. She nodded, and he opened the door. Five men filed in and stopped.

He'd described the men in detail. The elegant man's eyes widened. "Who are these gentlemen?"

"You may not remember Harry Marsh," Sebastian said. "He ran the gang for Jamison before, and this is Mr. Arnold, who took over while Harry was gone."

Anna narrowed her eyes as the men looked her over. Thank the Lord only one candle was lit, and it was on the table across the room.

Sebastian drew their attention away from her. "He's the one who negotiated the payment."

The man called Henry nodded. "Did a good job with that. Jamison saw red, but there was nothing he could do but agree."

Anna curtly inclined her head. Though her voice was low for a lady, and Harry had worked with her to make it lower, she didn't need to take any chances by speaking more than necessary.

"All right, then." Sebastian spread out the map. "We're here. We'll meet the smugglers on the beach just by this jetty."

He pointed to a spot on the map about three miles away. "If everything goes as planned, and there's no reason it shouldn't—the wind is in the right quarter, and we've no storms coming in—the ship should be off shore by around three in the morning."

He glanced at them. "We need to be in place in the next half hour."

Rutherford motioned toward Anna. "Mr. Arnold will meet with the smugglers an hour before the shipment is due. There's always a chance the ship could arrive early. Keep your distance from the smugglers until the packages arrive. I've been told they're glad for your help, but don't want you to be able to recognize them."

"There is a cave right about here." Harry pointed to the map. "You'll all stay there until we've received the signal from the ship."

He turned to Sebastian. "Do they know about the complication?"

"Yes, *our friend* will be at a shack down the beach toward town. When we arrive, we must lose one of the packages. I'm told it will be recognizable." He gave them the description Georges had given him. "Whoever has her needs to walk behind the others. We"—he waved to include Anna—"will be on the cliffs watching. If anything happens, we'll come down immediately."

"What about the gentleman from the Foreign Office?" one of the men asked.

"One of the smugglers is to bring him. What you do with him is no concern of mine." Rutherford glanced around. "Is everyone armed? Other than knives, the smugglers won't have weapons."

They all nodded. "Right then," Sebastian said. "Let's be off."

"Rutherford," a man drawled, "any chance of a warm drink after this is over?"

He stopped and looked back. "Curry, you'll be on your way to

London when this is over. Have Jamison make you a nice rum punch when you return. Or better yet, go to Brook's."

"I'll tell you what." Curry slapped Rutherford on his back. "We'll go out when you come back to Town."

"Sorry, I'm getting married next week. I'll have better things to do." Anna turned to hide her smile.

Harry cuffed her arm. "Come on."

She followed him out in the direction of the stables, but Curry's voice trailed behind. "What's marriage got to do with it?"

Harry swung up on to Devil. "I'll relieve Rutherford so he can saddle his horse."

"I'll wait here," Anna replied. Sebastian had been concerned that one of the gentlemen might follow them back to the stables.

"See you shortly." Harry rode around to the front to keep the other men company, while Anna waited on Thunderer for Sebastian.

He grabbed her around her waist and pulled her down.

Anna gazed up, concerned. "What?"

"This." He hauled her to him, and for a brief moment his hard lips pressed down on hers. He helped her mount again. "Keep yourself safe."

She cupped his cheek. "I will. You do the same."

They rode out to meet the others. Other than the sound of horses' hooves beating a tattoo on the frozen ground, the night was silent. When they reached the copse of trees, Anna signaled for them to stop and dismount. She ran to the cliff, dropped down and peered over the side. The beach was empty.

Waving her arm, Anna led the way down the path to the cave. "You gents can wait here with his lordship."

Harry followed her as she strode toward the beach.

"It's going well."

Anna turned to him. "When it's finished, it will be."

"Superstitious?"

"No, experienced. You forget. I ran this gang for over two years during the war. I kept everything going. They made larger profits because *I* bargained harder. And I did it all, while still managing to be in London for the Seasons, without the freedom of movement you had. Just because I know I cannot continue doesn't mean I don't want to."

Harry made a move to put an arm around her.

"Don't," she hissed. "You've got five men watching who *you* have decided should not know I am a female."

He dropped his arm and nodded. "I'm sorry. I just don't want you hurt by this. Those men are all members of the *ton*. I am not convinced your involvement wouldn't leak out."

Anna bit her lip. He was right. It would be disastrous to not only her but Sebastian if it got around. "I know," she said bitterly. "What they would keep as a secret for a man might not hold true for a woman."

"Anna, do you ever wish I hadn't made you responsible?"

"No. Truth be told, I enjoy it," she said. "I learned from it. I only wish you'd not taken so long coming home."

Anna turned her head to the sounds of men walking on the beach. "Kev and the rest of them are coming with our traitor."

The London gent glanced at her and then at Harry. "Who is this?" he asked haughtily.

"Me brother," Anna said, slipping into dialect. "Just come back from a long trip."

"Oh, well then, I suppose it's all right."

Anna pulled Kev aside. "The Home Office men are in the cave. When you see the signal, go back there and get them. We'll take the turncoat there shortly."

Kev smiled broadly. "As you say. We'll all be sorry to have you leave."

Anna touched his arm. "Thank you for that."

She sauntered over to the gent. "Why don't you come with me while we're waiting. You'll be warmer."

"Yes, yes. It is a bit cold."

"This way."

When they reached the cave, she stepped aside to allow him to enter. In the dark, even she couldn't see the men. "Go in the cave. It's not wet, and ye'll be out of the wind. I'll call when we're ready."

Anna quickly walked away. She heard a startled shout and a thump, then low chuckles, a shush, and silence. She nodded her head once and smiled.

"Well?" Kev asked her.

"They have him."

She stood with Harry and Kev watching for the signal. When it came she strode back to the cave and said to Sebastian, "Game's on."

"If there are any questions, address them to Marsh," Sebastian told the men, and joined Anna.

She scrambled up the path with him following, and took her place on the cliff. He lay beside her. The gang pushed the boats out.

"Anna."

"No, don't talk. Sound carries." She waited the same way she had for the past two years. "Here they come."

"How can you tell?"

Anna smiled. "You'll see them in a minute." The boats rowed in. Four huddled figures in skirts were helped from them.... All women? "What's this? Did you know they'd be females?"

Rutherford shook his head. "No. I only knew about the one that had to be rescued."

Women? A light dawned. Of course. What a brilliant idea. "Whores."

"That would be my guess. They're not here for the Season."

"A good plan."

"Brilliant. Too many men tend to talk under certain circumstances." He coughed. "Let's get the horses."

"No. Wait until they've cleared this area." Someone waving caught her eye. "Sebastian, look."

"Stay here."

"No." She made her way down the path like a goat. He followed, and Kev met them.

"They was none too smart, your Home Office nobs. They left that gent alone, and he got away when the boats came back in."

Anna turned to Sebastian and fixed him with a narrow-eyed look as she asked Kev, "Did he go back toward town?"

"Not sure exactly."

"We need to find him." Anna frowned. "Can our men take the women back?"

Kev met her gaze and rolled his eyes. Not a good idea.

Anna nodded. "Kev, tell Harry we need him. You're in charge. Make sure nothing happens to stop the nobs from taking the women. We'll meet Harry on top."

She turned to Rutherford. "We should go. We need to get the horses to the inn and look for the gent."

* * *

Madeleine had gotten into the small boat and crossed herself. *Mon Dieu.* She tried to cover her hair with the hood of her cloak. Instead, she clung to the seat, trembling. If it wasn't for her sister, she'd throw herself in the icy water. Death would be preferable to being defiled.

When she got to the beach, she was handed out with a tenderness that surprised her. A man took her arm and swiftly walked her down the beach. She stumbled. "I am sorry. My shoes are not made for this."

"You have no need to worry. We may walk as slowly as you wish."

Madeleine glanced up at him. "Thank you. You are very kind."

She noted that they fell farther and farther behind the others. Fear pricked her. "Why are we so far behind the others?"

"You'll see in a few minutes," the man answered. "There is no need for you to be afraid."

Tears started, and she blinked them back. "Very well." After several minutes of walking, a shack came into view, and another man stepped out from behind it.

"Madeleine?" Her heart stopped. *Mon Dieu.* She crossed herself, again. "Georges? How? Oh, no, you cannot see me like this. *I am ruined.*"

Her escort stepped back. Georges wrapped his arms around her. "Did anyone touch you?" he asked. His voice was hard as stone.

"No, they are saving me for a highly placed . . ."

He placed a finger on her lips. "Then all is well."

"Georges, you do not understand. If I do not do this, they will take my sister. She is only thirteen." The tears came again, washing down her cheeks. He held her and stroked her as if she were a child to be comforted.

"I'll save her. If I have to go to rescue her myself, I promise you she'll be safe."

Georges turned to the other man. "Thank you. Tell your boss, if there is ever anything I can do . . ."

"He'll be pleased to hear that. You'd better go. I was told the path is just behind you."

Georges kept his arm around her until they reached a small trail. "Keep hold of my coat."

Madeleine nodded. When they got to the top he let her rest. After a few moments she asked. "Where now?"

"I have a coach. We'll go to the inn at which I am staying."

"Who were those men?"

"English agents. The other women will never reach the brothel. Or, if they do, they will no longer work for the Corsican."

Chapter 29

Over an hour later, Anna and Sebastian arrived back at the cottage. She sagged with fatigue as he helped her down from Thunderer. Harry was waiting for them inside.

"Nothing of the traitor," Harry said disgustedly. "I take it you didn't find him either."

"No," Sebastian said. "But after the women were put in the coaches, Anna sent Kev ahead. The man rode to Thanport from wherever he was staying, so he'll probably go back there."

"Our associates' horses?"

Anna glanced up at him. "We left them at the inn."

Harry had a crooked smile on his face. "Other than losing our traitor, it was a successful night."

Anna furrowed her brow for a moment. "Yes, I guess you could say that."

Sebastian put an arm around her. "You need to change."

Harry left while Anna scrambled back into her habit.

Sebastian regarded her for a long while. "You'll miss it, won't you?"

"Yes, I shall." She had just enough energy for a smile. "You'll just have to keep me busy."

"I'll keep you as busy as you like." He put her cloak around her shoulders. "Come, my love." Sebastian blew out the candles. "I . . ."

"Shush," Anna whispered. "Listen."

304 • *Ella Quinn*

"I say, you wouldn't happen to know how far back to Thanport it is?" a man asked Harry.

"The gent?"

Anna nodded.

"Not fer. 'Bout a couple o' miles." Harry dropped into the local dialect. "I'm gettin' ready to make some tea. If you'd like a cup o' scandal-broth."

Anna slipped silently to the fireplace, grabbed the poker. Taking up a place behind the door, she listened.

"It is rather cold. If you don't mind, I would love a cup of tea."

"Na, be me pleasure."

The door swung open. Rutherford drove his fist into the man's face. The man stumbled back, and Anna hit him with the poker. Harry lit the candles.

"There is rope in that chest." Anna pointed to a place near the window. Rutherford and Harry tied up their prisoner. "Now, one of us needs to ride to town."

Harry shook his head as if he couldn't believe what she'd done. "I'll do it. If he wakes, hit him again."

"I shall." Anna picked up a candle and brought it close to the man. "I don't recognize him."

Sebastian came to stand next to her. "I've seen him somewhere." He rubbed his jaw. "Looks like . . . I know what it is. He reminds me of someone I know. Wigmore's heir. I'll give you odds he's one of his brothers."

She glared at the man and wished she could do more than hit him. "I know his sister, Catherine. How *could* he do this to his family?"

Sebastian tried to pull her away, but she resisted. "Anna, I don't want him to see you."

Anna put her hands on her hips. "I am not leaving you alone with him."

Sebastian sighed. "We shall have to do as Harry said and keep him knocked out."

It was a good half hour before she heard the horses. "Harry's back, with someone."

"Pull up your hood," Sebastian said. "Keep your back to whomever it is. I'll stop him from taking a look at you."

Anna did as he asked and stepped into the corner of the room farthest from the sprawled out traitor.

"Well, well, if it isn't Lord Florian," the elegant man drawled.

"I thought he was one of Wigmore's sons," Sebastian said in a satisfied tone.

"If you don't mind, I think you should leave Lord Florian to me." The elegant man's lip curled in a sneer.

"Not at all," Sebastian said. "Just don't leave a mess here."

"No worries."

"If you need to sleep before you go back, you are welcome to come to the Hill," Harry said.

Rutherford put his hand out. "No, there are too many people there. Go to the Priory. I'll send a message. Ride west, and you'll see a tower."

"Thank you," the elegant man said. "I might do that. It's been a long night. Who is that?"

His gaze bore into her. She stayed as still as she could.

"No one you need concern yourself with." Sebastian walked over to her and his arm circled her waist.

Anna kept her head down as he directed her toward the door and said, "Harry, I'll see you later."

They were half-way home before Anna slowed. "Do you think the man will figure it out?"

"I don't know. He's not stupid."

"No, I don't suppose he is. I've seen him before," Anna said.

"Yes, you must have. Not one of our circle, of course, but he's always present for the larger entertainments," Sebastian said grimly. "I have no doubt he would have recognized you."

"Why, Sebastian, are you jealous?"

"No, but I plan to make sure everyone knows this is a love match."

Anna slowed Thunderer as they neared the stable yard. Thankfully the house was still dark. They unsaddled their horses and took the tack to be cleaned. Rutherford fetched a bucket of water. They were brushing the horses when Humphrey came out.

"Here now, I'll do that. You two get."

"Thank you," Anna said.

Rutherford nodded and took her hand. He silently opened the side door. They made as little noise as possible while climbing the stairs.

Lizzy was asleep on the sofa when Anna walked into her parlor. She shook her maid gently by the shoulder. "Lizzy, go to bed."

She sat up and yawned. "Miss Emma is still in your bed. We thought it better."

"That's fine. Leave her there."

Lizzy left, and Anna opened the door to Rutherford's room. For the second time that night, she removed her habit.

He'd stripped quickly and was already in bed holding up the covers for her as she settled in beside him.

"What do you think that man will do to the turncoat?" Anna asked.

"I don't know if we'll ever find out."

November 24th, 1814, Marsh Hill, Kent

He fluttered kisses down her neck. She moved her head as if to encourage them. She sighed and looked as if her eyes might open. They didn't. He moved down over her body, kissing and nibbling. She gave another sigh.

If he hadn't been so intent on pleasuring her, he would have laughed. Her sighs and moans formed a symphony. She was warm and limp. A smile played on her lips. Then they formed an *O* as he moved his fingers in between her thighs. A strange, soft keening sound accompanied her shudder.

Rutherford thought about turning her onto her stomach, but he wanted to see Anna's face when she woke and found him making love to her. He slid his finger into her and rubbed the pearl hidden in her curls. Her hips arched. She thrashed her head back and forth. One of her hands found his shoulder and clung, nails digging into him. Her mouth opened to allow a high, breathy sound to escape.

He replaced his finger with his shaft and slowly filled her. Anna smiled. He withdrew and entered her again, repeating the movement until her body was tense. God, she was beautiful. Suddenly a gush of liquid silk ran over him. Her body shook. Her tremors closed around him until he lost control, and spilled his seed into her. Anna opened her mouth. Rutherford covered it quickly with his and swallowed her scream of pleasure.

The tension in her face gave way to Madonna-like calm, and her breathing deepened. Rutherford wondered if she'd remember anything in the morning.

When he awoke again, Anna was cuddled into his side, and the weak winter sun was no longer streaming through the window. He glanced to the clock on the mantel. Anna stirred.

"What time is it?"

"Two o'clock. How do you feel?"

Anna stretched. "Wonderful. I'm so relaxed."

He propped himself on his elbow and gazed down at her. "Anything else?"

"I had a strange dream. But I can't remember all of it."

"Hmm?"

"Yes, I was hot and wet and . . ." She blushed.

He kissed her. "Let me help you remember."

Harry woke up to someone knocking on his door.

"Sir, there is a gentleman downstairs wishing to see either Lord Rutherford or you. Lord Rutherford is . . . indisposed."

Harry wished he were indisposed. He and Emma hadn't had a minute alone since she had got to the Hill. "Come in, Farley, and help me dress. Send a message that I'll be down in a few minutes. I'd like a pot of tea as well."

"Yes, sir, I'll see to it."

His valet returned a few minutes later. "Sir, I wish you would allow me to shave you."

"We don't have time this morning."

Farley took out fresh linen and a pair of Harry's buckskin breeches. A few minutes later, Harry went downstairs to the front parlor. He opened the door to find the elegant gentleman from early this morning. Harry shook his hand and offered him a cup of tea.

"Thank you. I left our friend's house before they could offer me a meal or ask any questions."

The door opened to a footman carrying a tray with meat, cheese, and bread. "You can eat here." Once the door closed Harry asked, "Where is our Lord Florian?"

The gentleman sipped his tea and assumed a distressed look. "Sadly, he did not survive the night. A boating accident. I'm sure you understand how that can happen."

"Yes. Not suicide?" Harry asked, wanting clarification.

"Ah, no," the man replied. "That, as you might imagine, would be terribly hard on his family. He has a sister coming out next year. We wouldn't want any hint of scandal attached to her. I find it unaccountable the things people do when near the sea. He didn't swim at all well."

Harry watched the other man's calm demeanor and wondered if he could carry it off so well. "Should I expect to find the body washed up?"

The man finished his tea and began to place a slice of cheese between two pieces of bread. "Perhaps, but he was quite far out. I expect the current may take him."

"You do know Rutherford is the magistrate?"

The man had taken a bite of his sandwich and swallowed. "I do not think he should be unnecessarily bothered. Where is Rutherford by the way?"

"I'm here," he said as he entered the room. "I take it there's been a boating accident?"

The man rose and shook Rutherford's hand. "Indeed. So very sad. Please send a message to Jamison should the body, er, appear."

"I shall. How are you traveling back to London?"

The gentleman smiled thinly. "The mail. I have been visiting my father in Suffolk the past few days."

Emma knocked and entered the room. The gentlemen stood. "Harry, there you are."

Harry repressed a sigh. At least it wasn't Anna. "My love, we just have some unfinished business from last night."

She glanced around, and her gaze stopped at the elegant man. "I understand. I came to tell you that your parents should return soon. Your father suggested he and your mother spend the day in Dover. I'll be with the housekeeper if you need me."

Harry walked her to the door and shut it.

"Who was the lady?" the gentleman asked.

"My affianced wife, Miss Spencer-Jones."

"She was not the woman from this morning."

"No." Rutherford's lips tightened. "Thank you for the information concerning the accident. I think you should be going. Now."

The gentleman finished his meal and rose. "Yes, perhaps I should. I'll see myself out."

"I'll walk with you." Rutherford held the door open. "I wouldn't want you to lose your way."

Once the gentleman had mounted his horse and was trotting down the drive, Harry joined Rutherford. "Do you think he's going to be a problem?"

Rutherford shrugged. "Not if he's half as smart as he thinks he is. I suggested to him that he forget there was a female present last night."

Harry scowled. "Let's hope he does, for Anna's sake."

Anna finished eating in her parlor and was sipping the last of the tea when Emma knocked on the door. "May I come in?"

Anna looked up and smiled. "Of course you may. Would you like some tea?"

Her soon-to-be sister-in-law nervously smoothed her skirts before taking a seat on the sofa near the window. "No, thank you. Tea will be served within the hour."

Anna glanced briefly at the clock. She'd not known it was already so late. "Have you come to chat? Or do you have something to ask me?"

A light blush rose in Emma's cheeks. "I have a question."

Anna put her cup down. "What is it?"

Emma looked down at her hands for a few moments before continuing. "I understand that you and Lord Rutherford are . . ."

Anna couldn't keep from grinning happily. "Yes."

Emma raised her eyes and sat up straighter. Worry lines formed on her forehead. "You know I was betrothed before and that he died?"

Anna nodded.

Emma swallowed and her blush deepened. "We never—Well, he wanted to—to wait. Needless to say, *it* never happened."

Anna put her tea down and leaned forward. "Ah, and now you don't wish to wait until you are married."

"I do not," Emma replied.

"I can't say I blame you." Anna tapped her chin. "But as you are here, at Marsh Hill, Harry will not go to you. You'll have to do it."

Emma opened and closed her mouth. "Why—why will he not?"

"Because you're in his home," Anna said. "It is some sort of male code. He may not *take advantage* of you under his roof. Even though it is actually my father's roof." Anna frowned for a moment. "Consequently, my dear sister-to-be, you must go to him."

Emma's eyes widened. "Oh dear. Did you go to...?" She waved her arm.

Anna nodded and frowned. "Yes, because for some reason quite unintelligible to me, Rutherford would not have. Truly, I find it all very strange. Nonetheless, those are the rules."

Emma was clutching her hands together so tightly, her knuckles turned white. "I-I see. I never thought... it would... that I must. Oh my. Did you feel very wanton?"

Anna gave a gurgle of laughter. "No, but we'd, er..."

Emma nodded and said briskly, "Oh, I see how that would make a difference. *How* many days are there until the weddings?"

"Well, today is almost gone, so five days."

"Five days?" Emma moaned in despair.

"Rutherford would have gone for a special license, but I didn't know how long it would take my mother to return," Anna said. "Emma, you need not wait for us. You have a license. You may be married tomorrow if you like."

Emma brightened, then frowned. "I cannot. Lady Rutherford expects to see me married."

It was really too bad that Harry wouldn't do anything. "Hmm. I see. Would you like me to talk to Harry?"

"Oh my, no. What would he think of me?"

"I suppose you couldn't mention it to him?"

Emma shook her head.

What a pickle. "Let me think on it." Anna's brow wrinkled. "If I come up with anything, I'll let you know."

Emma grabbed Anna's hands. "Thank you."

Anna retrieved one hand and patted Emma's. "I only hope I *can* be of help."

Once Emma left, Anna thought of and rejected solutions to Emma's problem. Finally, she found one she thought would work. A short while later, Anna rang for Lizzy and gave her instructions. When Lizzy returned about an hour later, Anna sent a message to Sebastian asking if it was convenient for her to come down.

Receiving an answer in the affirmative, she descended the stairs and found her betrothed in the morning room. "Where is Mama?" Anna asked. "I can't believe she allowed us to sleep for so long."

Sebastian kissed her hand. "Harry took your father into his confidence, and Sir William suggested a trip to Dover."

That was a shock. "Indeed? What did Harry say?"

Grinning, Sebastian said, "Harry ended up having to tell your father everything about the smuggling, and our activities last night with the spies. Sir William rang a peel over his head about your involvement, but agreed to keep your mother out of the way."

"Well, I'm glad Papa decided to help," Anna said, "but I don't like it that he blamed Harry. By the by, where *are* Harry and Emma?"

Taking Anna in his arms, Sebastian replied, "I believe they're entertaining the children."

She touched her lips to his. "Hmm, I think we should take over for them."

Sebastian eyed her intently. "What are you up to?"

Shrugging lightly, Anna responded, "They need some time alone."

"Are you scheming, my love?"

"Only a little and for a very good cause."

Anna caught Emma's gaze as she and Rutherford entered the children's parlor. "Have you been inside all day? Harry, you should take Emma for a walk. I'm quite sure she has not seen all the grounds. We can easily put off tea for a while yet."

Cece, sprawled on the floor reading a book, looked up. "We'll come with you."

"No, no," Anna replied. "Emma wants to see the wood and beyond. You will be happier visiting the children's garden." Anna glanced at Sebastian. "Don't you agree?"

Without blinking an eye, he replied, "Absolutely. Harry, Emma, please go without us. We'll stay with the children."

Anna raised a suggestive brow. "Emma, you'll need your cloak. It may be a little cold. Do you know where it's kept?"

Emma rose. "No, I don't. Perhaps you'd better show me."

Anna led her out into the hall and showed her the large wardrobe just off the main entrance. "Have Harry take you to the folly in the wood. It's not as nice as the one overlooking the lake, but it's much easier to heat."

Emma took Anna's hands. "Thank you. I hope I'm doing the right thing."

Chapter 30

Harry sent the girls away to fetch their cloaks from the schoolroom. "Rutherford, would you mind very much if Emma and I married tomorrow?"

"Not in the least." He grinned. "Why so soon?"

Harry glowered. "If you can't figure it out, I'm not going to tell you."

Rutherford gave a bark of laughter. "It's the very devil to be in your own home, eh? Well, I'm not the one to ask. I don't even know what's going on with the activities at the Priory. You must speak with your betrothed, and then discuss it with your sister. Good luck to you. I'm happy to share a glass of daffy with you after you've had those conversations."

The ladies returned with Emma bundled against the cold and Anna carrying Harry's coat, gloves, and hat. Once he'd donned these items, he and Emma left through the French doors to the terrace.

Emma twined her arm in Harry's. "Anna said there was a folly in the wood that I should like to see."

There *was* a folly in the wood, and it would be too damn cold in this weather to do anything but look at it. "Yes, it was her spot when she was a child. I'll show it to you if you'd like."

Emma eyes shone softly as she gazed up at him. "I'd enjoy it very much."

He led her across a corner of the meadow, to a path in the wood. They walked along a stream until reaching a footbridge. The cabin was set in a clearing a little ways from the water's edge.

"Oh, Harry, it's charming," Emma exclaimed.

Harry grinned at her, then stopped. "I smell smoke. Stay here."

"Not likely," she said under her breath as she followed him to the cabin door.

He pushed it open cautiously, stepped in, and stared. What the devil? The fireplace was lit as well as some of the candles. A pot of what smelled like spiced wine warmed on a braiser. Bread, cheese, and fruit were on a platter that took up most of the small table. And the bed—the old rustic four-poster bed—was covered with a feather duvet and blankets and pillows. "It looks like Anna's made some changes."

Emma stepped around him into the room. "It's lovely, and so warm."

Harry took her cloak to hang it up on one of the pegs fixed on the wall. Her hand trembled. "You should warm up near the fire."

"I'm not cold."

He removed his cloak, his gloves, and hat. "Then what . . ." Emma gazed up at him, and he suddenly understood. "This is for us."

She nodded.

"Anna?"

Emma nodded again.

He narrowed his eyes. Was Anna meddling or . . . ? "My love, did you know about this?"

His beloved blushed. "I, er, might have mentioned something to her."

Of course, the minute Emma alluded to it, Anna would make it happen. So much for his decision to wait until after they were wed. He couldn't hurt Emma's feelings. "Then we shan't let it go to waste."

He untied the ribbons of her bonnet and pulled off her gloves, kissing her wrist as each finger was freed. "Emma, I want you."

"I want you, too." She stepped into his arms.

His lips touched hers, and all his intentions of taking this slowly fled. Her desire and urgency matched his. When he sought to claim her mouth, she claimed his first. His heart pounded, and his fingers fumbled with her laces. "Damn. Oh, I'm sorry. Here, turn around."

Emma's laugh was only a little nervous as her bodice, flannel petticoat, and stays dropped to the floor in a series of soft whooshes. Her blush extended down her neck and chest.

"You're beautiful." His voice deepened. "More beautiful than I remember."

She slid her hands over his shoulders. "It hasn't been that long."

Teasing the long column of her neck with his lips, he said, "It's been an eternity."

"Here, let me." She pushed open his jacket.

He shrugged out of it as she unlaced his shirt and pulled it out from his breeches. Harry picked Emma up, carrying her to the bed, where he unlaced and removed her boots.

Gooseflesh appeared on her creamy skin. He found a warming pan in the fireplace and ran it between the sheets. "You need to get under the covers until it's warmer in here."

"It is a little chilly." Emma slid under the now warm sheets.

He quickly stripped off his stockings and breeches. Emma had seen many half-naked men before working in the fields, but none had looked better than Harry. She took in his broad, muscular chest, which was covered with thick, dark, curly hair. Small scars were on his chest and arms. She raised the covers for him as he climbed on to the bed, causing her to roll against him.

She gently touched the marks. "Are they from the shipwreck?"

"Yes."

Emma traced the larger ones with the tips of her fingers. "You were lucky."

"I was the only one to survive." He gazed at her, desire smoldering in his eyes. "Emma?"

She ran her hands over the soft hair and leaned over him, pressing her lips to his. "Love me."

He groaned and flipped her on to her back without breaking the kiss. Need rose from between her legs. The ribbons of her chemise fell loose.

"Do you need this?" he asked.

"No."

He helped her pull the thin muslin off.

When she was finally free of all her clothing, Harry lightly caressed her breasts.

She tried to deepen the kiss, but his mouth moved down over her neck to her tight nipples. Desire shot through her when he took one in his mouth and sucked.

He held her down firmly but gently as she twisted and squirmed, trying to find relief. Soon his fingers found her wet folds and stroked.

Emma shuddered when he inserted a finger in her. The tremors were like swells coming into shore, one after the other, each one stronger. Warmth surrounded her. She cried out as the eddy took her.

She was still floating on the waves of pleasure when Harry entered her. His slow movements in and out caused her craving to build. She wrapped her legs around him and was gulping for air as he filled her.

She'd been told it would hurt and was suddenly afraid. "Harry, kiss me."

He captured her mouth. Emma clung to him, digging her fingers into his bunched and straining muscles. Harry stopped his slow thrusting and deepened the kiss. Emma found herself breathing through him.

Suddenly, there was a brief sharp pain, and he stopped. "Are you all right, my love?"

"Yes, I'm fine." And happy, so happy.

One hand possessed a breast, and she relaxed as he kneaded. He moved again, thrusting and retreating slowly. Tiny flames licked her skin, and her need grew. She arched against him as frissons of pleasure shot through her.

Harry still filled her slowly, but with each stroke, her need and desire for him grew. The convulsions took Emma unawares, and she arched up to meet him. His muscles relaxed, and he pressed deeper, possessing her completely, until he shook and a different warmth filled her.

She was bare and open to him. Nothing hidden. Their hearts pounded together as he held her so closely not even air could pass between them. This was what it was like to be possessed by a man who loved you. What it meant to become one. Tears pricked her eyes, and a welling in her heart caused her to sob.

"Emma, my love, what is it?" His voice rumbled against her cheek.

"I'm just so full of joy."

"You're crying."

A tear made its way down her cheek, and Harry kissed it away. She smiled. "It's not really crying."

Harry brushed her damp hair back from her face. Her knot was destroyed, and long golden curls spilt over her shoulders. His, she was finally his. Nothing could happen to her. Harry's throat closed. He wouldn't let anything hurt her. "Wait here."

Harry gently laid her down, slipped out of the bed, and covered her. The cabin was still not warm enough for his Emma. He took a small table and set it close to the bed, then filled a plate with cheese and cold meat, and poured two mugs of the spiced wine. After he'd set food and drink on the table, he arranged the pillows so she could sit up.

Harry slid in next to her. They ate, drank, and talked.

"Would you mind if we married tomorrow?" he asked.

"My darling, I would love to marry you tomorrow, but I promised Lady Rutherford I'd wait until she returned. She told Anna she'd be back for their wedding."

Harry couldn't imagine not having her with him. Five days. How often could they come out here?

"Is there a reason I cannot come to you at night?" Emma asked.

He wouldn't have asked it of her, but . . . "No, if you're sure that's what you want."

His arm tightened around her.

"Harry, have a care for the wine." Emma laughed, holding her mug out to steady it.

He took it from her and kissed her.

Whilst Emma dozed, Harry took out his pocket watch and checked the time. They needed to go back soon.

He dressed and took her now cold chemise to hang by the fire. Harry watched her. Helplessness washed over him. He'd almost withdrawn and not spilled his seed in her. Maybe he should have asked. Though he was sure Emma would scoff at any notion she not have children. She wanted a lot of them. He prayed she'd survive childbirth. He couldn't lose her like he had lost Marcella and his child. He'd rather not have children at all. He blinked away the tears, then woke Emma.

They returned slowly through the darkening landscape. He held her hand in his, helping her over small rocks and dips in the ground until they reached the gate to the formal gardens. They'd missed tea, but were in time to dress for dinner.

When they entered the drawing room an hour later, his mother was full of plans for the renovation of their chambers, which Emma entered into fully.

He joined Anna, Rutherford, and his father's political discussion.

"Harry, my boy, have you decided to run for the seat?" his father asked.

"Yes, yes, I have."

November 26th, 1814, Kent

Harry knocked on the door of his father's study and walked in. "Papa, you wanted to see me?"

Sir William reached for a sheet of paper on his desk and passed it to Harry.

He frowned. "What's this?"

"Read it."

Harry looked down at it. "It's from the Prime Minister's office. *Vienna?*" The letter requested his father accept a post in Vienna. "Are you going to take it, sir?"

"It depends on your mother. She is thinking it over, but I don't know how she'll feel leaving so soon after you've returned. If I accept it, we will be in London until we leave."

He sat back and gave a low whistle. "That's what all the secrecy's been about."

"I am surprised your sister didn't share the news with you."

Harry carefully kept an innocent expression on his face. "Anna knows? Well, she has got into the habit of keeping her own counsel."

"I plan to discuss it with your mother today."

"How did this come about?"

His father picked up a pen and toyed with it. "After you left, I formed a much greater interest in foreign affairs. I've been asked before." He sighed. "But, as you know, one's wife must accompany one. Your mother wouldn't have gone. Though I think Anna would have enjoyed it."

Harry had a vision of Rutherford racing across the continent to find Anna and choked.

"Anything wrong, my boy?" Papa looked at him in concern.

Harry struggled not to smile. "No, nothing at all. Please go on."

"Yes, well, this latest offer came just before you came back. I put them off until I knew what you wanted to do."

"Thank you, Papa. I hope Mama agrees to go. I think you'd be very happy."

Harry went to the morning room where he'd agreed to meet Emma, Rutherford, and Anna.

"Well?" Anna asked.

"He knows you went through his drawer."

She frowned. "Drat. I thought he might have discovered it."

Harry raised a brow. "Do you do it often?"

Anna assumed her wide-eyed, innocent mien. "Only when there is something I need to know, and he doesn't tell me."

Rutherford shook his head sadly, but there was a glimmer of mischief in his eyes. "I see there will be no keeping secrets from you."

Anna raised her head haughtily. "You have no need to keep secrets from me, my lord."

Harry grinned. "You two are a pair. Do you want to know what he said or not?"

"Yes," three voices chorused.

"He has a firm offer for a position in Vienna. If Mama doesn't want to accept it, they'll remain here."

"What do you think Lady Marsh will do?" Emma asked.

"Mama has never liked the country unless we were entertaining." Anna rubbed her forehead and frowned. "The only time Mama ever came here was when you had school holidays, Harry."

"No, you're right. She always wanted to be in London or at some fashionable resort."

"She's been moping around here as if there were nothing to do." Anna gave an exasperated sigh. "I think Vienna would be a good change for her."

Rutherford placed a seal on a billet he'd just written before crossing to Anna and putting his arm around her. "Speaking of mothers, mine married her gentleman. He will accompany her when she returns on Monday."

"I sincerely hope this is what she wants," Anna said. "I'm curious to meet him."

"Will her absence be awkward for you at church tomorrow?" Emma asked.

Rutherford responded. "I hope it's not commented upon. I shall rely on all of you to fill the pew."

Before dinner that evening, as they gathered in the drawing room, Sir William announced he would accept the post in Vienna. Mama had written to recall the London servants from holiday, as they would post to Town the day after the wedding.

"Mama, how wonderful and exciting," Anna said. "Sebastian and I must visit while you're there."

Mama's eyes sparkled with happiness. "Yes, it is very exciting. I shall expect all of you to come. We are to be given a house and an allowance to furnish it."

She turned to her future daughter-in-law. "You see, my dear Emma, you will not have to worry about my taking anything from the town house at all."

Emma hugged Mama. "I'm so happy for you. How long will you be gone?"

His father replied. "The initial posting is for five years, but, if all is going well, we can extend it."

Mama added, "Harry, you and Emma must treat the house as your own."

"That we will."

Anna cast him a sidelong glance, and said in an undertone, "We got over that fence easily enough. Now you'll have to firm up your plans."

"You mean, convince Emma she wants to be a political hostess," he said quietly.

Chapter 31

November 29th, 1814, Marsh Hill, Kent

Anna stared up at the bed hangings. "We are in agreement," Anna said. "Sebastian, you and Harry will spend the night at the Priory. Emma and I shall remain here with the girls."

"Did I agree to that?" he said. "It doesn't sound like something I'd do."

She'd been awake for the past hour, making plans. Anna turned to study her intended's face and became distracted by his chest. She propped herself up on one arm. With her free hand, she stroked his soft curling hair. "Did Worthington accept your invitation?"

Sebastian kissed the top of her head and shifted her over him. "Yes, and Huntley."

Anna shifted over to lie prone on top of him, folded her arms, and gazed into his eyes, molten silver. Small lines crinkled from the corners.

She loved how desire and humor mingled in his expression. "I wish Phoebe and Marcus could be here, but they're still in Paris."

Sebastian's hand, warm and heavy, stroked down her back and over her bottom. She sighed. "We have much to do today. Your mother and her husband are arriving today."

She lost her train of thought as his fingers slid into her. Oh, that was good. Then suddenly, she was underneath him, her legs spread wide. The head of his erect shaft thrusting in and out, teasing her. Anna moaned with pleasure and tried to gather her wits. "But, we need . . ."

"Later." Sebastian plunged fully into her.

Anna held him close as tremor upon tremor exploded through her. This time, instead of whirling off into oblivion, she stayed with him. Anna wondered how it was that an act so physical could, at the same time, be so ethereal. She concentrated on the sensations, then let go to join him as he came.

He held her close to him, trying not to think about tonight when he'd sleep without her. The last time hadn't worked at all well, for either of them. Anna was everything to him now. His lover, friend, confidante, and, tomorrow, his wife. He needed to make this moment last. Rutherford tucked her next to him.

"As I was about to say," Anna continued as if there had been no interruption, "I think your mother and her husband, I will be glad to know his last name, should dine with us this evening."

Rutherford fixed her with a look. "Tell me that was not what you were thinking about a few moments ago."

She turned to meet his gaze with a soft, loving look. "No, I thought of you, of us."

"Good. I'll meet you in the breakfast room." He kissed her one last time. "We can go over your lists then."

When he entered the breakfast room, Harry and Emma were just sitting down, but Anna wasn't there. "Have you seen my affianced wife?"

Harry's eyes sparkled with mischief. "Have you lost her already?"

Emma shook her head at Harry in admonishment, but ruined the effect by giggling. "She breezed in and out again, saying she'd forgotten something. Why don't you let me pour you a cup of tea? I'm sure she'll be back in a few minutes."

Rutherford would be damned if he'd sit with the two of them laughing at him. "Thank you, but I'm going to find her."

Before he was down the corridor, Harry gave a bark of laughter. Rutherford finally tracked Anna down at the stables handing a missive to one of the grooms. "What are you doing?" That came out rougher than he'd wanted. "I thought we were to meet in the breakfast room?"

Anna smiled. "I needed to send a note to your cook. I want her to arrange an initial store of foodstuffs for the dower-house. I'm ready now."

He escorted her to the breakfast room, but for all the time he was able to spend with her, he might just as well have left her in the stables or, better yet, not let her out of bed.

A steady stream of people, from servants to family members, all seemed to need her attention. At any other time, he would have enjoyed the competent picture of Anna as she sent her minions about their duties. This morning, all he wanted was her attention.

"I'm sorry, my love." She put down her cup and stood. "I need to go attend to some issues that have arisen. We'll leave for the dower-house soon."

He heaved a sigh. "I'll be ready when you come back down. How are my clothes being taken to the Priory?"

"By cart. Robertson is packing your trunk and shall take them over. My maid will ride with him to settle my things." Anna left.

Rutherford nodded to the empty room. Even his valet knew which side his bread was buttered on.

Harry joined him and sat down. "Did you know we're being banished?"

"So I've been informed. I was told I agreed to it, but I don't remember."

"It was probably at a weak moment," Harry said in sympathy. "I'm sure I wasn't asked at all."

"I take it we're to spend a convivial evening with Huntley and Worthington."

"Yes, but not too convivial. I've been told, quite bluntly, that if I arrive at the church under the hatches, it will be the worse for me."

"I wonder why it is," Rutherford said, "that neither of us could have had the good sense to choose a biddable miss?"

Harry's eyes gleamed with laughter. "We'd have been bored to death within a fortnight."

Rutherford's lips twitched. "If it took that long."

"Sebastian, are you ready?"

"Coming now, my love."

Anna was half-way down the side corridor leading to the stable yard when he caught up with her, grabbed her around the waist, and hauled her to him.

"Sebastian, what?"

"This." He bent Anna back against his arm and kissed her deeply. When he raised his head, her eyes were dazed.

"What was that for?"

"For being who you are." *My own personal harridan.*

"Oh." She smiled. "How nice."

"Let's try to accomplish what's on your list. With any luck at all, we may contrive to find some time for ourselves."

They arrived at the dower-house to find wisps of smoke escaping from the chimneys.

"Who would be here?" Rutherford asked.

"The staff I hired," she replied as he handed her down from the carriage.

"You hired the staff?"

Her eyes opened wide. "Yes, why not? It doesn't do your mother a bit of good to hire them in London. Griffin, Mrs. Thurston, and I got together and made up a list of what we thought necessary."

Anna took his arm and led him through the gate to the house. "The butler and housekeeper are local but used to a London household. I think your mother will like them."

Rutherford took in the newly painted black door and shining brass knocker. The dower-house was a small manor with two floors above the ground level, cellars, and attics. Ornamental gardens surrounded it to the front and sides, bordered by a low stone wall. The back housed a large, walled kitchen garden. It was on a walking path to Thanport. The door opened, and the butler called the staff to assemble in the hall.

Rutherford bent and whispered in Anna's ear, "I take it we are paying their salaries?"

"Yes. Your mother admitted to me she has never had to hold house. I thought it better."

"I quite agree, but how do you know all of this?"

Her brows rose in surprise. "Naturally, I've been corresponding with your mother."

"Of course." Rutherford met the staff and was surprised by the size of the two footmen and a military-looking valet. Though, when he found a chair on wheels with footrests in one of the parlors, he understood. "An invalid chair. Can he walk at all?" Rutherford asked Anna.

"He now has a prosthesis for one leg, and he is starting to get around on a cane."

"The valet, I take it, was in the military?"

Anna nodded. "His old batman."

"Do we know John's full name yet?"

Grinning, she responded, "Yes. I had a letter waiting from your mother this morning. Colonel John Forthsyth."

She greeted the butler and the rest of the staff, before being taken on an inspection of the house.

When they'd finished, Rutherford glanced at the clock on the mantel. "Where are we taking luncheon?"

"At the Priory," Anna replied. "Emma and Harry are joining us."

Anna put her hand on his arm. "My lord?"

Rutherford led her back to the carriage.

They arrived at the Priory to find not only Harry and Emma but Rutherford's two friends, Gervais, Earl of Huntley, and Mattheus, Earl of Worthington.

"You two are here early," Rutherford said. There went any hope he'd have some time today with Anna. "What time did you leave this morning?"

Worthington bowed to Anna and shook Rutherford's hand. "Eight o'clock. We had a ding-dong race. Famous sport."

"You will have to tell Rutherford and Harry all about it this evening." Anna took Rutherford's arm and led him to the family dining room.

Emma turned to Harry. "Ding-dong race?"

"It means they are well matched and the betting was running high."

"Ah." She sat in the chair he held out for her.

Anna signaled for the staff to serve and turned to Worthington on her left. "Tell us all the *on dits*."

Worthington and Huntley entertained them with several stories, including a scandal involving a young couple who had run off to Scotland to marry. It was mid-afternoon before they rose from the table.

A footman brought a message to Anna from the dower-house that Colonel and Mrs. Forthsyth had arrived. "Please tell Mrs. Forthsyth that I hope her trip was not very tedious and, if they are not too fagged, I'd love to see them at the Hill for dinner. If not, we shall see them in church tomorrow at ten o'clock."

"Yes, miss."

When Anna turned back to the table, Lord Huntley was staring at her. She returned his look with a challenging one of her own. Rutherford held back his laughter. His friend had never seen Anna in her element before.

"Is there anything wrong, my lord?" Anna asked.

Huntley gave an imperceptible shake of his head. "No, no, nothing at all. I just—well—who is Mrs. Forthsyth?"

"Rutherford's mother," Anna said. "She married late last week. As much as I wish we could remain, Miss Spencer-Jones and I must leave."

"It seems like everyone is getting married." Worthington rubbed his jaw. "It might be time for me to think about it as well."

Huntley looked at him aghast. "I wish you joy. I believe I shall wait a while yet."

A footman pulled Anna's chair out, and the gentlemen rose when Anna and Emma did.

"My love, I'll escort you to the door." Rutherford swiftly reached her and placed her hand on his arm.

"I shall come as well," Harry added.

Rutherford looked at Worthington and Huntley. "Harry and I will be back shortly."

He pulled Anna into a parlor, locked the door, and kissed her. "I love you. You won't be late tomorrow, will you?"

"No." She pulled him back down to her. "How can you even ask? I'll make sure we all leave in good time."

He released his erection and kept her distracted until her gown was rucked up. Rutherford lifted her and mumbled into her mouth, "Put your legs around me." He lowered her on to him and moaned. There was nothing better than being inside Anna. She was his haven, his home.

Heated from his kisses, Anna didn't even think to question him. Her need and her love for him had become so powerful she couldn't imagine a life without her Sebastian. She spun out of control as he drove deeper into her, filling her and showing his love.

Lifting her off him, he set her gently on the floor. Anna's legs wobbled, and she clung to him for a bit. "Tonight is going to be awful."

"Hellish," he agreed.

"I'm so used to waking up with you."

He kissed her again. "Stay with me."

Anna shook her head. "It's not fair to tease me. You know I cannot."

"I know." He unlocked the door, and they entered the corridor arm in arm.

Emma and Harry walked out from another room. It occurred to Anna she must look quite as disheveled as her soon-to-be-sister did.

"I'm going to escort you," Rutherford said.

"You don't need to, really," Anna protested. "It is not that far."

"No, I do need to, and the light is failing. I'll ask if Huntley and Worthington want to come."

Anna gave an order to have four horses saddled and Harry's curricle brought around. Griffin helped her into her mantle and cloak. She'd just finished donning her gloves when the men walked into the hall. With great bonhomie they escorted the ladies home and invited themselves in for tea.

The gentlemen were getting ready to leave when a footman entered the room. "My lord, a letter just arrived from London for you."

Rutherford held out his hand, took the missive, broke open the seal, and perused the letter's contents. "I'll meet you at the stables," he said to the gentlemen.

Once they'd left, Sebastian handed Anna the letter. "It's from Jamison. He wishes us all happy on our wedding day. Harry is to be made a baronet. He says he hopes you'll understand, my love, that he could not give you a similar honor, but trusts that the amount the government paid your smugglers will be compensation enough."

Anna refused to be upset about the snub to herself. "I understand. I think it's wonderful about Harry, but why is Harry receiving a baronetcy?"

"Partially for his hardship," Sebastian replied. "Harry is the only one of us he could reward. No, wait." Sebastian took the letter back and read down farther.

"He's asked Prinny to elevate me to Viscount. I don't place much hope in that happening. Georges allowed the woman he saved to speak to Jamison. She'd been recruited by none other than Napoleon's spymaster, himself, Fouché."

"Who is she? Did Jamison say?"

"No, only that she was threatened into joining them."

"Sebastian," Anna asked. "who *is* Georges?"

"He, my dear, is the Marquis Cruzy-le-Châtel. Louis has promised him his lands back, but he still needs Georges, so it hasn't happened yet."

"You mean he is really working for the French king?"

Sebastian nodded. "Yes, though only a very few people know, and it must remain that way. Georges managed to get his mother and sisters out. His father was murdered."

Anna couldn't imagine going through all the terror of having her family in danger and her father killed. "Of course, I understand. How—how sad for him."

Rutherford drew her close. "I'm grateful I never had to make that choice. It's been hard for both him and his family."

If Anna thought dinner would be a quiet affair, she would have been wrong. Although her future mother-in-law sent her regrets, the wedding plans caused a great deal of discussion and excitement with the girls.

After it was explained to them that Harry and Rutherford had to spend the night elsewhere, Cece looked up at Anna sitting next to her and said, "But won't you be lonely?"

Anna choked. How had the child known?

Emma hurriedly occupied Sir William.

Fortunately, Anna's mother hadn't seemed to hear. Anna said, "Yes, my dear, but that's not something we need to discuss now."

Jenny, their governess, mumbled, "From the mouths of babes," and took the two younger girls from the table with the promise that sweets would be sent up to them.

Anna and Emma sat up talking with Anna's mother, who had decided that it was time they should be told what to expect from their husbands tomorrow evening.

The clock struck midnight before Emma and Anna could escape her mother and ready themselves for bed. Dressed in nightgowns and wrappers, they met in Anna's parlor.

328 • *Ella Quinn*

Lizzy was setting out wine and biscuits. "I thought you might like something. Don't stay up too much longer. You don't want to look haggard come morning."

"No, we won't," Anna promised. "It's so strange. This is the last night I'll be here. My room is all but empty."

Emma grinned. "You'll like it at the Priory."

"I'm already at home there." Anna smiled. "How do you feel about being here?"

"For the most part, I'll be fine." Emma frowned a little. "It will be strange not having everyone around."

Anna held a finger to her lip and pointed to the door.

Emma's eyes widened.

Soft footsteps stopped outside the door. Anna grabbed the fireplace poker and rose to go to the door, when it opened.

Harry and Rutherford stood crowded in the doorway, smiling sheepishly.

"The others went to bed, and neither of us could sleep." Rutherford stepped forward and folded Anna in his arms.

She dropped the poker and returned his embrace. "Then we should go to bed. You'll have to get up early to leave without being seen."

When she awoke, he was gone, and Lizzy was preparing her bathwater.

November 30th, Berkshire, England

Georges held Madeleine, wracked with tears, sobbing in his arms. She'd been so brave, even during the interrogation with Jamison. Only when he'd taken her to his mother and sisters had she broken down. "You are safe, my sweet."

Madeleine took huge gulps of air. "I know. This is not worthy of me. Not fair to you."

He stroked her hair and waited for her to calm. "I shall leave in a few days to go to your mother and sister. You will wait here for them."

"I am going with you," she said.

"Madeleine, no," Georges replied harshly. He would not lose her again. France was too dangerous for her. "You cannot. I forbid it."

Her jaw firmed, and she replied, "Only I know the house. You will not find or be able to enter it without me."

"You'll tell me all you know." Georges's hands tightened on her. What she was proposing was impossible.

"No, no, no, I tell you. I shall go with you."

Somehow he'd find a way to keep her safe and in England. He tipped her face up to his and kissed her. "We'll discuss this later."

November 30th, 1814, St. Clement's Church, Thanport, Kent

The day dawned cold and crisp. Papa escorted Anna and Emma to the church in one coach, and Mama rode with the girls in the other. Anna had never been so excited to go to church before.

Julia was present, but her new husband was still resting from the exertions of the previous day's trip. She'd never looked happier. Tears started in her eyes as she embraced Anna and then Emma. "How pleased I am for both of you."

Huntley and Worthington stood up in front with Harry and Rutherford.

"Here they are. Shall we begin?" The Right Reverend Thompson grinned.

Sebastian took Anna's hand. "You are radiant."

Anna found herself smiling shyly. "Thank you. You look wonderful as well."

Someone coughed, and she turned to face the vicar.

Anna gazed into Rutherford's warm, molten silver eyes as they said their vows. This was the wedding she'd always dreamed of and had been afraid would never come to pass. When it was over and they were pronounced man and wife, she could scarcely believe it.

Rutherford placed his hand on her waist, even through her pelisse it was warm, as they witnessed Harry and Emma's vows.

Emma's hands shook as Harry held them in his steady ones. She'd been so afraid something would keep them apart. He held her eyes with his, calming her as they repeated their vows. She barely remembered what they'd said. That morning, she'd taken the ring off her right hand, and, now, he was sliding it over the knuckle of her left.

330 • *Ella Quinn*

"Mrs. Marsh."

It took her a moment to realize she was being addressed.

The vicar smiled. "You must sign the register."

Harry put his arm around her. "Come, Mrs. Marsh."

Anna suddenly turned and put her hand to her mouth. "Oh, Harry, we forgot to tell you. You've been made a baronet. It's Lady Marsh."

Please turn the page for an exciting sneak peek of
Ella Quinn's next dazzling historical romance,
THE TEMPTATION OF LADY SERENA,
coming in January 2014!

1814, Scottish border region

The Earl of Weir scowled. "Damn it, Serena, you can't back out now. Not after the plans have been made. If you don't go to London, who will you marry? What do you have left here?"

Lady Serena Weir stared out the solar's window, studying the bleak late February landscape. Snow covered the ground, more gray than white, the trees lifeless and black against the gloom. She glanced over her shoulder at her brother, James. "I could marry Cameron."

"Do you even care for him more than moderately?"

"No, but he needs to marry, and he likes me." She turned back to the window. In another month the hills would be the feeding ground for the castle's sheep and cattle. But if Mattie, her new sister-in-law, had her way, Serena would not be there to see it.

James snorted with derision. "Cameron likes your dowry. Mattie has made all the plans. She assures me you'll have a wonderful time."

Serena pressed her lips tightly together. *The plans,* he'd said, as if they had taken on a life. *The plans* for her to go to London for her first Season at six and twenty years of age. A little old to be making a come-out. *The plans* meant she would leave her home. The place she had been born and raised and had never before left. Tears pricked her eyelids. She would not cry. Not in front of James. If a London Season was such a good idea, why hadn't he sold out of the army after their father died, when she was still young? Instead, he'd left her here to manage the estate while he remained on Wellington's staff.

James had returned shortly before Christmas, with his bride, Madeleine—Mattie, as she liked to be called—and Serena's ordered life had been thrown into turmoil. She no longer knew what her future held.

Despite her warm cashmere dress and woolen shawl, Serena shivered. No matter how many fires were lit, Vere was always cold and damp, even in the solar, the warmest room in the castle. London would probably be warmer. That might be a good reason to go.

James teased her in the local dialect. "Serena, lass . . ."

She bit her lip. "James Weir, I *know* you did not speak Scots with Wellington."

"Please, Sissy?" her brother said, reverting to his childhood name for her. "Stop looking out the window, and talk to me."

Serena sighed, but turned. Her brother was tall with dark brown hair, like their mother's, whereas she had her father's auburn curls. She'd known her brother would marry, but it had never occurred to her he would bring a wife home with him. Or that Serena would be forced to leave.

Serena fought her sudden panic, but there truly was nothing here for her anymore. "Fine. I'll go."

"Good girl!" He smiled. "I'll tell Mattie it's settled."

James gave Serena a peck on the cheek and strode out the door.

"Do. Go tell Mattie," Serena muttered in frustration. *What didn't he tell Mattie?*

London was Mattie's idea to rid herself of her unwanted sister-in-law. Serena had been presented with the plans *au fait accompli.* Somehow, she would have to make the best of it.

Early the next day, Serena and James left on the weeklong journey from the Cheviot Hills to the home of their aunt Catherine, the Dowager Marchioness of Ware. James spent the night, but left early the next morning.

Mary, Serena's lady's maid, was still unpacking Serena's trunk when her aunt entered the bedchamber.

"Let me see what you've brought with you," Aunt Catherine said.

Serena tried to smile, but tears filled her eyes. Aunt Catherine was her mother's twin, and Serena wished her mother were here to reassure her. In answer to her aunt's question, she replied, "I'm afraid none of it is fashionable."

"You've had no reason to think about being fashionable, have you?"

Serena shook her head.

"Will it hurt your feelings if I told you I'd suspected that?"

Serena was still too numb to feel much of anything. "No."

Mary stood aside as Aunt Catherine sorted through the clothes, discarding most of them. She held up Serena's riding habit. "Well, this, at least, seems to be in good condition and not too out of date."

Serena grimaced. "It's probably the newest piece of clothing I own."

"No matter at all, my child. I knew you would need a new wardrobe. It will be much easier to toss everything and begin anew. A visit to a good modiste in York will start you. When we arrive in London, we shall visit Madame Lisette on Bruton Street." Aunt Catherine paused. "Have you danced at all?"

"I had a dancing master when Papa was well."

"When was that? No, don't tell me. It was too long ago to have mattered. We'll hire one in London." Aunt Catherine made a face at the pile of clothes on the floor. "Other than your riding habit, is there anything you wish to keep?"

Serena glanced at the now empty trunks and shook her head. "No, only something to wear until I have new gowns to replace the old."

Her aunt's kind, patient gaze stayed on Serena for a few moments. "Good. I am glad to hear it. There is nothing more unfortunate than being attached to a gown that is quite out of style and in no way useful." Aunt Catherine turned to go. "We'll visit York tomorrow."

After she left, Serena said, "Mary, please leave me for a while."

"Yes, my lady. Is there anything I can get you?"

"No, I'm fine." Serena sat on the window seat. Her throat hurt from holding back the tears she would not allow to fall. How anyone thought she was going to find a husband at her age, she didn't know. It was as if she'd been set adrift. How was she going to learn everything required when she'd only been in small villages? She'd

336 • *Ella Quinn*

never attended a proper ball or been to a modiste. Serena bit her lip to keep the tears at bay.

Darkness seemed to surround her. She pressed her head against the cold glass. Eventually the weak winter sun faded, and the room dimmed. By the time a knock sounded on the door, Serena had stopped feeling sorry for herself and vowed to carry on. She was the daughter of an earl and the granddaughter of an English marquis. Rising, she went to the basin and splashed water on her face. "Come."

"Her ladyship wants to know if you'll join her for dinner." Mary lit the candles. "If you're not up to it, she'll send a tray."

"No, I'll be down shortly, unless she expects me to change."

"No, my lady, she said to come as you are."

The next few days were spent in such a whirl of shopping that Serena felt she'd been turned upside down. Never in her life had another person made Serena a priority.

She gazed at her aunt, then at the large pile of new gowns and packages, and laughed. "I'm sure I cannot wear half so many."

"Well, I'm happy to hear you laugh, my dear, which you haven't done since you arrived." Aunt Catherine's humorous gray eyes sparkled. "You will need many more when we arrive in Town. You will have routs, balls, dinners, afternoon teas, and morning visits to occupy you, as well as other entertainments."

Serena trembled. A Season would be worse than she'd thought. "I had no idea."

"No, I daresay you did not, but there is no need to take fright." Her aunt smiled warmly. "I am extremely pleased with you. Your manners are very pretty and self-assured, and your mind is well informed. You will do splendidly."

"But *my age*. I'm no longer in my salad days."

"Serena, my dear," Aunt Catherine said in a no-nonsense tone, "even your age may be put to advantage. Not every gentleman wants a young miss. You know how to manage a great house and an estate, and you do not want for sense. I can think of any number of gentlemen who will not look upon you amiss."

Unconvinced, Serena merely agreed and allowed the matter to drop.

* * *

Early the next morning, Serena ordered a stableboy to saddle Shamir.

After he'd done as she bid, he glanced toward the stable. "I'll just get your groom, Will, to go with ye, my lady."

Serena's nerves were strung too tightly for company. She needed a good gallop this morning, and Will would slow her down. "No, I'll be fine without him."

The boy helped her mount without arguing. After she'd cleared the stable yard, Serena cantered south up a rise and gazed out over the still barren fields. The frost was not as heavy this morning, nor the air quite as cold. It was late, but spring was coming. The land tugged at her. She'd rather be planting than dancing.

A man on a large black horse appeared in the valley and stared up at her. He looked tall, but it was hard to tell at this distance. A breeze ruffled his fair hair as he rode toward her. After a few moments, Serena realized he was riding not simply in her direction, but to her. Her aunt had warned her not to ride alone. Was this man the reason for the warning? Whirling Shamir around, she gave the horse his head and rode back to her aunt's house as if someone were chasing her.

Robert Beaumont rode toward the woman on the crest of the hill. She sat atop a raking roan, much too large for a lady. Her riding habit, a dull rust color, reminded him of autumn leaves. Her long auburn hair curled down her back, and she wore a small hat with some sort of feather—pheasant by the way it stuck out. He wondered how the devil she kept the hat on her head with her hair down. His interest piqued, he urged his horse to a trot. As he neared, she took off at a fast gallop.

She was gone when he reached the top of the hill. Beaumont looked out over the valley. A horse and rider were in the north. How had she gotten that far so quickly? Disgruntled, he turned and rode home. After throwing his reins to a groom, he strode through the doors into the main hall and called to his housekeeper, "Norry!"

She came out from a parlor. "I'm here, my lord. There's no reason to shout."

"Who lives to the north?"

"Well, my lord," she muttered, "if you were here more often, you'd know. It's a widow lady. I can't remember her name right off my head. Why?"

Ignoring Norry's all too familiar complaint, he pressed for more information. "Does she have any children?"

The housekeeper narrowed her eyes. "I heard all her children are grown. She moved here after her son married. Now, if you'll excuse me, my lord, I have work to do."

"Norry, let me know if you remember. Especially if it concerns an auburn-haired female."

"Master Robert," she began in a censorious tone, "we'll have none of your carrying on up here. You leave it in London." She nodded her head curtly and left.

Beaumont clenched his jaw and stormed off to his study, cursing the fact that so many of his servants had been with him since childhood and never let him forget it.

Shamir's hooves clattered on the brick of the stable yard. Serena slid down from her horse and, hoping to avoid her aunt, hurried to a door on the side of the house. Serena had not yet found a way to explain to her aunt how riding calmed her fears so that her aunt would understand.

"Serena," Aunt Catherine called from the breakfast room.

Serena jumped. *Damn,* caught again. "Yes, Aunt Catherine?"

"Come here, my dear."

She was certain her aunt planned, once again, to kindly explain why Serena could not ride alone. Though, after seeing the man on horseback this morning, she acknowledged her aunt might be right.

Well, there was no avoiding it. Serena straightened her shoulders and entered the breakfast room braced for a reprimand.

Her jaw dropped.

Two very fashionable couples were with her aunt—one older, about her aunt's age, the other couple near her age. The men wore close-fitting dark coats and beautifully arranged cravats. They and the younger woman, shorter than Serena by a few inches, rose. Her gown was of a light brown cashmere, trimmed with dark brown ribbon, and tied under her bosom with a darker brown and gold twisted cord.

Serena shut her mouth and stood, rooted in place. The younger woman approached, smiling and holding out her hands. Serena, in her dull russet riding habit, felt like a duck to this lady's swan.

"I am so happy to finally meet you," the woman said. "I'm your cousin Phoebe. May I call you Serena? It is such a lovely name. We are here to help you make your debut."

When Phoebe embraced Serena warmly, she awkwardly returned the gesture. Serena blinked back tears and her tension seeped out as Phoebe then led the way to the table.

"You're surprised, I'm sure," Phoebe said in a warm voice. "I've just been told your aunt did not inform you we were coming."

Serena glanced toward her aunt, who immediately introduced the others present. "Serena, do you remember your uncle Henry and his wife, Ester? Phoebe is their niece. Her husband is Marcus, Earl of Evesham."

The tall, dark-haired man inclined his head.

"Your uncle Henry has been very interested to hear of you over the years and has invited us to stay at St. Eth House for the Season." Aunt Catherine smiled. "There is no one more able to help you through your Season."

Serena's throat ached. She did remember her uncle Henry, the Marquess of St. Eth, her mama's brother. He'd come to her mother's funeral. But her father hadn't liked her mother's family, and there had been very little contact after her mother's passing. When her father died, Uncle Henry had written her with an offer of help. She wished she'd taken it and desperately wished she'd made her come-out when she was younger. "I–I don't know what to say. Your generosity is almost too good to be true."

Phoebe took her hand. "Please, don't let us frighten you. We truly only wish to help. When Uncle Henry told Marcus and me about you, and asked that we accompany him here, we couldn't allow the opportunity to pass us by."

"I am just stunned. I had no idea Aunt Catherine would . . ."

Phoebe glanced at her husband and grinned. "Yes, isn't that the nice thing about family? They are always there to help one, whether they tell you or not."

Serena smiled. She'd moped long enough. She would make the best of her new life, and she had help now, when she needed it. Running an estate was nothing compared to entering the *ton*. "I–I am a fish out of water. I never thought to have a London Season.

I've never really been in a town, except for Edinburgh as a child and recently in York to shop. My whole life has changed."

Phoebe nodded. "Your aunt said you have never been in Polite Society."

Serena gave a short, mirthless laugh. "I've never been in *any* society. We have no towns near the castle and no close neighbors. Except for my dependents, I've spent the last twelve years alone."

Phoebe smiled reassuringly. "You're not alone anymore. We'll make your come-out as easy for you as we are able. And you may surprise yourself by having fun."

The next morning, Serena rode out with Phoebe and Marcus. Unlike Will, Serena's groom, her cousin and her cousin's husband didn't complain when Serena wanted to gallop ahead. She waited for them at the rise she'd visited the day before. "I like having you two as company. I usually ride alone, although Aunt Catherine is not at all happy about it."

Phoebe bit her lip. "Serena, in London you may not ride alone. It's considered fast for an unmarried lady to ride or indeed to walk unaccompanied. It will harm your reputation, and you'll not be able to obtain vouchers for Almack's."

Marcus smiled at Phoebe. "Phoebe didn't like to ride with a groom, either. It enabled me to escort her."

She met his gaze. "Yes, that did greatly advance your cause, my love."

The small signs of affection between Marcus and Phoebe, and between her aunt Ester and uncle Henry, intrigued Serena. "I have no wish to seem impertinent, but yours is a love match, is it not?"

Phoebe glanced warmly at Marcus. "Yes, indeed. I was out for over six years before I married."

"And Aunt Ester and Uncle Henry are a love match as well?"

Phoebe nodded. "It is the tradition in my family."

"And a very good tradition it is," Marcus said. "Else she'd have been snapped up long before I returned to England."

A love match seemed to be a very nice thing to have. "Do either of you know the area here? I was riding alone yesterday morning and stopped here, on the crest. A man upon a great black horse was in the valley." She frowned. "I left when he rode toward me."

Phoebe shook her head. "No, I don't know the area well. Marcus, do you know anyone up here?"

Marcus cast a gaze around again. "A large black horse?"

Serena nodded.

"Was the man fair and tall?"

"Yes."

"Most likely Robert Beaumont."

"Hmm," Phoebe said. "Very proper for you to have ridden off. There is no knowing what a gentleman encountering a lady alone would do."

One week later, Serena arrived at St. Eth House.

Phoebe met her on the pavement. "We'll visit Madame Lisette in the morning. I've already written her, and she'll be happy to design a wardrobe for you."

Serena admired all of Phoebe's clothes. "If she's the one who designs your gowns, I very much look forward to visiting her."

"I shall leave you to settle in and see you in the morning." Phoebe bussed Serena's cheek and left.

The comfort and opulence of St. Eth House amazed Serena. Built in the last century, it was one of the larger residences gracing Grosvenor Square and one of the few freestanding houses. The nicely laid-out gardens in the back and the smaller ones on each side of the house softened the imposing aspect. Serena's room had a view of the fountain in the back. She stood gazing out a window when her maid entered.

"Have you ever seen anything like this?" Serena smiled happily. "Feel how warm it is. What I'd have given for this comfort at Vere Castle."

"Aye, verra warm it tis." Mary ducked into the dressing room.

"I am beginning to feel as though this adventure was meant to be. Everyone has been so very kind." Serena sat on the window seat and called to Mary, "How have you fared?"

Her maid had been with her for many years. Serena had been grateful, and surprised, when Mary had agreed to leave Scotland and accompany her south. With matters as they were at Vere Castle, Serena did not think she would ever return home. Her goal now was to find a husband, and she had decided it must be a love match.

"I'm getting on well, my lady. Rose, Lady Evesham's maid, has been so good as to show me the newest ways to dress hair and care for your new clothes. And Lady St. Eth's grand dresser, Perkins, is as well."

"Are you comfortable here?"

"Aye, my lady, and happy, now that I havena got Lady Vere's French maid telling me I'm doing it all wrong."

Serena was concerned about the answer to her next question. Her groom, an older man, not used to traveling, had insisted on remaining with her. "Has Will said anything to you about how he's doing?"

"He'll miss Vere, but he's happy to stay with you. Says the other grooms know what they're about."

London was indeed warmer and friendlier than Vere Castle, for everyone.